The music stopp is arms as they stared at each other. In those ... ... s, Luke knew something changed, and he knew she felt it too. He'd been ready to shoot a man over a dance and he knew why. He wanted her. Taking her by the hand, he led her through the throng of people and he didn't stop until he reached the back of the church. Once he found the most secluded area he took her in his arms.

"You're beautiful in the moonlight," he whispered, cupping her face in his large hand.

Mary Ann's heart was thumping loudly, and she quickly forgot all of the reasons she wanted to stay away from him. His arms tightened around her, crushing her to his chest and she couldn't think of anything other than how good it felt being so close to him.

When he lowered his lips to hers she didn't resist . . .

Books by Scarlett Dunn

PROMISES KEPT

FINDING PROMISE

LAST PROMISE

Published by Kensington Publishing Corporation

Last Promise

SCARLETT DUNN

ZEBRA BOOKS
KENSINGTON PUBLISHING CORP.
http://www.kensingtonbooks.com

ZEBRA BOOKS are published by

Kensington Publishing Corp.
119 West 40th Street
New York, NY 10018

All Kensington titles, imprints, and distributed lines are available at special quantity discounts for bulk purchases for sales promotion, premiums, fund-raising, educational, or institutional use.

Special book excerpts or customized printings can also be created to fit specific needs. For details, write or phone the office of the Kensington Sales Manager: Attn.: Sales Department. Kensington Publishing Corp., 119 West 40th Street, New York, NY 10018. Phone: 1-800-221-2647.

Zebra and the Z logo Reg. U.S. Pat. & TM Off.

First Printing: May 2016
ISBN-13: 978-1-4201-3893-1
ISBN-10: 1-4201-3893-6

eISBN-13: 978-1-4201-3894-8
eISBN-10: 1-4201-3894-4

10 9 8 7 6 5 4 3 2 1

Printed in the United States of America

To Morgan—

I'm so proud of the person you are. You have a generous heart, and I admire your approach as well as your outlook on life. Our conversations and laughter mean more to me than you will ever know. My one pearl of wisdom for you is to never settle for less than you deserve.

Life brings changes, and people come and go, but no one, no matter how hard they try, can change the love I have felt for you from the first breath. No one will ever love you more.

Prologue

London, England

Dearest Mother,

I simply cannot allow Father to force me to marry Edmund Stafford. Contrary to Father's belief, I was not compromised by the rake, but he would not even allow me to explain. While Father professes to be a man of God, he displays no hesitation in judging his own daughter. Are we not taught, "Judge not, that ye be not judged."

Edmund was forcing his attentions on me, and in my struggle to get away from him, my dress was ripped. If anyone should be called to account, it should be Edmund! It does not matter one whit to me if he is as rich as Croesus himself; I cannot abide the man, and I am baffled why he wants to marry a woman who finds him totally insufferable.

I am sorry, Mother, but I must leave.

Mary Ann

Chapter One

What a piece of work is a man!
SHAKESPEARE

Promise, Wyoming

The soiled doves were hanging over the second-floor balcony of L. B. Ditty's Saloon, wearing nothing but their chemises and bloomers. When Luke McBride exited the bank across the street, one gal gave a shrill whistle, louder than any man could make, causing all of the gals to burst into laughter.

"Hi, Luke, honey, you sure look handsome this morning," one gal hollered. The other women chorused their agreement.

"Where you going, darling? It's noon, ya know, not too early to come in," another gal offered.

Luke glanced up to see the bevy of beauties displaying their wares to anyone who happened to be passing by. He had to hand it to L. B. Ditty, she hired the most attractive girls she could find, and he knew each one by name. He stopped and tipped his hat to the women.

"Hello, ladies. I can't join you today. I'm picking up some supplies." There wasn't a man on earth who appreciated God's design of the female form more than Luke McBride. And he took time to show his appreciation whenever possible. Looking at them from his vantage point, he couldn't decide if he preferred the more voluptuous figures or the tall, lanky gals with less cleavage to display. The way he saw it, they each had their advantages. And here they were lined up like colorful blossoms ready to be plucked.

"Are you sure, honey? We was just getting dressed to go downstairs."

Before he told them they shouldn't bother to change because they sure looked lovely in what they were wearing, he heard the voice of L. B. filtering down to the street.

"Girls, what in heaven's name are you doing out here on the balcony when you should be getting dressed?" L. B. Ditty didn't abide the girls making a spectacle of themselves outside the saloon. It wasn't good for business, at least not with the ladies in town on a Saturday morning. L. B. was adamant her girls maintain decorum so the local ladies wouldn't complain to their husbands. Inside the saloon, they could walk around half-dressed if they chose, she figured that was good for business.

"We was just saying hello to Luke," one gal answered.

"Come look, L. B., Luke looks so handsome today," another gal said.

"The way you're carrying on, I'd expect him to be walking down the street buck naked." Even as the words left her mouth, she couldn't resist walking to the rail and leaning over to see if Luke happened to be in his birthday suit. That sure would give the ladies in town something to talk about instead of her girls.

Hearing the exchange between L. B. and the girls, Luke saw L. B.'s bright red curls appear over the railing. He tipped his hat, smiled, and spread his arms wide. "Sorry to disappoint, L. B., but as you can see, I'm fully clothed."

Grinning, L. B. shook her head at him. "And that's a good thing, Luke McBride, or you'd have all the ladies in town in a dither. But the gals are right; you surely are a sight to behold."

The gals flocked over the railing again, each exposing more bosom than the next.

Luke couldn't help but chuckle at the lineup of well-endowed females. "Thank you, ma'am. And might I say, you ladies look mighty fetching today."

"You are full of nonsense, but it's a pleasure to see you this fine morning," L. B. retorted. To her way of thinking, Luke McBride had the world by the tail, and he often liked to twirl it on a whim. She figured he would take exception if anyone ever said he strutted down the sidewalk, but there wasn't a man or woman who didn't take notice when he passed. Of course, that was partly due to his size. Like his brothers, Colt and Jake, Luke was well over six feet, had a rock-hard muscled body, and broad shoulders that naturally demanded a wide berth. His handsome face sported the same signature McBride square jaw, but where his brothers had black eyes, Luke's eyes were a vivid turquoise blue. She imagined that blue shirt he was wearing really made those blue eyes sparkle. He was definitely spit-shined, his shirt starched and pressed to perfection, not a speck of dirt on his pants, boots polished to a high sheen, his black Stetson brushed, even his holster was gleaming. Luke always looked attractive, yet there was something special about him today. Maybe it was his cocksure attitude that made him look exceptionally handsome.

No one could deny Luke McBride was a charmer, and he had a full calendar of Friday-night dinner dates to prove it. Women loved him, and there wasn't a man who didn't envy his carefree approach to life. Luke's motto was simple: He loved to laugh, loved horses, and loved women. Depending on the availability of the latter, he often rearranged the order.

Sally Detrick was shopping in the mercantile when she spotted Luke through the window talking to some-one across the street. Hurrying to the door, she saw what was drawing his attention. Seeing those saloon women in their undergarments hanging over the rail-ing, oohing and aahing over Luke, made her see red. Marching over to him, she hooked her arm through his and pulled him toward her. "Why, Luke McBride, you sure do look handsome today, even if you are just full of the devil!"

L. B. saw the look on Sally's face when she'd looked at the girls. That did it; Sally was sure to run to her daddy and tell him about the evil ways of her girls. Knowing Detrick would raise a ruckus, L. B. quickly ushered the girls away from the balcony.

"Hello, Sally," Luke replied, glancing at the balcony one last time to see the girls' backsides as they were being herded inside. With some regret he turned his attention on Sally.

Sally pushed her lower lip out in a pout. "Why did you turn down my dinner invitation?"

Luke knew that question would be coming. The

main reason he'd declined her invitation was due to her daddy. Every time he went to dinner at their ranch, Old Man Detrick stuck to him like glue once his feet were over the threshold. Detrick wanted a husband for his girl, and no cowboy was going to do anything untoward until he had that ring through his nose. But he was confident the old man wasn't aware of all of Sally's shenanigans or he'd lock her in her room until she walked down the aisle. He couldn't blame Detrick for trying to keep a tight rein on Sally. He'd seen firsthand on his last date with her that she certainly wasn't the prim and proper young woman she presented to the world.

She'd invited him to go for a ride and picnic by the lake, telling him that her daddy would not be joining them. Within minutes after they reached the lake, and without any coaxing from him, Sally surprised him by stripping down to her bloomers and chemise and jumping into the water. Luke was the one who usually pushed the boundaries of propriety in good fun, but she'd turned the tables on him. That day, she was the devil on his shoulder encouraging him to remove his pants and jump in. He jumped in, but he'd wisely kept his pants on. He wondered how many men she'd *picnicked* with in the past since she seemed way too comfortable being nearly naked with him. He'd seen uninhibited women, but not even the gals hanging over the balcony could hold a candle to Sally in that department. All afternoon she'd tried every move in her vast repertoire to get him in a compromising position. As much as he was tempted, and he was sorely tempted, he didn't want Old Man Detrick to take a horsewhip to him if he found them. He could always shoot the old buzzard, but if he did something as stupid as compromise his oldest daughter, he figured

Detrick would have every right to demand a shotgun wedding. Luke leaned over and whispered in her ear. "You want to go for a ride?"

Sally pressed closer and seductively batted her eyelashes at him. "Yes, I want to! I didn't want to leave the lake the last time. You know what I want, but I can't go. I'm shopping with Lucinda Sawyer. We came to town together."

It was probably for the best, Luke thought, because he did know what she wanted. It was a puzzle to him why he was still playing with fire, as his big brother Colt had warned him. One of Colt's favorite sayings played in his mind. *If you play with fire you are going to get burned.* He wondered if this was a Shakespeare quote. Colt was fond of quoting Shakespeare. Playing with fire seemed to be a recurring theme for him lately. And Luke knew if Sally used the same tactics as last time, he wouldn't have the willpower to stop her even if he wanted to. He wouldn't be playing with fire, he'd be in flames. While he wouldn't mind knowing her in the biblical sense, he thought it would be wise to listen to that little voice in his head. Or was that his brother talking? It was pure torture trying to clean up his act, as his brothers had been haranguing him to do. Just because God had blessed them with beautiful wives and they'd settled down didn't mean he wanted to follow their lead. He didn't want to be hog-tied into marriage either, so he altered course with Sally. "If you can't go for a ride, I'll take you two lovely ladies to lunch instead."

Glancing through the window of the mercantile, Sally saw Lucinda walking to the door. She leaned closer to Luke and whispered, "Meet me at noon tomorrow at the river. I have something special I ordered from Paris, France, that I want to show you."

Luke almost groaned aloud at his imaginings. He

figured something from Paris, France, meant silky and see-through. Sally might not be as beautiful as his two sisters-in-law, but she did have a nice full figure, and judging by her display at the lake, she liked to show it off. And he didn't mind looking. He still couldn't get the image of her in a wet chemise out of his mind. Before he had time to respond, he felt a warm body press against his other side.

"Hello, handsome. What are you doing in town on a Saturday afternoon?" Lucinda inquired. Lucinda had been trying to wrangle a date with Luke after she met him at Sally's house last winter. She was aware of Sally's plans to marry the very handsome and available McBride brother, but to her way of thinking, if a proposal hadn't been made, he was fair game.

"I'm here to take two lovely ladies to lunch," he replied smoothly. Neither woman was what he would call beautiful, but in his opinion all women were lovely in some way. In his experience, a little gallantry went a long way with the ladies. What did it hurt to do a little harmless flirting?

"How wonderful!" Lucinda leaned around him to look at Sally, managing to keep in close contact with his chest. "You're a dear to share your handsome man."

Sally didn't want to share Luke, but she had no control over him. Yet. That wouldn't be the case much longer; she planned to have him standing at the altar before he knew what hit him. She'd set her sights on him when he'd returned to Wyoming a year earlier. Everyone knew he was the most eligible bachelor in the state after his brothers finally married. Her father told her Luke had made a small fortune while he was traveling around the country busting broncs. She couldn't remember exactly how he'd made so much money—seemed like her father mentioned it had something to do with silver mining. The details weren't important. He was handsome and he was well-off. Her father wasn't a pauper by any means, but even their ranch paled in comparison to the McBride Cattle Company. Sally gave Lucinda a knowing smile. "Isn't it wonderful of him to surprise *me* this way?"

Luke picked up on the feminine undercurrents, but he didn't know what it was about, and he was smart enough not to ask. "Would you two ladies like to go to the boardinghouse or the hotel?" While he was in town, he figured he might as well eat and enjoy some female companionship. His favorite pastime.

They'd started to cross the street when the stagecoach came barreling down the road. At the same time, Mrs. Rogers came out of the mercantile trying to hail them by waving a package in the air. Sally realized she'd left her package in her haste to join Luke and hurried back to Mrs. Rogers. Lucinda took advantage of that moment to tell Luke she wanted him to call on her, but Luke wasn't really listening. His attention was on the stagecoach that pulled to a halt a few feet in front of them. The driver scampered down from his perch to open the door for the passengers. A man stepped from the coach and helped the driver assist an elderly woman to the ground. Both men quickly redirected their attention to the interior of the coach. Their faces were beaming when a young woman placed her hands in theirs, allowing them to assist her from the coach. She was looking down and the wide brim of the pink hat she wore hid her face. Luke stared at her pink hat. He liked the vibrant color; and the brim was decorated with lace and an array of feathers. His sisters-in-law would love that hat. Victoria and Promise were lovely women and they enjoyed keeping up with the latest fashions. He just knew a woman who wore such a stylish hat would be beautiful.

Sally rejoined them and curled her arm through his again. "Mrs. Rogers saved me a trip. I can't believe I forgot this." When Luke didn't look at her, she flapped the package in his face. "This is the one from France," she reminded him playfully.

Luke couldn't help but glance at the parcel that was blocking his view of that pink hat. It was small, real small. That meant whatever was inside of that package was really small. His mind started imagining again, but his illicit thoughts were disrupted by a feminine voice with a distinct British accent. It was the woman in the pink hat conversing with the stagecoach driver. She was facing the driver and Luke still couldn't see her face.

The next moment changed Luke's perfect day. A man came flying through the batwing doors of the saloon behind him. He slammed into Sally's back, causing her to stumble forward. Thankfully, she was still holding on to Luke's arm and he managed to keep her from hitting the ground. Luke turned around to see what was going on and he saw Tubby Jenkins on the ground. It didn't take long for Luke to see how he got there. Clyde Slater, the town troublemaker, came charging out of the saloon after Tubby.

"You need to mind your manners, Clyde," Luke said in a no-nonsense tone. It wasn't the first time he'd exchanged words with Clyde.

"Why don't you mind your own business, McBride?"

Clyde was a big man, but he spent too much of his time drinking to stay in tip-top form, unlike Luke, who kept his body in excellent condition working on the ranch. Still, when Clyde was drinking, he thought he was invincible, and most times, he was.

"Tubby almost knocked me down!" Sally yelled her indignation to Clyde.

Clyde smirked. "Honey, from what I hear, you like to do a little rolling around."

This isn't how I planned my day, Luke thought.

"How dare you!" Sally rushed forward with the intention of giving Clyde a good slap.

Luke wasn't going to allow a woman to defend herself as long as he was drawing breath. It was one thing if Clyde thought his comments about Sally were true, but it was another thing to express them in the middle of the street with everyone gawking. Luke grabbed Sally by the waist and pulled her back. He took a step forward. "You might be drunk, Clyde, but that doesn't give you the right to be rude to a lady. Apologize."

Clyde was grinning like a half-wit. "I'm sure you know firsthand how she likes her skirts tossed up."

And that was when the first fist slammed into Clyde's bulbous nose. Luke followed up with three good punches to Clyde's jaw, sending him reeling backward. Tubby, still on the ground, managed to get to his knees in an effort to gain his feet and stumbled into Luke's back, knocking him off balance. Clyde took that opportunity to land a right hook to Luke's jaw. Staggering backward, Luke fell over Tubby and hit the dirt. He jumped up and plowed head first into Clyde's stomach, both of them going to the earth in a heap. They rolled around in the dirt, each landing punches, neither able to get to their feet since Tubby was groveling in the dirt trying to stand and getting in their way. The women were yelling for Tubby to get out of the way so Luke could finish off Clyde. Tubby wasn't really trying to help Clyde, but you couldn't prove it by Luke. The man made a habit of teetering into Luke when he was about to land another blow. Luke tried to stand to put some leverage into his punches, but Tubby bounced into him again. Frustrated with this unintentional interference, Luke turned around and rammed his fist into Tubby's jaw, hitting him so hard he reeled back several feet and landed in the water trough. With Tubby out of the way, Luke traded a few more punches with Clyde before he finally landed the giant-slaying blow. Clyde hit the ground and stayed there like a dead carcass. Luke grabbed him by the shirt and dragged his dead weight to the water trough and dunked his head in the murky water a few times. Water sloshed over the sides of the trough and landed on Luke's perfectly polished boots. He muttered a string of cuss words under his breath.

"What'd ya hit me for? I didn't do nothin'." Tubby struggled in vain to get out of the trough.

"Shut up and stay down," Luke warned.

Tubby flopped back down in the water and glared at Luke with bloodshot eyes. Luke released Clyde's shirt, and watched as he slid down beside the water trough in a filthy heap.

Running his fingers through his black wavy hair to get it out of his eyes, Luke spotted his Stetson a few feet away. Snatching it off the ground, he had to smack it against his thigh a few times to remove a fraction of the dust before he slammed it on his head. There was blood on his favorite blue shirt, and he was covered in dust from head to toe. And the day had started out so perfectly.

Sally and Lucinda ran to him.

"Oh, Luke, are you hurt?" Sally ran her hands all over him, half pretending to dust off his shirt.

"You are so brave," Lucinda said. "You certainly taught Clyde a thing or two!" She pulled a handkerchief out of her sleeve and dabbed at Luke's split lip.

They were giving him so much attention, he quickly forgot about his appearance and thought maybe he should get into a fight every time he came to town. "Ladies, unless you are too embarrassed to be seen with me, I'd still like to take you to lunch. I promise to show you two a good time." Maybe he should take them both to the lake and salvage his day in a more delightful way.

"We're proud to be seen with you, Luke McBride," Sally said. She meant every word. She'd rather be with Luke than any man she knew.

"We certainly are. It was high time someone put that bully in his place," Lucinda agreed.

Once the women finished dusting him off, they started toward the hotel, but were brought up short when they nearly collided with the people from the stagecoach. From the looks on their faces they'd obviously witnessed the encounter with Clyde. Luke finally saw the face of the woman under that pink hat. She was staring directly at him, and she didn't look nearly as impressed as Sally and Lucinda.

Luke couldn't tell what she was thinking, but whatever it was, it wasn't good. He stood there as if he'd grown roots. All he could do was stare at her large eyes, the color of quicksilver, he thought. His eyes skittered over her face, noting her delicate features. Her complexion was so fair he figured she'd never spent one day in the sun. He was right about a woman wearing such a flamboyant hat: She was one beautiful woman. Remembering his manners, he reached up to tip the brim of his black Stetson, dragging Sally's arm up with his. He'd forgotten she was hanging on to him like a leech.

The woman's eyes widened when Luke acknowledged her, and her gaze made a slow traverse down his body, stopping at the Colt .45 on his hip. She didn't respond to his greeting, she simply turned and addressed the stagecoach driver. "My trunk and portmanteaus."

"I'll bring them right along," the stagecoach driver promised.

"Thank you."

The gentleman who had assisted her from the stagecoach stepped to her side. "I'll escort you to the hotel, ma'am."

For the first time in his life, Luke McBride had been snubbed by a female. That in itself was an unusual circumstance as the McBride brothers were legendary for their appeal to the ladies. Before his brothers married, women had flocked to them like they had magnetic poles in their holsters instead of six-guns. Unlike his brothers, Luke didn't run from the ladies, he ran *to* them. While he wasn't one to kiss and tell, he was one to love 'em and leave 'em, as he often reminded his brothers. And he'd left plenty in his wake. But he couldn't remember a time when a woman had rebuffed him.

It was a mystery to Luke why the woman looked at him like she couldn't decide if he was Satan himself or a scorpion to be squashed. Admittedly he looked pretty grubby after the fight, but if she'd seen the whole thing, she had to realize he was defending a lady's honor.

Luke and the ladies had no choice but to follow the woman being escorted to the hotel. It gave Luke ample time to think about her snub and to take in her shapely backside.

"That dress is lovely," Lucinda said.

"Fine quality too," Sally added.

"And that hat is surely a Parisian design."

"No doubt, and the color is delightful," Sally agreed.

Luke wondered what it was about Paris that seemed
to get women all lathered up like racehorses. He'd
heard more than he cared to know about fashion from
his sisters-in-law, who were forever expounding on the
virtues of clothing from Paris. His appreciation of
women's garments was generally based on how easily
they could be removed. Although he did notice the
woman was wearing a silky-looking silver dress that
matched her eyes. And of course he couldn't help but
notice how it complemented her petite trim figure.
She certainly didn't have Sally's more than ample
curves, but he liked the way her little backside swayed
to and fro.

"British," Lucinda said.

"Rather rude, if you ask me," Sally said.

"I can't believe she didn't even acknowledge us."

On that point, Luke silently agreed with them. If he
were as intimidating as his brother Colt, with that black
stare of his, he might have understood the woman's
slight. But Luke knew he was considered the charming
brother, and not bragging, he was—as even his sisters-
in-law would attest.

Once inside the hotel, Luke and the ladies veered
toward the dining room, as the British woman walked
to the desk. Luke noted it was the clerk, Eb, behind the
desk and not the owner of the hotel. When they entered the dining room, he was too far away to hear the
conversation between the woman and Eb, particularly
with Sally and Lucinda chatting away. He held the
chairs for the women and positioned himself so he had
a clear view of the front desk. Straightaway the stagecoach driver and another man walked into the hotel
sharing the weight of a large trunk with several pieces
of luggage on top. The woman turned and smiled at
the driver, and Luke was held spellbound. He couldn't

think of a word for her, but *beautiful* didn't even come close. She was more than beautiful, her face looked like a magnificent work of art. He watched as she pointed out the pieces of luggage that belonged to her. After thanking the men, she accepted the key from the clerk and walked to the staircase.

Lunch ended and Luke was eager to escort the two women to their buggy. Generally, he might have stretched out the lunch, taking pleasure in the subtle way the women flirted with him, but today he had another matter on his mind, and it was wearing a pink hat. Besides that, Sally was making it obvious she had big plans for him. During lunch she'd made several remarks to Lucinda that led him to believe she was gearing up for marriage. And it sure as Hades wasn't going to be him in the church wearing a string tie that was certain to feel like a noose.

"Tomorrow, then?" Sally asked, squeezing his hand as he assisted her into the buggy, her silent message promising another intimate encounter.

"Sorry, tomorrow is Sunday. Church with the family, then dinner. And I promised the twins I would take them riding afterward." He knew his refusal wouldn't please her, but he thought his brothers were right when they told him to limit his womanizing to the gals at the saloon. Good advice he intended to follow from now on.

That promise to himself lasted about a second, then Sally waggled the itty-bitty package in his face again. He was spared from his weakening resolve when Lucinda thanked him for lunch, and he said his good-byes and quickly took his leave before he changed his mind about Sunday.

Luke hurried back to the hotel, but Eb wasn't behind the desk. Instead of waiting, he spun the register around to read the names of the guests who had just arrived. He figured the elderly woman on the stage had registered before the British woman, so he glanced at the next signature. Miss Mary Ann Hardwicke. He looked at the name of the man who had escorted Miss Hardwicke to the hotel to see if he had the same last name. He didn't. Just then, Eb returned to the desk, and Luke asked him about the woman. Always ready to deliver some gossip, Eb told him Miss Hardwicke asked to speak with the owner, Mr. Granville, but she didn't state her business. Eb also indicated Mr. Granville wouldn't be back until later that evening.

Spying her trunk and valises still piled by the front door, Luke figured Eb couldn't lift them alone. The way he saw it, he was presented with another golden opportunity for a little more harmless flirting, ignoring his vow to mind his ways. One of his favorite sayings was *don't look a gift horse in the mouth.* "Want me to get that luggage for you, Eb?"

"I would appreciate it, Luke. My back can't handle anything so heavy."

"Is she traveling alone?"

"Yessir, that's what she said."

Perfect. Luke hoisted the large trunk on his shoulder, leaving a free hand to carry the three valises. "Which room?"

"Number six at the top of the stairs to the right."

His lucky number.

Chapter Two

Reaching her room, Mary Ann hurried inside and quickly turned the lock. For the first time in months she felt like she could actually breathe. Since she'd left England she'd been forced to ward off the advances of strange men. She'd even been forced to strike one man with her parasol, holding him at bay until a constable came to her aid. She counted on God to protect her, but she also felt like He wanted her to do her part. She'd purchased a pistol in one town for her own peace of mind. She knew how to use it and she wouldn't hesitate if she had no alternative.

She found the men in this new country crude and overall quite distasteful. Other than her last fateful encounter with Edmund Stafford, she had never been pressed to protect her person from unwanted attention. And look how that had ended; with her running away so she would not be forced into a loveless marriage. She should have called Edmund out instead of expecting her father to exact satisfaction. Her father would not even listen to the truth of what happened that night. His mind was made up and he was going to force her to marry Edmund. Perhaps after she left, Edmund had told her father the truth about that night, but she wasn't inclined to wait and see. She made the decision rather quickly to leave England, and told herself once she arrived in Wyoming she would live the life she wanted.

Her uncle George, the proprietor of this hotel, had written in his letters how much he loved this country and she'd been excited to find out for herself. Uncle George had failed to mention that America was filled with ruffians. Upon her arrival to this very town, the first person she sees is that miscreant brawling in the middle of the street. The man was truly fearsome with his large black hat and pistol riding low on his hip. He must be a . . . what did they call them out here . . . oh yes, a *pistolier*. Granted, she'd been startled by his twinkling blue eyes when he stared directly at her, but make no mistake, that man was a scoundrel if she ever saw one. Just the memory of him fighting those men made her shiver. And the way those two women were putting their hands all over him! By displaying such a lack of breeding, one could only conclude they were surely not ladies. The rogue didn't seem surprised by their behavior, she'd heard him promise to show those women a good time! Of all the nerve. If he lived in Promise, she prayed she wouldn't encounter him often. Surely there were gentlemen in this town who understood proper comportment.

Aside from the ill-bred men in this country, she was mesmerized by the sheer beauty of the West. She'd never seen anything as magnificent as the mountains in the distance, or the thousands of stars twinkling in the infinite night sky.

Standing with her back to the door, Mary Ann inspected her quarters. It was a very well-appointed room and much larger than she expected. The four-poster bed was covered with a pristine white quilt embroidered with lilies of the field. Spanning one wall was an ornately carved wardrobe, and a writing desk filled one corner. A round mahogany dining table with four deep blue velvet upholstered chairs, along with a lovely crystal chandelier above, were cleverly positioned by a window overlooking the street below. The massive stone fireplace covered the wall nearest the bed, and she imagined it would be warm and cozy with a fire blazing in the hearth on a chilly night. She'd heard about the frigid Wyoming winters, and this room would be perfect for cold winter nights. All of the wood was polished to a glossy finish and the room was spotless, not a speck of dust could be seen. The room was lovely, and even though it was only a quarter of the size of her bedroom at home, she knew she would be comfortable here.

Her uncle had written he'd built a hotel that any Englishman would be proud to own in the new country. She certainly couldn't disagree. When she'd hurriedly made her decision to depart England, this was the only place she thought she could go to escape the long reach of her father and Edmund Stafford. But as members of the peerage, they had vast resources at their disposal. She had to face the fact that if they wanted to track her down, she would be found sooner or later. She hoped it was later.

Luke made it up the stairway without running into any walls or dropping her trunk. The blasted thing was so heavy he thought that lovely little lady might have dead bodies stored in there. It was large enough to hold three or four. When he reached door number six he didn't have a free hand so he banged on the door with the toe of his boot.

Standing at the mirror brushing her hair, Mary Ann jumped at the knock. Collecting herself, she said through the door, "Yes?"

"Your luggage."

"Oh, certainly." She hurried across the room and turned the key in the lock. To her dismay, when she cracked the door open there stood the very man she'd faced outside. The desperado. What in heaven's name was *he* doing with her luggage?

Once again, when Luke looked at her face, her sheer beauty caught him off guard. She had removed her hat, and he didn't know what he expected, but it definitely wasn't the wealth of red hair hanging over her shoulder. It wasn't a bright red like L. B. Ditty's, but a soft red, with strands of gold running throughout it. The kind of hair that gave a man a lot of thoughts. Thoughts he shouldn't be having right now. After he stopped staring at her hair, his eyes moved back to her unusual silver eyes. If he was reading her expression correctly, she was surprised and not pleasantly so, that he was the one carrying her luggage. He thought she might slam the door in his face. "Do you reckon I can put this inside your room? I don't think I can hold it much longer."

Not only was the man a mischief-maker, he was also quite forward. She assumed he must work at the hotel, so surely her uncle wouldn't hire someone who was a danger to his guests. But at the first opportunity tonight, she planned to let Uncle George know that this . . . this scoundrel needed his manners polished like the glistening furniture. Opening the door wider, she stood back to allow Luke entry.

Luke had been in this room before with another

young woman, but right now he couldn't even recall her face much less her name. He placed the trunk on the floor near the wardrobe thinking it would be convenient for her, and the valises on the long bench at the foot of the bed. He noticed her pink hat on the bedspread. Finished with his task, he didn't want to leave. What he really wanted to do was turn around and get a good long look at her. He glanced at the fireplace and saw the wood was already laid and ready to be lit. "The nights can be a bit chilly this time of year, would you like me to go ahead and light the fire? Eb probably won't make it up here anytime soon." He was proud of himself for thinking of that. Yep, gallantry could go a long way.

Perhaps he wasn't as ill-mannered as she first thought. She appreciated his consideration. "Yes, thank you, a fire would be lovely."

Luke noticed how she hovered by the open door, looking something akin to a lost calf, a bit skittish, uncertain of which way to go. It was understandable why a little thing like her wouldn't want to close the door with a man in her room. He thought maybe if he talked to her it would put her at ease. Plus he liked the sound of her proper English accent. After removing his hat, he tossed it on the bed and it landed right beside her frilly pink hat making the feathers flutter. "You must have traveled a long way," he said conversationally.

She wasn't accustomed to servants speaking so freely. That didn't happen in her father's home, no one dared speak out of turn. But she must remember she was in America now, and attitudes here, as she had learned, were vastly different. As Luke went about lighting the fire, Mary Ann covertly observed his physique. He was a very large man, tall and muscular, with legs that seemed to go on forever. When he squatted down in front of the fireplace and leaned over to add more logs, his shirt stretched over his broad, muscled shoulders and she half expected the seams to tear apart. She hadn't noticed his wavy raven black hair when he was brawling in the street. Once he removed his hat, she noticed he wore his hair a bit longer than most men, but on him it somehow seemed fitting. With his dark bronze complexion and black hair, she thought it most unusual his eyes were bright blue. A very attractive combination, she grudgingly admitted.

Luke waited for an answer, but when none was forthcoming, he turned to her. "Did you travel a long way?"

"What would give you that impression?"

Ignoring her frosty tone, Luke pointed to the luggage. "That much luggage says either you've been traveling for some time, or you're planning to stay awhile. Plus your accent is a dead giveaway." He gave her a smile, hoping something about him impressed her. His smile always worked with the ladies.

"Hmm."

So much for trying to engage her in conversation. Once the fire was blazing, Luke stood and grabbed his Stetson from the bed and his eyes lingered on her hat. He really wanted to pick it up and look at it. He wasn't sure why, other than it was so feminine, and well . . . pink. One of his favorite pastimes was watching a woman at her toilette. He prided himself on being a man who appreciated the time women took with their appearance. It was all of the little things women did that he treasured, whether it was the way they fixed their hair, or how they applied perfume in strategic places, or how they pulled on their stockings. He loved watching them dress and undress, and all of the various stages in between. He liked how they chose their hats to match their dresses. Actually, he loved everything about the opposite sex. That was one of the reasons women were drawn to him; he made them feel appreciated. Right now, he admired one particular pink hat worn by one particularly beautiful woman. He slowly sauntered to the door. "That's a beautiful hat."

It surprised her a scoundrel like him even noticed her hat. How unexpected. "Thank you."

Standing just a foot from her, Luke smelled her subtle perfume. He had the urge to nuzzle her neck like a dog and get a good whiff. Looking down at her he realized she was just a little thing. He figured she couldn't have been over five feet tall, but it was hard to tell because she had her head lowered looking for something in her reticule. Luke wasn't sure, but he thought the bag she was digging through might have been designed by his sister-in-law Victoria. He'd never really paid much attention to the little bags before he'd seen Victoria's artistic designs. The intricate detailed work involved in creating them gave him a whole new appreciation for her creations. He was really surprised to learn that some women paid more for those little things than a man did for a good horse.

He lingered, trying to think of something else to say to her so he could hang around a little longer. It was unusual for him to be so tongue-tied around a woman and he didn't know why it was happening now. Maybe it had something to do with the fact that she was the most beautiful woman he'd ever seen. He thought he'd start with the basics and not try so hard to impress her. "I'm Luke McBride."

"Mr. McBride."

"Call me Luke."

When she found what she was looking for she looked up at him and their eyes met, and his brain stopped working again. Everything about her face was flawless; smooth pale skin, a small straight nose, even her pink lips were perfectly formed, and her silver eyes sparkled like stars. *Don't stand here like a dummy. Say something, impress her.* He nervously twirled his hat in his hands. "So are you staying a long time?" He hoped so.

Standing so close to her, she found his size most intimidating, and the display of fisticuffs in the street earlier didn't help matters. And she certainly didn't understand his interest in her travel plans. Still, she couldn't help but notice what a handsome man he was even with a swollen bloody lip. "I believe so."

Lord she was a beauty, but she was definitely on edge. She reminded him of a baby bird, and he was the hawk flying overhead. "Do you want to have dinner?" His question was impulsive, but he was proud of himself for mustering the courage to ask.

She took a step forward. "I'll require some later."

Luke thought it was an odd response, but he didn't have time to comment since she was slowly inching him toward the threshold as she pulled the door with her. He had no choice but to step back or have the door smack him in the face. What she did next really threw him. She reached out and placed some coins in his hand. "Thank you," she said and promptly closed the door in his face. He heard the key turn in the lock with a loud click. Only then did he realize that she had masterfully shuffled him over the threshold and he was standing on the wrong side of the closed door. He stood there speechless. That little gal had actually shoved him out the door without touching him. He opened his palm and looked at the silver dollars. Yeah, he made an impression all right. She thought it was his job to carry up her luggage. He chuckled all the way down the stairs.

On his ride home, Miss Mary Ann Hardwicke occupied Luke's thoughts. Eb said she had business with George Granville, the owner of the hotel. He knew George had only been in Wyoming for a few years, hailing from England. Luke's brother told him that once George purchased the hotel he'd spent months and a lot of money renovating the place until it was one of the nicest hotels in the West. Luke hoped George made it to church tomorrow so he could ask him about the mysterious lady in the pink hat. It seemed odd a young woman like her would be traveling alone. She couldn't have possibly traveled all the way from England without an escort.

"Don't you want me to stay, Uncle George?" The reunion with her uncle hadn't gone as well as Mary Ann had expected. After she'd told him of her reasons for leaving London, he seemed concerned her father would come to America to find her. Perhaps her uncle thought he might face her father's wrath and be held responsible for her decision to come to Wyoming.

George's sister, Coreen, had married Hardwicke for his money. Coreen was a great beauty in her day, just like his niece, and Hardwicke had been persistent in wooing her. George's family were on the same social level as Hardwicke, but their estate was not nearly as large. George knew when his sister married Hardwicke it wasn't a love match, but his sister wanted the life his wealth could provide. When George inherited the Granville estate he chose a different path than his sister. He gave control of the estate to his younger brother and he left England. He yearned for a different life, one filled with adventure and knew he would find what he was looking for in America. He could sympathize with Mary Ann for desperately wanting to get away from the life she was destined to lead. She feared her life would mirror Coreen's if she stayed in England.

"Of course I want you to stay, but you know your father. He'll send someone to find you, and I would expect if they are not already on their way, they soon will be. I just don't want you to be disappointed if he forces you to return."

"I left Mother a note and told her I was leaving. I didn't say where I was going."

She looked so devastated that George tried to relieve her concerns. He didn't have the heart to tell her that it would only be a matter of time before they discovered she'd left England. Hardwicke had a legion of detectives and barristers at his disposal. "Let's not worry about it tonight. I certainly don't mind if you stay forever. If your father's agents appear on our doorstep, then we will deal with the situation when and if it happens. But if you decide you want to go home before then, I will escort you." It troubled him that his beautiful young niece had traveled so far with no escort. Why, all manner of evil could have befallen her. Her guardian angel must have been keeping a close watch over her.

"I will not be going home. I have some funds, but I need to find a position, or a building where I can establish a business. Once I arrived in America, I discovered I could start a small shop. As a matter of fact, while I was waiting for you to return today I had time to look around your hotel and there is a perfect little spot I could utilize for a shop I have in mind."

George couldn't believe his ears. Mary Ann was nearly royalty in England, he wouldn't hear of her looking for a position, or working for that matter. "My dear, that is impossible for someone of your position. If your father does show up here he will have me drawn and quartered if he finds you among the working class."

"Uncle, I don't need to remind you that this is a different country and I am determined to support myself. I am no longer dependent on Father and I have not come all this way to be a burden on you."

"My dear, you have never been forced to earn a coin and I assure you I can certainly see to your needs. I do not consider you a burden." Her desire to work was the last thing George expected out of a young woman who had been coddled her entire life.

"I want to work. I want to live life like everyone else. I'm sorry, but I cannot exist like Mother." She'd given her future a lot of thought, and if her uncle wouldn't assist in her effort, she would find another way.

They discussed this point for over an hour until George finally relented. If she was determined to do this, then he would help her in any way possible. He actually admired her resolve. "What kind of shop do you have in mind?"

"A small shop to carry products for women."

"What kind of products?"

"On my journey here I noticed the farther west I came that there were fewer stores that sell items necessary for a woman's toilette; powders, tinted rouges, perfumes, and such.

"You are so beautiful, surely you have no need of such potions."

"Thank you, but I assure you all women will use such products if they are available. I will carry the finest perfumes, as well as undergarments from France. Such items are only found now in the larger towns."

"You'll not find the women here will buy such foolishness. I thought apothecaries mixed the powders for women. As far as undergarments, these are items that can be purchased at the mercantile."

"I assure you it is not foolishness as all women enjoy looking their best. Apothecaries do mix various powders, but they are not equal to the products from Paris. The undergarments certainly are not what you will find in the local mercantile. They will be designed from the finest silks and satins." She wasn't comfortable discussing intimate apparel with her uncle, but he needed to know what she had in mind, and he seemed truly interested. "I am quite determined. If you do not have space to spare in the hotel I will find another spot."

He quickly concluded his niece was not just a lovely woman, she also had a sharp mind. Far be it from him to know what interested the fairer sex. He would have to take her word for that. It seemed her mind was made up, and he wasn't one to squash her dreams of independence. "What space did you see that you fancied?"

"The space to the right as you walk through the door. The alcove under the staircase is quite large and I can use a partition should the ladies prefer privacy while they are shopping."

"Quite right. That is a space not utilized. While you are getting your shop underway, perhaps you would be interested to learn about managing the hotel. I am building a house on some land outside of town, and it is taking me away from my responsibilities at the hotel on a regular basis. You can register the guests when Eb is occupied with his other duties, and supervise the two ladies who handle the cleaning of the hotel. Mrs. Howe does the cooking in the restaurant. You may need to help her in the dining room when we are busy, nothing too demanding, maybe refill coffee cups, things of that sort."

Mary Ann jumped up and threw her arms around his neck. "Oh thank you! I don't know what I would do without you. I will pay you rent for the space."

"Now, now, this is not something you need to concern yourself with. As I said, the space is not used at present. Let me know what you will need in the way of construction for shelving, painting, or whatever, and I will see to it. We will install a door to have a private entrance."

Her uncle hadn't mentioned the man who carried her luggage to her room. The man with the stunning blue eyes. "Uncle, you didn't mention Mr. McBride. What is his position at the hotel?"

George gave her a puzzled look. "Mr. McBride?"

"Yes, he carried my luggage to my room."

"I have no Mr. McBride employed here."

"That is strange. I'm quite sure he said his name was Luke McBride. He's a very tall man and quite the ruffian."

George laughed. "Luke is not one of the employees. He is one of the owners of the McBride Cattle Company. He is the youngest of the three brothers. Fine men." He furrowed his brow at her. "Ruffian, you say?"

"Indeed. He was brawling in the street when I arrived. I thought he was one of those *pistoliers* I've heard so much about."

"Most men here carry guns and make no mistake, the McBride brothers know how to use them. But they are good men, certainly not gunslingers. I consider them friends, they've been very kind to me."

She had tipped a man who didn't even work for her uncle. "You say they have a ranch here?"

"They own one of the largest cattle ranches in Wyoming. And Luke carried your luggage?"

"Yes, I'm afraid I made a dreadful mistake. I thought he was in your employ and I tipped him." She'd probably insulted one of her uncle's friends.

"No worries, honey. I'm sure he took no offense. Luke is a good-natured man."

She remembered when Mr. McBride was in the room she hadn't been very friendly. He was such a large man that he made her nervous. "I will apologize, of course."

"Don't give it another thought. These men out here don't consider such slights as serious transgressions." He smiled at her. "Particularly if the transgressor is someone as lovely as you."

She hoped her uncle was right and she hadn't offended Mr. McBride. While she didn't countenance his behavior, she wouldn't want her uncle's friends to think ill of him due to her mistake.

George stood and walked to the door. "You best get some rest, we will talk some more over breakfast and make plans for your shop. In the morning I'll have Eb take your things to the third floor. Those are my living quarters for a few more months until my home is completed. You will find the space more accommodating than this room."

Mary Ann hadn't realized he lived on the premises. "The entire third floor is your personal living quarters?"

"Yes, you will have all the room you require. Your bedroom is much larger than this room," George informed her.

"This room is quite lovely. Why are you building a home?"

"I've an interest in trying my hand at cattle ranching. So perhaps your arrival will be most opportune for me if you find you enjoy managing a hotel."

"I am sure I will enjoy it very much and I will start tomorrow." She was anxious to get started now that she had a plan for her future.

"There is no hurry, take some time to rest." George had made the trip from England and it was a grueling journey.

Mary Ann didn't need rest. She was invigorated knowing she would no longer be forced to attend parties gossiping with bored women, or be forced into a marriage she didn't want. "I do not need to rest. Tomorrow is the beginning of my new life."

Chapter Three

"What do you mean you got in a fight with Clyde Slater?" Colt asked. The three brothers were sitting on the porch waiting for the women to get ready to go to church, and it was the first chance Colt had to ask Luke about his busted lip.

"I told you, he was rude to Sally Detrick and I kicked his butt," Luke answered.

"Bad words," Jake reminded his brother.

Luke gave him a sheepish grin. "A synonym for donkey is in the Bible; just ask Cade and Cody." His twin nephews had a way of letting him know what words were in the Bible, and what he could get away with saying and what were *bad words*.

Jake chuckled. "You better put a *jack* in front of it then."

Colt gave them both a hard look. "Luke, you need to stop brawling in the streets."

Luke took a deep breath and expelled it loudly. "Just tell me what you would have done, big brother."

"Yeah, Colt, tell him what you would have done," Jake said. Both Jake and Luke knew Colt would have done the same thing.

Colt couldn't help but laugh. Sometimes his brothers were like dealing with his twin boys. "I know, I know. But it seems to me you have a way of finding trouble, Luke."

"I was taking Sally and Lucinda to lunch, I wasn't looking for trouble, at least not the kind you're thinking about," Luke explained.

Jake shook his head at Luke. "Both of them? Dang, brother, don't you ever get tired?"

"I'm not married." Luke grinned at them. "Remember me? I'm the smart brother."

As soon as the entire family reached church, Luke looked around for George Granville. Almost every Sunday George arrived at the same time they did, but not today. Once inside, Luke looked at every person in the pews, but still no George. He didn't pay attention to the preacher's sermon, his mind kept going back to the beautiful woman he'd met yesterday. Finally, the last hymn ended and everyone filed out of the church. Colt stopped to speak with the preacher at the door, and Jake grabbed Luke by the arm and pulled him aside.

"What are you looking for, little brother?"

"I was looking for George Granville."

Colt walked up behind them and overheard Luke. "Why are you looking for George?" He'd also noticed his brother's lack of attention during the sermon.

"I had something to ask him."

"Well, I imagine he's at the hotel. Come on, the family's having dinner there," Colt said.

The men preferred to eat at home, but Colt liked to surprise the ladies with a dinner in town when they had the time. Victoria hadn't been out of the house much since little Tate was born and it was a treat for her.

The ladies and boys joined them, and Colt took the baby from Victoria. "Are you ladies ready to go to the hotel?"

"Yes," Victoria and Promise answered together.

"Mrs. Howe makes a delicious apple dumpling," Promise said.

"Your apple pies are better," Jake told her.

Promise stood on her tiptoes and kissed her husband's cheek. "You eat so many you are going to turn into an apple pie one of these days." It pleased her that he still preferred her cooking.

Luke took the twin boys by the hand and led the way to the hotel. As soon as they entered the restaurant, Luke spotted two young women who had been vying for his time, Emma and Lorraine, sitting on the other side of the room. He glanced at Jake and told him he'd be right back.

Jake glanced across the room and knew what his brother was up to. "Don't take too long, we want to order before midnight."

Luke approached the table and removed his hat. "Hello, ladies."

"Please join us, Luke," Emma said.

"Thanks, but I'm having Sunday dinner with the family. I just wanted to come over and say hello."

"Are we going to see you at the church social at the end of the month?" Lorraine asked.

"I'll see you before then. You are still planning to come to dinner next week, aren't you?" Emma was excited that Luke had accepted her dinner invitation. Everyone thought Sally Detrick had her hooks in him and no one else stood a chance.

Luke was so busy flaunting his charms to Emma and Lorraine that he didn't notice Mary Ann Hardwicke walking from the kitchen. She stopped to place some plates and silverware on top of the sideboard, and saw Luke conversing with two ladies just a few feet away. She thought she would apologize to him for mistaking him for a hotel employee, but when she heard his conversation with the women, she changed her mind.

"Emma, I'm looking forward to dinner next week, and I promise, honey, I won't be late. And yes, Lorraine, you can count on me to be at the social. I won't forget and I promise I'll show both of you ladies a good time. We'll dance the night away."

Mary Ann rolled her eyes at his comments, thinking every time she saw him he was making promises to show women a good time. Mr. McBride was a lothario of the worst kind. Her uncle might be friends with the man, but she didn't want to have anything to do with him.

"We heard about your day at the lake with Sally. Was she really wearing only her shimmy?" Emma asked.

Luke couldn't believe Sally would have confided in two of the town's biggest gossips about their day at the lake. He leaned over and whispered, "I never kiss and tell, ladies."

"Emma and I like to swim in the lake, why don't you take us?" Lorraine asked.

Lorraine's implicit meaning wasn't lost on Luke. "Maybe next time."

Mary Ann's mouth dropped open. She didn't know what was most disturbing: the seducer's behavior, or the lack of propriety by the women fawning all over him. She turned from the sideboard and hurried across the room before he saw her.

Mary Ann's uncle intercepted her as she neared the McBride table. George introduced her to the family, and after an exchange of a few pleasantries, Mary Ann left to check on the ladies cleaning the rooms upstairs. She was taking her new position at the hotel very seriously, determined not to disappoint her uncle.

"Your niece is absolutely lovely," Victoria said to George.

"She is widely regarded as the beauty of London," George replied.

"Is she staying in Promise long?" Victoria asked.

"Unless her father comes after her, she says she's planning on making this her home."

Before the women could ask more questions, Colt spoke up. "I think Luke wanted to see you about something, George."

"Where is Luke, I haven't seen him?"

Jake pointed across the room. "He's over there flirting with the ladies, where else?"

George smiled. "If only I could be half as popular with the ladies." He gave a knowing look to Colt and Jake and added, "Not to mention his stamina."

"Would you tell him I'm going to order for him in two minutes?" Colt was hungry and tired of waiting on Luke to return. As long as there were women to impress, Luke might be gone for hours.

"Certainly."

"That was an odd response," Promise said.

"What was odd?" Colt asked.

"George said his niece was staying unless her father came for her. He made it sound as if her father might not be keen on her being here."

* * *

"Luke, your brother said you wanted to see me," George said.

"Excuse me, ladies." Luke pulled George a few feet away so the women couldn't hear his conversation. "I wanted to ask you about a young woman who registered at your hotel yesterday."

George chuckled. "You must be referring to my niece. I just introduced her to your family. She told me about meeting you."

"Your niece?" Luke wasn't expecting this news. His eyes flickered to the table across the room, but he didn't see her.

"Yes, my niece, Mary Ann. I hope she didn't offend you by thinking you were employed at the hotel."

"Not at all." Hearing George was her uncle put a whole new twist on things.

"What did you want to ask?"

Luke didn't directly answer the question. "Did she travel from England all alone?"

"Yes, I wasn't aware of her plans to come here. It's probably a good thing as I would have been worried to death. She experienced a few harrowing situations along the way."

Luke couldn't believe it, a pretty little thing like her traveling all the way from England alone. She had to be scared to death. In his mind, it would have been surprising if she hadn't received some unwanted attention since she was so beautiful. That probably accounted for her wariness around him yesterday.

"She wanted to apologize to you about yesterday."

"That's not necessary; no harm done."

"I told her no man could be angry with someone so lovely." George started to walk away, but he remembered Colt's request. "Your brother said he would be ordering for you in two minutes."

Luke laughed and headed to the table. After they ordered dinner, Victoria told him about meeting George's niece while he was off flirting with Emma and Lorraine. "She's a very lovely woman."

"I saw her yesterday," Luke informed them.

"And you don't have a dinner date yet?" Jake asked him.

Luke wasn't about to admit to his brothers that the woman they were discussing had absolutely no interest in him. "No, I really didn't get the chance to spend any time with her." That was sort of the truth; he didn't spend the amount of time he'd wanted to when they were alone in her room.

"Was this before or after the fight with Clyde?" Colt asked.

"After." Maybe she was repulsed by his appearance yesterday. That thought gave him hope.

"I hope we get the chance to know her better, I would love for her to meet Mrs. Wellington and hear all about her journey," Victoria said. She thought her surrogate mother would enjoy the opportunity to speak with one of her countrywomen.

"Mrs. Wellington would enjoy a visit with her," Colt agreed.

"We should invite her to dinner," Promise said.

"Did you know she traveled all the way from England alone?" Victoria directed her question at Luke.

"That's what George told me."

"I can't believe she traveled all that way unchaperoned," Promise said.

Victoria told Luke about George's comment regarding Mary Ann's father, and Luke recalled Mary Ann's response when he asked if she was staying a long time. The entire time Luke was eating, his eyes remained fixed on the staircase hoping she would come back downstairs. Just as they were about to leave the hotel, his wish was granted. As soon as Luke spotted her on the staircase, he told his family he would catch up with them at the livery.

He stopped at the landing, blocking Mary Ann's path. "Hello again."

Reaching the last step, Mary Ann's gaze swept to his hips, noticing he was absent his gun today.

"Mr. McBride."

"So you're George's niece?" He liked her yellow dress and he really liked the way it hugged her curves.

"Yes, I am." She hesitated, not really wanting to engage in a conversation with him, but she needed to apologize. "Please forgive me for thinking . . . well . . . that you were in my uncle's employ. He informed me of my mistake."

Luke, never one to waste what he saw as an opportunity, said, "I know how you can make it up to me."

Mary Ann was surprised by his response. "Excuse me?"

Luke moved an inch closer. She was still on the second step so they were nearly at eye level. "You can make it up to me by having dinner with me."

Mary Ann backed up a step. "Certainly not. I've apologized, and you, sir, if you were a gentleman, would accept."

Luke arched his brow at her. "Who said I was a gentleman?"

His comment really flustered her. Her uncle had said the McBride brothers were fine men, and his brothers appeared to be gentlemen when she met them. They even stood to greet her, but this McBride brother was something else altogether. "I should have known by your behavior yesterday that you are certainly not a gentleman."

What in Hades was she talking about? He thought

he was the perfect gentleman in her room yesterday. He'd prided himself on not even trying to steal a kiss. He usually worked faster than that. "What's that supposed to mean?"

She narrowed her silver eyes on him. "Brawling in the streets. Real gentlemen don't behave like common ruffians in England."

God had definitely blessed her in the beauty department, but she might be lacking in common sense. She must think him a real country bumpkin. Well, she had another think coming. "I suppose I could have demanded satisfaction for insulting a lady and killed him in a duel for his bad manners."

Did he really think those two women he was sashaying around were ladies? She'd seen the way they put their hands all over him. She arched her perfectly shaped little eyebrow at him. "Ladies? I assure you they haven't a nodding acquaintance with the word!" With that said, she presented him with her back and promptly marched back upstairs.

Chapter Four

Luke was so busy at the ranch it prevented him from going back to town for over a week. He'd even been forced to cancel his dinner with Emma on Friday night. He hoped by Saturday night he would have time to go to dinner at the hotel in hopes of seeing Mary Ann. After his last encounter with her he might just be a glutton for punishment, but he was confident he would eventually charm her. He'd yet to meet a woman he couldn't win over. In his mind he saw himself having a nice dinner, of course he'd ask her to join him, and then, if he played his cards right, she'd invite him up to her room. If the night didn't turn out as he planned, he would head to the saloon and play some poker with the men and then . . . well, he'd see what he had the energy for after that. Either way, he was going to enjoy his Saturday night.

Mary Ann spent the week at her uncle's side learning the hotel business. Her nights were occupied with writing to merchants in France where she had once shopped, to place orders for her inventory. True to his word, her uncle had men build shelves and paint the space. He'd even supplied her with a display case that he had stored in the hotel. She'd visited the mercantile and purchased some dress forms to display her garments. Things were going along quite nicely, and she was eager to have her little shop open.

Mary Ann was behind the front desk when her uncle approached. "Mary Ann, Mrs. Howe has taken ill and I had Eb see her home and fetch the doctor. I don't know what we will do about the people already coming in for dinner. The maids have left for the evening, and Eb doesn't know the first thing about cooking. It's Saturday night and that is our busiest time."

"Shall I give it a go, Uncle?" Mary Ann had never cooked a meal in her life, but she felt certain it couldn't be that difficult. She was more than willing to give it a try.

George was skeptical; he wasn't sure Mary Ann had ever stepped foot in a kitchen. "Do you think you could handle the cooking? We could have a large crowd."

"Certainly. When Eb returns he can take the orders and I shall see to the preparations."

George was pleased with her willingness to pitch in and help. "If you are certain you can handle it, I will keep an eye on the desk and help Eb in the dining room."

Luke had taken time with his appearance before he left home, making sure he had a very close shave and his boots were shined. By the time he arrived at the restaurant there were already a few diners sitting at the tables. Once he took a seat where he could see everyone coming and going, he heard one of the diners complain to Eb in a louder than necessary voice,

"If I wanted my steak this rare I would have walked to the range and sliced a piece off its rear end while he was still moving." The man shoved the platter back toward Eb. "I want rare, not raw."

"I'm sorry, I'll take care of it," Eb stammered. He grabbed the platter and headed back to the kitchen.

George approached Luke when he passed his table. "Luke, I'm sorry but this might not be the best night to have dinner. Mrs. Howe is ill and my niece is trying to do the cooking." He inclined his head toward the table where the complaining patron was sitting. "As you can tell, I don't think it is going well."

Luke heard the murmurs of discontent from the other diners and he saw his opportunity. "Tell you what, George, you just keep it simple tonight. Tell everyone they are getting steaks and spuds, and I'll lend a hand with the cooking."

"You can cook?" George didn't think the McBride brothers looked like the kind of men who would ever need to cook their own meals.

"I can manage to cook a good steak. I'm a bachelor who lived alone in the middle of nowhere." He stood and slapped George on the back. "No worries. But remember, steaks and spuds, nothing else."

George smiled. "That'll be fine. Almost everyone orders that meal anyway."

Luke walked through the kitchen door and came to a halt. Smoke was filling the room, and Mary Ann was leaning over the stove fanning something. Her hair was hanging in disarray, half up and half down, and her dress sleeves were pushed to her elbows. She certainly didn't look as proper as the last time he had seen her.

Without turning around she asked, "Eb, what do you need?"

I need you, Luke thought. "I think I should ask what you need."

Mary Ann whirled around to see Luke standing in the doorway. She didn't know what he wanted, probably to complain about something like the other diners. She didn't have time for him. "Not now, Mr. McBride, I'm busy."

"I can see that." Luke put his hat on a hook.

Mary Ann glanced back at him to see he was still in the room. "What?" Her tone wasn't patient.

"I told George I would help you out in here."

She whirled around to face him, and the look she gave him might have made a lesser man turn tail and run. "You what?"

He walked beside her and glanced at the stove. "I'm going to help you out in here. First, let's open this damper more."

She watched as he started opening latches he had no business opening. "What do you think you are doing?"

He grinned at her. "You don't want the whole restaurant to fill up with smoke, do you?"

She shook her head, feeling every bit the fool. She had no idea why the room was smoky.

"Now, we are going to cook steak and potatoes."

She stared at him like he was speaking in a foreign tongue. His face was mere inches from hers and all she could think about was how handsome he looked.

Luke grinned. "Potatoes?"

Collecting her thoughts, she pointed to the pot on the stove. "Eb boiled them earlier and they are ready to mash."

"Good. We need to add more wood to the stove to get the temperature up for the steaks," Luke said as he turned and walked to the table.

Mary Ann turned around and saw him lean over and untie the leather thong around his thigh. When his large hands moved to unbuckle his gun belt, she couldn't take her eyes off him. She'd never seen a man remove an article of clothing, other than perhaps a jacket, certainly never a gun. There was something about his movements that almost seemed intimate, and she shouldn't be watching. But it was such an utterly masculine gesture that she ignored her own commands.

Luke was aware of those silver eyes on him. After he placed his holster over the back of a chair, he walked back to the stove. When she looked up to meet his gaze they simply stared at each other. He would give anything to know what she was thinking. He spotted a streak of flour on her cheek and when he brushed it off, her eyes widened in surprise. He wondered if she realized the top three buttons of her high-neck shirt were open. He wasn't going to tell her since he was imagining his lips following that trail of buttons. *Get control,* he told himself. "Firewood?"

His touch left her breathless, and it took her a minute to realize he'd said something to her. "Pardon?"

"Wood for the stove?"

"Oh." She pointed to the corner of the room where Eb had stacked some wood earlier.

Luke grabbed a couple pieces of wood, returned to the stove, and tossed it inside. "Now we're in business." He looked around the room. It was a nice kitchen with the latest stove and the largest ice chest he'd ever seen. George had spared no expense outfitting the place. He glanced at the long wood table and saw a pan of beautifully browned biscuits. "Did you make those?"

"Yes, I can do that much, but I'm afraid I've made a mess of everything else." He seemed to fill the room

with his manly presence. Just watching him move
about the kitchen made her heart start pounding
faster. It was a new experience for her to have such a
physical reaction to a man. She could almost understand why those women had their hands all over him.
He was undeniably handsome and so physically appealing she could understand why women were naturally
attracted to him.

"They look delicious. You did the hard part. The
steaks are easy." He saw the platter that Eb had brought
back to the kitchen with the undercooked steak. "First,
let's cook this one a bit more." He threw the steak back
into the iron skillet. "Do you want to watch this steak
while I mash the potatoes? It'll just take one turn and
I'll tell you when."

"Yes." She was still confused by her reaction to him.
She reminded herself that he was a rake, but that didn't
seem to make a difference as she tried to control her
runaway emotions. His arm brushed against hers with
his every movement and she felt her skin getting warm
and her hands started to shake. She'd never responded
to a man the way she was responding to him and she
was flustered by the entire situation.

Picking up the butter on the table, Luke plopped
a large amount into the potatoes. He knew he was
making her nervous by standing so close, but that only
fueled his actions. He reached around her to grab a
spoon and brushed against her back, but his plan backfired. He was the one that became rattled by the contact. He had the urge to wrap his arms around her
waist and pull her to him. She smelled good, almost
good enough to eat. He saw himself leaning over and
planting small kisses on her neck. "You smell better
than these mashed potatoes."

She kept her eyes on the steak. "Thank you." He

smelled good too, like sunshine and leather. She could feel the muscles flexing in his arm as he worked.

"Time to turn."

She stared up at him and he smiled at her. His teeth were perfectly straight and very white. *Is there anything about him that isn't attractive?* "Turn?" she questioned.

He put his hand over hers and speared the steak in her skillet and flipped it over.

"Oh." His large hand on top of hers was surprisingly gentle.

Eb walked into the room and handed Luke another returned steak. "We have orders for eight more steaks."

"We'll get them done," Luke told him. He grabbed another huge iron skillet hanging over the stove and placed it over the flames.

"Isn't anyone ordering anything other than steaks?" Mary Ann asked.

"No," Luke answered.

"Luke said they could only order steaks tonight," Eb put in.

"But why?"

Luke winked at Mary Ann. "That's the best thing I can cook."

This was a night filled with firsts for Mary Ann. No man had ever winked at her, and she didn't know what it was about that particular gesture, but it stirred her insides. She told herself that he probably winked at every woman he saw, but her heart started doing flip-flops all the same.

Luke stabbed the sizzling steak in the skillet and tossed it on a plate, adding some potatoes and a biscuit before passing it to Eb. "This is for that loudmouth in the dining room, Eb."

Eb's eyes lit up. "Thanks, Luke. Maybe this will shut him up."

"If it doesn't, come and get me."

Mary Ann turned her eyes on him. "Was someone upset?"

"Nothing to worry about." He picked up a fork, scooped it into the potatoes and then held the creamy mound to her mouth. "Tell me if they're good."

She nibbled the potatoes off the fork. "Oh, yes, very good."

When she licked her lips Luke wanted to pick her up and start nibbling on her. "More?" His voice sounded strange to his own ears.

The way Luke was looking at her mouth, she was certain he was about to kiss her. And to her surprise, she didn't think she would have objected. "Later, we need to get started on the other steaks."

I'd like to start on you, he thought.

"How did you learn to cook?"

"I've traveled around some and if I didn't cook, I didn't eat. Sometimes we are out on the range for weeks at a time and we don't always bring a cook with us. Did you cook at home?"

Mary Ann laughed. "Heavens no. Father would have never allowed that. We had several cooks."

He turned from the stove and reached for a biscuit off the table. When he saw her watching him, he said, "I need to keep up my strength." He took a big bite and offered the remainder to her.

"No, thank you."

He loved a good biscuit and these were soft and fluffy on the inside and the top perfectly golden brown. He could have eaten the whole platter. "How did you learn to make biscuits?"

"Lillian taught me. She's the wife of the man who managed the way station in Missouri where we spent

the night. I told her they were the best biscuits I ever
ate and she was kind enough to show me how to make
them. We didn't sleep at all that night, we just talked.
I don't think she sees many women and she was thrilled
to have company. She was a lovely woman."

If he was with her all night they wouldn't be talking.
"Will you make more so I can have some for dinner
later?"

"Of course." She was delighted he liked them. "It's
the least I can do for what you are doing tonight. I'm
sure you came in for a nice dinner and not to do more
work after a long day at the ranch."

He finished the biscuit and turned his gaze on her,
his teasing demeanor was replaced by a sincere request. "I want you to make them only if you want to
make them for me. I don't want you to feel indebted.
I'll cook you a steak and then we can enjoy a nice
dinner after the last customer is served."

Her heart started thumping again when she looked
into his turquoise eyes. At that moment she feared she
would do anything he asked. Just like all the women
she'd seen with him since she arrived in town, she
was succumbing to his charms. She nodded her
agreement.

They worked companionably for two hours, only interrupted from their cooking when Eb came in with
new orders. While they worked Mary Ann asked questions about his life. She learned what it meant to bust
broncs, and about the many places he'd traveled. Luke
noticed she didn't talk much about her life in England
and what she did tell him, he thought it sounded stifling. He couldn't imagine days structured around
parties and teas. She did mention some of the details
of her journey when she left England. Just as he'd

suspected, she hadn't escaped male attention along the way.

"You didn't say why you decided to come to Wyoming." Luke was curious as to why she traveled all that way by herself.

Before she responded, George walked into the kitchen. "We're done for the night. Why don't we have a late dinner?"

"That was my plan." While Luke enjoyed George's company, he was disappointed that he wouldn't be dining alone with Mary Ann. "I'll cook four steaks. I bet Eb has worked up a hunger, he did the hard work putting up with the customers."

Mary Ann was busy cutting out the biscuits and thinking over everything she'd discussed with Luke. It was fun listening to his stories, but she thought it prudent that her uncle would be dining with them. It was proving difficult to be indifferent to his masculine appeal.

"I've smelled those steaks all night, and judging by the reaction of the customers they were delicious. I can't wait to dig into one."

Eb walked in with some dishes from the dining room. "I'm starving."

Everyone laughed. "Four steaks coming up," Luke said.

Chapter Five

George finished his steak and leaned back in his chair enjoying his glass of wine. "Luke, I don't know how to thank you. Not only for all of your hard work tonight, but also for that wonderful steak. It's the best I've ever eaten, but I dare not tell Mrs. Howe." He had a feeling that Luke enjoyed his evening with Mary Ann even though they were working in the kitchen. He'd seen the way he looked at his niece. If he wasn't mistaken, Luke was smitten.

Luke gazed at Mary Ann when he answered. "It was my pleasure, George." It didn't feel like work to Luke, he'd enjoyed every moment he spent with Mary Ann. It didn't matter what he was doing, he just liked being near her. What man alive would tire of looking at her? It was a bonus that she was much more than a pretty face. He stuffed his sixth biscuit in his mouth. "I would cook for you every night if Mary Ann made the biscuits."

"They are delicious," Eb agreed. "I like Mrs. Howe's, but these are even better than hers."

"I think we'd best be careful about our success

tonight when Mrs. Howe returns. She might not feel like she is needed."

"Uncle, if not for Luke, dinner would have been a disaster."

"The three of you saved the day," George replied. "By the way, Mary Ann, did you tell Luke about the shop you are setting up?"

"No, I'm sure that wouldn't interest him."

"It will certainly interest his sisters-in-law," George replied.

"Now I'm curious," Luke said, directing his gaze on her.

"Mary Ann is setting up a small shop to carry items for the ladies," George told him.

Luke wasn't surprised to hear of her plans. He'd already figured out she was an intelligent woman by the many questions she'd asked tonight.

"Actually, I'll carry items from France. I will have powders, perfumes, and ladies' wear." She wasn't about to mention undergarments in mixed company. It was one thing to talk to her uncle about her plans privately, but she wasn't comfortable discussing such things with Luke.

Luke grinned. "That might not be just for the ladies." He wouldn't mind dabbing perfume on her in all the right places.

Before Mary Ann could ask what he meant by that statement, the door to the hotel opened and in walked Clyde Slater with two of his friends.

This can't be happening again, Luke thought.

Seeing they were headed to a table, George stood and moved toward them. "I'm sorry, the restaurant is closed."

"It ain't closed until we had our supper," Clyde

growled. The three men pulled the chairs out and plopped down. "We want steaks."

"The kitchen is closed, everyone has gone home. You gentlemen need to come back tomorrow," George said sternly.

"Then you cook us something."

"Clyde, go on back to the saloon. The restaurant is closed," Luke said in a no-nonsense tone from across the room.

Clyde looked up and tried to focus his bleary eyes on Luke. "Stay out of this, McBride."

Luke pushed his chair back and walked across the room to stand beside George. "Clyde, it's late and I'm tired and these fine people are ready to go to bed. So why don't you boys go on back to the saloon."

"We're hungry," one of the men whined.

"Then go home and fix yourself something to eat," Luke suggested.

Clyde stood and glared at Luke. "You're always butting into my business."

Luke knew Clyde was drunk by the way he was slurring his words. "Do you really want to do this now? Or do you want to go on back to the saloon?" Luke wished he hadn't left his pistol in the kitchen, he didn't feel like having another fistfight. But he didn't want Clyde to leave the hotel thinking he could come back at any time and harass George, particularly with Mary Ann around.

One of Clyde's friends stood. "Come on, Clyde. Let's go on back to the saloon."

Remembering the last outcome of the fight with Luke, Clyde decided to leave. "We'll settle this another time, McBride."

Luke was relieved he wasn't going to have to break any furniture or windows. Not to mention, he didn't want another busted lip. He followed the three men to the door and locked it behind them, with George right behind him.

"Thanks again, Luke," George said.

Luke spoke quietly to George before they walked back to the table. He didn't like the fact that he couldn't protect Mary Ann if necessary. "George, you should start carrying a gun."

"I'm not sure I would be comfortable using one."

"What if Mary Ann's safety is at stake?"

"I see your point."

"If nothing else you might place some weapons strategically around the hotel so you could get to them in a hurry if necessary."

"Good practical advice, Luke. I will see to it."

"I'm going to go home," Eb said.

"Come in later tomorrow, Eb, you've earned some time off," George told him.

When Eb left, George locked the door behind him before walking back to the table. "I think I will retire for the night. You two take your time."

Mary Ann started clearing the table. "I'll just wash these before I go up."

Luke picked up the remaining dishes and followed her to the kitchen.

"It seems that man is always drunk." Mary Ann recognized Clyde as the man whom Luke was fighting with the first day she saw him.

Luke chuckled. "He does his fair share of drinking."

Mary Ann washed the dishes as Luke dried. "The saloon does a booming business. They start early and are open very late." She'd heard noise from the saloon at all hours.

Luke had to agree with that. "Most saloons do a fair

trade. That's the only place men can go and let off a little steam."

She wasn't familiar with all of the phrases used by people in this country. "What do you mean *let off steam?*"

It surprised him she'd never heard the term. "It means to relax, have some whiskey and play poker and . . ." He almost said visit with the gals, but he didn't think that would be wise.

"I see. My uncle says saloons are similar to the clubs men frequent at home to play cards and have their spirits."

"I imagine they are the same thing." Luke had never been to England and he wondered if the clubs had women serving liquor.

"Do the women who work there play poker and drink whiskey too?" She'd never seen the inside of a saloon so she wasn't familiar with what went on.

"Sometimes. L. B., she's the owner and she's a fine poker player and she drinks whiskey. The gals serve the drinks and . . . provide the entertainment."

"Oh, so the women are playing the piano I hear every night?"

"No, they have a man that plays the piano."

"Do they sing?"

Luke could hardly believe she didn't know what went on in a saloon. She obviously hadn't seen L. B.'s gals hanging over the balcony yet. He guessed her uncle didn't tell her everything that went on across the street and he wasn't going to be the one to enlighten her. "Ah . . . no."

"Do they have plays?"

Oh, they play all right. "No, it's not that type entertainment."

She looked up at him with those large quizzical silver eyes and handed him the last plate.

When she looked at him like that all he wanted to do was kiss her. He thought he'd best change the topic of conversation before his baser thoughts got the best of him. "We're finished here so why don't you show me your shop?"

She wasn't sure why he didn't want to answer her question, but she didn't think it was wise to ask. It surprised her that he was interested in her little shop. "Certainly."

Before they left the kitchen Luke stoked the stove for the next morning and made sure the back door was locked. He grabbed his gun belt and buckled it around his waist, then grabbed his hat. As they walked through the dining room he turned off the oil lamps and Mary Ann extinguished the candles on the tables. Reaching the area under the staircase, Mary Ann pulled back a drape that Eb had hung for her until the door was installed. "The drapery is temporary. We will have a lovely door with a glass oval here. I'm afraid there's not much to see since I don't have all of my inventory."

Luke struck a match to the oil lamp sitting on the display case and the soft light illuminated the room. The room was more spacious than he'd expected and she had arranged the space nicely. His gaze went to the dress forms in the corner. "Are you going to sell ladies dresses?"

"No, those are for . . . ah . . . ladies' undergarments." Her skin started to get hot again and she blushed.

Luke smiled when he saw her turning pink. He couldn't resist asking, "You mean like corsets and chemises?"

She nodded.

His eyes automatically went to the bodice of her dress and he wondered if she was wearing a corset. "These things are coming from France?"

"Hmm, yes."

He remembered the small package Sally had showed him that day. It was from France and it was very small. "When will the items be here?"

She wondered what he was thinking. "In a couple of weeks."

He'd like to see her model a corset for him. He needed to get control of his thoughts. "I guess it's not like the things sold at the mercantile. I have a feeling Mr. Foster will not be too happy with his new competition."

"I purchased the dress forms from his wife. She inquired if I was selling ready-made dresses. To tell you the truth I hadn't thought of selling dresses, but her question made me consider ordering dresses from Paris. Of course, they would be for special occasions." She thought she might be boring him to tears with talk of fashion, but he made her nervous.

"You may want to talk to my sister-in-law Victoria. She makes those bags you ladies carry. She has orders from shops in London and Paris."

"Reticules?"

He nodded. "Yeah, that's what they're called."

"Oh, I would love to see them. They would look lovely in the display case."

Luke turned his attention to the shelves lining the wall behind the display case. "This is where you will put the perfumes and powders?"

"Yes, I thought it would be wise to have the expensive crystal bottles on the higher shelves."

"I expect you might have some male customers." He didn't know how he'd like men coming in to look at ladies' undergarments and Mary Ann helping them. He knew men and he knew what they would be thinking. Exactly what he was thinking.

She hadn't thought men would be interested in the items she carried. "There will be nothing for men here."

Luke almost laughed. He tapped the mahogany display case that was glistening under the light. "What will be in here?"

"More items for ladies."

"Like?" What else did women wear besides corsets and camisoles? He mentally stripped off her clothing. Oh, maybe she was talking about bloomers and . . . "Ah . . . stockings and garters." And she thought there wasn't going to be anything in here for men.

He certainly knew his way around a woman's wardrobe. "I've also ordered some jewelry."

Luke liked the way she thought, she'd make a fine shop owner. She was full of good ideas and he expected she'd have a booming business before long. "You could place advertisements in the newspaper."

She was thrilled that he truly seemed interested. "That is a wonderful idea!"

His eyes met hers and he thought about moving closer and taking her in his arms. But he didn't want to hurry things along. Things had gone well tonight and he didn't want to jeopardize the progress he'd made. "I think you'll have a nice business here. There's a shop at a hotel in Denver that is similar."

"You've been there?"

"Yes, but I like yours better."

"Do they carry items for men?"

"No, but men like to give presents." He didn't dare tell her he'd bought many delicate items for women in the past.

"I see." She had a feeling that he'd purchased gifts in that shop in Denver. Probably for one of the women he'd been making promises to the first day she saw him. Or for all of them.

"I best get out of here, I'm sure you're tired." He didn't really want to leave, but it had been a good night and he didn't want to make a wrong move.

She turned around and led him to the door. She was sorry to see him go, and that thought surprised her.

Luke tapped the lock on the door. "Lock this behind me."

"I will. Thank you so much for your help tonight."

"You're welcome. Maybe you'll make biscuits for me again."

"I will."

He leaned over and she thought he was going to kiss her, but he didn't. He pulled the comb from her hair, allowing all of it to tumble past her shoulders. "It looks beautiful down."

When he held the comb to her she took it with trembling fingers. He set her nerves on end. "I'm afraid my hair wouldn't stay up tonight in the heat."

Luke wondered if she was talking about the heat radiating from him as he stood next to her smelling her sweet scent or from the fire. He really wanted to kiss her, but he wasn't sure how receptive she would be. Funny, he'd never questioned whether a woman wanted to be kissed. He'd always been able to read their signals. He thought he'd made some headway with her so he decided to take it nice and slow. At least she didn't tell him he wasn't a gentleman tonight.

He opened the door and settled his Stetson on his head. "Sweet dreams."

"Good night."

Before he walked away he watched her through the glass as she turned the lock in the door. He winked at her and she gave him a little wave.

Luke thought about heading to the saloon, but he'd nixed that idea just as he heard a voice call out.

"Hi, Luke, honey, what are you doing at the hotel so late?"

He looked up to see three of L. B.'s gals on the balcony. It looked like every light in the place was lit and he could see the girls were half dressed. He didn't turn around, he knew without looking that Mary Ann was still at the door and if he could see the girls in their state of undress, so could she. "Enjoying a late dinner."

"Well come on over, honey. It's not too late for us to show you a good time."

"Too late for poker tonight." It seemed Mary Ann didn't know what went on in a saloon so maybe he would pull off that response without her being any the wiser.

"We ain't talking about poker, Luke, honey." The gal's comment made the other girls laugh.

Oh Lord, could this get any worse? "Night, ladies."

He walked fast toward the livery to get his horse with female catcalls echoing down the vacant street.

Chapter Six

Colt held up a piece of paper when Luke walked in his office. "This telegram came for you."

Luke took the telegram and read the few lines. "This is strange."

"Yeah?"

"I told you about my partner in the Lucky Sunday silver mine, Sam White," he reminded Colt.

"You've mentioned him several times."

"The telegram is from his wife, Arina. It says she will be here on the fifteenth."

"Did she say why?"

"No, just that she would be in on the noon stage." Luke had only seen Arina a few times before his partner married her. He had only been partners with Sam for two years, and while he considered Sam a friend, they rarely discussed anything other than business. He was aware Sam was courting a younger woman, but he hadn't pried into his personal life. His partnership with Sam happened mostly by accident when they met at a poker table. Sam struck up a conversation with him about training horses on his ranch after he'd heard of Luke's skill with horses. Not long after Luke started working with the horses, Sam approached him with an offer of paying him in the form of stock in the mine, saying it would save him an outlay of cash while the mine was just getting started. Luke knew it was a bit of a gamble, he might never see a cent for all of his hard work, but he was in a position to take some risks. Sam also liked to gamble at the poker table, and Luke liked to win. Over the course of a year, Luke had won half of the Lucky Sunday mine off Sam, which was now turning attractive profits.

Right after Luke attended Sam's wedding he'd left for Wyoming, and he hadn't seen Sam since that day. They'd stayed in touch by telegrams and letters over the last year, but now that he thought about it, he hadn't heard from Sam in a few months.

"Is she coming alone?" Colt asked.

"It sounds like it. I wonder why Sam isn't coming with her. I don't know her very well. I left for Wyoming right after they married."

Jake walked in and heard the last part of their conversation. "Maybe she got tired of old Sam and is looking for a new husband."

"Not likely. Sam's a fine man and he's not that old, mid-fifties. Besides, he has more than enough money to make up for his age." Luke had heard talk among the ranch hands that Arina was marrying Sam for his money. She was an attractive young woman who could have had her choice of many younger suitors. It wasn't much of a stretch to think Sam's money was a factor in her decision-making. But that was none of his business, then or now.

Luke was truly perplexed. He thought about sending a telegram to Sam, but if he was coming with his wife, they would already be on the way. And meeting the stage gave him a good reason to go to town in the middle of the week, and he could see Mary Ann again. He hadn't seen her since the night they cooked together because he'd been busy at the ranch. Well, if he was totally honest with himself, ranch work wasn't the only reason he hadn't been back to town. Knowing Mary Ann had heard every word L. B.'s gals said to him that night, he expected she would give him a cool reception. Then again, he always did like a challenge.

George moved Mary Ann's belongings to the third-floor private residence. For the first time they were enjoying a nice private dinner away from the hotel restaurant. "Mary Ann, I never dined up here until you arrived."

"Why not? The quarters are lovely. I never expected anything as grand in a hotel." He wasn't exaggerating when he'd mentioned in his letters that his hotel was exquisite. Her bedroom was every bit as luxurious as the one she had at home, plus she felt much more relaxed here with her uncle.

George looked around the room as though he'd never seen it before. "It always seemed too lonely, but now that you are here, we will do so much more often while the home is being built. We should invite guests, too." He was thrilled to have his niece living with him. He'd left England several years ago, and this was the first time he had the opportunity to really get to know her. She was an amazing young woman, quick to learn everything he'd taught her about the hotel business, and she was particularly adept with mathematical calculations. "We could invite Luke. I haven't seen him since the night he helped you cook."

Mary Ann had tried not to think about Luke after the last time she'd seen him. She'd started to second-guess her opinion of him that night, thinking she had misjudged him. Right up until they said good-bye. Then she saw those women at the saloon in their underclothes conversing with him. She may not have understood what those women did at the saloon when she was discussing it with Luke, but she was no longer in the dark. Listening to their comments to him that night, there was no doubt in her mind what type of entertainment they provided upstairs. Subsequently, she'd had ample time to observe the saloon women, and the many men coming and going. Her bedroom window faced the saloon, and she had seen and heard the men upstairs with the women on warm nights when the windows were open. She couldn't have been more shocked. And to think they knew Luke well enough to speak to him on the street. He must have had a good laugh at her naïveté. Her first impression was right on target. He was a scoundrel. "Uncle, what exactly do the women at the saloon do?"

George choked on his steak. "Pardon?"

"I want to know what type of entertainment the women at the saloon provide. I assume you go there to play cards."

George couldn't stop coughing.

"Are you quite okay?" It was all Mary Ann could do not to laugh at her uncle's discomposure.

Unable to speak, George nodded.

She waited and watched as he sipped his tea.

"The women serve drinks." He thought that response should appease her.

"And what do they do upstairs?" she asked sweetly.

"Well . . . they . . . ah . . . provide companionship with men that desire their . . . that sort of thing."

"Companionship?" *Is that what it's called here in America?*

Once he composed himself, he wanted to find out the reason for her inquiry. "Why do you ask, my dear?"

"When Luke was leaving the hotel that night, the women at the saloon were talking to him. They were on the balcony in their undergarments asking him to come upstairs. It seemed most inappropriate."

"Yes, that behavior is most inappropriate, but they are not conventional young women. They haven't had the benefit of education and family, so we must allow for that."

"Hmm. They seemed to know Luke quite well."

"I'm sure they do. The men from all of the ranches go in to play poker most weekends. That is their form of entertainment."

"Do the women also offer him their *companionship* upstairs?"

He saw no good end to this conversation, so he wanted to change course. "I don't think that is for me to answer. Now, would you like to go out and see the house at the ranch? It is really coming along nicely."

"I would love to see it." She didn't mind the change of subject, she knew she was making him uncomfortable. As a matter of fact she was trying hard not to laugh. She was reminded of Luke's discomfort when they discussed the saloon women.

"Wonderful. We will ride out there soon one morning so you can see where we will be living. You do still ride, don't you?"

"Yes, I love to ride, but I didn't bring my sidesaddle." She'd considered adding her saddle to her trunk, but she didn't have room.

"Not a problem, I have one here somewhere I am sure."

Luke wasn't able to leave the ranch as early as he'd wanted to go meet the stagecoach, but he still hoped to have time to go to the hotel first to see if he might persuade Mary Ann to have lunch with him. He was pushing his horse to go faster when he saw two riders ahead of him. Recognizing one of the horses as belonging to George Granville, he figured the other person riding sidesaddle and wearing a blue hat with feathers had to be the very woman he wanted to see.

When he caught up to them he slowed his horse next to Mary Ann's. "Good morning, folks."

"Why, Luke, what a nice surprise," George said.

Luke waited a beat to see if Mary Ann was going to say hello. Obviously not. "Were you out to see the ranch?"

"Yes, I was showing Mary Ann around. I was just telling her how helpful you and your brothers have been with my venture into cattle ranching."

Luke nudged his horse so close to Mary Ann's that his thigh was actually touching her leg. He looked over at her. "How do you like George's ranch?" Just as he expected, she was acting very cool. No doubt she was going to hold it against him for the behavior of the gals at the saloon.

She made an attempt to get her horse to sidestep closer to her uncle's horse, but the contrary animal wouldn't heed the command. "It's a beautiful place, and my uncle picked a perfect spot for his home."

Luke grinned at her attempt to move away. Maybe she thought he couldn't get his horse to make the same move. He didn't know how he was going to get back in her good graces, but he was determined to find a way. "George, I have to meet the stagecoach today, but I'm early so why don't you and Mary Ann have lunch with me."

"I'm sorry, Mr. McBride, but I have responsibilities to see to upon my return." She'd called him Luke that night in the kitchen. She really was miffed.

George didn't have the same objections. "My dear, as your employer I think we can take time to lunch with Luke."

"Excellent." *Score one for me,* Luke thought. He had a feeling not many people could outmaneuver this little lady. He glanced her way again. She sure did look fetching in her blue hat and riding habit. "I like your blue hat."

That comment made her look his way. He had an uncanny way of surprising her by complimenting her wardrobe. She wondered if he complimented the lack of wardrobe on the saloon women. Mary Ann decided when they reached the hotel, she would go to her quarters to freshen up and take her sweet time doing so. And remove her blue hat. She didn't give a hoot if he liked it or not, she was certain he didn't like it half as much as he liked seeing those women in their corsets. If he thought he could force his unwanted attention on her as he did with the tarts from that saloon he was sorely mistaken. She wouldn't do anything to offend her uncle, but she was determined not to be in the company of this scoundrel.

"Are you expecting a relative on the stage?" George asked, oblivious to the undercurrents between Mary Ann and Luke.

"No, I have a business partner in Arizona, and his wife telegraphed me saying she is coming to Promise, but she didn't say if he would be with her."

Arriving at the hotel, Luke and George walked to George's preferred table in the restaurant while Mary Ann excused herself to go upstairs. The men waited so long for Mary Ann's return that George finally sent Eb upstairs to fetch her.

She joined them at the table a few minutes later and smiled sweetly at her uncle. "I do apologize, but I needed to change. I fear I collected more dust than I thought possible."

Luke liked the pink dress she was now wearing, it reminded him of her pretty pink hat she'd worn the day she came to town. He stood and helped her with her chair. "You look lovely in your pink dress, it was well worth the wait." He'd already figured out her game, but George was completely clueless. He'd bought her innocent little explanation without question.

"As Luke says, it was worth the wait, my dear. But we must order soon, the stagecoach is due and I want Luke to be able to appreciate his lunch."

No such luck. They heard the stagecoach while they were placing their orders. Luke stood and reached for his hat. "I am sorry, but you will have to excuse me."

"No need to apologize. I assume your guest will be staying at the hotel, so we will go with you to greet her and she can lunch with us." George stood and held out his arm to Mary Ann. "Come along, my dear, let's go with Luke."

Luke grinned at the pained expression on Mary Ann's face. Without a word she walked with them to meet the stagecoach, positioning herself very close to her uncle's side and far away from Luke.

A man jumped down from the stage first, and when Luke saw the driver hold his hand to assist the next passenger, he stepped forward. Before Arina stepped to the ground she looked at Luke and literally leaped into his arms. "Oh, Luke." She proceeded to wrap her arms around his neck and kiss him on the lips.

Luke automatically put his hands on her waist when he caught her in the air. When he recovered from the shock of her lips on his, he tried to lean backward to break contact, but her body and her lips followed him. He eased her to the ground, released her waist, and leaned back so their lips were forced to part. His eyes, as if they had a will of their own, drifted down to her cleavage . . . he couldn't help it, her chest was bare and on display and her . . . well . . . they were right there under his nose. He had never noticed how well-endowed she was, but he was certain it wasn't proper for a lady to display so much skin in public. He hadn't seen that much cleavage since the night the gals were hanging over the balcony at L. B. Ditty's. Remembering George and Mary Ann were standing behind him, he glanced their way. It came as no surprise to see their faces mirrored his own shock as they interpreted this strange greeting.

"This is my partner's wife, Arina White. Arina, this is George Granville and his niece, Mary Ann Hardwicke." Luke could tell by Mary Ann's appalled expression that Arina's kiss just put the final nail in his coffin. As if he needed a final nail. Even though they had spent a pleasant evening together that night in the kitchen, the gals at the saloon had rekindled her ill opinion of him. And now there was no telling what she thought seeing his partner's wife land a big kiss on him.

George greeted the woman politely, but Mary Ann remained silent. She wasn't sure she could even form a civil reply. How could a married woman throw herself at a man in the middle of the street in broad daylight? Actually, she was amazed the woman didn't pop out of her dress when she hurled herself through the air at

Luke. Did Luke McBride have any female acquaintances who were not tarts? *His partner's wife indeed!*

"Arina, where is Sam?" Luke asked, but what he
really wanted to ask was what in Hades was that kiss
about. Normally, he might have been excited to have
an attractive woman throw herself at him, but not
Sam's wife under any circumstances.

"That's what I need to see you about, Luke darling."

Luke frowned. *Darling? Darling?* Where did that
come from?

"Mrs. White, we were just going to have lunch,
please join us," George said.

Arina looked Mary Ann up and down, and immedi-
ately came to the conclusion she was involved with Luke.
"I'm sorry, but I need to speak with Luke privately and
I'm afraid it is quite urgent."

Mary Ann breathed a sigh of relief. She didn't want
to be at the same table with the rogue or his . . . his . . .
whatever she was to him. He was the worst sort of cad
to behave that way with his partner's wife.

"I understand," George held his arm for Mary Ann.
"Come, my dear, let's give these two some privacy."

"I apologize, George." He turned his gaze on Mary
Ann. "I was looking forward to our lunch." He wasn't a
man who normally worried about what people thought
about him, but at this very moment he was very concerned. It was inexplicable to him why Mary Ann
Hardwicke's opinion of him mattered, but he couldn't
deny it mattered very much.

"Don't give it another thought, we'll do it another
time." George said as they walked into the hotel.

Luke picked up Arina's luggage that the stagecoach
driver had placed beside them. Arina linked her arm
through Luke's and together they followed George
and Mary Ann to the hotel.

"Could we talk over lunch, Luke?"

"Yes, we'll just get you checked in." He'd allow her time to tell him what was going on before he asked her about the greeting she'd just given him.

George and Mary Ann sat at the table and waited for their order. "She certainly is a lovely young woman, although not extremely circumspect."

Her uncle seemed to be reading her mind, and Mary Ann couldn't disagree with his assessment. The blond woman's apparel, though costly, looked more suitable for the women she'd seen on the balcony at the saloon. Her bodice was way too tight and far too revealing for day. "I should say she is certainly not circumspect. But it appears Mr. McBride prefers that type of woman. You should have seen the behavior of the two women he was escorting when he was brawling in the street the day I arrived." Mary Ann finally leveled with her uncle and gave him her true opinion of Luke McBride. "Uncle, I know you like the man, but he is a rake, make no mistake."

"My dear, I heard from the lady who owns the mercantile that Luke was defending the honor of a lady."

Mary Ann frowned at her uncle. "Lady my foot." She did recall Mr. McBride had said those very words to her. But if those women were ladies, why, she would eat her hat, feathers and all.

George chuckled. He wondered if the true reason she had a bad opinion of Luke stemmed from the gals at the saloon talking to him that night. Perhaps it was because of what happened with Edmund Stafford that made her wary of men in general. "Mary Ann, you will see that the men here are very different than in England. Here they often handle their differences with fists or guns in the street. It's the same in England, only we do it in a more gentlemanly fashion, we fight duels at dawn so no one can see."

What had happened to her uncle? Surely he didn't condone such behavior as brawling in the streets, and women dressing indecently and generally behaving like harlots. "It all seems rather uncivilized."

George remembered he'd felt the same way when he first arrived in America so he could appreciate her perspective. "It can be, but the good men here will not allow the rowdies to disrespect ladies. I think they feel it is the most expedient way to handle a problem. Many men carry guns, and good men like Luke McBride must be prepared for any situation. Give him a chance. I think you will come to appreciate a man like Luke."

Before her last encounter with Edmund, Mary Ann may have thought the men in England were different from these men in America. She was no longer that naïve young woman. She'd seen Luke's true colors, he used his charms indiscriminately on every woman he knew. If he were a woman he would be called fickle. She supposed the term for him would be *skirt chaser*. "I'm afraid if you are waiting on the day when I appreciate a man like Luke McBride, you will surely be in for a disappointment, Uncle."

After Luke checked Arina into the hotel, they walked into the restaurant. They sat just a few tables away from George and Mary Ann, and Luke positioned himself so he could watch Mary Ann. After he turned his attention on Arina, he thought she was much lovelier than he remembered with her long blond hair and dark blue eyes. They placed their orders and Luke got right to the point. "Where's Sam?"

"I don't know."

This stunned Luke more than her kiss. "What do you mean you don't know?"

"That's why I came here, I thought he might be with you."

"Maybe you better start at the beginning and tell me everything."

"Sam told me he had to go to Denver on business and I haven't seen or heard from him in three months."

"Did he mention what kind of business?" Luke wasn't aware of any reason Sam would need to be in Denver.

"No, he didn't say. He'd been acting very strange, but I don't know what was wrong with him."

"What do you mean he was acting strange?"

"He wasn't coming home at night. He said he was staying in his office." Arina pulled a handkerchief from her reticule and dabbed at her eyes. "I just don't know what has happened to him."

"Why didn't you telegraph me earlier?"

"I thought he would come back before now."

Luke thought if Sam was in trouble or needed help he would have contacted him. "I haven't heard from Sam for some time. Did you two have an argument?"

"No, we didn't. I was sure he would contact you."

She wasn't telling him something. "Did you ask the sheriff for his help?"

"He said there was nothing he could do if a man wanted to go somewhere without telling anyone."

Luke could understand the sheriff's position, particularly if there was no evidence of foul play. "What about his foreman, Buck?"

"Buck is dead."

Luke leaned forward with his arms on the table. "What happened to him?"

"He was shot just before Sam left."

That was an odd coincidence, Luke thought. "Who killed him?"

"No one knows."

"Arina, I need to ask you about the kiss you gave me. What was that about?"

She reached over and placed her hand over his and stared into his eyes. "I was just so glad to see a familiar face. I'm sorry if I overreacted, but I always felt a connection with you."

Her comment threw him. *Connection?* "We've never even been alone for five minutes, Arina."

Squeezing his hand, she looked at him with sad eyes. "I want to be friends with you, Luke. I know Sam trusted you. Please don't turn me away. I need someone I can trust."

Luke looked away, feeling uncomfortable with Arina's unusual behavior. It had been his plan to ask her if she preferred to stay at the ranch, but after the kiss she'd landed on him, he thought better of that. None of this was making sense to him. He really didn't know anything about Arina, other than the fact she was his partner's wife. Sam had never confided in him about his relationship with her, and it came as a complete surprise when Sam told him he was getting married. The whole situation was confounding. Luke glanced up and found himself staring directly into large silver disapproving eyes. He quickly jerked his hand from Arina's grip.

Chapter Seven

Later that evening, Luke was alone with his brothers and he told them about his meeting with Arina and her strange behavior.

"I can see why you didn't invite her to stay at the ranch," Colt said.

"The way you like to flirt around, are you sure you didn't give her the wrong impression at some point?" Jake asked.

Luke didn't take exception to Jake's question, he didn't hide the fact he liked women. "I don't think I've said more than ten words to her before today. She never paid me the least bit of attention at the wedding, and I left Arizona right after that."

"Did the sky fall?" Jake teased. "You met a woman who wasn't all over you in five minutes. I can't believe it!"

"Very funny," Luke countered. "Sam didn't talk much about her, so I know very little. I don't even know how they met."

"What are you planning on doing?" Colt asked.

"First, I'm going to telegraph the sheriff and see what he can tell me. I'll also telegraph the supervisor at the mine. He worked for Sam before I became a partner."

"Doesn't he have a foreman at the ranch you could contact?" Jake asked.

"That's another strange thing. The foreman I knew at Sam's ranch is dead. He was shot and apparently there are no leads on his killer. Odd coincidence, don't you think?"

"There are no coincidences," Colt and Jake said in unison.

Luke laughed. "I knew you were going to say that. And in this case, I have to agree."

"What are you going to do about the wife?" Colt asked.

"She wants my help, but I'm not sure what I can do from here."

"If you're asking my opinion, I think this is exactly where you need to be," Colt told him.

"Why is that?"

"Think about it, if Sam is not dead, he must have had a purpose for leaving. It stands to reason a man would protect his wife, but as he didn't confide in her, it makes me think he didn't trust her."

Luke hadn't thought about it from that angle. "I'm not sure we can go that far in our thinking."

"Do you think your friend would have left his wife to fend for herself if there was trouble?" Colt asked.

"Not the Sam I know."

"Then if he is alive, do you think his actions indicate he is protecting her or suspecting her of something?"

"Colt has a point," Jake cut in. "Maybe you should keep her here and get to know her a little better. If she has something to hide maybe she'll accidentally say the wrong thing. I'll make some inquiries, too."

"Thanks, Jake. It comes in handy to have an ex-U.S.

Marshal for a brother. Colt might be right. Sam had to have a reason to leave without telling her what was going on." Luke hoped his friend was alive, but he couldn't figure out why he hadn't heard from him if he was.

Luke knocked on the door to room number six. He wasn't so foolish that he expected Mary Ann would be thrilled to see him. She'd made it perfectly clear she was determined not to give him the time of day, but he was equally determined to change her opinion of him once he figured out a way to accomplish that goal.

The door opened and Arina was standing there in a silky robe which was loosely belted. Her hair was disheveled, and Luke thought she looked like she'd just left her bed. "Luke!" Like yesterday, she snuggled up to him and wrapped her arms around his neck. "Why didn't you tell me you were coming?"

With her pressed so tightly to his body he didn't need to ask what she was wearing under her robe. He almost forgot that she wasn't the woman he expected to open the door. "What are you doing here?" Hearing footsteps coming down the hall, he halfway turned to see who it was. Arina was still hanging onto his neck.

He groaned when he saw it was Mary Ann. How could this be happening? She couldn't miss Arina cozied up to him. *Again.* Thank goodness Arina wasn't kissing him this time.

Arina released his neck and took his hand, trying to pull him into her room. "I told you I would be staying for a few days."

He turned to face Mary Ann and tipped his hat when she neared the door. "Mary Ann, I was just coming to see you."

Mary Ann's gaze shifted from him to Arina, and Luke could tell by those silver eyes darkening like a storm cloud that she didn't approve of what she was seeing.

His head whipped around and there was Arina with her hands on her hips and her robe gaping wide above the belt, leaving little to the imagination.

"Yes, I can see that," Mary Ann snapped. She didn't miss a step as she continued down the hallway.

"Wait a minute!" Luke tried to go after her but Arina was holding tight to his hand.

"Luke, come in, honey," Arina said.

"Hold on." Luke pulled away and hurried down the hallway after Mary Ann. He reached her at the top of the staircase. "Would you wait a da . . . dang minute?"

She stopped so fast that he bumped into her and almost knocked her down the stairs. He grabbed her arm to steady her. "Careful."

"You curse at me and you expect me to stop and converse with you?"

"I didn't curse at you! I just . . . I just . . . well, I almost cursed, but it wasn't at you. I have a habit of saying some bad words." That sounded lame even to his own ears.

"Bad words?" If he wasn't such a cad she might have smiled at his choice of words.

"Ah, yeah. That's what my nephews call them." He blessed her with his famous McBride grin. "They told me their ma would wash my mouth out with soap. And if they are really bad words, they told me God won't let me into heaven."

For a flicker of a moment, she saw the same charming man she'd seen that night in the kitchen when they were cooking together. He might be a scoundrel, but at least he spoke about his nephews with unabashed affection. "As well she should wash your mouth out with soap. What kind of influence is your language on young boys? However, I'm not sure our Maker would keep you out of heaven for that transgression."

He didn't care that she was dressing him down, at least she was talking to him. "I've been cleaning up my language for them. Working around men who are rough as cobs most of the time it's hard to remember your manners in polite company." He saw she was staring at something past him, so he turned around to see Arina standing in the hallway watching them, and she hadn't bothered to pull her robe together. Before Mary Ann took off again, he spoke quickly, "I wanted to explain about yesterday. I didn't want you to get the impression there was something going on between Arina and me. And I thought I was knocking on your door this morning."

She felt like telling the woman that the hotel was a respectable business and not a brothel, and if she wanted to act like a common tart she could jolly well go to the saloon. She held her tongue, but instead addressed the man in front of her who was creating the problems in the first place. "Mr. McBride, you certainly don't owe me any explanation. I have no interest in your personal life." She glanced back down the hallway. "I think your . . . *friend* is waiting for you." She turned and descended the staircase as regally as a queen. Her thoughts, on the other hand, were far from noble.

Taking a deep breath, Luke wanted to let out a stream of bad words. Trying to talk to Mary Ann was like trying to grasp the wind. He turned around and walked back toward Arina's door. When he reached her, she was still standing there with her arms on her hips, robe barely clinging to her every curve. A very enticing package if she wasn't a married woman. He'd prefer it was Mary Ann in that getup.

"I don't think your girl likes me."

Luke hooked his thumbs in his belt and gave Arina a no-nonsense look. "She's not my girl. But I'd sure like to know why you keep throwing yourself at me."

Arina reached for his hand and brought it to her chest, right over her heart. "Oh Luke, I just feel all alone and I'm scared. I don't know what's going on and I'm afraid to be here alone."

Luke looked at his hand pressed against her bare skin. Just an inch or two one way or the other . . . no . . . don't go there. He tried to concentrate on what she was saying. He could understand if she was frightened, particularly not knowing what had happened to her husband. She was a beautiful young woman and vulnerable. He sure wouldn't like his wife traipsing all over the country alone. Sam should have made some sort of arrangements for her. Colt might have thought she was involved with whatever was going on, but he had a hard time believing that. She'd never acted so forward in Arizona, so maybe she was really scared.

"Please don't be angry with me. You make me feel safe, even when you were in Arizona I wanted to be friends with you, but you left so soon after the wedding we didn't have a chance to get to know each other."

This was news to him. He couldn't recall having much of a conversation with her the day of the wedding. After he'd talked to his brothers he'd done some reflecting on the few times he had been around Arina. He remembered catching her staring at him once or twice, but she certainly never did anything inappropriate. "You shouldn't be in the hallway dressed so . . . in your nightclothes."

She looked down at her robe, but made no move to pull it together. "What's wrong with the way I'm dressed?"

"You shouldn't wear your robe outside your room. Another man might walk by and get the wrong impression."

"Then come in for a minute while I change. There's a dressing screen so it would be proper."

"I can't, I need to get back to the ranch."

She wrapped her arms around his neck again. "Please don't leave me alone here, Luke."

He couldn't help feeling sorry for her and found himself saying, "I'll come pick you up and take you to the ranch for dinner tonight."

"Oh, thank you." She cupped his face and kissed him on the lips again. "I'll be waiting."

Within minutes Luke was downstairs, but instead of walking out the door he decided to have breakfast in the restaurant. If Mary Ann didn't want to see him . . . well, that was too bad. He'd left home without eating, and he was hungry. When he didn't have food in his gut he wasn't a happy man. Right now that wasn't the only reason he was in a foul mood.

He sat where he had a good view of the front desk and the staircase. If Arina came downstairs he planned to gulp his food and get out of there in a hurry. He didn't even intend to try to talk to Mary Ann again. He wanted a few minutes alone to think things over. Thinking back to Sam's wedding, he did recall Arina was very affectionate with Sam. Since they were newly-weds, he thought Sam was lucky to have such a loving woman. Granted, her clothing had probably been more revealing than most ladies wore, but at the time he didn't give it a second thought. He figured he should take her at her word that she was scared. People often acted in strange ways when they were frightened.

The waitress delivered his steak and eggs and warmed his coffee. He glanced up and saw Mary Ann walking behind the desk while she conversed with Eb. She glanced his way, but for once, he didn't bother to acknowledge her. To show his indifference, he picked up his coffee and took a healthy gulp and nearly burned his tongue off. Thankfully, Mary Ann wasn't watching, her attention was on a cowboy who walked in and approached the desk. Luke kept his eye on the drifter. He was taking his own sweet time if he was checking into the hotel. He stood there chatting with Mary Ann before he turned the register around and signed his name. He saw Mary Ann hold out a key to him, but the cowboy grasped her hand along with the key. Luke stood, threw some coins on the table for his meal, grabbed his hat, and strolled to the desk.

"Let go of my hand, sir," Mary Ann said.

"Honey, I want you to show me to my room," the man said.

George approached the desk and overheard what the man said to his niece. "Sir, release her immediately."

The man elbowed George out of his way. "Mind your own business, old man."

Luke clamped down on the man's shoulder with a firm grip. "I think you should listen to him."

The man held on to Mary Ann as he turned to Luke. "Like I told him, mind your own business, cowboy."

Breakfast hadn't helped Luke's mood. He reached down and grabbed the man's hand and removed it from Mary Ann's in a grip so tight he thought he might break a knuckle or two if he was lucky.

The man took a swing with his free arm and Luke was late in blocking his fist before it connected with his lip in the exact spot where Clyde Slater had hit him days ago. Fresh blood dripped on his clean shirt. That did it! Luke threw one punch to the man's jaw that sent him reeling into the staircase. The man gained his balance and charged Luke, knocking him into the door leading to the dining room. Luke didn't think about the damage he would cause when he hauled back and caught the man squarely in his mouth. The man went skittering across a table in the dining room and dishes went flying. Fortunately no one was sitting at the table. Realizing what damage could be done if he continued this fight inside, Luke grabbed the man by the shirt and dragged him out the door and tossed him in the street. George and Mary Ann ran from the hotel to the sidewalk in time to hear what Luke had to say. "If I were you I would mount up and keep on riding until I reached Mexico."

Sprawled on his back the man leaned up on one elbow. "I paid for the room."

Luke reached into his pocket, pulled out enough money to cover the room, and threw it next to the man. "As I said, keep riding." Luke turned and saw Mary Ann and George were right behind him.

"Luke!" George shouted.

Hearing the urgency in George's voice, Luke spun around and drew his gun in the process. Seeing the man had drawn his pistol and was ready to shoot him in the back, Luke shot the gun from his hand. The man clutched his hand and started yelling obscenities at Luke. Luke walked to him and kicked the gun from his reach. "You want to get on your horse, or do you want to be tied over him? Your choice."

The man managed to walk to his horse under his own steam. After he pulled himself into the saddle with one hand he slowly rode out of town. Luke turned to George. "Thanks, George."

"Think nothing of it, I'm the one who should be thanking you for coming to Mary Ann's defense."

Luke glanced at Mary Ann, fully expecting her to look at him like she did the first day she'd arrived. But what he saw was a look of shock.

"That man was going to shoot you in the back," she said in a shaky voice.

"Thanks to George he didn't have the chance," Luke responded.

George took Mary Ann by the elbow and led her to the door. "Let's get some breakfast, my dear, and take your mind off of all of this unpleasantness." He glanced back at Luke. "Can I offer you some coffee?"

"No, I need to get back to the ranch." Luke tipped his hat and walked to his horse.

"McBride, thank you," Mary Ann said.

Luke turned back to her, tipped his hat again. "Yes, ma'am."

Chapter Eight

"Not again." Colt spotted Luke's split lip when he reined in beside him. "Slater?"

Luke was in no mood to take any more grief today and that included from his brothers. "No, not Slater, a drifter."

"What did he do?" Jake asked.

"He grabbed Mary Ann and shoved George."

Colt couldn't argue over a man defending a lady. "How was the meeting with Arina?"

"I'm not convinced she's involved in anything nefarious. I think she's really scared. I'm going back to town later and bring her back out to the ranch for dinner."

"Really? What does this gal look like?" Jake asked. He knew his brother was a sucker for a pretty face and a sad story. Luke wasn't naïve, but he had a weakness, and that weakness was the fairer sex. Luke's attraction to the opposite sex was legendary and he'd take bets his younger brother could be fooled by Sam's wife. Jake wasn't as easily hoodwinked by women. As a U.S. Marshal he'd arrested some women before who were every bit as dangerous and shrewd as their male counterparts.

Luke thought about Arina's curves in her robe.

"She's real pretty, but that's not why I'm bringing her to the ranch. She's here all alone and she's frightened. I'm sure you wouldn't like the thought of your wife being in a strange town all alone."

"You're right about that," Jake agreed. "But if you invite her to stay here she might get the wrong idea."

"I'm going to talk to her about that on the ride back. If she's an innocent in whatever is going on, I owe it to Sam to take care of her. As pretty as she is she probably wouldn't be safe in town alone." *Especially with the way she dresses,* he thought. After seeing that cowboy grab Mary Ann, he realized single women were at the mercy of any man who got out of hand. Mary Ann had George to defend her, but he wasn't certain what George would have done if he hadn't intervened. He hoped George listened to him and started wearing a gun. His mind went to Mary Ann and how she'd thanked him. That was the kindest thing she'd said to him and it came right after he'd told himself to ignore her. Maybe he should consider that approach since trying to persuade her to give him a chance wasn't gaining traction. She hadn't even given him the opportunity to ask why she was no longer in room six.

During breakfast, Mary Ann was still in shock over the events that had just taken place on the street. "I can't believe that man would have shot Mr. McBride."

"We were fortunate Mr. McBride was in the restaurant," George told her. "Now perhaps you can see for yourself the kind of man he is." George had hoped she would come around and see what a fine man Luke was. It was surprising his niece was the only woman he'd seen who was impervious to Luke's charms.

"He is so fast with that gun, I didn't even see it leave his holster."

"His brother Colt is even faster. But please don't think they are men seeking trouble, they are not like that, but they are prepared when necessary."

Each time Mary Ann was tempted to think she may have jumped to the wrong conclusion about Luke, she thought about that married woman hanging all over him in the hallway. In the short time she'd been in town, she'd seen him flirting with several women and she'd be wise not to forget that. *When did the man have time to work?* "While I did appreciate his assistance, I still think he is a scoundrel. I saw him with *that* woman this morning in the hallway, and she was improperly dressed for entertaining a man other than her husband. It was quite scandalous."

"I spoke to Mrs. White last night. She told me Luke is her husband's partner just as Luke mentioned. She said her husband is missing and she came here to seek Luke's help. She obviously knows she can trust him. It wasn't as if he was in the woman's room, was he?"

"No, he wasn't in her room." She wasn't sure that was an indication there wasn't something illicit going on between them.

"I can't imagine there is anything improper there." George appreciated his niece's genteel comportment, but he feared she had a lot to learn about the West. Seeing the women from L. B. Ditty's hanging over the balcony probably distorted her view of all women in town.

"You didn't see how she was dressed, nor how she was draped over him. If you had I'm quite sure you would agree it was shockingly indecent. Mr. McBride didn't seem to have a problem with her state of undress or her attentions." It wasn't that she wanted to think ill of Luke, particularly since he was nearly shot in the back for defending her. She found it infuriating that her opinion vacillated back and forth about Luke McBride. One moment he was a scoundrel and the next moment a hero.

When Luke rode back to town to pick up Arina he stopped at the livery to leave his horse and rent a buggy. He thought Arina might be in the reception area of the hotel waiting for him, but seeing no one around he walked upstairs and tapped on her door.

"Come in."

Luke was surprised she didn't keep her door locked. Maybe she had unlocked it knowing he would be arriving soon. He walked through the door and received another surprise. She was wearing a different robe, even thinner than the one she'd worn that morning.

Arina hurried to him and kissed him on the cheek. "Just give me one minute to finish dressing."

"I'll wait downstairs."

"Don't be silly." She pointed to the dressing screen. "As you can see I have a screen, so please have a seat. Would you like a whiskey? I was just going to pour myself one."

Luke glanced at the screen thinking that should offer enough privacy. He walked to the chair by the table and saw two glasses and the bottle of whiskey. He didn't know she drank. "Do you want one?"

"Yes, please." She walked to the wardrobe and pulled out a dress.

As Luke poured the whiskey he wondered if she was going to wear anything under her dress. He certainly didn't think she was wearing underclothes right now.

He picked up both glasses and held one to her as she passed. "I didn't know you drank whiskey."

"I rarely did before the last few months. I find it calms my nerves." She clinked her glass to his. "I'm so grateful to you for helping me, Luke." She drank the contents in one gulp and sat her glass on the table. "I mean it, Luke, thank you. Now have a seat, I'll just be a minute. Would you pour me another?"

Her voice sounded low and sultry, and he knew this was a dangerous situation. "I think I should wait downstairs."

"No, I won't be long, I promise."

Luke gulped his glass of whiskey down as he watched her walk to the screen. She started removing her robe before she was behind the screen and he watched as it drifted down past her waist. He averted his eyes before it fell to the floor. He poured another shot of whiskey in both glasses and drained one. His eyes automatically moved to the screen again, and saw she had turned the light up behind the screen and he could see her silhouette. Her naked silhouette. Nope, no underclothes. He poured another shot and gulped it down. His eyes roamed to the screen again, and he saw her pick up her robe and toss it to a chair before grabbing the corset and stockings that were hanging over the top of the screen. After she pulled her stockings on and secured them with garters, she arched her back to put her corset around her midriff and he couldn't look away. Lord help him, did she have a body! Maybe another shot. Gulp. He held the bottle over his glass, ready to pour one more, but he put the bottle on the table. One more drink and he might forget she was the wife of a friend. He prided himself on self-control, but when a woman had a body like hers it would be easy to forget just about anything if too much whiskey was in the equation. Reluctantly, he pulled his eyes away from the screen. He looked at the wardrobe, the fireplace, the window, everyplace . . . anyplace . . . to keep from looking at the screen. Finally, he stood and walked to the window overlooking the street. He needed a plan, he couldn't sit around and wait for Sam to contact him, if he was even alive. None of this made sense, least of all Arina's behavior.

Arina moved from the screen wearing a flattering blue dress, but again the neckline was cut very low. Luke knew what was beneath the fabric. He couldn't deny she looked beautiful, but he thought his sisters-in-law would think he'd brought one of the gals from L. B. Ditty's to dine. He couldn't even imagine what his brothers would think. At that thought, he was tempted to pour another drink.

Arina moved in front of him and twirled around. "How do you like my dress?"

"You look fine."

She frowned at him. "Fine? Is that the best you can do?"

Luke seemed to recall his sisters-in-law had told him *fine* was a word women abhorred when it came to questions about their appearance, but he wasn't willing to allow Arina to goad him into saying more. He had a feeling she knew exactly what she was doing when she turned the light up behind the screen.

Arina handed him her shawl and turned around and lifted her hair so he could place the shawl around her shoulders. "Now I see why you aren't married. You need to work on your flattery, cowboy."

"I've never had any complaints." His knuckles grazed her shoulders, and he saw her shiver at the contact. *She's my partner's wife*, he reminded himself.

"It's so nice to spend the evening with you."

He didn't want to correct her, but this wasn't a date, so he thought he would remind her other people would be dining with them. "My sisters-in-law are great cooks. I promise you will have a nice dinner."

Luke was relieved Mary Ann wasn't at the desk when they left the hotel. If Mary Ann saw the dress Arina was wearing she'd never speak to him again. As if he had some say in what Arina chose to wear. *Women!* As much as he loved them, he didn't always understand them. He just hoped he could ride away before Mary Ann appeared.

After assisting Arina into the buggy, he pulled out the blanket to place it beside her in case she needed it before they reached the ranch. He walked to the rail to remove the reins, and just as he was about to climb into the buggy he heard a voice behind him.

"Hello, Luke."

He knew without turning around the voice belonged to Sally Detrick. Uh-oh, a catfight was imminent. When he did turn around, he was almost relieved to see Sally was in the company of her father. It was the first time he'd ever been happy to see Old Man Detrick. He tipped his hat. "Sally." His eyes slid to Old Man Detrick. "Sir."

"Are you coming or going?" Sally asked, not looking at him but eyeing the woman in the buggy. And it wasn't a friendly eye. Luke figured Arina made certain Sally got a good view of her neckline.

"Let me introduce my partner's wife. Arina White. Arina, this is Sally Detrick and her father." Arina had him so flustered he couldn't even remember Old Man Detrick's given name. "Their ranch borders the McBride ranch." Luke thought he was seeing things when Detrick rushed to the buggy and extended his hand to Arina.

"I'm Judd Detrick," he said, and actually smiled.

Arina smiled back at Detrick and accepted his hand. "It's a pleasure to meet you."

Luke glanced at Sally to see if she was as surprised as he was at her father's behavior. She was. He'd never even seen the old man crack a smile.

"Where is *Mr.* White?" Sally asked.

"Actually my husband is missing and that is the reason for my visit, to enlist Luke's help," Arina answered.

"I'm sorry to hear that. If there is anything I can do for you, do not hesitate to call upon me," Detrick said.

Arina gave Detrick a brilliant smile. "How kind of you, Mr. Detrick."

"Judd, please."

Luke thought his mouth probably hit the ground when the old man kissed the back of Arina's hand.

"Luke, you are coming to the social tomorrow night, aren't you?" Sally asked.

"Of course, you must come and bring your lovely guest," Detrick added. "I'm sure she could use some entertainment to take her mind off her troubles."

Sally rolled her eyes. She didn't want her daddy to attend the social, he was certain to put a damper on her activities. Especially where Luke was concerned. And she sure as heck didn't want that woman to attend.

Before Luke responded, Arina spoke up, "Oh, I would love to go. You will escort me, won't you, Luke?"

"If he can't, I will certainly come for you," Detrick told her.

"Daddy, give Luke a chance to answer," Sally said.

"If Arina would like to go, I will make sure she gets there," Luke replied.

Both Sally and her daddy glared at him. *What did I do now?* He thought he answered the question like a true gentleman.

Sally turned her attention on Arina. "Luke has promised the first dance with me. Don't be surprised if all of the local gals take up most of his time."

"I'm sure he will live up to that promise, but I'll have to make sure he'll find time for one dance with me," Arina countered sweetly. "You will certainly save a dance for me, won't you, Judd?"

"You can count on it."

Arina smirked at Sally.

Luke wasn't sure, but he thought Old Man Detrick was blushing. His chest had definitely puffed up like he was the cock of the henhouse. Luke could hardly find his tongue. He'd had enough surprises for one night. "If you folks will excuse us, they are expecting us at the ranch."

Chapter Nine

Colt walked in the kitchen and saw his wife pulling pies from the oven. When she placed the pies on the counter, Colt leaned over and kissed her neck.

Victoria turned around and looped her arms around his neck. "I've invited George and his niece to dinner tonight."

"But Luke is bringing his partner's wife to dinner tonight." Colt hadn't told his wife what Luke had revealed about Arina's inappropriate behavior. "I hope that is a good idea."

"What do you mean? Why wouldn't it be a good idea?"

"Luke said his partner's wife is acting strangely."

"Strangely? How so?"

Victoria was surprised when Colt repeated what Luke had told him about Arina. "Is he certain he hasn't given this woman some indication he has an interest in her?"

"Jake had asked Luke that very question. He assured us he hadn't, but even if he did somewhere along the line, she's still a married woman."

"True enough. Well, nothing can be done about the invitation now."

Colt kissed his wife before he left the kitchen. "Jake and I will be back in plenty of time to clean up before dinner."

As soon as Luke and Arina walked through the door, Luke wanted to turn around and head to the range. The last thing he expected was to see Mary Ann and George sitting in the parlor. Dang his luck. Luke made the introductions and Arina promptly turned to him. "Would you take my shawl, Luke, honey?" Luke didn't look at his brothers, but he felt certain he heard eyeballs popping out.

Colt was standing near Jake and Jake heard him utter, *Aw, no.* There was little chitchat in the parlor before Victoria and Promise walked to the kitchen to finish the dinner preparations. Colt saw Promise lean over and whisper something to Victoria, and from the look on their faces, he was certain they weren't discussing the food.

When dinner was on the table, Luke hoped Colt would escort Arina to the dining room. But no, he wasn't that lucky. Arina linked her arm through his and walked with him. Always the optimist, he thought he might seat Arina near Jake or George, somewhere far away from him.

"Mary Ann, why don't you sit here?" Victoria pointed to a chair next to Colt's, at the head of the table. She planned to sit Luke next to Mary Ann, and George could sit next to Arina and keep her occupied. It certainly wasn't going to be her husband.

Luke was definitely going to take the seat next to Mary Ann, but when he moved in that direction, Arina had plans for his other side. "I'll just sit here right next to Luke."

"That's fine," Colt responded. He knew he didn't want to sit next to her if he wanted to sleep beside his wife tonight.

Luke looked at Colt like he wanted to shoot him. And Jake didn't look any happier since he was sitting directly across from Arina, and he was going to have a difficult time averting his eyes for the next hour.

Colt said grace and Luke silently prayed for a peaceful dinner after seeing the visual daggers Victoria and Promise were sending his way. Colt was trying to think of a way to start the conversation at the table, but darned if he knew how to begin. Even he'd been distracted by Arina's buxom display. Thankfully his dilemma was short-lived when his wife addressed Mary Ann.

"Mary Ann, Luke told us about your shop, I think it sounds lovely. Promise and I will be in as soon as you're open."

"Some of my inventory has already arrived so I will have it open in a few days. Luke told me about your reticules and if you are agreeable I would love to display some in my shop."

"I certainly am agreeable. I will bring some with me when we come and we can work out the details then."

"I suppose you don't have shops here that carry expensive items like the shops in Denver," Arina said.

Luke started to speak up, but Mary Ann beat him to it. "Actually, all of my items are coming from France. And Victoria's reticules are carried by shops in Paris. I think we may give Denver some competition soon."

"Oh, what a surprise. But I doubt the women here would be interested in the latest fashions like you find in Denver."

Mary Ann didn't know if this woman came from

wealth, but she thought she could teach her a thing or two about handling insufferable snobs. She'd been exposed to the best of them in England's upper class. But she was a guest, not the hostess, so she remained silent.

"We are very much interested in fashion," Promise said curtly.

Arina eyed her high-necked dress. "Yes, I can see that." She touched Luke's arm. "The dress I'm wearing was designed in France and Luke said he liked it, didn't you, Luke, darling?"

All eyes landed on Luke. He cleared his throat while he tried to think of a diplomatic response. Being a single man he enjoyed looking, but if he were her husband he wouldn't let her out of the house in that getup. "As I said earlier, it's fine." He took a long drink of water, wishing it was a double shot of whiskey.

I'll just bet he likes it, Mary Ann thought.

Of course, Arina's comment drew everyone's eyes to her dress, but no one had a response. It didn't appear Arina was aware of the venomous looks from the women at the table as she continued on. "I find men appreciate dresses which flatter one's figure. But of course one must have a good figure for the latest styles."

Colt thought he could hear his wife's teeth grinding together, so he thought he would redirect the conversation. He asked George about his new house.

While George was talking, Luke took that opportunity to speak to Mary Ann. "You look real pretty tonight."

"Thank you." He looked handsome too and she was angry with herself for noticing. After all, he knew he was picking up Arina for dinner so he obviously wanted to look good for her.

Luke told himself not to allow her brusque tone

to dissuade him. "I didn't know you were coming to dinner tonight."

"That's obvious."

"Mary Ann . . ." Luke started but was interrupted by Arina.

"Luke, darling, would you pass me the green beans?" Arina asked.

Luke snatched the bowl from the table and thrust it into her hands. He glanced across the table and saw Jake grinning at him. He rolled his eyes. Jake's eyes moved to Arina, and Promise thought he was looking overlong at her bosom and gave him an elbow in his ribs.

"Luke has promised to help me and I am so grateful," Arina said, responding to George's question about her plans, and turned to give Luke an adoring smile. "I don't know what I would do without him."

Mary Ann almost gasped aloud when she saw Arina place her hand on Luke's thigh. She glanced up at Victoria, and her expression said she knew something was going on.

Luke jumped like someone had put a cattle prod on his rear. He didn't know what to do, so he ignored Arina's hand and took another drink of water. His voice sounded two octaves higher when he spoke. "This dinner is delicious." He discreetly pushed Arina's hand off his leg.

Colt and Jake looked at him wondering what in the devil was wrong with him.

"Thank you," Victoria replied. She certainly hoped her brother-in-law didn't have something going on with Arina because she never wanted to see the woman again.

Luke was so on edge he couldn't even enjoy the fine meal. The situation might have been humorous if he didn't have to face the wrath of his sisters-in-law later. His brothers would be a piece of cake compared to them.

George asked Arina another question and she turned to him when she responded, but she placed her hand on Luke's arm.

"Could we speak privately later?" Luke whispered to Mary Ann.

She glanced at Arina's hand on his arm again and then glared at him. "I rather think you will be occupied." Mary Ann could hardly believe what was happening at the dinner table of all places. That woman had actually put her hand on Luke's leg. Of all the nerve! Now she had her hand on his arm. At least his arm was on top of the table. Luke seemed oblivious to Arina's indecent behavior. Mary Ann felt like walking out, but her good manners kept her in her seat.

Luke knew Mary Ann saw Arina's hand on his thigh. It wasn't as if he was asking for Arina's attentions. "If I planned on being occupied, I would not have asked you."

Overhearing part of Luke's exchange with Mary Ann, Colt looked at Victoria and arched his brow in silent communication. Victoria already sensed there was tension between Mary Ann and Luke. Hearing their conversation, she knew it wasn't much of a stretch to see it had something to do with Arina.

Luke couldn't take the tension of not knowing what Arina would do next. It wouldn't surprise him if she crawled in his lap during dinner. He jumped from his seat and everyone stared at him. "I need some more water." It was a lame explanation, but he needed to get out of the room for a few minutes. Victoria started to get up but Luke told her to stay seated. He walked to the kitchen and grabbed the whiskey bottle. He didn't bother to find a glass, he just took a large swig.

The dinner ended and Mary Ann and George left before Luke and Arina. But as soon as Luke and Arina were out the door Colt poured a large whiskey for himself and Jake and they walked to the porch. "What do you make of her?"

"I don't know, but Luke has his hands full," Jake said.

"You can say that again. She acts mighty strange for a married woman." Colt was sure the women were in the kitchen discussing the very same thing.

"I'll say. She's obviously a woman who likes men. And she is a looker, no doubt about it."

"You better not let Promise hear you say that."

Dinner proved to be quite interesting, but not exactly what Luke would call successful. Luke's sisters-in-law were fit to be tied by the time he put Arina in the buggy. If there had been room in George's buggy he would have had him take Arina back to the hotel. Arina hadn't helped matters with the ladies. He thought she went out of her way to be rude to them. On the other hand, she was very friendly with his brothers and made it very clear she preferred their company. Before Luke climbed into the buggy, Victoria pulled him aside and reminded him he was a God-fearing man, and he'd better not do anything that he wouldn't mind being repeated in church. On their way to town, Arina cuddled up next to him like it was thirty below zero instead of an unusually warm evening.

He'd driven home slowly, not so he could spend

time with Arina, but he hoped Mary Ann would have already retired to her quarters by the time they arrived. No such luck. When he reined in at the hotel he saw Mary Ann walk behind the desk.

Arina was still hanging on to him when they walked inside the hotel. "Luke, honey, thank you for keeping me so warm on the way back."

Mary Ann didn't take her bait. She didn't even look at the couple.

Her apparent indifference didn't thwart Arina from making her point. "You are so thoughtful to walk me to my door."

He'd actually thought about saying good night at the staircase but he didn't want Arina to plant another kiss on him in front of Mary Ann.

"Did you enjoy your dinner, Mary Ann?" he asked as they passed the desk.

"Yes, I did, Mr. McBride. Your sisters-in-law are lovely ladies." Which was more than she could say for the creature on his arm.

Reaching Arina's door, Luke said a hurried good night hoping to catch Mary Ann before she went to her room.

"Come in for a little while, Luke." Arina wasn't ready to let him go.

"I need to get back to the ranch."

"If you light a fire for me I will fix you one drink before you go." She walked inside and dropped her shawl on the floor.

He thought now might be the opportune time to talk to her about her flirting. He had tried to be understanding of her situation and make allowances, but he'd had enough. At this point things couldn't get much worse between him and Mary Ann, or his family for that matter. He followed her inside and closed the door. After tossing his hat on the table he grabbed some logs and started stacking them in the fireplace. It reminded him of the day he'd started a fire for Mary Ann. He chuckled to himself when he remembered she had tipped him for his efforts. It took him a few minutes to get the fire raging, but once the job was done he saw a glass appear over his shoulder. He rose and turned around to see Arina standing there holding two glasses of whiskey. She'd changed out of her dress and was wearing her robe again. She must save a lot of money on underclothes since she rarely had them on. Taking the glass from her he quickly gulped the contents down. He couldn't have a talk with her while she was wearing next to nothing. It was all he could do to keep his eyes above her neck.

"I should go."

Arina moved closer. "Stay, Luke."

He took a deep breath. He had no choice but to have this discussion now. "Arina, I don't understand what you are doing."

"You don't?" She ran her fingers over his chest to the back of his neck. "I want you to stay the night with me."

"Are you forgetting you are a married woman?"

"I'm not forgetting, but I haven't seen my husband in months. I'm not a woman who wants to be alone." She stood on her toes and pressed her lips against his.

Luke pulled away from her. "Arina, I can't forget you are the wife of my friend and partner. I don't understand you. By the way you are acting, I don't think you're really concerned about Sam's disappearance. He could be dead! Doesn't that bother you?"

"Of course it bothers me. But he obviously didn't care what happened to me, did he?"

Now he was getting somewhere, he thought. Colt had said the same thing. Did that mean Sam suspected her of something? "Why is it Sam wasn't worried about you? That's not like the Sam I know. Are you telling me everything, Arina?"

"I don't know what was going on! He said he had to go away on business. He didn't tell me why. I'm not hiding anything!"

Luke thought she sounded truthful, either that, or she was a good liar.

"Sam and I married mostly for convenience. I wanted respectability and Sam wanted a wife. It wasn't a love match if that is what you are thinking. I thought he would have told you."

"No, Sam didn't talk about you very much." He didn't understand why Sam would marry a woman for convenience. He must have cared about her.

Arina walked across the room and grabbed the bottle of whiskey. She refilled both of their glasses. "Sam knew what I needed."

He wasn't going to ask what she needed, he wasn't about to give her the opening to show him. He didn't want another drink either, he'd already had too many. At least, he still had his senses about him if he could refuse what Arina was offering. "How did you meet Sam?"

"In a Denver saloon. I was working there." She stared at him with unrepentant blue eyes. "Now do you understand?"

"Understand what?" He didn't understand any of this and he was tired of being in the dark. "I want to understand and I want the truth."

"I'm used to being with men and I want to be with you. I've tried to make that clear."

She was blunt, but he'd asked for the truth and no matter how ugly it sounded, she was very clear. "Didn't you love Sam?"

"No. He always treated me good when he came into the saloon. When I moved to Arizona he told me he wanted a wife and I told him I would marry him. It's simple really. Sam was like a lot of men, he wanted a warm body next to him at night and I wanted what he could provide." She sipped her whiskey as she stared at him.

He wondered if Sam loved her. "Whether it was a marriage of convenience or not, it doesn't change who I am. I can't forget Sam is my partner."

"I'm not asking you to forget anything. Sam knew I would eventually be with someone else, but I told him I would be discreet as long as we were married." She walked closer to him and started to untie the sash to her robe. "He wouldn't care."

Luke reached out and put his hand on hers to keep her from taking off her robe. He thought any husband would care if another man touched his wife, whether he loved her or not. He turned away and grabbed his hat from the table. "I care."

Chapter Ten

Luke drove the buggy back to the livery to get his horse. He didn't regret walking away from Arina, but that didn't mean it wasn't difficult. He was a man and he had needs, and it wasn't every day a pretty woman threw herself at him. It'd been a long frustrating night and he wasn't ready to ride home so he headed back to the saloon. He didn't notice the woman in the window of the hotel watching him walk into L. B. Ditty's Saloon.

Thankfully, Eb had returned to the desk so Mary Ann fled to her quarters to avoid facing Luke when he came downstairs. Room number six was directly below Mary Ann's bedroom and she knew the moment Luke left Arina's room. He'd been with Arina a long time. It annoyed her that he had accompanied her to her room in the first place. She didn't know why Luke's actions were affecting her, it wasn't as if she didn't know what he was like.

She walked to her window and watched Luke take the buggy to the livery. She was still standing there

waiting to see him ride out of town, but when he left
the livery he rode back toward the hotel. He tied his
horse at the rail in front of the saloon. From her vantage
point she could see the inside of the saloon when he
walked through the doors. Two women rushed over
to greet him and he hooked an arm around each one.
The piano music started and Mary Ann stood there listening to the tunes, and wondering if Luke was playing
poker, or if he went upstairs with one of the women.
Just as she had that thought, her attention was diverted
to the second-floor window by someone lighting a
lamp. The curtains were too thin to hide the identity of
the occupants. It was Luke. As soon as he placed the
globe on the lamp, a woman appeared in front of him
and linked her arms around his neck and pulled his
head down so she could kiss him. When the woman released him, Luke started unbuttoning his shirt. The
woman ran her hands over his muscled chest and
helped him out of his shirt. Mary Ann turned away
and crawled into bed.

A few hours later Mary Ann awoke to the sound of
people talking on the street. She lit the lamp on the
bedside table and carried it to the window. There was
a full moon and she clearly saw Luke standing beside
his beautiful horse, a buckskin with a showy white
mane and tail. Just like his master, the horse was magnificent. Luke was looking up at the balcony of the
saloon talking with several of the scantily clad women.
She heard one of the women say, "Good night, Luke,
honey. We had a real good time just like you promised." They all blew him kisses. He tipped his hat to the
women before he jumped into the saddle. "Good night,

ladies." When he turned his horse, he looked directly up at the light in the window of the hotel and saw Mary Ann. He didn't know if she was wearing a camisole or a nightgown, but it was the first thing he'd seen on her that wasn't buttoned up to the chin. She was a vision with her tousled red hair falling over her bare shoulders. He moved his prancing horse into the middle of the street and tipped his hat to her before he rode off.

Early the next morning George was having breakfast with Mary Ann and he thought she was unusually quiet. He'd already noticed the circles under her eyes.

"Didn't you sleep well, my dear?"

Mary Ann couldn't go back to sleep after she watched Luke ride away. He'd spent hours with the women at the saloon. The man obviously had his choice of women, but she wouldn't dare say those things to her uncle. "The saloon was a bit noisy last night."

"We can put you in another room if you prefer. I chose the largest one for you, but I am sure another one will suffice."

If she slept in another bedroom she wouldn't see Luke coming and going. Perhaps that would be the wisest thing to do, but she couldn't bring herself to do it. "That's not necessary. It isn't so noisy every night."

"Fridays and Saturdays are the worst." George handed a piece of paper to her. "Your mother wrote to me."

Mary Ann was not at all surprised her mother had written George. "When was it written?"

"Not long after you left England. She thought you might come here. She told me about the incident with Stafford and your father's insistence you marry the bounder."

"She didn't argue with Father, so I assume she agrees

with his plan." At the time her mother had greatly
disappointed her by not standing up to her father.
With the passing of time she'd been more forgiving of
her mother. Her father ruled with an iron fist, and her
mother had long ago learned it saved a lot of heart-
ache to comply with his wishes. "Did she say Father
suspects I am here?"

"No, but she did say he has hired detectives to find
you." George understood Mary Ann's feelings about
her father. The man was a tyrant. He'd tried to dissuade his sister from marrying the man in the first
place. "Don't be too harsh on your mother, she has
little choice in the matter as you well know."

Mary Ann didn't want to be unforgiving, but she
wished her mother had the courage to speak up and
confront her father. "I know, Uncle. But I do wish
Mother would give him a piece of her mind on occasion."

George chuckled. "That's not the way it is done in
England, my dear. You of all people should know that."

She knew all too well. What she didn't know was if
she had a choice if her father found her. "Could he
force me to return to England?"

"I don't think so as you are of legal majority." George
had discussed her situation with an attorney, but her
father was a powerful man with friends in high places,
so he might find a way to force her to return. "I don't
have to tell you that your father is a determined man
when he wants to have his way. He has the means and
is perfectly capable of having men whisk you away
without anyone's knowledge."

"I know." She prayed her father wouldn't send
anyone to America to look for her.

"I feel I should write to your mother to tell her you are well. I can't let her worry."

"I'll write to her, but I will tell her not to tell Father." Mary Ann didn't enjoy hurting her mother by allowing her to worry about her safety. Still, she didn't want her to tell her father where she was.

George didn't want to raise her hopes. "I'm afraid it's only a matter of time until he finds out."

"Let's not make it easy for him."

Not wanting to worry her, George changed the subject. "I don't know what to make of Mrs. White."

Mary Ann knew what to make of her. "She is certainly attached to Mr. McBride."

"I don't think Luke has an interest in her other than helping her. I appreciate the difficult situation he is in."

"What do you mean he's in a difficult situation?"

"She is his partner's wife and the man is missing. I think Luke probably feels he needs to take care of her for his friend, and at the same time try to find out what happened to him. I doubt it can be good news considering the husband has been missing for such a long time."

"She doesn't appear to be too worried about her husband the way she flaunts her wares in front of other men." Mary Ann knew she sounded like a jealous harpy, but she couldn't help saying what she thought.

George tried to be more gracious considering the circumstances. "She is dealing with her worries in an unusual fashion, I agree. But we all handle situations differently."

Her uncle was much too charitable in Mary Ann's opinion. It was clear to her Arina didn't care that her husband was missing or she'd be out looking for him and not snuggled up to Luke at every opportunity.

"I can't wait to introduce you to everyone at the social." George was excited to show off his beautiful niece, and he fully expected she would have a selection of suitors once the men got a look at her.

Mary Ann had thought about telling her uncle she didn't want to go since she was sure Luke would be there with Arina, but she hated to disappoint him. "I'm looking forward to meeting your friends."

"I feel I should warn you there will be men lined up waiting to dance with you. There are many more men than women in this town. I expect you will be dancing every dance."

Colt and Jake were saddling their horses when Luke walked into the stable.

"What time did you get in last night?" Colt asked.

Jake laughed. "Last night? He got in about four in the morning."

"Do you have to talk so loud?" Luke asked.

Colt exchanged a look with Jake before he folded his arms over his saddle and glared at Luke. "Tell me you didn't spend the night with Arina."

"I didn't spend the night with Arina," Luke said softly. His head was pounding and Colt's deep voice was reverberating in his skull.

Colt frowned at his brother. "I'm serious, Luke." He'd seen Arina with Luke, and he thought it would be difficult for any man to turn away from a woman who was basically offering herself up on a silky platter.

"I'm serious, too. I left Arina after we discussed her behavior and I went to the saloon. And I had too dang much to drink." He remembered being upstairs with one of the gals and drinking way too much whiskey. He also remembered seeing Mary Ann standing in her window when he left the saloon in the wee hours of the morning. He'd really stepped in it this time.

"Good," Colt said. "You need to do something about *that* woman. I don't know what her game is, but I can tell you it's not good."

"I think you need to talk to her about her wardrobe," Jake said.

"I can talk until I'm blue in the face, but she doesn't hear."

"Well, just so you know, the wives are mad at you."

"I didn't dress her." Why was everyone giving him the devil about the way Arina dressed? He wasn't her husband, even though that might be her intent. "She told me last night that she worked in a saloon before she married Sam. Sam never mentioned that to me."

"I guess that explains a lot of things," Colt said. "She doesn't go out of her way to befriend the women."

"I didn't notice that about her when Sam married her. She told me she didn't love Sam and they married more or less for convenience. She married him for his money."

"And Sam never mentioned that?"

"Not a word. I guess I just assumed he got married because he loved her."

"Do you think Sam could have been tired of being married to her and just walked away? Maybe he tired of her flirting, or maybe he caught her with another man," Jake theorized.

Luke hadn't thought of that, but it didn't sound like something Sam would do. "I can't imagine Sam walking away. He's a decent man. But I don't know what he would've done if he caught her with another man. I've sent a telegram to the supervisor of the mine to see what he can tell me about this whole situation."

"Well, there's no indication that anything happened to him yet," Colt said. "Maybe they had an argument and he went away to cool off. If there is another man involved maybe he thought he'd give her some time to think things over."

"But why would she come here?" Jake asked.

"She said she thought Sam probably came here to see me because we are friends as well as business partners."

"She could have sent a telegram. It would have been a heck of a lot faster," Jake added.

"The way she acts, you'd think she has a thing for Luke. And everyone at the table saw how she couldn't keep her hands off you," Colt said.

Luke felt his face turning red.

"Yeah. What I want to know is what happened under the table?" Jake teased.

"Yeah, I'm curious about that, too. Thank goodness the boys were at Mrs. Wellington's," Colt added.

"I didn't know what to do," Luke admitted. "She is the most forward female, including the gals at L. B. Ditty's, I've ever seen."

"She is that," Jake agreed.

"What's your plan?" Colt asked.

"I thought I would go to Denver and see if Sam made it that far. If I can't find him there, I think I have to go to Arizona and see what I can find out."

"Luke, I don't like this. Nothing is adding up here other than the fact you are not getting the whole story from her," Colt told him.

"I agree with Colt. She's not telling you everything, but I'm not sure you'll get the truth out of her. Do you think it's possible she had an interest in you when you first met her?" Jake asked.

"As I told Colt, we hardly even talked before. She didn't show the least bit of interest in me. I'm as puzzled as you two are by this. She says she's scared and lonely."

"Maybe she's looking for another husband if she thinks Sam is dead," Colt said.

Luke wondered if there might be something to Colt's words. From the moment Arina got off the stagecoach, she'd been throwing herself at him. He couldn't even tell his brothers that she'd nearly disrobed last night and admitted she wanted him to spend the night. He could hardly believe it himself. If she was looking for a new husband, she'd best keep looking since it sure as heck wasn't going to be him.

Chapter Eleven

It was a perfect evening for the social in town. The McBride brothers were on the porch enjoying the warm breeze and a sky full of twinkling stars while they waited for Victoria and Promise. The ladies had kept them waiting so long, the men decided to go inside and have a drink. They were sitting in the parlor sipping on their whiskey when the women finally appeared.

Colt nearly dropped his glass when his wife walked in front of him. "I haven't seen that dress before." He would have remembered a dress that showed so much flesh.

"It's the latest fashion from Paris. Mrs. Wellington brought me a sketch from a catalog advertisement so Promise and I could make our dresses for tonight."

Promise walked in behind Victoria and Jake frowned.

"How do you like it, honey?" Promise asked, twirling in front of her husband.

Jake didn't smile and his tone confirmed his displeasure. "You two are showing a lot of skin. We'll be fighting every cowboy at the dance."

"Jake's right, it seems like the latest fashion doesn't look suitable for a simple ranchers' social," Colt added.

Luke was grinning from ear to ear. He couldn't believe how his brothers were acting over a couple of dresses. Personally, he was enjoying the view. Maybe he shouldn't have judged Arina's low-cut gowns now that he knew they were the latest styles from France. And their dresses were not nearly as low as Arina's. He walked forward and held his arms out to escort the ladies to the front porch. "Don't pay any attention to them. They are crazy; you two are beautiful."

Colt and Jake followed them out the door. "I didn't say they weren't beautiful, I just don't want every rancher from here to Montana enjoying the view," Colt grumbled.

Victoria turned to make a face at Colt. "Husband, don't be an old fuddy-duddy, you need to keep up with the times."

From his vantage point, Colt thought he might be able to see her toes. "I don't think anyone has ever called me a fuddy-duddy. Besides, what's wrong with the old times? I like the old times."

"You and Jake seemed to enjoy Arina's dress when she came for dinner," Victoria said sweetly. She knew none of them knew the color of Arina's eyes.

"The last time I checked I wasn't married to Arina," Colt replied.

"So you can gawk at other women, but you don't want to appreciate your wife's figure?"

Colt heard his father in his head. *Don't argue with a woman, son.* He knew he couldn't win this battle.

"We didn't gawk at her dress," Jake added.

"That's right, and I don't want to hear one word out of you if I knock some cowboy's teeth down his throat for ogling my wife." Colt pulled his pistol and checked the chamber just to let Victoria know he meant business.

She grinned at his theatrics. "I'm sure you can control yourself. By the way, do you know the color of Arina's eyes?" Victoria asked.

Colt didn't know the answer and he looked at Jake hoping he could bail him out.

"Jake, what color are Arina's eyes?" Promise asked.

Jake didn't respond. He didn't know. Point made.

"Luke?" Victoria asked.

"Blue." Luke knew where the women were going with this question and he was thankful he had the answer. He looked at his brothers and told them they were acting like jealous morons. To his way of thinking their wives had lovely figures and there was no sense hiding them. "I'm going to pick up Arina, I'll see you there."

"Try to keep her under control," Colt warned.

By the time Luke arrived with Arina on his arm everyone was already dancing. He spotted Colt and Jake and made his way through the crowd to them. Everyone acknowledged Arina politely, and he was sure his brothers were comparing dresses. He already knew Arina's was, by far, the most revealing so Colt and Jake should be happy about that. But the women were not pleased. Victoria and Promise pulled their husbands to the dance floor before Arina started flirting with them.

"Dance with me, Luke," Arina said.

Luke figured enough cowboys had seen Arina when they walked in so he would have men cutting in right away once they started dancing. Not only that, but the dance floor was a good place to look for Mary Ann. "Okay." He took her in his arms, making an effort to keep her at a respectable distance, but she quickly closed the gap between them.

"I'm so happy to be here with you," she purred in his ear. "It's been so long since I've had an exciting evening."

He didn't want to say or do anything that would encourage her to make more advances. That thought made him shake his head. He never thought he'd see the day he would want to discourage a woman from flirting with him. If she wasn't Sam's wife, he might be singing a different tune. "I'm not sure how exciting it will be, but it is a lovely evening for a dance."

Arina's hand moved to the back of his neck and she ran her fingers through his hair. "I guess it will depend on how it ends."

Before Luke could respond he felt a tap on his shoulder. "Could I dance with your lovely partner?" Judd Detrick asked.

For the second time Luke was happy to see Old Man Detrick. "Certainly." He relinquished Arina's hand.

"Sally was looking for you," Detrick said before Luke walked away.

That had to be a first, Luke thought, Detrick trying to push him on Sally. The old man must be truly smitten with Arina if he was trying to get him out of the way. He looked around for his brothers, but seeing they were dancing with their wives, he decided to find the punch bowl. Walking through the crowd, he saw Mary Ann dancing with one of the ranchers. He watched for a minute as the two of them laughed and moved around the floor. They seemed to be having a good time. Forgetting the punch, he pushed through the dancing couples and tapped the rancher on the shoulder. "I'm cutting in."

The cowboy didn't like it, but he nodded and

walked away. Luke took Mary Ann's hand in his and pulled her close. She looked beautiful in her white dress, which was designed very much like the dresses his sisters-in-law were wearing. He couldn't believe she would wear such a low-cut gown. It was much too provocative and he hadn't realized she had such an abundance of curves. "You look beautiful tonight, but don't you think your dress is too . . . revealing?" No wonder the cowboy she had been dancing with was all smiles.

"Not compared to your date's dress," she countered coolly. She'd seen him when he walked through the crowd with Arina. Even though he had Arina on his arm, she thought he was the most handsome man she had ever seen. Everyone in the town greeted him like he was the prodigal son. And she saw him take Arina in his arms for the first dance. She reminded herself Arina wasn't the only woman on his list. She hadn't forgotten he was upstairs in the saloon with a different woman. If he thought she was going to be on his long list of conquests, she had news for him.

Uh-oh, he didn't want the conversation to go in that direction. Still he didn't want all the cowboys drooling over her. "Your hair looks really pretty down." He remembered how her hair looked the night she was watching him from her bedroom window. It was draped over one creamy pale shoulder and he'd never seen such a lovely sight. He started to mention it until he realized she'd seen him talking with the gals from the saloon. Now that he knew where her bedroom window was located, he wondered what else she saw that night. It occurred to him that she had a bird's-eye view of the second floor of the saloon.

"Mr. McBride, do not waste your flowery words on me. I do not intend to be on the list of women vying for your attentions." It wasn't as if she couldn't see why women flocked to him. Not only was he devastatingly handsome, those mischievous blue eyes of his twinkled brighter than the stars. Even she couldn't deny he had charm to spare. And if that wasn't enough for any woman to fall into his trap, he danced divinely. But he was still a scoundrel, she reminded herself, and she would do well not to forget that fact.

"Miss Hardwicke, I was simply stating a fact, not trying to add you to a list." He had to be the biggest kind of fool for cutting in on her dance. The way she was laughing with that cowboy he thought she might be in a more agreeable mood tonight. But she seemed heaven-bent on keeping him from making any headway with her. He didn't know why he was wasting his time.

Mary Ann felt a little bit guilty for her sharp tongue. "In that case, thank you."

Luke was tapped on the shoulder and he was forced to relinquish Mary Ann to another cowboy. Before he took two steps, Sally Detrick appeared and asked him to dance. He maneuvered Sally near Mary Ann and her partner. Considering the gown she was wearing, he thought he should keep an eye on her to make sure none of the men got out of line. The tall cowboy she was dancing with didn't take his eyes off her, just like the last one. The dance with Sally ended, but before he could ask Mary Ann for another, Lucinda grabbed his hand. Another man had Mary Ann in his arms and he was holding her way too close. Luke stayed near, ignoring his respective partner to make sure the cowboy minded his manners. Two more women asked him to dance, but by the end of the next dance, he'd formed a plan. With some maneuvering, he managed to be right beside Mary Ann and her partner when the dance ended. He looked at the man and said, "Let's change partners." In the middle of his dance with Mary Ann, the first cowboy he'd tapped on the shoulder returned the favor. Luke said, "No."

"Hey cowboy, that's not the way this works."

"That's the way it's working during this dance." Luke was determined he was going to finish this dance.

"I'm cutting in," the man said more forcefully.

Luke stopped dancing and glared at him. "You've had your dance, now find another partner."

The cowboy wasn't going to back away easy. "If this ain't your wife, I'm cutting in."

Luke pulled his arms from Mary Ann, and the cowboy smiled thinking he'd won this round, until he saw Luke's eyes.

Luke had the look of a man who wasn't going to take any guff. "You want to walk out of here tonight, or be carried? Your choice."

The cowboy didn't like what he saw and took a step back. "No sense getting in a huff over a dance." He turned around and walked away.

Luke was glaring at Mary Ann when he took her in his arms. "See, that darn dress is like fanning the flames of a fire."

Mary Ann couldn't believe Luke was going to fight over a dance, even if she didn't want to dance with anyone but him. And the way he acted about her dress confused her. He didn't seem to mind Arina's dresses. By comparison she could be nominated for sainthood. "You don't like my dress?"

"I like it too dang much. Along with every other cowboy here." After a few moments he'd calmed down enough to say what he felt. "You're the most beautiful woman here." She was the most beautiful woman he'd ever seen. Period.

She didn't want to be susceptible to his charms like

the other women in town. Still, when she looked up at him she was lost and she couldn't force her eyes from his. Did he lure every woman into his web so easily?

The music stopped, but Luke still held her in his arms as they stared at each other. In those few seconds, Luke knew something changed, and he knew she felt it too. He'd been ready to shoot a man over a dance and he knew why. He wanted her. Taking her by the hand, he led her through the throng of people and he didn't stop until he reached the back of the church. Once he found the most secluded area called *the sparkin' corner*, he took her in his arms.

"You're beautiful in the moonlight," he whispered, cupping her face in his large hand.

Mary Ann's heart was thumping loudly, and she quickly forgot all of the reasons she wanted to stay away from him. His arms tightened around her, crushing her to his chest and she couldn't think of anything other than how good it felt being so close to him.

When he lowered his lips to hers she didn't resist.

Luke was lost in the kiss, he pulled her even closer to his body, not giving a thought that someone might see them. His kiss was long and she clung to him. He pulled his lips from hers so he could nibble his way down her neck, over her bare shoulders to the soft skin along the neckline of her dress. She smelled so good, tasted even better, and he wanted more. He wanted it all.

Having never experienced anything like Luke's kisses, Mary Ann was ill-prepared for her own raging desires. Everything about him enticed her; his smell, his powerful body, his warm skin, his very talented mouth. His lips seared her skin and it felt so wonderful she offered no resistance. She was on fire, and begging for more, weaving her fingers through his hair and holding him to her. It wasn't until she felt him tug at her dress, trying to pull it lower, that sanity returned. Realizing what he was about to do, she placed her hands on his chest and pushed him away. "You must not."

Luke stopped, his breathing was labored as he stared at her trying to make sense of what just happened. He had to focus on reining in his insatiable desire. He'd been so caught up in his craving for her that in another moment he would have had her dress half off, not giving a thought to where they were or who might see them. He was ashamed he'd let his hunger for her get the best of him. "I'm sorry. I shouldn't have gone that far." He fully expected her to berate him for his behavior, and it would have been well-deserved.

"The fault is not yours alone," she said. "I'm afraid I was as caught up in the moment as you." She silently scolded herself for behaving as shamelessly as Arina.

Her admission surprised him. Still, he was embarrassed that he'd allowed himself to go so far. But when he looked at her swollen pink lips, all he wanted to do was kiss her again. And he did.

As before, she wrapped her arms around his neck meeting his passion with equal intensity.

Reluctantly, he forced himself to pull away. Another moment and he wouldn't be able to walk away. "We should get back."

Mary Ann couldn't speak. She longed for more of his kisses, but she knew they needed to stop before something disastrous happened. She straightened her hair and her dress before Luke took her by the elbow and walked back to the dance floor. He spotted his brothers standing like sentinels beside their wives and steered Mary Ann toward them. His sisters-in-law were thrilled to see Mary Ann and they immediately started discussing their dresses. Luke found it difficult to converse with his brothers, he was trying to process what just happened behind the church of all places. *What was wrong with him?* He knew what was wrong. He wanted to take Mary Ann to her room, lock the door, and not surface for a week.

A man approached Mary Ann asking her to dance and she accepted. Luke noticed no one asked his sisters-in-law to dance. He wondered if these cowboys didn't think he was as mean as his brothers when he got riled. Maybe he should just go out there on the floor and knock that cowboy's bulging eyes back into their sockets and show him just how mean he could be.

"What do you think, Luke?" Colt asked.

Luke didn't respond and Jake jabbed him in the ribs with his elbow.

"Huh?"

"What are you thinking about, little brother?" Colt asked, knowing full well where his mind was. All he had to do was follow his eyes.

"Nothing." He wasn't about to tell them what he was thinking when he couldn't even get it straight in his own mind. He needed to get his thoughts off Mary Ann before he went plumb loco. He glanced around the dance floor and saw Arina dancing with Detrick. He thought he'd be wise to take Arina up on her offer before contemplating getting involved with a woman like Mary Ann. She was a woman he'd have to wed.

Suddenly, Sally Detrick was standing in front of him. "I haven't seen enough of you tonight."

"Sorry." Sally was another one who was offering herself up for the taking, and by the way she was dressed he was surprised her old man let her out of the house.

"Well, it's time you made good on your promise to

dance all night." Sally grabbed his hand and pulled him to the dance floor a second time.

Mary Ann tried to keep from glancing at Luke as he danced with Sally, but it was as if her eyes had a mind of their own. She wondered if he was holding Sally as tightly as he'd held her. She wondered if he was telling her she looked beautiful. Would he take her behind the church and kiss her?

The whole time Luke danced with Sally, he tried to remember how she looked that day on the lake where she was all but naked to see if he might work up some desire for her. Nothing. He saw his lips on Mary Ann's delicate skin, smelled her fragrance, felt his fingers threading through her hair. Before the dance ended, a cowboy tapped him on the shoulder, cutting in. Luke started to walk back to where his brothers were standing, but instead made his way to the table to get a drink. He hoped someone spiked the punch. He needed a good stiff drink.

"Would you pour me some punch?" Arina asked.

Luke hadn't even seen her approach. "I think it's spiked."

"Good, that'll make it better."

He handed her a full cup. "Are you having a good time?"

"Yes, I am. Judd is a wonderful dancer and I haven't been to a dance in a long time. It's nice to put my troubles aside for a while."

Luke didn't respond. His eyes were on Sally approaching and she looked to be in a snit. Thanks to Jake he didn't have to stand around and listen to the sparring between the two women.

"Luke, can you come with me a minute, I need to talk to you about something."

"Sure thing." Luke took his drink with him and followed Jake away from the crowd.

"I saw Sally walking your way and I figured you needed a way out of that squabble," Jake told him.

"I owe you." Luke scanned the crowd for Mary Ann and he found her on the dance floor with yet another man.

"I actually had another reason to find you. Joey, from the telegraph office, was looking for you to give you this." Jake handed him a telegram.

Opening the piece of paper, Luke scanned the contents. It was the news he'd dreaded, but suspected would come. He wished Sam would have contacted him if he had a problem, but Sam was a lot like his brother Colt. They were both men who thought they could handle anything without help. Luke figured that was one of the reasons he thought so highly of Sam. It saddened him to know that his friend died alone. He deserved better. "Sam's dead."

Chapter Twelve

"I can't find Arina," Luke told his brothers. He looked around the dance floor and he didn't see Arina, but he spotted Mary Ann dancing with a different cowboy. The man looked like he'd died and gone to heaven by the way he was staring at her. He didn't like her dress one little bit. He thought about going over and cutting in, but he needed to find Arina and tell her about the fate of her husband.

"The last time I saw her she was dancing with Detrick," Jake said.

Luke saw Detrick in the crowd so he headed in his direction. "Have you seen Arina?"

"I was dancing with her when some cowboy cut in." Detrick looked among the dancing couples. "I don't know who he was, but I don't see them now."

Sally walked up and her father asked if she had seen Arina. "I saw her headed around the back of the church with some cowboy."

"Did you know him?" Luke asked.

"I've never seen him before."

Luke and his brothers looked everywhere for Arina, but they couldn't find her. He walked back to the hotel thinking whoever she was with may have escorted her back to her room. When he entered the hotel Eb was behind the desk but he said he hadn't seen Arina. But Luke thought he would check her room anyway. Her door was locked and she didn't answer, so he decided to go back to the dance to see if she had surfaced.

On his way back he thought about Sam. He owed it to his friend to find out what happened to him. He decided he had to go to Arizona to get some answers. The way he saw it, that might be the best thing to do for many reasons. He needed to get away from Mary Ann anyway so he could get his head on straight. It was apparent tonight that she wasn't as indifferent to him as he had thought. Her reaction surprised him, and he'd never been as close as he was tonight to taking advantage of a lady. She was fogging up his brain, and while he wanted her, he wasn't ready to settle down. Arizona seemed like the answer to a lot of his problems.

He reached the dance just as Mary Ann and her uncle were leaving. "Did you enjoy the dance?" Luke tried to keep his eyes off Mary Ann.

"Very much," George responded.

Finally, he couldn't resist and he looked at her. "Did you dance every dance?" He hoped he didn't sound like a spurned lover.

Mary Ann thought Luke sounded angry, which puzzled her considering he'd disappeared with Arina. Perhaps Arina refused his advances. "Almost."

"I think she did, I had to plead for one dance. After tonight she's going to have her choice of beaus," George added.

In that dress, Luke didn't doubt it for one moment, and that suited him just fine. Let other cowboys fight over her. "I'm glad you had a lovely evening. I'll say good night." He tipped his hat and turned toward the livery. He didn't know why he was angry, he loved being a bachelor and chasing women. He liked having them chase after him, too. Let other men fight over Mary Ann. He didn't care.

Mary Ann didn't know what to make of Luke's attitude, especially considering what had passed between them tonight. What right did he have to be angry with her? She should have never allowed him to take such liberties. Not only had she allowed it, she enjoyed every moment. She didn't know what she would have done had he not been the one to pull away. Yes she did. She would have been disgraced. He didn't even ask to dance with her again. She hadn't lacked for partners to be sure, but the whole time she was dancing with the other men, her mind had been on Luke and his kisses. When he disappeared she was confident he was with Arina since she disappeared at the same time. Then Luke came back acting like nothing had happened between them. Those few moments with him had been life-changing, and now all she wanted to do was cry.

Before dawn the next morning, Mary Ann was on the staircase poised to step on the second-floor landing when she heard a door opening. She stopped when she realized that it was Arina's room and she didn't want to talk to the woman. She saw a tall, dark-haired man wearing a blue shirt backing out of Arina's door with his holster hung over his shoulder. Luke had worn a blue shirt last night. The lanterns were turned low and the hallway was dim and all she saw was his back, but she knew it was Luke sneaking out at that hour of the morning. She heard Arina's voice before the door closed. "Bye, handsome, come back soon."

Mary Ann was furious, not with Luke, but herself for being upset. It wasn't as if she didn't know he was a rake. He'd done nothing to hide his philandering ways. Why he wanted or needed additional conquests was beyond her. She'd yielded to his seduction willingly, and sadly she couldn't blame him alone. Thank goodness their encounter had ended before she made a fool of herself. A tear streaked down her cheek and she swiped at it with the back of her hand. She'd been awake all night berating herself for allowing what had transpired between them. It was time she faced facts. Luke didn't want any kind of relationship, he just wanted her like he wanted every other woman in town. She was nothing special to him, no matter how he flattered her. From now on she wouldn't give Luke McBride another thought, or the time of day.

Luke was sitting in the kitchen having a cup of coffee with Colt at dawn while everyone else was still sleeping.

"I didn't find Arina last night," Luke told him.

"I wonder who she was with if it wasn't Detrick."

"I don't know, but one thing is certain, Arina would have no problem attracting a man." He couldn't deny he would be relieved if she found another man to flirt with other than him. He'd questioned if he would be attracted to her if she wasn't Sam's wife. If he met her in a saloon he might have spent some time with her, but she wasn't the kind of woman a man would take home to meet his mother. It didn't come as a great surprise that she'd left the dance with a stranger. He'd learned how aggressive she could be when it came to men and what she wanted.

"She might have spent the night in some man's room somewhere," Colt said as if he knew what Luke was thinking. "I'm sure she'll turn up today."

"Yeah." Luke stood and walked to the stove. "What do you say we start Sunday breakfast? I'm sure Victoria and Promise wouldn't mind."

Colt smiled at him. "I'm sure they wouldn't."

It was Jake's turn to drive the buckboard to church with the women and children in the back. Colt and Luke were on horseback riding alongside the buckboard.

"I noticed no one asked your wives to dance last night," Luke commented to his brothers.

"They knew better," Colt replied.

"Everyone was too afraid of Colt," Promise cut in.

"Afraid of Colt? What about me?" Jake asked.

"You know Colt looks more intimidating than you two," Victoria added. She frowned at her husband. "And he had that scowl on his face the entire evening."

Her comment ruffled Jake. "He might look more intimidating, but it doesn't mean he is."

Luke didn't pay attention to their banter. "Every man there asked Mary Ann. They must have thought I'm not intimidating. Did you see that dress she had on? I can't believe she wore something like that."

Colt and Jake exchanged a glance. Their little brother sure had changed his tune. He certainly enjoyed what his sisters-in-law were wearing before he saw Mary Ann's dress. "There's a difference. Mary Ann is not your wife."

Luke processed that observation. "Well, men should be more polite. She's new to this country and they should keep their . . . darn eyes above the neck."

Before Colt had a chance to caution Luke about his language, Cade asked, "Uncle Luke, are you marrying 'Rina?"

That question got Luke's attention. "Marrying who?"

"Arina," Cody clarified.

"The lady who has the bosoms," Cade said.

"Where did you get a notion like that?" Luke asked the twins.

"Where did you hear that word?" Colt asked at the same time.

"Ma said you brought 'Rina and her bosoms to dinner. When Uncle Jake brought Aunt Promise home, he married her," Cade explained.

"No, I was just being nice bringing her to dinner. I'm not marrying Arina."

"What's bosoms?" Cade asked. "We didn't get to see 'em because we was with Mrs. Wellington."

"You'll find out when you get older," Jake said, laughing.

"A lot older," Colt told them.

"Ma and Aunt Promise says she likes to show her bosoms. Whatever they are," Cody said.

"Yeah. Why can't we see them?" Cade asked.

"Ma said they were about to fall out," Cody said.

Cade furrowed his brow. "Fall out of what?"

"I dunno. All I know is Ma said, 'I've never seen anyone who likes to show her bosoms so much and if she leaned over they are sure to fall out all over the place.'" Cody repeated Victoria's words in a falsetto voice.

Colt nearly fell off his horse he was laughing so hard.

"That will be quite enough," Victoria said. Though her voice was stern, she turned her head so they wouldn't see her smiling.

Seeing the reaction they were receiving from the

adults, Cade said, "Aunt Promise said Uncle Jake and Pa sure had a good time looking at her bosoms, so I don't know why we can't see 'em."

"Enough," Victoria said.

Hearing his ma was not happy, Cody moved on to another topic. "Who's Mary Ann?"

Colt and Jake were very interested in Luke's response to this question.

"She's a lady at the hotel," Luke said.

"Who was dancing with her?" Cade asked.

"Do you boys hear everything?" Luke asked, waiting for Colt to tell them to quit asking so many questions.

"What was wrong with her dress?" Cody asked.

This time Victoria answered before Luke. "Nothing was wrong with her dress; it was lovely."

"But Uncle Luke didn't like it," Cade said.

"I liked it fine, but so did every other cowboy."

"Shouldn't they like her dress?" Cody asked, confused by Luke's explanation.

"Well . . ." Luke started, but Cade interrupted.

"Is she real pretty like Ma? Ma said she was real pretty."

"Yeah, she's real pretty," Luke said.

"Why don't you invite her to dinner? Does she have bosoms?" Cody asked. "Maybe we can see hers."

Luke rolled his eyes when Colt and Jake started laughing again. Their question reminded him of Mary Ann's low-cut gown, and her bosoms, and what almost happened behind the church. Last night's kisses changed everything. "I think I've invited enough ladies to dinner."

"Nope, you got to bring them home so you can get married," Cade instructed.

"I'm not wanting to get married," Luke told them.

"Why not?" both boys asked at the same time.

"I like to enjoy all the ladies."

"Luke." Colt's tone was a warning that he was talking to impressionable young ears.

Luke shrugged at him.

"Maybe you can marry lots of 'em," Cody said.

"It doesn't work that way," Colt told them.

"What if you like lots of 'em, like Uncle Luke?" Cade asked.

"You have to narrow it down," Colt explained.

"Did you have to narrow down Ma?" Cody asked.

Colt knew his wife was listening. "Nope, I knew the moment I saw your ma she was the one for me."

"What a good answer, husband." Victoria smiled at him. "But as I recall there were several women vying for your attention."

"What's vying?" Cade asked.

"Your father was very much like Uncle Luke and Uncle Jake, popular with the ladies."

"Then why can't you marry more than one?" Cody questioned.

"Grown-ups make it hard to understand," Cade told his brother.

"That they do. But I don't want to marry one or ten." Luke leaned over to ruffle Cody's hair just as a shot rang out.

"Down!" Colt yelled. Jake pulled the buckboard near a clump of trees and jumped over the seat to position himself over the boys and the women. Colt and Luke backed their horses to the side of the buckboard shielding them the best they could.

"Where?" Colt asked.

Jake and Luke understood he was asking what direction the shot came from, but they didn't know. Within seconds they heard a horse in the distance. Luke and Colt took off after the sound of the hoofbeats. Jake jumped from the buckboard and helped everyone to the ground. Thirty minutes passed before Colt and Luke came back.

"See anything?" Jake asked.

"No, we lost him," Luke said.

Jake handed Luke his hat with his finger in the bullet hole through the crown. "I think someone was aiming for you, little brother."

"Looks like I moved at the right time." He inspected the hole in his hat. "Dang, this was my Sunday hat."

"Any ideas?" Colt asked as he helped the women in the buckboard.

"Not a one," Luke answered.

"You haven't been sniffing around any married women, have you?" Jake asked.

"No way. Besides the dance, I haven't been anywhere but the saloon. And I only danced with single women last night."

"Except one," Colt said.

Luke quickly went through the list of women he'd danced with. "Yeah, Arina."

"Do you think this has anything to do with Sam's death?" Colt asked.

"I have no idea. I'm in the dark on this and I'm not sure what I can do about it from here. If that bullet was meant for me, how did the shooter tell us apart?" He might not be mistaken for Colt since he was the largest of the three, but he could certainly be mistaken for Jake.

"Your horse," Colt and Jake answered at the same time. Colt and Jake both had black horses and Luke's was a buckskin.

Colt looked at his wife and boys. "Honey, is everyone still wanting to go to church?"

"Absolutely," Victoria responded. "I'm confident you and your brothers can handle any problems."

Colt winked at her. His wife always made him feel invincible by her confidence in him. "Jake, let's go."

They arrived late to church so Luke had to wait until the service was over to tell Arina about Sam. When the family entered the hotel, Luke headed for the stairs. "I'll be down in a few minutes." Mary Ann was behind the desk when Luke passed and he stopped to say hello, forgetting about his decision to let other cowboys fight over her. This morning she was dressed in a pristine white shirt and a black skirt and he noticed she was buttoned up to her neck again. Luke thought she looked even lovelier than she did last night. She didn't need to show so much skin.

Mary Ann saw Luke and his family when they arrived, and she'd noticed Luke had changed his clothes. He certainly didn't have time to sleep after leaving the hotel at dawn. She didn't look up when he spoke to her. "Back so soon?"

Luke figured she was referring to the fact he'd picked up Arina for the dance last night. He thought it odd she wouldn't look at him. Perhaps she was embarrassed about what happened between them at the dance. "You look beautiful this morning."

"I'm sure you say such things to every woman you see. At all hours of the day or night."

She sure sounded testy this morning. "You're the first woman I've said it to today," he teased. She still refused to look at him, so he tried again. "How are you today?"

"Perfect." She walked from behind the desk without sparing him a glance and walked into the restaurant.

Luke stood there looking after her wondering what in the heck he'd done wrong this time. Were all women such a puzzle? He'd have to ask his brothers if their wives were as unpredictable as Mary Ann. He shook his head. No figuring women. He hustled up the stairs to get his business over with.

Arina answered her door on the first knock, and to Luke's surprise she was dressed.

"Oh . . . hello, Luke, do come in."

Luke thought she acted like she was expecting someone else. He walked in and closed the door. "Arina, I have bad news."

One look at Luke's face and she said, "Sam's dead."

Luke nodded. "I received a telegram from Tom Sparks, the supervisor at the mine. He said they found Sam in the desert. He'd apparently been there for some time."

Arina moved close to Luke and put her head on his chest and wrapped her arms around his waist. "That's terrible news."

Luke didn't know what to say or do, so he ended up patting her on the back. He heard her sniffling, but he didn't know if she was really crying.

She pulled back and looked up at him. "What does this mean? I know Sam had a will, but I don't know what this means."

Luke hadn't even thought that far ahead. "We'll find out all of the details when we get to Arizona."

"But what about the mine? Are you going back to oversee the mine?"

Luke thought about his contract with Sam. It stated if anything happened to either one of them, the surviving person was sole owner of the mine. Their agreement had been signed before Sam's marriage, and Luke never gave it another thought until this very moment. Interesting that it was the first thing Arina was asking about. It made him think about the incident earlier. *Was that shot this morning a coincidence?* Colt's words rang loudly in his head. *There are no coincidences.*

Mary Ann saw the McBride family at the table and she thought Luke was probably upstairs with his . . . whatever she was to him, so she stopped and talked to them. She genuinely liked Luke's family and adored his nephews.

"We didn't see you at church this morning," Victoria said.

"I'm afraid last night's dance was too much for my uncle, he's a bit under the weather this morning, so I was taking care of him."

"I do hope it's nothing serious," Victoria said.

"I think it's just a cold."

"Give him our best?" Colt said.

After she conversed with the women briefly, Mary Ann hurried to the kitchen. She didn't want to be at the McBride table if Luke and Arina were joining them.

Luke politely asked Arina if she wanted to have dinner with the family. He hated to leave her alone when she'd just heard the devastating news. While he wasn't positive he could trust her to display some decorum, his conscience wouldn't allow him to desert her at such a time. Arina declined his invitation, saying she preferred to be alone right now. Before he left he told her he would be back later to make plans to go to Arizona. He wanted to pay his respects to Sam and try to find out what happened to him. He'd need to attend to business while he was there.

When he left Arina's room, he realized two things: It was the first time Arina hadn't made any sexual overtures, and there was a black cowboy hat on one of the bedposts. He also noticed the coverings on the bed were in complete disarray. Obviously Arina didn't spend the night alone. His mind drifted to Detrick. He didn't think Detrick spent the night with her since he always wore a brown hat. So who belonged to the black Stetson? Arina didn't seem particularly surprised over the news of Sam's death. Of course Sam had been gone so long that she may have just accepted the fact that he was dead.

"How'd she take it?" Colt asked when Luke took a seat beside him.

"I think she'd already convinced herself that Sam was dead." Maybe it was easier for him to believe that she saw herself as a widow than it was to know she had a man in her bed while she thought she was still a married woman. He hated to think Sam's wife would dishonor him in such a way.

"And you don't think she knew Sam was dead when she arrived here?" Jake hadn't trusted her motives from the beginning.

Knowing Arina had actually acted on her physical desires without a care about Sam forced Luke to re-think the entire situation. He'd almost convinced himself that she was throwing herself at him out of fear. "I can't say one way or the other."

"No one had taken a shot at you until Arina came to town, so I'd say someone wants you out of the picture." Colt was worried for his brother, and logic told him Arina was involved with the incident this morning.

Luke thought his brother was closer to the truth than he realized. "Arina said something that reminded me of my contract with Sam. On his death, I inherited his half of the mine."

Jake whistled. "Well, little brother, I'd say that changes things. In the event both of you died at the same time, what happens then?"

"My half goes to you two. Sam's half would go to his next of kin. He wasn't married at the time of the agreement, but that would be Arina now."

"I don't want you going anywhere alone," Colt said.

"I've got to go to Arizona for Sam's burial, and to see if I can piece together what happened."

"Someone will go with you," Colt stated. He wasn't about to entertain any arguments. His brothers were both home now, and as far as he was concerned he was their guardian angel.

Luke didn't want to remind his big brother that he'd been on his own for ten years. He knew Colt was just being cautious and he was trying to protect him out of love. It meant a lot to Colt that the family was back together, and he was determined to keep them all safe.

Hearing someone enter the hotel, Luke glanced up to see if Mary Ann was at the desk. He saw a tall man walk directly up the staircase without stopping at the desk. He thought he had seen the man before, but he couldn't place where.

Chapter Thirteen

The family had just ordered dessert when Luke looked up and saw Arina coming down the staircase on the arm of the same man he'd noticed earlier. He finally remembered where he'd seen him before. He'd been on the stagecoach with Arina, but they didn't act like they knew each other. Luke noticed he was wearing the black hat he'd seen on Arina's bedpost.

"This is a strange twist." Luke looked at his brothers and nodded in the direction of the staircase. "I saw him get off the stagecoach before Arina and it didn't seem like they knew each other. I haven't seen him since he arrived."

Jake glanced at the man standing beside Arina. "Maybe he's staying at the boardinghouse."

Suddenly, Colt jumped to his feet, pulled his pistol, and checked the chamber.

Victoria glanced at her husband and saw the murderous look in his eyes. "Colt?"

"It's Creed Thomas," Colt growled.

Before Colt could walk away, both Luke and Jake jumped up and moved in front of him.

"Are you sure?" Luke asked.

Colt's eyes didn't leave Thomas. "I'm sure. He's older and added some weight, but it's him all right."

"Who is Creed Thomas?" Promise whispered to Victoria. She seemed to be the only adult at the table who didn't know the name.

Victoria jumped up and reached for Colt's arm. "Colt, what are you going to do?"

Hearing the fear in her voice was the only thing that momentarily stopped him. "Honey, take the boys out the back way and wait for me at the livery." He didn't want any stray bullets putting his family in danger like they did his mother years ago.

"But . . ." She wasn't sure what to say, the only thing on her mind was she didn't want to lose her husband.

Colt took her by the shoulders. "I promised I wouldn't go looking for him and I didn't. I never promised I wouldn't kill . . ." He glanced at his boys seated at the table with their large eyes glued on him and he amended his words. "I never promised I wouldn't face him if he came here."

She knew by the look on his face that she wouldn't deter him. "I'm afraid for you."

"I'll be fine. Now take the boys out." He gave her a light kiss on the lips and turned toward the lobby. Luke was right behind him, and Jake turned to his wife and told her to go with Victoria and the boys. "She will explain."

"I can't believe that's Thomas with Arina, and yet you don't believe in coincidences, Colt," Luke commented.

Colt didn't answer, he'd have to think about that later. Right now his mind was on one thing: killing Creed Thomas.

Arina and Thomas were standing outside the hotel when Colt stalked through the door. "Thomas!"

Luke and Jake exchanged a glance. Colt's voice was cold. Deadly. They'd never heard him sound so threatening.

Thomas turned around to see who called his name. "Yeah?"

Colt noticed he wasn't wearing a gun. "Do you remember me?"

Thomas looked the big man up and down. He didn't recognize him. "No, I don't know who you are."

Arina turned to see the three brothers standing side by side, and the look on their faces was truly frightening. "Luke, what is this about?"

"Maybe you should tell me how you know this hombre," Luke responded.

"This is our new ranch foreman, Alan Thomas," she said.

"This is Creed Thomas," Colt corrected. "The man who caused our mother's death."

"My name is Creed Alan Thomas," Thomas admitted. "No one calls me Creed now."

"What do you mean he caused your mother's death?" Arina asked.

To everyone's surprise it was Creed who answered the question. "I was in a gunfight in this town some years back and a woman was accidentally shot."

"That woman was our mother and it wasn't accidental. You were the cause of her death," Colt growled.

"I'm sorry about that, but it was a long time ago. I was young and I did a lot of things I'm not proud of, but I'm a different man today. I always regretted what happened to your mother," Thomas said.

Colt wasn't listening to excuses, all of the excuses in the world would never bring his mother back. "Luke, give him your gun."

Thomas held his hands in the air. "I'm not going to draw against you."

Luke unbuckled his belt. "You were heeled when you got off that stagecoach."

"This is the Sabbath, I don't generally arm myself on the Lord's Day."

"But you'll spend the night in a married woman's bed," Luke said.

It was an affront that someone like him even spoke the Lord's name, Colt thought. "Take the gun."

"I've got no quarrel with you. Look, I'm sorry about your mother, but as I said it was a long time ago. I made a lot of mistakes and I'm not making another one now. I ain't looking for trouble here and I won't take the gun."

Colt removed his holster and handed it to Jake. "Trouble just found you." He was determined to have his revenge. Colt's fist landed with a powerful thud against Thomas's jaw.

Thomas hit the ground hard and it took him a minute to regain his senses. He struggled to his feet and took a swing at Colt and missed. Colt slammed a right uppercut into him which sent Thomas staggering backward, though he managed to stay upright. Thomas took a run headfirst at Colt, but Colt knew what was coming. Bracing himself, Colt grabbed Thomas by the shirt and used his momentum to throw him over his head. Thomas crashed through the hotel door, shattering the oval glass insert. Colt went after him and jerked him off the floor and proceeded to give him a thorough thrashing.

Jake and Luke tried to pull Colt off Thomas when they saw he was no longer capable of fighting back. "That's enough, Colt, he's no match for you," Jake said.

Somewhere in his mind, Jake's words registered,

and Colt knew his brother was right. He would take no pleasure in beating a man to death who wasn't able to defend himself. He didn't say a word as he straightened, took his gun belt from Jake, and buckled it around his waist. Was it a coincidence he'd seen Creed Thomas after all of these years? At one time he might not have thought twice about beating Thomas within an inch of his life. But he'd changed. Loving Victoria and the boys had changed him. Having his brothers back at the ranch made a difference in his life. Old grudges were no longer important to him.

He realized that even though he was a boy when his mother was killed by that stray bullet, Thomas was also a young man. Thomas looked to be about ten years older than Colt, so when he started the gunfight that fateful day he was probably about twenty-one. Colt remembered his father told him that Thomas didn't have a pa to teach him right from wrong. Maybe Thomas had turned his life around, maybe not. But Colt figured it was up to the Good Lord to right the wrongs. He had to answer for his own soul, and he was glad he no longer had hate in his heart. Revenge didn't seem so sweet. No, it wasn't a coincidence seeing Thomas after all of these years. God had a way of opening his eyes at just the right time. He was a man who had a whole lot to be grateful for, and he wouldn't allow himself to take his blessings for granted. There couldn't be room in his heart for grudges or for hate.

Luke handed Colt his hat, then turned to Arina. "Aren't you going to help your boyfriend?"

"He's not my boyfriend," she countered.

Luke grinned. "Well, whatever he is to you, he's wearing the Stetson that was on your bedpost this morning."

"As I told you, he's our foreman on the ranch. We

were together last night, but that doesn't make him anything special to me. You can't say I didn't tell you what I wanted."

Luke had to give her credit, she didn't lie about sharing her bed with Thomas. "Maybe you should start at the beginning and tell me why he came here with you. More importantly, why you didn't mention you two were traveling together."

"He thought I needed protection. I didn't want you to get the wrong idea about us, so I didn't mention him."

Her explanation rang hollow. She obviously didn't care about his good opinion while she was coming on to him. "Did you two kill Sam?"

She looked at him like she was surprised he would suggest such a thing. "Of course not! I didn't know he was dead."

"How long have the two of you been sharing a bed? Before Sam disappeared?"

"No, last night was the first night."

Luke didn't believe her. "If I find out you had something to do with Sam's death I will see you hang."

"Let's go," Colt told them. He turned and saw Eb behind them. "Eb, tell George I will pay for a new door."

The brothers were quiet as they walked to the livery. Luke and Jake wanted to give Colt time to settle down. They were taken by surprise when Colt stopped suddenly and turned to them. "I remember Pa saying that Creed Thomas was always causing trouble when he was young. He might have changed, but we can't take his word as gospel. Someone took a shot at you this morning, Luke, and considering Thomas's past, he's the most likely candidate around. You own the mine now, and Thomas is sharing a bed with the new widow, so we can't ignore the fact that if they didn't kill Sam they could have paid someone to do it."

"That's what I was thinking. She doesn't strike me as the type who would sit back and let someone else inherit her husband's half of the mine. I don't believe a word out of her mouth. I'd say she had plans of being a wealthy widow," Jake added.

"Yeah, but how do I go about proving it?" Luke asked.

"I'll go to Arizona with you and we'll see what we can find out," Jake said.

Luke smiled. "Are you sure you want to leave your new wife?"

"Heck no, I don't want to, but I don't want a dead brother, either," Jake said.

Colt liked the idea of Jake going with Luke, but he also wanted Jake's former partner, Cole Becker, to go with them. Jake and Cole had been partners as U.S. Marshals for ten years. "I'd feel better if you two took Cole with you."

"Can you do without the three of us for a few weeks?" Luke asked.

"No, but we'll manage. I don't want either of you riding into a trap. Until we know what happened to Sam, we need to take precautions," Colt said. "If you leave soon you'll make better time than the stagecoach. You might have a better chance of finding out what happened before Arina gets there."

"If it's okay with Jake and Cole, we can leave tomorrow," Luke replied. He thought about Mary Ann even though he tried not to. She'd treated him like he had the black plague this morning, but he sure hated the thought of not seeing her for weeks.

Bob, the owner of the livery, walked from the stables and saw the McBride brothers coming his way. He turned around and motioned for the women to come out. "He's here and in one piece."

Victoria ran from the livery into Colt's arms.

Colt could feel her shaking as he hugged her to him. "I didn't kill him."

"Is this the end of it?" Victoria asked.

"It is for me."

The following morning Luke, Jake, and Cole were saddling their horses to leave. "I need to stop in town before we leave," Luke told them.

"Me too, I want to send a telegram and see if a Marshal can meet us there," Jake said.

Colt walked in to see them off. "Luke, is the mine supervisor up to running it without the owner on-site?" He'd stayed awake all night worried that his brother might need to move to Arizona to see to the day-to-day operations of the mine.

"He's more than capable, he's done a fine job." Luke knew what his brother was asking, and he'd thought about the same thing. "Don't worry, Colt, I'm staying on the ranch even if I have to sell the mine."

Jake laughed. "Colt, looks like we can't get rid of little brother."

"That suits me just fine." He slapped his brothers on the back. "Make sure you get yourselves back here in one piece."

"Colt, if you need us, just send a telegram to the mine," Luke told him before they rode away.

Reaching town, Jake headed for the telegraph office, and Cole accompanied Luke to the hotel.

Eb said Mary Ann was upstairs checking on her

uncle, and Luke headed for the stairs. He turned to Cole and said, "I'll just be a minute." He didn't want Cole to accompany him upstairs. What he wanted to say to Mary Ann was a private matter.

Mary Ann tried to appear indifferent when she answered the knock on the door and saw Luke standing there. "How may I help you?" No matter how many times she told herself to forget the kisses they had shared, she couldn't stop her reaction to him. Her heart was thumping wildly at the mere sight of him.

"How's George?"

"He's much better today. Did you need to see him?"

"No, I wanted to see you." He really wanted to sweep her up in his arms and kiss her like he did behind the church.

"Why? Aren't you at the wrong room?"

Her words were frosty, but it didn't deter him from stepping over the threshold without being invited. "No, I'm right where I want to be."

She backed up a step. "I told you I wasn't going to be one of your conquests."

Why did his brain turn to mush with just one look at her? "Yeah, you told me. I don't want to conquer you! I want to kiss you."

She started to say she didn't want to kiss him, but didn't have a chance. He pulled her to him and lowered his mouth to hers. Reacting the same way she did at the dance, her arms automatically wound around his neck as she returned his kiss with uninhibited passion.

When Luke pulled away from her mouth his breathing was ragged. "I came to tell you I'm leaving town."

Trying to gain her own composure, it took her a minute to respond. When she did she found herself asking, "With *that* woman?"

"No, but I am going to Arizona. I need to find out what happened to Sam. I will be back as soon as I can."

As long as his lips were not on hers she could think straight. And right now she was thinking he had spent the night with that woman after sharing intimate moments with her at the dance. "Why tell me?"

"When I come back we need to talk about this." He stepped even closer.

"About what?"

"This," he replied before kissing her again.

Chapter Fourteen

Luke had been gone for two weeks and while he was away Mary Ann worked diligently to complete her shop. She thought being busy would take her mind off of Luke, but it hadn't worked. Each time she stepped into the shop, she was reminded of the night Luke was standing at the display case asking her questions about the items she planned to carry. Tonight was no different. Luke had been on her mind the entire time she was putting the finishing touches on the shop. After she placed the last item on the shelf, she lit the blue opalescent oil lamps and stepped back to see how the shop would appear from the customers' vantage point when they entered. Under the warm glow of the lamps the room looked enchanting. The crystal perfume bottles adorning the shelves twinkled like diamonds. The garters, stockings, and camisoles were made of the finest silks and satins. Jewelry in lovely black velvet cases alongside a few of Victoria's beautifully designed reticules were as exquisite as anything she'd seen in the shops in Paris. The heliotrope and pink satin corsets displayed on the dress forms were sure to attract the ladies. She was so excited, she just knew women would love the shop, especially Victoria and Promise.

"This looks really nice," Colt said from behind her.

Mary Ann whirled around. She had been so absorbed checking every detail that she hadn't heard him approach. "Oh, Mr. McBride, thank you. I was just finishing up. Did you need something?"

"Yes, I did. Victoria told me while I was in town to invite you and George to dinner tomorrow night."

"That would be lovely, and I'm sure my uncle will be thrilled to have some male companionship. I'm afraid he's tired of hearing about ladies' fashion."

Colt chuckled. "I can appreciate how he feels. I will give him a break." His gaze surveyed the bottles of perfume lined up on the shelves before landing on the colorful corset in the corner. That was not something you typically saw displayed at the mercantile. He'd only seen such beautiful things on the women in the saloon and they ordered their clothing from the stores in Denver.

Seeing where he was looking, Mary Ann blushed. "I thought I would have mainly women customers. Your brother tried to warn me that I would have men coming in."

"It's arranged nicely." She had done a good job of placing the intimate items out of the view of hotel guests; one had to step inside to see them. He glanced back at the bottles. "Would you recommend one of those perfumes?"

"Yes, they are from France and smell divine." She reached for one bottle and handed it to him.

"I was thinking about something for Victoria's birthday next month." He took the ornate crystal bottle and pulled out the stopper and sniffed. "That does smell good."

Mary Ann smiled at him. "This is my favorite; I'm sure she would love it."

"I'll take it." He pointed to two white garters in the display case. "Give me two of those lacy garters and stockings."

He'd shocked Mary Ann to her toes. She'd never considered she would be waiting on a man, not only a man, but the most fearsome looking man she'd ever seen in the form of Colt McBride. She picked up the garters and handed them to him and watched as he felt the material. His hands were large and strong, just like Luke's, and the way he touched the garters was quite sensuous. She felt herself blushing even more.

He glanced at one of the corsets. He really liked the color and thought it would look beautiful on Victoria. He pointed to the heliotrope corset. "Would that fit my wife?"

He didn't seem the least bit embarrassed buying intimate items for his wife. She had a feeling Luke wasn't the only McBride who knew his way around a woman's wardrobe.

"I think it would be perfect for her."

"Good. The perfume is for her and the corset and garters are for . . ." He hesitated as he pulled out some bills.

Mary Ann was stunned. Surely he wasn't buying a present for some other female when his wife was one of the most beautiful women she'd ever seen. "They are for?"

"Me." He smiled as he handed her the money.

Mary Ann returned his smile, and placed the items in a box and tied it with a large pink ribbon.

Colt picked up the box. "Don't forget about dinner."

* * *

Mary Ann's friendship with Victoria and Promise had blossomed over the weeks, and she was thrilled to have friends in the town she was beginning to call home. She had been to the McBride ranch several times for dinner and had the wives to tea at the hotel. Spending so much time with the McBride women, as well as Colt, she was also gaining a fresh perspective on the men in this country. Quite naturally, they all gave glowing accounts of Luke. To listen to Colt's twin boys, their uncle Luke hung the moon and the stars.

No matter what they said, or how hard she tried, she couldn't forget seeing Luke leave Arina's room that morning. Admittedly, she was infatuated with him, but she wouldn't allow herself to forget that he wasn't a one-woman man. When he came back she promised herself she would stay away from him. If she got close enough for him to kiss her, she wouldn't forget all the reasons she needed to keep her distance. It saddened her that she probably wouldn't be invited to the ranch when he returned, but she could always invite Victoria and Promise to the hotel.

Mary Ann and George were sitting in the parlor having a pleasant conversation with the McBrides when an unexpected visitor appeared on their doorstep. Mary Ann had seen the woman from a distance, but never in her life had she ever thought she would meet her.

Colt and his wife greeted L. B. Ditty, the owner of the saloon, warmly and invited her into the parlor where Colt introduced her to Mary Ann.

L. B. turned her attention on Mary Ann. "I hear you've set up a fine shop in your uncle's hotel. I'll be coming to see you for some perfume and powders.

You'll save me waiting for things I usually order from Denver."

"That would be lovely." Mary Ann wondered how she knew about her little shop.

"Promise and I can't wait to see it," Victoria said. "I've been wanting some pearl powder."

L. B. was still staring at Mary Ann. "You sure are a beauty and I'm sure you have no need of your own potions."

"Thank you." She blushed under the woman's scrutiny.

L. B. turned to Colt. "I guess that means another one will be added to the McBride clan."

"I wouldn't be surprised." Colt had to agree with his wife. Mary Ann did seem like the perfect woman for Luke. He had a suspicion that Luke cared for her, but Luke was buck wild, and hadn't yet figured out that once he settled down he'd be happier than he could ever imagine. He figured every man had to come to terms with such an important decision in his own time.

Mary Ann hadn't even heard what L. B. said, she was too busy staring at her vivid red hair.

"It's good to see you again, L. B.," George said.

"I've wondered where you've been keeping yourself," L. B. retorted.

If Mary Ann was shocked when she saw the buxom red-haired saloon owner in the McBride parlor, she was stunned speechless that her uncle knew this woman.

"Building that blasted house has been keeping me busy. Thank goodness my niece came here when she did, she's been a great help to me at the hotel. But if today is any indication, she's going to be so busy in her shop that she will no longer be able to help me."

"It's going to be a fine home. Now you need to find yourself a wife and do everything up right."

Colt grinned as he walked to the bureau to pour some whiskey. L. B. was always talking marriage, but she had never married. Still she was like every woman he'd ever met, always trying to marry off the men.

"Colt, I don't want to take up too much of your time. I'm sorry I came out here unannounced, but I heard something from one of my gals that I thought you should know."

"Before you begin, George and I were just about to have a whiskey, can I get one for you?"

"Please," she automatically replied. She glanced at the ladies thinking she may have spoken too quickly.

Victoria caught L. B.'s concerned look. "I'll have one too, dear. The boys are visiting Mrs. Wellington, so there's no reason we can't all enjoy one tonight."

Colt turned to his wife and stared at her. First it was that low-cut dress, and now whiskey. What was happening to his sweet little wife?

Promise realized Victoria was trying to make L. B. feel comfortable. "I'll have one too, Colt."

Colt finally caught on and he glanced at Mary Ann. "How about you, Mary Ann?"

Mary Ann was moved by their kindness to L. B., and she could do no less. "Certainly, that sounds lovely." She responded as smoothly as though she ordered whiskey every day of the week.

As Colt poured the drinks he figured he'd have a lot of whiskey to finish tonight. Once again, he said thanks to God for giving him such a wonderful woman. She was one of a kind, and she'd taught him so much about love and compassion. He passed the drinks around and winked at his wife when he handed her the whiskey. "You were saying, L. B.?"

"Just before I came out here one of my gals was telling me about a fellow she was . . . ah . . . entertaining last evening. It seems this man said some things that I thought you should hear. He said a woman had paid him two hundred dollars to shoot Luke. He said the woman even pointed Luke out to him and told him the best time to see the deed was done. He also said she told him when it was done . . . well, she promised him *something else.*" L. B. gave Colt a knowing look.

Colt didn't have to ask what the *something else* was. After what Luke told him about Arina, it wasn't hard to figure out. "Did your gal say when this was supposed to have happened?" Colt asked.

"It was a few weeks ago on a Sunday. Anyway, he apparently ran into a problem, and when he went to see the woman she had checked out of the hotel. I didn't know if it was just drunken talk, but my gal said she didn't think he was making up this story."

"Is he still in town?" Colt asked.

"No, he rode out when he was finished with . . . when his business was complete."

"Someone took a shot at Luke on the way to church with the family, and he would've been hit if he hadn't moved at the right moment. Fortunately, his hat came up with the hole and not his head," Colt said.

"Oh, my goodness, I didn't know. I'm happy he wasn't hurt." L. B. held a special fondness for Luke. He was always in a fine mood, and congenial to everyone he met.

"It was the Sunday before Luke left," Victoria said.

Mary Ann's heart was in her throat hearing how close Luke had come to being shot. He'd never said a word to her about the incident. Just the thought of anything happening to him scared her to death. But Colt had to be mistaken about the day it happened. That was the Sunday she'd seen Luke sneaking out of Arina's room. "But that was the morning Luke was with . . ." She almost blurted out Arina's name before she caught herself. Luke might not want his family to know the nature of his relationship with Arina. And while she didn't approve, and seeing him that morning had hurt her terribly, she had no right to tell his secrets.

"What?" Colt asked.

Mary Ann didn't reply. She didn't want to reveal something private.

"It may be important," Colt urged.

Still she hesitated until she saw the determined look on Colt's face. "I probably shouldn't say anything, but I saw Luke leave Arina's room at dawn."

"It wasn't Luke you saw that morning, it was Creed Thomas," Colt told her.

"But I was so sure it was him," Mary Ann insisted.

"I assure you it wasn't him. Luke and I talked late into the night, and I saw him at dawn on Sunday morning. We were having a cup of coffee and we even cooked breakfast for the family."

Victoria could see the surprise on Mary Ann's face. "Did you get a clear look at the man?"

Mary Ann saw the morning clearly in her mind. She realized she'd only seen the man from the back. "Only from the back. He was tall, had black hair, and was wearing a blue shirt. Luke had on a blue shirt at the dance."

"There you go. Thomas is Luke's size, has dark hair, and a similar physique. It would be easy to confuse the two of them from the back."

"I made a terrible mistake." She was relieved it wasn't Luke coming from Arina's room that morning, but at the same time she felt horribly guilty for assuming the worst about him.

Seeing the tears welling in Mary Ann's eyes, Victoria had her confirmation of what she had been suspecting for weeks. Mary Ann was in love with Luke McBride. "Nothing that can't be undone."

Without thinking, Mary Ann took a big gulp from the glass she was holding. Never having tasted whiskey before, she couldn't believe how it burned her throat. She gasped and looked at her uncle who was trying hard not to laugh.

Colt learned from Mary Ann that Arina had taken the stagecoach the day after Luke left for Arizona. She was probably in Arizona by now, and he needed to get word to Luke to tell him he was still in danger. Hearing what L. B. had to say didn't really surprise Colt, he'd had a feeling Arina either wanted to marry Luke, or wanted him out of the picture. Luke needed to know that Arina was behind the attempt on his life, but it couldn't have been Creed Thomas who pulled the trigger if he'd been in bed with Arina. That didn't mean Thomas wasn't involved, it just meant that Arina had no aversion to recruiting complete strangers to carry out her nefarious plan. The cowboy from the saloon was probably long gone, so they couldn't prove anything in court, but at least they knew what Arina was trying to do. Colt didn't want to wait to get word to Luke. "Excuse me, I'm going to get T. J. and have him ride to town and send a telegram to Luke."

"I can do it for you, Colt," L. B. said as she stood to leave.

"Nonsense, dinner is about ready and we want you to join us," Victoria said.

L. B. looked at Mary Ann and George. She didn't want Victoria and Colt to feel the need to invite her to stay when they had other visitors. She knew firsthand how straitlaced people got their nose out of joint if anyone as much as spoke to her. "I need to get back."

"I was just going to put dinner on the table and I

won't hear of you leaving. We promise not to keep you too long," Victoria insisted.

"Listen to my wife, L. B., she won't take no for an answer." Colt walked out the door to find T. J.

"This is so nice of you." L. B. couldn't believe how kind the McBride women were to her.

"We'd love to have you," Promise added, taking a tiny sip of whiskey. She couldn't wait for Jake to return so she could tell him she'd drunk some whiskey.

"Indeed, and Promise has made a lovely dessert," Victoria said.

Mary Ann was worried about Luke's safety. She prayed nothing would happen to him before he received Colt's message. Hopefully, he hadn't been spending time with Arina, not only for his safety, but she worried that the woman would lure him into her bed. She was so lost in her thoughts that she absently took another drink of whiskey. The second sip wasn't nearly as bad.

"May I help you?" Mary Ann asked Victoria.

"I would love your help. Promise can keep L. B. company while we take the platters to the table."

Once they were out of the room Mary Ann told Victoria that Luke hadn't told her about someone taking a shot at him.

"I'm sure he didn't want to worry you," Victoria replied. "The McBride brothers do not discuss their troubles."

"I feel terrible for the way I have treated him. I thought he had an intimate relationship with Arina."

"No, there is nothing between them. He felt it was his responsibility to look out for her since she was his partner's wife. He told us he didn't even know her very well, and he was as surprised as everyone else at her forward behavior."

"I didn't understand. Luke seems to have so many women he's interested in, and I thought he was a rake." It felt good to share her feelings with someone.

Victoria smiled at her. "Luke has a lot of women chasing after him, that's a fact. And he has a soft place in his heart for women, but his character would never allow him to betray a friend."

"He frequents the women at the saloon." Mary Ann whispered her comment out of respect for the lady in the parlor.

"Many men visit the saloon."

"I mean upstairs," Mary Ann clarified.

Victoria understood what Mary Ann was talking about. "I see. Many men have done the same thing before they were married." Victoria remembered how she felt knowing Colt had visited the saloon before he met her. Victoria had even met the woman Colt had *visited* at the saloon before she came to Wyoming.

"Even Colt and Jake?" Mary Ann's hand flew to her mouth, she didn't know what made her ask such an impertinent question. "I'm sorry. It was utterly rude of me to discuss such a private matter."

Victoria glanced at the glass in Mary Ann's hand. There was only a small amount of whiskey left in the glass so that probably accounted for her loose tongue. But she wasn't offended, she'd often discussed the same subject with Mrs. Wellington. "I don't mind your question and the answer is yes, even Colt. I can't speak for Jake."

"Oh, my. Didn't it upset you to know that he was . . ." Worried she would offend Victoria, she didn't finish her question.

"To be sure! But that was before I came to town. He was a single man and well, he wasn't the first man to visit women at a saloon. But when we decided we cared for each other, he put an end to whatever type of relationship he had with the woman at L. B.'s."

Mary Ann was surprised by Victoria's honest admission. "From my bedroom window I can see into the upstairs windows of the saloon. I saw Luke upstairs with a woman."

Victoria was beginning to understand Mary Ann's mixed emotions about Luke. "I wouldn't worry about such things if you have an interest in Luke. Once he realizes he's found the woman he doesn't want to risk losing, he will stop frequenting the saloon. Colt said the women who work there need to earn a living, and as long as the men weren't married, he saw nothing wrong with visiting them."

Mary Ann appreciated Victoria's candor. She would never have felt comfortable discussing such a personal matter with anyone else. Her mother would have fainted if she'd ever broached a personal subject. "Thank you for explaining this to me." While she might not agree with Colt's point of view about the saloon women entertaining men, she shouldn't judge Luke. They weren't married, they didn't even have a relationship, implied or otherwise. He'd wanted some kisses and whatever else she was willing to offer. Plain and simple.

Victoria hugged Mary Ann. "I'm glad we are friends. It's difficult to find friends here. I'm sure things were different in England."

"Yes, it was easier to make friends, but I'm not sure the friendships were as meaningful. We were always socializing and having teas, but we certainly never discussed anything so personal."

Mary Ann proceeded to tell her about her life in England and the reason she came to Wyoming.

"Your parents must be worried sick about you,"

Victoria said. She would have been distraught if her boys left home and she didn't hear from them.

"I wrote to Mother and told her where I am. Actually, I'm surprised Father hasn't made his way here. I have a feeling I will see him soon."

"He wouldn't really make you marry that man, would he?" Victoria was appalled that Mary Ann's father had treated her so shabbily. She couldn't imagine being married to a man she didn't love.

"He most certainly would insist I marry Edmund."

Victoria thought of her husband's favorite saying, and thought it worth repeating to Mary Ann. "Let's not borrow trouble, he may not even come here."

Chapter Fifteen

Arizona

Luke read Colt's telegram to Jake and Cole. "I guess we have an answer now. It doesn't look like we can prove Arina's involvement, but we have more information than we did." He'd already found out from the mine supervisor, Tom Sparks, that the gossip around town was Arina had been entertaining other men after she married Sam. Tom conveyed he'd heard a lot of rumors about her, and he understandably wasn't a fan of the woman. Every man Luke had spoken with told him Sam had been troubled for months, but he hadn't confided in anyone. Luke figured Sam was troubled because he was aware of his wife's philandering. If he'd been in Sam's position he didn't know what he would have done. He voiced his thoughts to Jake and Cole. "Maybe she wanted to replace Sam with another man."

"Are you thinking it could be Creed Thomas?" Jake asked.

"Possibly. As far as I'm concerned everyone is a suspect in Sam's death." He knew Arina and Thomas had arrived back at the ranch, but he hadn't seen her yet. "It might be time for a confrontation with Arina."

"Now that you have all the documentation on the ranch, it wouldn't hurt to let her know that you are sole owner of the mine now and have a will, so she will gain nothing by having you killed," Cole offered.

"Yeah, we need to tell her before she has a chance to hire someone else," Jake agreed.

"If she was willing to hire someone to kill you, it's reasonable to think she hired the person who killed Sam," Cole mused.

"Yeah," Jake agreed.

"Now all we have to do is prove it," Luke told them.

"Luke, how nice to see you again," Arina said when she opened the door. Luke wasn't surprised she was wearing one of her silky figure-hugging robes even though it was nearly noon. It certainly didn't prevent her from answering the door and inviting three men inside. She acknowledged Jake and then turned her attention on the third man she hadn't met. "I don't believe we've met."

"No ma'am, I'm Cole Becker."

"Luke, why haven't you introduced me before?" She thought this man was every bit as handsome as Luke.

"I figured you had enough men in your quiver," Luke responded.

"Where's Thomas?" Jake asked. He hadn't liked Arina from the start, and he wasn't going to waste his time with her.

"I'm sure he's out on the range, did you need to see him?"

"Not really, just trying to keep track of him," Luke said.

"Why don't you have a seat?" She walked across the room to the sideboard and grabbed the whiskey bottle. "Can I get you some whiskey?"

"We won't be here long." Luke came right to the point of their visit. "I'm aware that you hired a man to shoot me."

"What?" She whirled around to face him and put her hands on her hips. "I did no such thing! What are you talking about?"

Her robe parted just enough with her movements to make them all take a look. She was good at feigning her innocence and using her assets to redirect attention, Luke had to give her that. She should have been on stage.

"The cowboy described you perfectly," Jake added.

Her cold eyes met Jake's. "Well, where is this cowboy?"

"He's in jail in Wyoming," Cole told her.

Luke could see why Jake and Cole had been successful U.S. Marshals. They were as smooth as she was in the cat-and-mouse game.

She actually smiled at them. "Then bring him here and see if he recognizes me." Her words sounded like a challenge.

"We might do that, or we might take you back to Wyoming," Cole said.

"It depends on what we find out here about Sam's death," Jake said to her. "You might as well tell us what happened. You have my guarantee we will find out sooner or later."

She turned around and poured herself a full glass of

whiskey. "I'll tell you the same thing I told Luke, I don't know what happened to Sam."

"I've heard gossip around town that you hadn't been faithful to Sam even before he disappeared," Luke said.

She swirled the whiskey in her glass before she took a drink. "I told you, Sam knew I would see other men; I've made no secret of that."

Luke could tell she wasn't embarrassed to have this conversation with them. "Were you discreet, or did he know?"

She shrugged. "Well, I never came out and told him, if that is what you are asking. As I said, I told him I wouldn't advertise it on the street. I could have gotten a job in a saloon if I wanted everyone to know."

Luke didn't understand her heartless attitude. Sam had given her respectability and he was a kind, decent man, and this was how she showed her gratitude. He'd never thought he'd feel like he could smack a woman, but at that moment he was sorely tempted. "It doesn't seem to bother you much that your husband was shot in the desert and left to the animals. I was told there was little left of him to identify."

Arina looked at him, void of emotion. "He's dead. I'm alive. I have a life to live."

Jake could appreciate the anger he heard in his brother's voice. He knew it was difficult for Luke to believe that a woman could be so ruthless. Jake saw Arina for what she was, a cold-hearted, evil woman. She wasn't the first woman he'd seen who was completely without conscience, but he had a feeling she might be the most cunning. It'd serve her right to hang. "Before you make plans to finish the job that cowboy started in Wyoming, you should know that Luke has full control of the mine and he has a will. It will not benefit you in any way to kill him."

Arina drained her glass and slammed it on the table. "Are you finished?"

"One more thing. Who's been in your bed besides Thomas?" Luke asked.

The question didn't ruffle her. "I told you I've been discreet."

"You might as well tell us, Arina. Jake and Cole were U.S. Marshals and they will find out."

"I have nothing else to say." She turned and led the way to the front door.

"I never thought I would want to see a woman hang, but I might make an exception in Arina's case," Luke said as they were riding away from the ranch.

"I wonder what made her marry Sam in the first place if she didn't want to settle down," Cole said.

"Sam was a good man and he didn't deserve someone like her. I have a hard time believing that he would agree to her seeing other men," Luke told them.

"It doesn't seem logical any man would agree to his wife bedding other men," Cole said.

"Yeah." She wasn't the kind of woman Luke would have married, but obviously Sam saw something he liked. If Sam had been lured by her body, he sure as heck wouldn't have accepted another man touching her. "Unless we have a witness willing to come forward, I don't know how we will ever find out what happened." The only thing that cheered Luke was knowing Arina would have a lot to answer for when she met her Maker.

After breakfast the next morning, Luke, Jake, and Cole met with U.S. Marshal Rafe Colston, who had just arrived at Jake's request.

Jake outlined the situation to Rafe. "I think the only thing we can do is start talking to the men in this town to find out if the gossip is true. If she has a lover maybe she slipped up and said something that might incriminate her."

"There is always the chance a man was working with her," Cole said.

"She sounds like a woman one of our guys has been tracking for a few years. She was a soiled dove in Santa Fe. Everyone said she was very young and beautiful," Rafe offered.

"What did she do?" Luke asked.

"She married a much older man who was to be her ticket out of the saloon. It seems like married life didn't agree with her either. She poisoned the groom three months after they said their *I do's*. Somehow word got out that the sheriff was going to question her for murder and she took off. She didn't even get the old man's money."

"How long ago did this happen?" Luke asked.

"About four years ago," Rafe replied.

"How old was this gal?" Jake asked.

"About seventeen when she married the old man," Rafe told them.

"That's young to be a murderer," Luke said.

"That's not all. She's supposed to be one heck of a shot," Rafe said.

Luke glanced at Jake. "Do you think Arina could have shot Sam? They said he'd been dead for some time."

"The woman we talked to yesterday is cold enough to shoot anyone," Jake replied. "I wouldn't turn my back on her."

"I agree," Cole said. "She could have killed him before she left for Wyoming."

"If the woman we've been searching for is Arina, she's dangerous, particularly if she's done this twice," Rafe suggested. "I'll send a telegram and see if we have a photograph of the woman from Santa Fe, or get a better description other than a *beautiful woman*."

"Arina is beautiful, at least until you get to know her. Let's keep this information to ourselves. Until we find out if she is the woman from Santa Fe, we don't want her taking off," Jake said.

The men nodded their agreement. Rafe headed toward the telegraph office and Luke, Jake, and Cole decided to speak to Tom Sparks again to see if he could shed some light on Arina's lover.

"I hate to give you a name on just hearsay," Tom told them.

Luke gave him a level look. "Tom, this is all we have to go on right now. I want Sam's killer."

"We need to find out if she may have said something which would incriminate her," Jake explained.

Tom ran his fingers through his hair. While he didn't like carrying tales, if this was the only way to find out what happened to his friend, he felt it was his duty to help. "There was gossip that she was real friendly with the circuit judge and the sheriff. I also heard there was another man, but no one ever mentioned his name."

"Do you think the sheriff or the judge would be involved with her?" Luke asked.

"At one time I would have said that it was real hard for me to believe, the judge is a fine man. But more than one man I trusted carried that tale and swore it was the truth. I just don't know about the sheriff," Tom said. "It's a real shame, Sam was good to that gal."

"Did you ever see her with anyone else?" Luke asked.

"Nope," Tom responded. "What I couldn't figure out, if the gossip was true, is why did she marry Sam in the first place?"

"Good question," Luke said.

When Luke, Jake, and Cole reached town to meet up with Rafe, they were side-tracked when they spotted Arina and Creed Thomas walking out of the church. "Look at that. You think the church will still have a roof?"

"Doubtful," Jake said.

They reined in beside the couple as they were getting into a buggy. "You getting baptized, Arina?" Luke asked.

Arina laughed. "Not hardly. We just got married."

Her response left them momentarily speechless. Luke was the first to comment. "This is kind of sudden, isn't it?"

Thomas put his arm around Arina's waist and pulled her close. "She's honored me by becoming my wife. I know it's sudden considering Sam's death, but after we were together in Wyoming, we decided we loved each other."

Luke exchanged a glance with Jake. Creed Thomas wasn't their favorite person, but they didn't think he deserved someone like Arina. "You're a brave man."

Thomas looked up at the men. "I know what you're thinking and you're right. Both of us have a past we're not proud of. You know better than anyone that I was trouble, but I swear I've changed. Arina's changed, too."

Arina pulled his face to hers and kissed him. "That's right. You're all the man need."

Luke wondered if she'd said the same words to Sam.

She looked directly at Luke when she said, "Sam was too old for me and you know it's the truth."

"That's your truth." Luke took a long look at Thomas. He inclined his head in Thomas' direction and said, "He's at least twenty years older than you."

"You'd never know it," she shot back.

No one had to ask what she meant by the comment.

Thomas and Arina rode away like a normal newly-wed couple. "I wonder if she married him because of the marital communication law," Jake said.

"What's that?" Luke asked.

"It's a law which says a man or wife cannot be forced to testify against their spouse even if they have incriminating evidence against them," Jake told him.

"If that was her reasoning she's even smarter than I thought," Cole said.

"Hopefully, we can outsmart her," Luke said.

Chapter Sixteen

Luke headed to the telegraph office to send Colt a message. He started to leave, but decided to send one more telegram. When he was finished, he met up with the other men and they walked to the sheriff's office. They confronted the sheriff with the rumors they'd heard about him and Arina. He denied having a relationship with Arina, swearing he'd only seen her in town a few times.

They finished questioning the sheriff and when they left they saw the judge walking into the saloon. At first, Judge Rivers was not forthcoming about the nature of his relationship with Arina, but after they plied him with whiskey, he became more talkative. He insisted his relationship with Arina was strictly platonic. He said he hadn't heard the rumors that Arina was seeing other men while Sam was alive, and he wouldn't have listened to the gossip. He also told them that he knew Sam, and he had never heard an ill word spoken about the man.

Luke thought the judge genuinely liked Arina. When he talked about her his whole demeanor changed and his face lit up. Not many people had good things to say about her, but the judge was one of them. But to be fair to the judge, Luke had to admit he also spoke highly of Sam.

The judge pointed out three men in the saloon who worked for Sam, so Luke spent some time talking to them. The three men did not share the judge's opinion of Arina. They admitted they heard the gossip she was seeing another man, but no one could give them a name. They also insinuated the judge's relationship with her seemed more than neighborly.

"You know, Luke, the way Arina was throwing herself at you I think it was her intent to make you her next husband. That would have been the best of both worlds, she'd have the mine and a younger man," Jake told him when they left the saloon.

"Yeah and I wonder how she would have eliminated me," Luke replied.

"I don't think she likes men," Cole said.

Luke, Jake, and Rafe stared at him in disbelief. "Well, if she doesn't she sure spends a lot of time with them," Rafe said.

"I know. But if she really liked men don't you think she could settle down with one who treated her well?" Cole questioned.

"You may have a point," Luke said.

"We still need to find the man she was seeing before Thomas, if he wasn't the one helping her," Jake told them.

Mary Ann sat down at a table in the corner of the restaurant and opened the letter she had dreaded receiving.

My dearest daughter,

I was so happy to receive your letter and to know you are safe with my dear brother. I cannot believe you dared such a journey alone. What would I have done had something happened to you? And I cannot even consider some ill fate befalling you and forever wondering where you were. Daughter, this was a foolhardy decision on your part, but I thank God for seeing you safely to your destination.

Your father is on his way to America, and I would expect him to make his way to Wyoming soon. He departed before I received your letter, but after his men searched London, they found you had sailed to America. I am not without sympathy for you, dear. I know you think you do not want to marry Edmund, but I am certain you will grow fond of him in time. There are many reasons your father wants you to marry Edmund, and you must think of your duty. We all have our role to play and we must put aside foolish romantic notions. You and Edmund are well suited and Edmund will not be dissuaded.

I pray I will see you soon. Please give my love to my brother and express my deepest appreciation for caring for you.

> *Loving thoughts,*
> *Mother*

Victoria walked into the hotel and saw Mary Ann sitting at a table in the restaurant looking very sad. She walked toward her but stopped when she saw Mary Ann wipe tears from her face. Victoria didn't want to intrude on her, yet she couldn't help thinking she might need to talk with a friend.

"May I sit down?" Victoria asked.

Mary Ann was surprised to see Victoria standing there. "Of course. Shall I get you some tea?"

"No, Colt will be coming for me soon, he may want something then. I came ahead to give you this." She handed Mary Ann a piece of paper. "It's a telegram from Luke."

"What does it say?"

"I don't know, it's for you. He sent Colt one as well." Victoria watched as Mary Ann tentatively unfolded the paper. A sad smile crossed her face as she read. "Are you okay?"

Mary Ann picked up the letter and handed it to Victoria. "I received this from Mother. "Now, I fear all of my plans will be for naught."

After Victoria read the letter she placed it aside. "They cannot force you back to England, or to marry this Edmund! If he comes here tell him you refuse to go back if you don't want to go."

"It's not so simple. Things are so different in England. Everyone expects us to marry."

She sounded so dejected that Victoria didn't know what to say. "Did Luke have good news?"

Mary Ann opened the telegram and placed it on the table. Victoria glanced down and saw three words. *I miss you.*

"That is sweet of him. Luke's a man of few words."

Her comment made Mary Ann smile. "He's talkative enough when he's making promises to women. When I first came here every time I saw him he was making a promise to a different woman. Usually he was promising to show them a good time."

Victoria laughed. "Luke is a unique man. He has a real appreciation for women. He will be the first one to notice if Promise or I change our hair, or if we are wearing a new dress. We always ask his opinion when we are selecting a new hat. As a matter of fact, he told us about the beautiful pink hat you were wearing the first day he saw you. He said you were the most beautiful woman he'd ever seen."

"Really?" She didn't know why that surprised her. He had told her several times he thought she was beautiful, but she thought he probably said the same thing to all women. She'd never expected him to discuss her with his family.

"He's never said such things about another woman."

"I find that difficult to believe considering the way he flirts."

"It is true. I've never seen him so taken with another woman."

"It's flattering to be sure, but it will make no difference." She pointed to the letter. "It looks like I will be going back to England."

"Don't let your father determine your future." Victoria didn't know if she should say more, but she couldn't resist. "Do you care for Luke?"

Since Luke had been gone she could think of nothing else. She'd never felt the way she did when she was in his arms, or when he was kissing her. From the first day she saw him, her feelings had vacillated between indignation over his behavior with women and a desire to be the woman wrapped in his arms. "I'm enamored with Luke, but I'm not certain he is husband material."

Luke and Jake were on Sam's ranch talking to some of his men about Arina. One man told them Arina had mentioned she couldn't wait to get rid of her husband. She told him Sam was too old and she didn't want to be tied down to him forever. Still, she hadn't approached him to murder her husband. But every man on the ranch seemed to think it could easily have been Arina who pulled the trigger on Sam. They all felt she was a woman with few scruples.

One man told them he saw her with a man at the lake on the ranch a few times, but he couldn't identify the man.

"If you were so far away, how did you know it was Arina?" Luke asked.

"You've seen her. Do you think I wouldn't recognize her body a mile away?" the man replied. "The man had his back to me."

Before they rode back to town, Luke and Jake decided to ride to the lake. They didn't expect to see anything, but as Jake had learned as a Marshal, sometimes you just got lucky when you weren't expecting it. They were talking about home and barely paying attention to their surroundings when they rode around the bend of the lake. Luke glanced ahead and saw two saddled horses standing at the water's edge a few hundred yards away. He motioned to Jake and they slowly backed up their horses to a copse of trees, all the while scanning the area for the riders.

Luke spotted two people walking toward the horses. "Can you see them?"

"Yeah."

"It's Arina, but I can't make out who the man is. Maybe it's her new husband."

"I don't think so, he's not tall enough. Let's ride in slow, maybe they won't notice us," Jake suggested.

Luke leaned closer to his brother. "Are you sure you just don't want to get a good look at Arina if she has her clothes off? I'm going to tell Promise."

"I'll tell Mary Ann," Jake replied.

Luke stared at his brother. How did he know he had feelings for Mary Ann?

"Don't look so shocked, little brother. Any fool could see she has you chasing your tail."

On that point, he could agree. He winked at Jake. "I won't tell if you don't." Together they moved slowly in the direction of the couple by the water.

They hadn't expected the man with Arina would be the judge. By the look on the judge's face, he was equally surprised to see them. True to form, it didn't seem to concern Arina one way or the other. It looked as though they'd caught the two of them in the middle of an argument.

"Does your new husband know where you are?" Luke asked.

"New husband?" the judge repeated, and grabbed Arina by the arm, whirling her around to face him.

"Looks like you let the cat out of the bag, Luke," Jake said. He glanced at the judge. "You mean she didn't tell you she got married?"

The judge was not only surprised, he was angry. "Arina?"

Arina pulled away from his bruising grip. "It's true, I got married. I came out here to tell you."

"She married her new foreman, Creed Thomas." Luke wondered why this news upset the judge if his relationship with Arina was simply platonic.

"But why? I thought you didn't want to be married," the judge asked.

Arina's impatience with him was evident. "You didn't want me working in a saloon."

"What does Thomas have that you need? You have the ranch now. There's no need to marry another man you don't love," the judge said.

She didn't respond to the judge's question. Instead she turned her attention on Luke. "Now why are you here?"

"Just waiting for you to slip up."

She walked to get her horse. Once she was in the saddle, she turned to Luke. "As he said, this is my ranch now and you are trespassing. Get off my land."

Luke watched the judge as he grappled with the news of Arina's nuptials.

"Why is her marriage so upsetting to you if you are not involved with her?" Luke asked.

Running his fingers through his white hair, the judge just shook his head, but he didn't answer the question.

"I have a feeling you haven't been honest with us about your relationship with Arina. Are you the man she has been seeing in secret?" Jake asked.

The judge looked appalled. "Of course not. I'm her father."

Chapter Seventeen

Luke and Jake rode to town with the judge and listened to his story. The judge told them he'd been married when he was a young man studying law. His wife died giving birth to a daughter and in his grief he didn't think he was capable of raising a baby alone. He relinquished the care of his daughter to his sister and her husband.

"I left town and never went back. That little girl grew up and never knew her real father. My sister and brother-in-law provided for her quite well, and I sent them money to supplement her care. They weren't wealthy people, but they had a comfortable home and they loved her as one of their own. Over the years I received letters from my sister telling me my child was lovely, but very troubled and they were unable to handle her wild ways. When she was thirteen she ran away from home and they never saw her again." The pain of the past was evident in the judge's voice.

"How did you find her?" Luke asked.

"I didn't, she found me two years ago. I was in Denver and she came to see me and told me she was my daughter. All of those intervening years, we didn't know where she was or what happened to her," the judge explained.

"Did she say why she wanted to see you after all this time?" Luke asked.

"She said she was always curious about me, and wanted to know why I didn't love her enough to ever visit."

The judge was quiet for a minute. Luke and Jake could tell he was trying to control his emotions.

"She made it sound like her life was terrible with my sister and she blamed me. I wrote my brother-in-law and asked about Arina's accusations, but he said they weren't true. He said Arina never told the truth. It didn't really matter since Arina blamed me for leaving. Rightly so."

"Did you bring her to Arizona?"

"It took me some time to talk her into coming here. I tried to make up for all of the things I should have done for her. She was working in a saloon, and I took her out of there, bought her a new wardrobe so she would look like a lady. I told her I would buy her a home here in Arizona and she could start over. She had already met Sam in Denver, and when she came here she married him. She didn't need the home I offered, but I continued to give her money."

"Did she say where she had been all of these years since she ran away from home?" Jake asked.

"She wouldn't talk about her past other than to blame me. She said it brought back too many sad memories."

When they reached town, they stopped at the judge's office. The judge dismounted but he didn't move. "I've done a lot wrong in my life, I shouldn't have left her. My sister died never knowing what happened to her and I know she loved that girl. I'll regret that the rest of my life."

When Luke and Jake met up with Cole and Rafe, Rafe had news about the woman who'd poisoned her husband in Santa Fe. He'd received a telegram with a description of the woman and it seemed to match Arina.

"But with those general descriptions it would probably match a few women in this town alone," Luke said.

"Maybe, if there are a few beautiful women in this town, but they are sending me a likeness of her by stagecoach. We'll have to wait, but at least we're going to know if it is her or not," Rafe told them.

"You mean she was photographed?" Jake asked.

"A photographer was traveling through Santa Fe and he photographed the women in the saloon where she worked."

Luke wanted to leave Arizona soon, but he couldn't leave before he knew if that was Arina in the photograph. "If it's Arina in the photograph, the judge is sure to be devastated."

"Yeah," Jake agreed.

Luke explained the judge's relationship with Arina to Cole and Rafe.

"Well, if that don't beat all," Cole said. "I sure never expected that."

"Since their relationship wasn't what everyone was gossiping about, maybe she's not involved with anyone," Rafe said.

"By the way Arina was acting in Wyoming, I'd bet there was another man," Luke said.

"Yeah, she had taken Thomas to her bed before she even knew she was a widow," Jake said. "Maybe they are both lying and they'd been together all along, before Sam's death."

As much as Luke didn't like Thomas, he thought he'd been telling the truth about the first time he was with Arina. "I guess waiting on the likeness will give us more time to see if we can find the man if there was one." He wasn't happy about waiting, but he didn't want to leave with unanswered questions. Still, he couldn't stop thinking about going home and seeing Mary Ann.

"Well, as my pa always said, *where there's smoke, there's fire,*" Cole said.

"I agree. I wouldn't trust that woman out of my sight," Luke replied.

Mary Ann listened to the piano music from the saloon, a nightly ritual as sleep was eluding her lately. Luke had been away for so long that she wondered if he would ever return. She hadn't heard anything from him other than those three little words, *I miss you.* She'd read his telegram so many times, trying to read between the lines, but always ended up with more questions than answers. Victoria had told her that the McBride brothers were known to be men of few words. That statement certainly applied to Luke. She worried he'd fallen under Arina's spell. It would be hard to compete with such a worldly woman. Victoria said Luke had felt responsible to look after Arina because she was the wife of his partner, and that they weren't involved. She wasn't so sure Victoria was right on that score. Even if she was right, with Arina's husband dead and buried, Luke had no reason to stay away from her now. But what would happen if he did come back without Arina? Now that her father was on his way to Wyoming she could never have a relationship with Luke. Her mother was right, it was her duty to marry Edmund Stafford. Her mother didn't come out and say the marriage would help the estate, but she knew it was the reason her father was so determined to find her. What would happen to the family estate if she didn't marry Edmund? Even knowing what the future held for her, it didn't lessen her desire to see Luke once again. She longed to feel his lips on hers, feel his strong, hard body holding her. These emotions were new to her, and no matter how she tried, she couldn't erase them from her memory. It saddened her to know she would never again feel like this once she was married to Edmund. Could a woman live her life with one man knowing she was in love with another? She had to find a way to get Luke McBride out of her mind for good.

She walked to the table beside her bed and picked up his telegram and read it again. It was possible Luke sent the same telegram to several women in town. She couldn't forget how adept he was at wooing women. That was one thing her mother had told her about the opposite sex. *If you allowed them to take liberties they wouldn't respect you. They will take what you offer, but they certainly won't marry you.* She hadn't exactly allowed him to take liberties, but it was a close call. She wasn't sorry for what occurred between them, they were memories that would have to last a lifetime.

Luke, Jake, and Cole were having breakfast at their hotel and were discussing the cowboys they had talked with about Arina. They were no closer to finding out the identity of the mysterious man said to have been Arina's lover.

"If there was another man, they were very discreet,

or just lucky. I'm not sure we are going to figure out who it is," Luke said.

"You might be right about that," Jake said.

"If the photograph doesn't arrive soon, I say we head home," Luke said.

Jake and Cole nodded their agreement. "Yeah, I'm ready to go. We can leave Rafe to find out the truth," Jake said.

Before they finished their breakfast, Rafe came into the restaurant and took a seat beside them. He placed a photograph on the table in front of Luke. "Here it is."

Grabbing the photograph, Luke studied the line of scantily clad women for Arina's likeness. "What? I don't believe this!"

Jake took the photograph from his brother's hand. "This is a big help." He handed the photograph to Cole.

"Impossible!" Cole said, looking at the women who were lined up in a row. Two women were standing side-by-side and they looked exactly alike in the photograph.

"I couldn't believe it, either," Rafe concurred. "I've never seen two women who looked so much alike. They could be twins."

"We can't even tell which one is Arina. How are we to know which one killed her husband?" Luke asked.

"I can't figure it out. I'm going to telegraph the office and see if there is something I'm missing," Rafe told them before he left.

Jake looked at the photograph again. "This is the strangest thing I've ever seen."

"Yeah. Maybe we should take this and show it to Arina and get her reaction," Cole said.

"At least she could give us the name of the other

woman. These gals get close working together in saloons," Luke suggested.

"You should know, little brother, as much time as you spend in them," Jake teased.

"I told you, I'm the smart, single brother," Luke retorted.

Two hours later, Rafe received his response. "They were no help. There is no way to tell which one is the murderer. All we know is it's one of the two women."

"Let's go show this to Arina and see what she has to say," Luke said.

"How will the Marshal's office know which one to arrest?" Jake asked.

"They don't. Both women left the saloon at the same time. No one had been able to identify which one married the older man. I guess they figure if they make an arrest then they will confess," Rafe answered.

Luke and Jake arrived at Arina's ranch to find the door ajar. Luke stuck his head inside and yelled, "Hello."

Hearing no response, they stepped inside. "Arina?" They were met with silence, and they both pulled their guns at the same time. Slowly, they walked through the house, and didn't see anything amiss until they reached a bedroom and heard what sounded like a man weeping. Luke pushed the bedroom door open wider with the barrel of his pistol. Creed Thomas was on his knees on the floor with his face in his hands leaning over Arina's lifeless body. The thin robe she was wearing was gaping open, leaving her nude body on display for all to see. Luke had seen her wearing that very robe the night he was in her room at the hotel in Wyoming.

They holstered their guns and walked to Thomas.

Luke kneeled down beside Arina and saw the belt from the robe was wrapped around her neck. He removed the belt and felt for a pulse. Dead. Someone had used the belt to strangle her to death. He looked up at Jake and shook his head.

"What happened here?" Luke asked Thomas.

Thomas looked up and seemed surprised they were in the room. "I found her like this."

Jake noticed the bed was unmade and the pillows and sheets were in disarray. Nothing else in the room had been disturbed.

"When did you find her?" Jake asked.

"I don't know. Not long ago."

"Where were you?" Luke asked as he reached for a quilt to cover her body.

"On the range. Why would anyone do this?"

"Was she seeing someone else?" Jake asked.

"What do you mean?" Thomas asked.

"I think you know. Look at the way she was dressed. It's not like most women would be dressed at this time of day."

Thomas slowly shook his head. "She might have thought to surprise me. She had no reason to be with another man; she said she was happy."

"But how would she know you would be coming in early?"

Thomas had no answer.

Jake pointed to two glasses on the table beside the bed. He walked over and picked up one glass and sniffed the small amount of liquid. The whiskey bottle next to the glasses was uncapped. "She was drinking whiskey with someone." He poured a shot into one of the glasses and handed it to Thomas. He looked like he could use a stiff drink.

Luke and Jake walked through the house to see

what they could find, but nothing gave them any clues as to who might have been in the home. Luke left Jake at the ranch with Thomas while he rode back to town to get Rafe. He reined in near the judge's office when he saw Cole talking with Rafe. Once he told them about Arina, Rafe rode out to the ranch and Luke and Cole walked inside the judge's office to tell him about her death.

As soon as they walked through the door they saw the judge sitting at his desk with a revolver lying in front of him. He didn't look at them as they approached.

"Judge," Luke said.

The judge didn't respond, he was staring at the gun. His face was pale and his eyes were vacant.

Luke thought the judge looked like he was in a trance. He reached over and removed the pistol from the judge's reach. "Judge, we need to talk to you."

The judge finally looked up and focused on the men in front of him. "I know."

"You know what?" Cole asked.

"Arina's dead," the judge responded, his voice flat and void of any emotion.

"Do you know how it happened?" Luke questioned.

"Yes."

"How do you know?" Cole asked.

"I killed her," he told them.

Luke and Cole exchanged a glance. They needed to get to the truth of what happened because Rafe was going to bring Thomas in for murder.

"Judge, why don't you start at the beginning," Cole said.

The judge nodded. "I went to the ranch to see Arina to ask her why she married Thomas." As if they wouldn't understand, he thought he would explain what happened when she arrived in Arizona. "You see when she came here she promised me she would make better decisions. I didn't want to see her go back to the kind of life she had in Denver. I'd seen how she lived in Denver, selling herself to any man who came along. She said she didn't choose that life, but it was the only way she could survive. But she lied. She couldn't stay away from men. She knew I was a churchgoing man and she said she would start attending church. She married Sam, telling him she loved him and wanted a family. I was happy for her, I thought she was going to turn her life around. I didn't learn the truth until later when I heard she wasn't being faithful to Sam. We had several arguments because I knew she wouldn't stop with one man. I was trying to do right by her after all the years I'd neglected her, tried to guide her to respectability. But she didn't want respect, she didn't want to change."

"I see. What happened when you went out to see her today?" Luke asked.

"When I arrived the door was open. I yelled out, but she didn't answer. I thought maybe something was wrong so I walked through the house and I heard a noise from the bedroom." He dropped his head in his hands and started to weep.

"What happened then?" Luke asked.

The judge pulled his handkerchief and wiped his face. "I don't know what I was thinking, maybe she was hurt or something. I opened the door and found her . . . with the sheriff."

Luke wondered if the sheriff was the elusive man whom Arina had been seeing before Sam's death.

"I started yelling and the sheriff got out of bed in a hurry and pulled his pants on and took off. He didn't even hang around to defend Arina's honor. Arina was furious with me. I was angry with her because at that moment I knew she was involved in Sam's death. It wasn't speculation any longer. I had no idea she was involved with the sheriff. If I had known I would have put a stop to it before Sam ended up dead."

"What happened then, Judge?" Cole asked.

"I told her I would tell Thomas. She laughed at me and said Thomas was so in love with her that he wouldn't believe anything I told him." He hesitated again and a tear slid down his cheek.

"What else did she say?" Luke was not without sympathy for the judge. He was one more person Arina had deceived and devastated.

"She said I was a crazy old man for believing she was my daughter. It seems she worked with my daughter in Santa Fe. She told me they looked so much alike that everyone thought they were sisters. She said my daughter told her the story of her life, and when she saw I was in Denver, she saw a way to change her circumstances. It was purely by accident we were in the same place at the same time."

"Did she say what happened to your daughter?" Luke asked.

"No, she wouldn't tell me. She admitted she had Sam shot and she laughed about it. She said I would never know what happened to my daughter. She insinuated that she may have shot her, too." He shook his head and looked away. "She was probably lying about my daughter, but . . . I lost my mind . . . I grabbed for her and my hand came away with the belt on her robe. She kept laughing and taunting me. I reached her and threw her on the bed and wrapped the belt around her neck. I don't know what I was thinking, I just wanted her to stop laughing. She wouldn't stop. She said such terrible, ugly things. I pulled harder and harder on the belt . . . she started gasping . . . we struggled and somehow we ended up on the floor. I didn't stop until she stopped fighting . . . God help me, I didn't stop." He couldn't continue. He wept uncontrollably.

"Judge, why didn't anyone know about your relationship with Arina?" Luke didn't understand why the judge didn't tell everyone she was his daughter instead of allowing people to speculate about their relationship.

"Arina told me not to say anything. She was worried that one day some man who had been with her in the past would recognize her and it would ruin me. It was just another lie, she didn't care if she ruined me."

Luke pulled the photograph from his pocket. "Take a look at this, Judge."

The judge wiped his eyes and stared at the images. "What does this mean? They look exactly alike. Who is the other girl?"

"I'm sorry, Judge, we don't know," Luke told him. "But we know she was alive a few years ago."

"Are you saying she could be my daughter? That Arina was telling the truth?"

"She may have been telling the truth for the first time in her life," Luke said.

Luke and Cole stood and helped the judge to his feet. "Let's go."

As they were walking to the jail, Jake and Rafe were riding into town with Creed Thomas. Once Luke told them about the judge's confession, Thomas was free to go back to the ranch. They reached the jail and Rafe made it clear to the sheriff that the judge was his prisoner. After he escorted the judge to a cell, Rafe questioned the sheriff. The sheriff admitted he was the man seeing Arina before Sam's death, but he swore he'd had nothing to do with Sam's death. He said he was in love with Arina and he thought she loved him.

"I would never have left the ranch had I known what would happen. I was furious. I thought she was involved with the judge, too. I'd had enough."

Luke, Jake, and Cole were saddling their horses to leave Arizona when Creed Thomas walked up. He handed a leather-bound book to Luke. "I found this in Arina's things and I thought you might want to see it."

Opening the book, Luke saw the inscription on the first page. It was Arina's journal. Stuffed between the pages were several letters and Thomas pointed to one in particular. "Read this one."

Luke read the letter and stuffed it back in the journal. "We need to find Rafe. The sheriff was lying to us. He shot Sam."

Before Luke, Jake, and Cole left Arizona they sent a telegram to Colt to tell him they were coming home. Luke thought about sending a telegram to Mary Ann, but decided he'd rather surprise her.

"Do you feel better knowing the truth?" Jake had given Luke a few hours on the trail before he'd asked his question.

"Yeah, I wanted justice for Sam."

"I feel bad for the judge," Cole stated. "He may never really know what happened to his daughter."

"People like Arina never think of the consequences of their actions," Jake said.

"I think she enjoyed destroying lives," Luke commented. "In one of the sheriff's letters he wrote to Arina, he said he loved her, and when he killed Sam he wanted to marry her. She used him to do her dirty work."

"It makes you wonder how she became so evil," Jake said.

"It doesn't really matter. People can always change if they want. She lived the life she wanted. I know one thing, she had a lot to answer for when she met her Maker." Luke had no sympathy for a deceitful woman who lied to everyone she knew. She didn't give one hoot about the lives she ruined. Everything was a game to her.

"Cole, I think you were right from the start when you said she didn't even like men," Jake said.

"That's the only thing which made sense. I have a feeling she might really be the judge's daughter and she had a grievance against all men," Cole replied.

Luke wasn't so certain it was the truth. "On the other hand, Arina didn't want the judge to tell anyone about their connection and that doesn't add up knowing her. She wasn't so noble. She could have been afraid the real daughter would show up and reveal the truth." He wasn't willing to believe Arina would do anything to benefit anyone other than herself.

"I know one thing: I'm glad to be going home," Cole said on a lighter note.

"Yeah." *Home. That word never sounded so good,* Luke thought. He couldn't wait to see Mary Ann and find out if what had passed between them that night at the dance was the real thing. He thought it was, but he wanted to know how she felt.

"Well, let's pick up the pace," Jake said.

Chapter Eighteen

Luke knew he looked rough having been on the trail for so long. He smiled to himself thinking he probably looked more like the desperado Mary Ann thought him to be when she first arrived in Promise. He hadn't shaved in a few days, his beard was thick and dark, and he was covered from head to toe in dust. Even though he looked like a saddle bum, he didn't want to take the time to ride to the ranch. He didn't want to wait that long to see Mary Ann. Jake and Cole teased him about going to town instead of to the ranch, but he didn't care. Let them think what they wanted. He didn't know how she would react since he'd been gone for so long, but he'd thought of nothing else but her beautiful face for weeks on end.

Before he left she'd told him she didn't want to be on his list of conquests, and he could understand why she thought he was just flirting with her like all of the other women in town. The night she'd seen him leave the saloon in the middle of the night probably hadn't helped his cause. At first, it might have been his intent to add her to his list of flirtations, but he'd had a lot of time to think while he was away. No doubt it was going to take him some time, and he would have to court her properly, but he would show her that he could be faithful to the right woman. And she was that woman.

As soon as he hit town he didn't stop until he pulled to a halt in front of the hotel. He quickly loosened the girth on his horse before he walked inside the hotel. Mary Ann was standing behind the desk speaking to some man when he interrupted. "Hello."

Mary Ann turned to ask the person interrupting her conversation to wait a moment and allow her to finish with the gentleman. When she saw it was Luke, she hurriedly handed the man his key. She turned to Luke and tried not to appear too excited to see him. "When did you get back?" Victoria had told her that Luke sent a telegram saying he was coming home, and that Arina was dead. She'd been worried how Luke would take Arina's death.

"I just got back." He took her hand and pulled her from behind the desk into his arms. "Did you miss me?"

"Should I have missed you?" She was delighted to see him, although with his scruffy beard he was barely recognizable.

"Maybe you missed this." He lowered his lips to hers.

Mary Ann felt like time stood still while the man of her dreams kissed her soundly. Like the night of the dance, she wrapped her arms around his neck and held him to her. She didn't spare a thought that they were in the middle of the hotel lobby and any passerby could see them. She didn't care. She was in Luke's arms again. Her plan to stay away from him upon his return melted away with his kisses.

Luke had thought about this moment so many times over the last few weeks that he could hardly believe it was happening just like he'd planned. It was too good to be true that she was responding just as he'd remembered. Nothing could feel this good. He didn't know if she missed him, but she for darn sure missed his kisses. The kiss went on and on, and then suddenly Mary Ann was ripped from his arms. Stunned, Luke opened his eyes in time to see a man slap Mary Ann so hard across her cheek she fell to the floor.

Without thinking, Luke lunged at the man and hit him with such force the man literally bounced through the front door onto the ground. Luke went through the door after him, but another man grabbed his arm before he could jump on the man. "What do you think you are doing, sir?"

"I suggest you take your hands off me," Luke warned.

"Do you not understand who you are hitting?" Another man joined him and tried to pin Luke's arms behind his back.

Luke broke free and landed his fist in one man's mouth, then turned and punched the other man in the gut. Both went down beside the first man. "Get up!" Luke growled to the three men.

A fourth man shouted, "Stop this right now!"

Luke turned to him, prepared to throw another punch. "If you can't do better than these three, I suggest you stay out of this."

"Luke, stop!" Mary Ann ran from the hotel and grabbed his shirt. "This is my father." She was terrified her father would have Luke arrested for assault.

Luke saw she was pointing to the man who had hit her. "I don't care if he is Saint Peter, no one will ever strike you!" Luke wanted to haul her old man up and give him the thrashing he deserved, but he saw one man on the ground stick his hand inside his coat and he figured he was going for a gun. Luke pulled his .45

so fast that the man didn't have time to react. "Leave it unless you'd like to eat lead."

The man removed his hand from his coat and helped Mary Ann's father to his feet.

Hardwicke turned to his daughter. "I see you are behaving like a common trollop, daughter. What do you mean by allowing this ne'er-do-well to put his hands on you?"

At that moment, Mary Ann's uncle hurried from the hotel. He'd heard Hardwicke's comment. "I see you haven't changed, Hardwicke. You're still a self-important fool."

"This son-of-a . . ." Luke glanced at Mary Ann. He was trying to clean up his language and he was making a poor showing. "He hit her." Luke was so angry he was ready to shoot Hardwicke on principle.

"She deserves to be thrashed after what she has put her mother and Stafford through," Hardwicke countered. He turned to George. "And upon our arrival we find her in a compromising situation with this . . ." he glared at Luke, trying to think of an appropriate word to impart his displeasure. "Miscreant." The look he gave Luke would have had any man in England quaking in their boots.

He didn't concern Luke. "You might be her father, but that doesn't give you the right to strike her. If you ever do it again, I won't stop with a beating, I will kill you."

"And if he doesn't, I will," George told him. "That is no way to treat your daughter."

Hardwicke eyed his brother-in-law. "I see you've become as barbaric as these Americans, and you've allowed my daughter to demean her station."

"Indeed. I'm proud to be in the company of the men in this country. I'll have you know this young man is not a miscreant, he is one of the local ranchers and a fine gentleman. And your daughter is the finest lady I have ever known." George had feared Hardwicke would come here and create havoc, and that was exactly what happened as soon as he got off the stagecoach.

Hardwicke turned his gaze on Luke. "Is this the way gentlemen dress in this country?"

"Gentlemen in this country work for a living, not live off the estates passed down to them, or marry for money to enhance their fortunes," George responded. He knew by the look in Hardwicke's eyes that he'd struck a nerve.

Luke didn't give a thought to how he was dressed, he wasn't there to impress this group of Englishmen. All he wanted at the moment was to give them a whipping they'd never forget. They might be proper in their dress, but there was one big difference between them. He'd never struck a woman. "You think the clothing makes the man, but I don't know a man who would strike a woman. You're either a coward or a fool, or both."

Hardwicke ignored him. "Mary Ann, what have you to say to Stafford? He's the one you have made a fool of by your philandering," her father snapped.

"Hello, Edmund," Mary Ann replied tamely. "You are well aware of the reason I left England. I'm not sure why you came here." Seeing Stafford with her father was unexpected. She'd never dreamed he would accompany her father to Wyoming, and her mother never mentioned that fact in her letter.

Before Stafford could respond, George spoke up. "Luke, as you have already heard, this is Mary Ann's father and"—he flung a hand in Stafford's direction—

"I assume this is Edmund Stafford." He'd never met Stafford, but he didn't like the looks of him. He glanced at the other two men. "I don't know who these gentlemen are, but I would venture a guess they are detectives."

"Stafford is my daughter's fiancé," Hardwicke added, taking pleasure in seeing Luke's eyes widen at hearing that fact. It looked like his daughter failed to mention she had a fiancé.

Luke looked at the man next to Hardwicke, taking in his countenance. He was tall and trim with dark blond hair and mustache, with the look and bearing of an aristocrat. The man didn't say a word when Mary Ann's father hit her so hard she still bore the imprint of his hand on her cheek. Was this the kind of man she wanted? He turned to Mary Ann. "Your fiancé?"

Mary Ann wished she could disappear. Just moments ago she'd never been so happy. Having Luke home and to be in his arms was sheer bliss. "Luke, it's not that simple."

He wasn't pleased by her equivocation. "The way I see it, it's pretty darn simple, it's either yes or no."

She so badly wanted to lie, but what good would it do. Her father would have his way, he'd already made that perfectly clear by stating Stafford was her fiancé. "Well, in a way, yes he is."

Luke stared at her a moment longer, his blue eyes searching hers. He thought of Arina. Still fresh in his mind were the many lies she'd told that had ruined countless lives. He shook his head and abruptly turned away and stalked to his horse. After he tightened his girth, he mounted and rode away and didn't look back. He took it slow riding to the ranch hoping to calm down before he arrived. He couldn't believe

Mary Ann allowed what had passed between them if she was engaged. She'd played him for a fool from the start. She was no different than Arina, just a different accent. Unlike Mary Ann, at least Arina was honest about what she wanted with men, she didn't hide who she was behind good manners and a virginal attitude. He hoped his brothers knew how lucky they were to have found guileless women. He'd wasted a lot of time thinking about Mary Ann since she came to town. Well, no more. There were plenty of women who chased him around, he didn't have to do the chasing. It would be a long time before he saw another woman who didn't work in a saloon, or didn't freely give what he wanted, without thoughts of matrimony.

Early the next morning Luke was in the corral getting ready to ride one of the four wild horses Colt had captured the week before. Colt walked to the fence as his brother roped the first uncooperative animal. No one was around so it was the perfect opportunity for Colt to find out what was bothering his brother. When Luke came into the house last night he'd barely said two words, which was totally out of character for him. Out of the three brothers, Luke was the most gregarious, so when he was quiet, there was a problem.

"You're up early," Colt said.

"Yep."

Colt folded his arms over the top rail. "Is something on your mind?"

"Nope." Luke jumped on the back of the horse and he was prepared when the animal started bucking.

Colt watched in silence, not wanting Luke to lose his concentration. His brother was a vision in the saddle, he hadn't seen a horse he couldn't ride. This animal was a fighter, giving Luke a bone-jarring ride, but he stayed with him. Even though it was a chilly morning Luke's shirt was soaked with sweat by the time the horse tired. Whatever was on Luke's mind, being on a horse might help him work it out. When the horse stopped bucking, Colt clapped. "Great ride."

"Thanks."

Colt was at a loss. If Luke didn't want to talk about what was bothering him he couldn't force him to. "Luke, are you upset that Arina was killed?"

"It's a shame she's dead, but she probably would have been in jail anyway. It was just a matter of time until all of her evildoing caught up with her."

"Jake said the same thing." Colt didn't want to harass his brother, but he was concerned. "Did you have dinner in town last night? Jake said you might have eaten with George and Mary Ann." They'd waited for him to come home for dinner, but he didn't get there until hours later and he went to bed without eating.

"Nope."

Colt didn't know what else to say. "Victoria said breakfast is almost ready. Are you coming in?"

"No, I'm going to ride a couple more."

Colt thought he should leave him alone. "Be careful with that chestnut, he's really rank."

"Isn't Luke coming in?" Victoria asked.

"No, he's breaking a few more," Colt told her.

"What's bothering him?"

"I don't know. He wouldn't say."

"It has to do with Mary Ann," Victoria said.

"Why do you say that?"

"He sent her a telegram telling her he missed her."

"Really?" Colt was surprised, but now that he thought

about it, Luke was very upset with Mary Ann's dress at the dance. That should have told him something."

"Yes, I think he's in love."

"Does she love him?" Colt figured if anyone knew the answer to that question it would be his wife.

"Yes, but she said her father has promised her to another man in England. She seems to think her father is going to come here and take her back, even if that is not what she wants."

"Why would he do such a thing?"

"From what she said, I think her family must be quite wealthy and influential. Mrs. Wellington told me it is common for the parents to choose the husbands for their daughters, often selecting very wealthy men so they can be assured of the future security of their estates, particularly if they are in financial difficulty."

"You can be sure if Luke loves her and she loves him, she won't be going anywhere unless she wants to," Colt said.

Jake walked into the room and went straight to the coffeepot. "Where's Luke?"

"In the corral," Colt replied.

"What's up with him?"

"Victoria said he's in love."

"Yeah, I figured," Jake said.

Colt wondered if he was the last person to find out what was going on around him. "What makes you say that?"

Jake looked at him like he was the dumbest son-of-a-buck around. "The way he acted about her dress. You and I carried on pretty much the same way, but we're married."

"Huh." At least he did notice that, Colt thought. "Do you think she was the reason he went into town yesterday instead of coming home?"

"Yeah. What did you think?" Jake asked.

Colt didn't want to say aloud that he thought Luke might have wanted to visit the gals at the saloon. "It's Sunday, and we're having dinner at the hotel, so I guess we will see what happens."

"Have the boys take him some coffee. If anyone can cheer him up it will be the boys," Victoria suggested.

"Good idea." Colt went in search of the boys.

"Here's some coffee, Uncle Luke," Cody said.

Luke walked to the fence and leaned down to take the half-filled cup from them. He saw them walking slowly from the house to keep from spilling whatever they had in the cup. He smiled at them. "Thanks, boys."

"Ma said you needed a break," Cade said.

Luke took a sip of the coffee. "This is really good. Did you make it this morning?"

The boys giggled, and said in unison, "No, Uncle Luke, we don't know how."

"How many horses are you gonna ride?" Cody asked.

"Just one more."

"Pa says men go for a ride when they need to think," Cade said. "You gotta lot of thinking to do?"

"Yeah, I guess I do," Luke admitted. He was crazy about these boys. How could anyone stay in a bad mood around them? He sure as heaven couldn't.

"You want us to go for a ride with you? We can help you think," Cody offered.

"I think that is a fine idea. Now let's go get some breakfast and then we'll take a ride."

"Pa said you need to come in and get ready for church. We can ride when we get home," Cade said.

Luke thought about telling the boys that he wasn't going to church, but he didn't have the heart to disappoint them. Besides, it wouldn't hurt him to have a talk with God this morning. If nothing else he needed to thank him for not letting him break his fool neck on that chestnut horse Colt warned him about.

Colt and Victoria were watching the three from the window. When they started walking toward the house, Colt looked down at his wife and winked.

Chapter Nineteen

Once again, Mary Ann tossed and turned all night, but this time it wasn't due to the noise from the saloon, it was because she couldn't stop crying. Her heart was broken. It was still hard for her to believe how one moment she felt like she was on top of the world, and in the next moment her life was in shambles. She'd been so thankful Luke was back safe and sound, and when he kissed her, she thought her heart would burst from happiness. Why did her father and Edmund have to show up at that life-changing moment? She would never forget the way Luke looked at her before he turned and mounted his horse. Each time she thought about him riding away, she started crying again. Once he was out of sight, she ran to her bedroom, locked the door, and hadn't come out. Her uncle tried to persuade her to have dinner alone with him last night, but she refused his offer. George had told her he rented rooms to her father, and she was thankful they were not staying in their residence. She didn't want to see anyone, particularly her father and Edmund Stafford. They had walked into her new life and torn it apart. Everything had changed in that one moment.

"Mary Ann, please open your door, I've brought you breakfast," her uncle said through her bedroom door.

She felt guilty over the way she'd shut her uncle out last night, he'd done nothing but help her. She put on her robe and opened the door and invited him in.

George placed the tray on the table by the window and took a seat. "Now you need to eat something."

Mary Ann poured the tea and sat in the chair opposite her uncle. "I'm sorry I've been such a coward."

"You certainly are no coward. Any woman who can travel all the way from England alone is very brave. After what happened yesterday, I don't blame you for retreating to your quarters to think things through." He sympathized with his niece. It was obvious she had feelings for Luke McBride, and the prospect of returning to England to marry Stafford had to be daunting.

"I wasn't prepared to face Father. I thought I had resigned myself to my fate, but when they showed up . . ." She stopped since she was tearing up again.

"I must say I wasn't prepared for him either." He'd talked briefly with Hardwicke last night and tried to make him see that Mary Ann was thriving here, but the man wouldn't listen. Hardwicke was securing the future of his dynasty and Mary Ann's happiness was the least of his concerns. He'd always found his sister's husband to be an overbearing tyrant and he wasn't improving with age. Hardwicke's mind was set and Mary Ann would return to England and be forced into a loveless marriage. Knowing his niece as he did now, he knew she would be miserable with that lifestyle. She shared his perspective on a life without purpose.

"I suppose Father is preparing to leave," she commented. She wished they would hop on a stagecoach and leave without her, but she knew it would never happen.

"It wouldn't surprise me. I told him they were welcome to stay here as long as they were civil."

Mary Ann thought about Luke knocking both her father and Edmund to the ground. "I doubt anyone ever hit Father in the jaw before."

"No doubt you are right about that," George agreed. "I must confess, it did my old heart good."

Mary Ann smiled at his admission. "I was surprised Edmund didn't call Luke out."

George wasn't surprised at all. He didn't think Edmund had ever faced a man like Luke McBride. "I don't think Edmund wants to tangle with Luke." He saw the look that passed over her face when they discussed Luke. He thought he would give her a bit more time before she had to speak with her father. "What do you say about walking to church with me this morning?" He winked at her. "You can avoid your father as long as possible."

She appreciated her uncle's efforts to give her some time before facing the inevitable. "Yes, I would like that. But do you think my cheek will be noticed?" Her cheek was sore and bruised from where her father had struck her.

"Put a bit of your special powder over it and I'm sure it will be fine." George wished he had Luke's muscle, he'd like to do the same thing to Hardwicke for leaving a mark on his beautiful niece.

Mary Ann hoped she might have the opportunity to apologize to Luke at church. He obviously thought she was trifling with his feelings and it was not her intent. She didn't know why she hadn't told him about Edmund. Her only excuse was that her feelings for him had developed so quickly, and before she knew it, he'd left for Arizona. At first, she didn't even think she liked Luke McBride much less love . . . yes, she loved him. She wasn't sure when it happened, but she finally admitted her feelings to herself.

Mary Ann spotted the McBride brothers as soon as they walked inside the church. Her uncle led her to the pew behind them, and she sat directly behind Luke. Instead of listening to the sermon, she couldn't take her eyes off Luke; the way his shiny black hair curled at the nape of his neck, the contrast of his white shirt against his tanned skin, the width of his broad shoulders, the muscles bulging under his shirt when he placed his arm along the back of the pew, and the bruised knuckles on his hand. Not only could she smell his scent of soap and leather, she thought she could feel the heat emanating from him. She wanted so badly to touch him and whisper her apology in his ear.

Luke saw Mary Ann when she entered the church. She was wearing the silver dress she had worn the first time he saw her get off the stagecoach. And the same pink hat. He remembered how he felt that day as he tried to get a look at her face under the brim of her hat. When he did get a glimpse of her beautiful face, he was sure his heart stopped beating. He was still blinded by her beauty and his heart still lurched at the sight of her, but he wasn't such a sap that he'd forget she'd played him for a fool. The moment she sat down behind him he got a whiff of her soft perfume. He wondered why her fiancé or her father didn't accompany her to church. He hoped their jaws were swollen shut. His knuckles were swollen and sore for his effort. He caught himself wanting to turn around just to look at her, but he didn't give in to the urge. There were plenty of attractive women in this church who wanted his attention, and he was determined to see that they got it as soon as the last hymn was pounded out on the organ. Now all he had to do was sit through the hour and try to get something out of the preacher's words.

Mary Ann realized the pastor was saying the final prayer so she bowed her head and closed her eyes. She prayed that God would give her the words to say to Luke so he would forgive her.

The worshipers said amen and everyone stood and turned to walk to the aisle at the end of the pews. Luke didn't look her way. Mary Ann followed George and when they reached the aisle she came face-to-face with Luke.

"Hello." She looked up at him silently pleading that he would allow her a moment to explain.

Luke nodded. "Miss Hardwicke." He didn't look at her, he simply walked around her and said hello to George before he walked away. He wasn't about to look into those silvery eyes of hers . . . beautiful, deceitful eyes, he reminded himself.

Victoria and Promise overheard the exchange. They stopped and talked to Mary Ann, but she barely heard a word spoken. Her eyes were on Luke's back as he walked down the aisle.

"Are you okay?" Victoria asked.

"Certainly." She tried to sound cheery, but her heart was breaking.

Victoria saw the direction of Mary Ann's eyes, as well as the bruise on her cheek, which she'd tried to cover with powder. What was going on here? How had she received such a bruise? "We are having dinner at the hotel, won't you and George join us today?"

Mary Ann saw Luke stop when he reached Sally

Detrick. He leaned over and whispered something in her ear. Sally laughed and pressed close to him as she gave him her response. Mary Ann glanced back at Victoria. "Not today, but thank you."

Leaning closer, Victoria whispered, "Did something happen between you and Luke?"

"Yes, you see my father is in town with Edmund Stafford. They told Luke of my engagement," she confided. She was on the verge of tears again and wanted to leave before she made a fool of herself.

"I see," Victoria said. "Is there anything I can do?"

Mary Ann didn't trust herself to say more, so she just shook her head and hurried down the aisle.

George was talking with Colt and Jake when he saw Mary Ann hurry past. He left them to catch up to his niece.

When Victoria walked to her husband, Colt asked, "What was that about?"

"Mary Ann's father is in town. Did Luke mention meeting him?"

"No, he didn't." Colt looked over and saw Luke in the center of several ladies, but he noticed his brother wasn't smiling. That in itself was unusual, particularly when he was surrounded by women. The twins interrupted Luke's conversation to ask him something. Luke said his good-byes to the women and he walked away with the boys.

"Everyone ready for dinner?" Colt asked, taking the baby from his wife's arms.

"Ready," Victoria said.

"Uncle Luke, can I ride?" Cade asked.

"Sure thing." Luke hoisted the boy on his shoulders.

Not to be outdone by his twin, Cody turned his eyes on Jake. "Uncle Jake?" Jake lifted Cody on his shoulders and they walked beside Luke and Cade to the hotel.

* * *

Mary Ann was sitting in the restaurant listening to her father berate her for leaving England. She'd tuned him out, her gaze was on the front door. It wasn't long before she saw Luke walk in with one of the boys on his shoulders. The smile on the boy's face said he was having the time of his life. *Luke would make a wonderful father,* she thought. Trailing that thought, she realized he would be a good husband to some lucky woman if he didn't cavort with other women once he married. She didn't think his brothers did that sort of thing, they seemed to be truly in love with their wives.

She looked at her father and wondered if he sought out other women. It was difficult to believe her father would be passionate with any woman, including her mother. If he had been, surely he would understand why she didn't want to marry a man she didn't love. What about Edmund? She doubted he would be faithful to a wife. Edmund was accustomed to having his way, and she had a feeling if he wanted another woman, then he would have her. If she were yoked to him, she didn't think his philandering would upset her. She couldn't say the same thing about Luke McBride.

Luke saw Mary Ann sitting at a table with her father and Stafford, and the two detectives were seated at a nearby table. No wonder she hurried out of the church, she was coming back to see her fiancé. He took a chair at the table with his back to them.

Colt also saw Mary Ann sitting across the room with two men. He figured one was her father. "Who is sitting with Mary Ann?"

Luke pretended not to hear his brother, he was busy teaching the twins how to pull a coin out of their ears.

Victoria shook her head at her husband, she didn't

want to tell him about her conversation with Mary Ann
in front of everyone. Jake and Promise turned to see
the men with Mary Ann. "I don't know who they are,"
Jake said. "Do you know, Luke?"

Luke didn't turn around. Seeing they weren't going
to let the subject drop, he decided to respond. "Yeah,
it's her father and her fiancé."

"Fiancé?" Jake repeated.

"Uncle Luke, what's a fiancé?" Cody asked.

Before anyone had a chance to answer Cody, George
stopped by their table.

"I didn't know Mary Ann's father was here," Colt said.

Glancing at Luke, George figured Luke was still
angry over yesterday. "Ah, yes, he arrived yesterday."

"Maybe they would like to join us," Promise said.

Obviously Luke didn't tell his brothers what had
transpired with Mary Ann's father. George thought it
was a good idea to keep Hardwicke far away from Luke.
Not that Hardwicke would join them if asked. "Her
father said he wanted to speak to her privately, so I
doubt they can join you right now."

Victoria had a feeling more had happened between
Luke and Mary Ann's father than Mary Ann indicated.
And what about that bruise on her face? By the way
Luke was acting, she knew he wasn't inclined to see
Mary Ann or her father. Certainly not Mary Ann's
fiancé.

"Why don't you join us, George," Colt suggested.

George pulled out a chair. "Thank you." He always
enjoyed the McBride family, and he wanted to stay in
the dining room to keep an eye on Hardwicke. He noticed Luke had his back to Mary Ann. He couldn't
blame him. It had to be quite a shock for him to find
out about Stafford.

Mary Ann kept glancing across the room at the

McBride table. How she longed to be sitting at that table engaged in the conversation and joining in the laughter. Instead, she sat nearly an hour listening to her father berate her. Edmund didn't utter a word in her defense. It occurred to her that Edmund might not have told her father the truth about that night when her dress was torn. She had a sick feeling Edmund led her father to believe that he did compromise her, which accounted for her father's insistence that she marry him. Whether Edmund told the truth or not, it didn't matter, her father would not listen to her explanation. She didn't think he would strike her again, but he'd raised his voice when she tried to explain, causing other diners to look in his direction. Not once did Luke turn around.

Mary Ann was barely listening to her father, but when he suddenly started coughing uncontrollably she turned her attention on him. "Father, are you ill?"

"I'm sure it wouldn't concern you. You certainly didn't care about my welfare when you left England."

That wasn't true, Mary Ann loved her parents, she simply couldn't agree with his dictates. She would never be able to make him understand that she dreamed of marrying a man she loved. No matter what he forced her to do, she would never love Edmund Stafford.

"We will be leaving in two days," Hardwicke told her. "So I suggest you wrap up whatever you need to do in that time frame."

"I can't possibly leave so soon, I need to find my replacement for Uncle George," Mary Ann replied.

"My dear, I am quite confident George can manage without you, he did so before you appeared in his life unannounced," Edmund said. He'd noticed Mary Ann's gaze drift to the table where that cowboy was sitting. "I daresay we will not see a repeat of yesterday's performance with that hooligan."

Mary Ann wanted to kick him in the shins for bringing up her kiss with Luke, and for calling him a hooligan. Her uncle was right; he was a pompous tyrant. To think she had put up with these people all of her life, and that was what her future held. She felt ill. "If you will excuse me, I have work to do."

"Two days, no longer," her father warned as she jumped up and walked away. She wanted to run, but she wouldn't give them the satisfaction of knowing they had upset her. She passed the McBride table without stopping.

"George, is Mary Ann okay? She seemed upset at church." Victoria really wanted to ask how Mary Ann received that bruise on her cheek.

Again, he glanced at Luke, but seeing he wasn't going to offer an explanation he knew he had to say something. "Her father is a difficult man. She will be leaving soon to return to London." It didn't really explain the entire situation, but he wasn't going to reveal what happened if Luke wasn't going to be forthcoming with his family.

"I'm sorry to hear that. Promise and I have enjoyed spending time with her. She is a lovely woman," Victoria told him.

"I'm sorry she will be leaving too. I've enjoyed having her here. It's nice to have family close," George told them.

"I couldn't agree more," Colt confirmed.

"And that man is her fiancé?" Jake asked.

"So it seems," George answered.

"I hadn't heard her mention a fiancé," Jake said.

"Exactly," Luke finally spoke up. Mary Ann hadn't even mentioned Stafford to anyone.

"What's a fiancé?" Cade repeated his brother's earlier question.

"It is a person that one is promised to marry," Victoria explained.

"Uncle Luke, do you have a fiancée?" Cody asked.

"Yeah, you're the only one not married," Cade added.

Luke smiled at the twins. "You two aren't married."

"Uncle Luke! 'Course not, we're little boys," they said together.

The food arrived at the perfect time, Luke thought.

Chapter Twenty

During lunch George explained the importance of the Hardwicke estates in England and the role of Mary Ann's father as landowner. George said Hardwicke was close to royalty and Edmund Stafford was one of England's wealthiest men.

"But why did Mary Ann come here if she was to be married?" Victoria didn't dare let on that she knew Mary Ann didn't want to marry the Englishman.

"There was a conflict with her father and she left," George responded.

George seemed reluctant to offer more information and no one pressed him.

Luke told himself he wasn't interested in Mary Ann's reason for failing to mention her impending marriage, but he listened intently to George's response.

Colt watched his brother during lunch. Luke didn't join in the conversation when the conversation centered on Mary Ann, but Colt knew he was interested.

When they were preparing to leave the hotel, Cody forgot his Bible and ran back to the table. When he reached the dining room, he accidentally ran into Edmund Stafford.

Stafford grabbed Cody by the shirt and held on to him. "Watch where you are going, you little hellion."

"I'm sorry, mister," Cody said.

"Let the boy go," Luke said from the doorway.

Stafford glared at Luke. "I should have known he would belong to you."

The two detectives walked up and flanked Stafford.

Luke glanced at both men and sneered. "Didn't get enough yesterday?"

Stafford roughly shoved Cody toward Luke. "I imagine that explains this little brat's breeding."

That was all it took. Luke lunged after Stafford and together they crashed through the window in the dining room. Once they hit the ground, Luke got to his feet and pulled Stafford with him, then hit him in the jaw knocking him to the dirt again. "Don't ever put your hands on that boy again!"

The two detectives followed through the doorway and jumped on Luke from behind. One man spun Luke around and got in a jab to Luke's lip before Luke managed to slam his fist in his nose. Luke heard a loud crack and the detective grabbed his broken nose. The other detective threw a punch at Luke, grazing his chin. Luke slammed his left to the man's gut and a right uppercut to his jaw knocking the man out cold.

"Luke," Colt said.

Luke was leaning over with his hands on his knees breathing hard from the exertion. He raised his head to look at Colt and held up his hand. "Don't say a darn word! He pushed Cody."

"I was just going to say thanks for looking after my boy. You saved me the trouble." Colt slapped him on the shoulder. He and Jake had seen the entire encounter, and when Jake started to jump in to lend Luke a hand, Colt told him to wait. Colt thought he'd let Luke handle it and get some of his anger out. He had a feeling Luke wanted to punch Stafford for no other reason than he was Mary Ann's fiancé. Lord, he loved his brothers. "Let's go home, unless you want to give your knuckles a few more bruises."

Hearing the commotion on the street, Mary Ann walked to her bedroom window and looked out. She saw Luke in a fight with Edmund and the two detectives. Not exactly a fight, Luke handled all three men quickly and efficiently. She'd learned to expect no less. She heard Luke tell his brother that Edmund shoved one of the boys. She wanted to run downstairs to him, but she didn't move. He'd made it clear at church that he didn't want to see her or talk to her. She watched him walk down the street with his family. He was walking out of her life.

The next morning Hardwicke did not come down for breakfast so George went to his room to check on him. When George came downstairs he told Mary Ann her father was ill and he was going to have the doctor take a look at him.

The doctor closed the door behind him and faced Mary Ann, Edmund, and her uncle.

"What is wrong with him?" Mary Ann asked.

"I'm afraid your father has developed pneumonia," he replied.

"He was coughing badly yesterday," she remembered.

"He is a very sick man right now."

"Will he be able to travel tomorrow?" Edmund asked.

"He won't be going anywhere for some time," the doctor said.

No matter how much she disagreed with her father, Mary Ann was worried about him. "He will get well, won't he?"

"With rest he should be fine, but he must not overdo. See to it that he stays in bed and gets some rest."

The doc patted Mary Ann on the shoulder. "A hot toddy each night won't hurt either."

Edmund went to his room and George walked downstairs with Mary Ann. "Perhaps this will give your father time to rethink what he is doing."

"Oh, Uncle, how I wish you were right! But Father is a determined man, and I think there are other reasons he is insistent on this marriage. Mother's letter indicated it was imperative that I marry Edmund. I have a feeling the estates are in jeopardy." She rarely paid attention to gossip, but more than once she'd heard her.

Her uncle hadn't considered that possibility. He remembered before he left England there was gossip Hardwicke was a heavy gambler at the clubs. Mary Ann could be right and that was the true reason Hardwicke came all this way to find her. If that was the case, Hardwicke wouldn't relent just because Mary Ann didn't want Stafford. Nothing was more important to Hardwicke than his estates and if they were in danger, Mary Ann's future was established.

At Edmund's insistence, Mary Ann relented and agreed to have dinner with him the following Friday night. She had successfully avoided speaking to

Edmund for a week, and she didn't want to dine with him tonight, but she knew she must face him at some point. She was tired and irritable after spending the week running up and down the stairs seeing to her father's needs. He was even more demanding when he was ill, but considering his condition, she tried to be understanding. Thankfully, he was recovering, but that also meant she would be leaving Wyoming soon.

She sat at the dressing table in her room and decided she wasn't inclined to care much about her appearance at dinner tonight. Her pale reflection in the mirror didn't surprise her, so she pinched her cheeks to add some color. She was pleased to see the bruise on her cheek had faded, but the memory of her father's cruelty had not. There was little she could do about the dark circles under her eyes, only a good night's rest would solve that problem, something that was eluding her at present. She picked up her French compact filled with pearl powder, but decided not to bother. Perhaps her frightful appearance might encourage Edmund to go back to England without her.

Stafford was waiting for her at a table in the corner, some distance from the other diners. Always the gentleman, he stood and held her chair as she approached. "I think it's time we had a private conversation. We haven't really had an opportunity to speak about our future."

She didn't see a reason not to speak the truth. What harm could it do? Knowing she would never love him might force him to question his determination to marry her. "Edmund, you know I do not wish to marry you."

"I think you made your point when you left England.

However, your future is settled so you might as well accept that fact."

Mary Ann had been accompanied by Edmund to many social events, yet she didn't find him as appealing as most of the women in her circles. He was handsome to be sure. His patrician features were perfectly formed, and he possessed refined manners as befitted a noble-born blue blood. The simple truth was nothing about him aroused her. He had kissed her in the past and it certainly engendered no passion from her. His kisses were cold, without emotion, nothing like Luke's kisses. Luke's kisses awakened a hunger she didn't know she possessed. No, she couldn't think about Luke right now. She had to try to find a way to forget Luke and everything that had passed between them. "Did you tell Father that you compromised me?"

Edmund smiled. "Is that what you think I did? Believe me, there are plenty of young women who want to marry me." Edmund had always wanted to marry the most beautiful woman in England and that was Mary Ann. It wasn't necessary for him to tell Hardwicke a lie about compromising his daughter. Hardwicke was desperate for an influx of funds to save his estates. Stafford had the money and that was all it was going to take for him to have Mary Ann.

Mary Ann didn't doubt that many women wanted to marry Edmund for his money, so the question remained why he was so determined to marry her. She decided to ask him outright. "Why do you want to marry a woman who doesn't love you?"

"You have such childish notions of marriage, my dear. Love is inconsequential. I care about land and titles, and the offspring of our union. I don't love you any more than you love me, but you are considered the great beauty of London. It will be no hardship on me to get you with child. After watching that encounter with your cowboy, I think we may need to marry quickly. I no longer hold the imprudent belief that you are without experience."

She didn't care what he believed. The thought of being intimate with him made her feel sick. Would she feel so uncomfortable if she was having this discussion with Luke? Why couldn't she stop thinking of him? She'd been very comfortable in Luke's arms, unlike the night she'd been in the garden with Edmund and he tried to force himself on her. She had done nothing to encourage his attentions and she found his touch revolting. In her haste to get away from him, he'd reached out to grab her dress and it ripped. That one incident sealed her fate. "I am not the only person you could marry who can give you what you want."

Edmund's ego would not allow him to settle for someone less desired by other men. "No you are not, that is true enough, but we will wed." He leaned closer and wrapped his fingers around her hand. "I will have what I want, you will bear my children and the Hardwicke estates will be mine in the future."

Mary Ann was no longer paying attention to Edmund. Luke had just walked in the restaurant with Sally Detrick clinging to his arm. He escorted Sally to the table at the very center of the room, held the chair for her and pulled his chair very close to hers. He was so close to Sally that she couldn't see a space between them. Mary Ann didn't think there was a chance Luke might come to the restaurant for dinner or she would have taken more time with her appearance. He looked so incredibly handsome and every other man paled by comparison.

Edmund glanced across the room to see what held Mary Ann's attention. "It didn't take him long to find your replacement."

"He is free to do what he pleases," she replied. If Edmund thought she would be a wife like her mother and cower to him, now was the perfect time to set him straight. If she was going to be forced into this marriage she would certainly speak her mind.

"I apologize, I assumed when he had his hands on you that the two of you had some sort of understanding," he said.

"You are wrong." She knew it would be fruitless to try to explain to Edmund her feelings for Luke when she didn't understand how quickly she had fallen in love with him. She hadn't even spent that much time with Luke, just a few intimate moments, but it had been enough for him to capture her heart.

Luke saw Mary Ann dining with Stafford when he walked in, and he made sure everyone saw him. Particularly Mary Ann. That was the reason he took the table in the center of the room. He was going to make a point to Miss Hardwicke that he didn't lack for female companionship. And Sally Detrick was the perfect woman to make that point, she was very affectionate and she liked to touch him. Several times through the week Luke thought about riding to town to see if Mary Ann had left for England, but talked himself out of it. Life would go on when she was gone. She'd intentionally deceived him, and the sooner she left for England, the better. He was going to get on with his life. Sally was right beside him and looking mighty good in his opinion. *Heck, tomorrow I might even take her to the lake.*

Having endured dinner with Edmund, Mary Ann excused herself saying she had work to complete before she retired. Fortunately, Edmund returned to his room and she hoped she had seen the last of him, at least for tonight. After she checked on her father one last time, she returned to the front desk to relieve Eb so he could have dinner. She tried not to glance in the dining room at Luke, but it was difficult. It seemed Luke and Sally were having the longest dinner in history. Luke was very attentive, and Sally couldn't seem to keep her hands to herself. Mary Ann happened to glance their way and saw Luke pull Sally to him and whisper in her ear. She figured Luke was whispering a promise to show her a good time. As difficult as it was to admit, Sally looked lovelier than usual, she'd even added a hint of rouge on her cheeks if Mary Ann wasn't mistaken. Of course, it was possible she was blushing over whatever Luke said to her. She remembered how often he commented on her dress, or her hat, or the way she smelled. The man knew how to give compliments. She remembered all too well how it felt to have his cheek brush against her skin when he would lean into her ear and whisper in his deep masculine voice how beautiful she looked.

All of the other patrons had left the dining room, leaving Luke and Sally alone in the large room. When Eb returned from dinner, Mary Ann helped Mrs. Howe clear the dining tables. After the dishes had been washed and the preparations for the next morning were complete, Mary Ann told the workers to go home. They'd had a long day and it wouldn't be fair to keep them longer than necessary. She had a feeling Luke was determined to make it a late evening. She considered going upstairs and have her uncle come down and wait for Luke to leave, but she thought he was probably in bed. Instead of sitting behind the desk and being forced to watch Luke drool over Sally, Mary Ann decided to go to her shop and put out some of the new stock that had arrived that day. She thought she would hear the front door close when they left and she would lock up then.

She worked for some time in the shop, covering one of the dress forms with a lovely pale pink silk and satin corset, and another one with a white corset. After she situated the forms where customers were sure to notice, she arranged the matching garters in the display case. Hearing a noise behind her, she turned to see Luke standing there.

"I wanted to tell you that we are leaving so you can lock up." He'd overheard Victoria and Promise talking about the lovely items Mary Ann had in her shop, so he glanced around the room.

"Thank you."

Luke walked over to the form displaying the pink corset. He ran his large finger along the top edge of the corset. His thoughts went back to the night when his lips blazed a trail along the low neckline of Mary Ann's dress. It made him angry he couldn't get that night out of his mind. "Is this what you wear for Stafford?"

"Luke . . ." she started, but he didn't give her a chance to finish, he turned to walk out, but Sally walked in.

"I thought I would come in and see the shop. I've heard so much about it," Sally said. "Oh Luke, look at that white corset, it's so pretty." Sally put her arm in Luke's and urged him across the room so she could see it up close. "Do you like that?"

"Yes, I do and with your figure it would look wonderful on you," Luke said loudly. He reached up and ran his hand over the smooth satin. "This would feel even better over your curves."

Mary Ann watched him touch the corset like a caress.

"I like that a lot," Luke said. He turned to the counter. "Sally, if you like it, I will buy it for you. Maybe you can model it for me."

Sally cuddled closer to him. "Why Luke! That is so sweet of you. But we would have to be married before I could model it for you."

Mary Ann wanted to throw the corset, form, and all at him. She knew he was doing this to hurt her, but that didn't make it hurt less. There was little she could do since he wouldn't allow her to apologize. Well, two could play his game. She would cook his goose. "That is so kind of you, Luke. You need to look at the matching garters in the display case, along with the silky stockings. I'm sure your lady would love these."

Sally pulled Luke to the display case. "Oh, I must have these, the garters are a perfect match."

Mary Ann pulled the stockings from the case. "Sally, you must feel these. They are divine."

Sally ran her hands over the stockings. "Oh, they are so soft. Yes, I do want them."

"Have you heard about the perfume I'm carrying?" Mary Ann reached on the shelf behind her and pulled down the most expensive bottle. "This just came in from Paris." She opened the crystal bottle and held it for Sally to sniff.

She glanced at Luke and could have sworn he was turning green. Good, it served him right.

"This is heavenly," Sally exclaimed.

Mary Ann also handed Sally the most expensive pearl powder. "This makes your skin look lovely."

"I've never had pearl powder." Sally looked at Mary Ann's face and thought the powder must be what made her skin look so luminous.

"It is an absolute must. I'm also carrying some jewelry," Mary Ann continued sweetly. She reached in the display case and pulled out a black velvet case that held a lovely pair of garnet earrings.

"I have never seen anything so lovely," Sally cooed.

Mary Ann gave Luke a wide smile. "I hope you brought a lot of money with you this evening." She opened the case again and pulled out a reticule. "And have you seen the reticules that Luke's sister-in-law makes? She usually sends them to shops in France, but she was kind enough to allow me to carry a few."

Luke glared at her and reached into his pocket. This wasn't going at all like he'd planned. This night was costing him a small fortune. Sally was sure to expect a proposal after this. If Old Man Detrick saw what he'd purchased for his daughter he'd have a shotgun stuck in his rear end before the sun came up.

"Oh, Luke, you are a sweetheart," Sally said.

Mary Ann took her time carefully wrapping each item individually and placing them into a large box. After she tied a pink ribbon around the box, she handed it to Luke. "I hope you enjoy your purchases." She noticed Luke wasn't saying much now.

Luke glared at her.

Mary Ann followed them to the front door. "Have a lovely night." Before she closed the door she heard Sally say, "Luke, honey, if you come to the lake tomorrow I'll model that corset for you and show you how much I appreciate this."

Luke didn't respond, he turned and saw Mary Ann hadn't shut the door and she was certain to have overheard Sally's comment. He almost told Sally he was looking forward to it, but he thought he'd dug that hole deep enough tonight. Still, Mary Ann was watching and without thinking it through, he grabbed Sally and kissed her.

Mary Ann slammed the door and doused the light.

Luke dropped Sally and her package off at her ranch and took his time going home. He didn't know what he'd been thinking kissing Sally the way he did in front of Mary Ann. Who was he kidding? In his mind he wasn't kissing Sally. He'd only acted out of sheer frustration. It was inexcusable to use Sally as a substitute and he felt bad about that. He'd lost his temper. When he entered Mary Ann's shop and saw that corset he saw red. All he could think about was Stafford seeing Mary Ann in something like that and it set him off. Before he got control of his temper he came up with the brilliant decision to buy that corset for Sally. He was wrong to try to hurt Mary Ann that way. But his plan backfired and Mary Ann had given him a dose of his own medicine. She'd made a nice penny off of him tonight and he had no one to blame but himself. He didn't know how he was going to get out of this fix with Sally. He'd only invited her to dinner to get back at Mary Ann. When he'd left Sally at the front door, he knew she was disappointed because she wanted more than he wanted to give. This had been an expensive night in more ways than one. He made a promise to himself right then to stay away from that hotel.

Mary Ann started crying as soon as she closed the door behind Sally and Luke. The kiss he'd given Sally was a crushing blow. He'd made his point. He didn't want to hear her explanation and he wouldn't forgive her. Maybe she should be happy for him that he could move on so easily. She was afraid she would never be able to forget him.

Chapter Twenty-One

Luke, Colt, and Jake were coming in off the range when Colt told them his plans for his wife's birthday. "Saturday is Victoria's birthday and I want to take her to town to dinner and we want you to join us."

"Sounds great," Luke said.

"You don't have a date?" Colt asked.

"No, I'm free," Luke answered.

This only confirmed to Colt that something was really bothering Luke, he didn't spend his Saturday nights alone. "I thought we'd go to the hotel."

"Why don't we go to the boardinghouse?" Luke asked, remembering his vow to stay away from the hotel.

"Victoria likes the hotel better and so does Promise," Jake chimed in. "So do I."

Colt wished Luke would open up, but he refused to discuss what was on his mind. "Luke, I'm not going to ask what is going on between you and Mary Ann, but it is Victoria's special day, so maybe you can put it aside for one night. It seems every time we go to the hotel lately there is trouble."

Luke started to remind him that he didn't start the

trouble, but Colt stopped him. "I'm not pointing the finger at you alone; I'm also to blame. Jake's the only one that hasn't been in a brawl there. I just want all of us to keep our tempers in check Saturday night so Victoria will have a nice birthday. Besides it'll give our knuckles a break and I can stop paying for windows."

Jake had no problem with that. "Agreed."

Luke wasn't sure he could agree to Colt's request. If Stafford was still in town and looked at him just right he might not be able to keep his promise.

"Luke?" Colt needed his word he wouldn't start trouble.

"I guess one night isn't too much to ask. But you better keep Stafford out of my sights."

Colt slapped him on the back. "Thanks, we'll have a good night. Mrs. Wellington is going to keep the boys. Luke, feel free to invite a date if you want." He just hoped if Luke brought a date it wasn't Sally Detrick, but he didn't voice his opinion.

After his last date was so expensive due to his own stubbornness, Luke thought he'd go solo. He still hadn't figured out a way to tell Sally he wasn't interested in marriage. It was his fault if she assumed their relationship was headed in that direction after he purchased those intimate items from Mary Ann. "Can I bring one of the gals from L. B.'s?"

"That would make for an interesting evening," Colt mused.

"If you did that, Colt and I would be sleeping in the bunkhouse for weeks," Jake added.

"Well, those are the only women I'm going to be seeing for a long time," Luke told him.

"Keep it discreet," Colt warned.

"Discreet is my middle name," Luke responded.

* * *

"I've never seen two more beautiful women." Luke was envious of his brothers. Not only were their wives beautiful, but they were loyal and honest.

"Now that is a fact," Colt said, and Jake agreed. Colt raised his glass of wine that George had poured and made a toast. "Happy birthday to my beautiful wife."

Everyone at the table raised their glasses, and Colt leaned over and kissed his wife. "I wanted to take you to Denver for a special birthday this year, but we couldn't be away that long."

"I love this so much more with family here," Victoria assured him.

"Would you like your present before dinner or after?" Colt asked.

"But you already gave me my presents," she replied.

"What did you get her?" Jake asked.

"A beautiful bottle of perfume, and . . ." Victoria stopped herself from revealing too much. She wasn't about to tell them about the corset he'd purchased for her.

Colt spoke up. "As I told Mary Ann the other items were really for me." He winked at his wife and whispered in her ear, "Can I see it again tonight?"

Victoria felt herself blushing. "You behave yourself, husband." She'd opened his presents while she was dressing to go to dinner and she'd never been so shocked in her life. The corset was the most divine undergarment she'd ever seen, and Colt was not satisfied until she modeled it for him along with the garters. She felt wanton and thrilled at the same time that her husband thought she looked beautiful. She didn't think he was ever going to let her get dressed for dinner.

Jake grinned at them. "Promise has told me about Mary Ann's shop, but I haven't been in there. I thought it was for women."

"Oh it is. It certainly is," Colt confirmed, still grinning. "But trust me, the men will get the most enjoyment from the merchandise she carries."

Luke was the only one not enjoying this conversation. He thought the undergarments looked more suitable for the gals working at L. B.'s.

"Have you been in there, Luke?" Jake asked.

"Yeah." Every time he thought about those corsets he felt his anger rising. Logic told him if Mary Ann sold those things that meant she wore them. And Edmund Stafford was the man that would be enjoying them, if he wasn't already.

Colt shook his head at Jake, silently telling him to leave the subject alone. He wanted everyone to enjoy the evening. He reached into his pocket and pulled out a beautifully wrapped box and placed it on the table in front of his wife. "This is your present. Your other gifts were really for me."

"You've done too much, Colt. Save this for my Christmas present." Victoria didn't want him spending so much money.

Colt reached for her hand and brought it to his lips. "I could never do too much for you."

Everyone at the table was moved by his loving gesture. It didn't surprise them, it was no secret he was crazy about his wife, but it was an amazing sight to see the intimidating Colt McBride's softer side with his wife.

Victoria opened the present. "Oh my goodness, how lovely!"

"What is it?" Promise asked.

With shaking hands Victoria pulled the turquoise and diamond necklace from the velvet box.

"You told me turquoise was the most beautiful stone you had ever seen," Colt reminded her.

She couldn't believe her husband had remembered what she said. "Yes, but wherever did you find anything as lovely as this?"

"Several years ago I trained some horses for a man who paid me with these stones. I sent the stones to a jeweler in Denver and told him what I wanted." Colt took the necklace from her hands and fastened it around her neck.

Earlier tonight when he asked if he could choose the dress she wore this evening she thought it was unusual. He'd never shown that much interest in her wardrobe, unless the dress was lower in the neckline, like the night of the social. But tonight he'd pulled out a white dress with a neckline lower than she thought he preferred.

"That is the most beautiful necklace I have ever seen," Promise told her.

"Brother, you are making it tough on the rest of us," Jake told him.

"A man needs to appreciate his wife," Colt replied.

Victoria ran her fingers over the necklace. "Colt, this is so beautiful." She leaned over and kissed him. "Thank you."

"It's not nearly as beautiful as you." Colt was thrilled he'd pleased his wife. This was going to be a great night.

"It's the color of Luke's eyes," Promise said.

"Luke wouldn't look as good with it around his neck," Jake teased.

Luke started to comment, but he saw Mary Ann walk into the dining room.

Spotting Luke at the same time, Mary Ann halted. She hadn't expected to see him again before she left for England. After that episode with Sally in her shop she felt certain she was the last person he wanted to see. The vision of him kissing Sally flooded her mind. That was a scene she would never forget.

"Mary Ann!" Victoria motioned for her to come to the table.

Seeing that Sally Detrick was not at the table, Mary Ann walked over. "Hello, everyone."

Colt stood and pulled a chair out. "Won't you join us, we were just toasting Victoria's birthday."

"Ah . . ." She hesitated seeing the unpleasant look on Luke's face.

"Please, we would love to have you join us for dinner too," Victoria said.

"No, thank you, I can only stay a minute." She sat in the seat opposite Luke. "Happy birthday, Victoria."

"Thank you, it's been a lovely day," Victoria said, glancing from Mary Ann to Luke. Colt had warned her about matchmaking, but she knew these two cared for each other.

"Colt just gave Victoria that beautiful necklace," Promise said.

Mary Ann looked at the necklace around Victoria's neck. "That is the most beautiful thing I have ever seen. Just the color of . . ." She was going to say Luke's eyes, but stopped herself. "The sky."

"The Indians say turquoise is the fallen sky," Jake told them.

"What a romantic notion," Mary Ann said.

"Promise said it is the color of Luke's eyes," Victoria said.

Mary Ann's gaze flicked to Luke's vivid blue eyes, eyes that were burning a hole through her.

"Maybe Luke fell from the sky," Jake teased.

"Nope, I was there when he was born. Even then he had the biggest, bluest eyes I've ever seen," Colt told them. "His eyes are just like our ma's."

Mary Ann glanced back at Luke but quickly looked away when Colt filled her glass with wine.

Colt held his glass in the air. "To beautiful women and men that are fortunate to find them."

"Amen to that," Jake added.

Luke raised his glass and glared at Mary Ann. "And may they be trustworthy." He gulped down his glassful of wine.

Seeing Mary Ann's crestfallen expression, Promise quickly asked, "Will you be leaving soon?"

Trying to maintain her composure, Mary Ann blinked back her tears. "As soon as Father is recovered. He is doing much better, so I'm sure it will just be a few days." Mary Ann tried to look anywhere except at Luke.

"I didn't know he was ill," Victoria said.

"Yes, he had pneumonia, but he has recovered. He's just a bit weak."

"I'm happy to hear he's better," Victoria said.

Mary Ann felt like she was putting a pall over their celebration, so she stood and said her good-byes. "Have a lovely evening."

"I do wish you would have dinner with us," Victoria told her.

"I'm sure she has to have dinner with her fiancé," Luke growled.

Mary Ann looked at him then and she knew there was no way this man would forgive her no matter how much she prayed. "I must take dinner to Father."

Colt made sure the conversation took another direction as soon as Mary Ann walked away. He didn't want anything to ruin Victoria's evening.

The dinner ended, and Colt couldn't have been more pleased with the whole evening. Everything had been perfect, from the food to the conversation and laughter.

"Thank you all so much for this lovely night," Victoria said to them as they were leaving the hotel. She stood on her toes and kissed her husband's cheek. "It's been a wonderful evening."

"I want a better thank-you than that. I want to see that corset again," he whispered in her ear.

Victoria started blushing. "Shhh, your deep voice carries," she admonished.

Luke overheard what his brother said, but he didn't say anything. He tried to avoid thinking about women's undergarments.

"Colt, it looks like we might get out of here unscathed," Jake teased. He held the door open for the women and Promise walked through first.

"Yeah, it's been a perfect . . ."

Before Colt finished his sentence, Promise bounced back into Jake's chest. Clyde Slater and his band of idiot friends burst through the door literally pushing Promise out of the way.

"You son-of-a . . ." Colt started, but stopped midsentence when Jake stepped in front of Slater. "Let me." He drew back his arm and hit Slater in the mouth knocking him back out the door. The three drunken men accompanying Clyde went after Jake, but Colt and Luke reached them first. And the brawl in the middle of the street began and ended just as quickly.

Colt picked his hat up off the ground and turned to his brothers. "I think that went well."

"Perfect," Jake agreed.

"At least we didn't break any windows this time," Luke added.

Chapter Twenty-Two

"We will be leaving day after tomorrow," Mary Ann's father told her.

Knowing it was hopeless for her to reason with him, Mary Ann had stopped trying. Now that Luke hated her she might as well go back to England. Even if her father left without her she didn't think she could bear staying here and seeing Luke frequently. It would be easier to forget him if she went back to England.

Mary Ann had another sleepless night. She only had one more day to try to explain to Luke and ask his forgiveness. If he wouldn't talk to her, she would at least have the opportunity to say good-bye to Victoria and Promise. She wanted to thank them for their friendship while she was here.

The next morning George escorted Mary Ann to the McBride ranch and arranged to come back for her in a few hours after he had a chance to check on the progress at his new ranch.

"Mary Ann, what a lovely surprise," Victoria said when she opened the door.

"I do apologize for coming unannounced, but my uncle was going to the ranch so I asked him to bring me here. He will pick me up in a couple of hours. I hope you don't mind." It was the first time Mary Ann had smiled in days. Every time she came to the McBride ranch she couldn't help but be cheered by the love she felt in the home.

"Mind? Of course not! I'm delighted to see you. Let me get Promise from the kitchen. We were just getting ready to make some pies."

"I brought some teacakes," Mary Ann said, handing Victoria the basket she was carrying.

"How thoughtful, I will make some tea."

When Victoria walked out of the room Mary Ann had time to look around the parlor. It was a warm, inviting room with oversize chairs that spoke to the large masculine men in the home, but they were softened by the colorful needlepoint pillows lending a feminine touch. Promise's painting of the family was the focal point hanging over the massive stone fireplace. But Mary Ann was drawn to the painting of the three brothers. The men were so similar in appearance with their dark weathered skin and their square McBride jawline, but it was Luke's blue eyes that jumped off the canvas. On her previous trips to the ranch she'd never had a chance to really study the painting. She stared at Luke until she heard Victoria and Promise walking down the hall.

The women sat in the parlor and chatted for over an hour and finally Mary Ann disclosed the reason for her visit. "One of the reasons I came by was to say good-bye. We are leaving tomorrow."

Victoria noticed Mary Ann kept looking out the window as though she was waiting on something. It could be her uncle, of course, but she had a feeling she was hoping Luke would walk through that door. "Your father hasn't changed his mind?"

"No, he hasn't. But it is probably for the best. I won't be coming back."

"Does this mean you will definitely marry Mr. Stafford?" Promise asked.

Mary Ann couldn't begin to discuss that subject without tearing up. "It seems so."

Victoria exchanged a glance with Promise. "We hate to hear that, we were hoping that your father would have a change of heart."

"I'm afraid that's not possible." Mary Ann had avoided the other reason she came to the ranch long enough. "I also wanted to see Luke. I need to apologize to him."

"Mary Ann, the men are out on the range moving cattle and they won't be back for a few weeks at least. We were doing some baking for the cook to take food out to them."

Mary Ann was disappointed, but she tried to hide her feelings "I didn't realize they stayed on the range that long."

"When I first came here, I remember Jake telling me he could stay on horseback for two weeks and never reach the western boundary," Promise told her.

"I had no idea the ranch was so large. Have you ever wanted to go with them and sleep out on the range?" Mary Ann thought the prospect of sleeping around a campfire with the right man sounded romantic. She'd never experienced such a thing.

"I came here with Jake on a cattle drive with twenty-five hundred head of longhorns. I think I prefer the comfort of my own bed," Promise responded.

Victoria and Promise shared their stories of how they arrived at the McBride ranch. By comparison

Mary Ann thought her story seemed rather dull. How she wished she could live on a ranch like this with a husband she loved and one who loved her. She could envision herself growing old here with her children and grandchildren. She wasn't so naïve as to think that this life came without hardships, but with a strong man by your side it was sure to be an interesting life.

"I'm sorry I won't be able to say good-bye to Luke . . ." She hesitated, trying to control her emotions. She would never see Luke again, and now it seemed so final. She didn't think she could feel worse than the night she saw Luke kissing Sally, but she was wrong.

"Let's go to Colt's office. You can use his desk to write Luke a note and tell him what you wanted to say," Victoria suggested.

"Mind if we join you?" Colt asked Luke.

Luke already had a fire going and was making some coffee. He enjoyed being out on the range and sleeping under the stars. It gave him time to think and put life into perspective. He'd spent a few nights off by himself away from the rest of the men so he didn't mind having the company of his brothers. "I'll make more coffee."

"Good. Jake shot dinner," Colt told him. Colt had given Luke some time alone since he understood that was what he needed. As much as Colt missed his wife and boys, he was happy to have the chance to be alone with his brothers. It reminded him of when they were young and they would spend time on the range with their father. Those were special memories that he enjoyed sharing with his brothers and he wanted to make more memories with them. It also gave them time to talk about the things men like to talk about without boring the women.

After they ate dinner they placed their bedrolls around the fire and Colt pulled a bottle of whiskey out of his saddlebag. He filled their cups and they settled around the fire and drank their whiskey.

"How do you like being out on the range again?" Jake asked Luke.

"I love it. I've really missed this place." He thought he might miss his rambling ways when he came home, but he didn't. It was the exact opposite, he loved being with his brothers, and he was crazy about his sisters-in-law and nephews. He'd forgotten how women made a house a real home. He questioned his sanity for leaving home in the first place. In his estimation Colt was the smart one for realizing early on in life what was important.

Colt was thrilled to be out here with his brothers, he had dreamed of this for ten years and he thanked God that his prayers came true. "I've never been as happy on the ranch as I am right now," he said in a rare expression of his feelings.

"You have a lot to be happy about with that wife of yours and those boys," Luke said. He glanced at Jake. "When are you going to catch up?"

Jake chuckled. "I'm working as hard as I can, we want some kids. At least I've got the wife now. The other part is easy and fun trying. Now what you need is to get a wife of your own, you're way behind, little brother."

Luke didn't smile. "That's going to be a long way off."

"I had thought there might be something happening between you and Mary Ann," Colt commented, trying to crack the door.

"You mean before she failed to mention her fiancé?" Luke replied.

Jake looked at Colt and arched his brow. "Yeah, that was sort of a surprise."

Colt saw his opportunity. "Victoria told me that Mary Ann's father arranged the marriage. Mary Ann told her he wouldn't take no for an answer."

"I'm sure Mary Ann agrees with the arrangement or she would say no," Luke said.

"She told Victoria this is not what she wants. And from what George said, her father doesn't seem like a man that takes no for an answer. George thinks Hardwicke is in financial difficulty and Stafford is a wealthy man. Hardwicke's estates may be in jeopardy."

"His daughter is being sold? Is that what you are saying?" Luke asked.

"I doubt they look at it like that, but I guess you could put it that way. Love doesn't enter into the equation," Colt said.

"What's the going price to sell your daughter to the highest bidder?" Luke asked.

Hearing the anger in Luke's question, Colt tried to explain. "Stafford has the money and Mary Ann's father has the title and land. The practice is accepted there."

"You know, Luke, you're a wealthy man now," Jake added.

Luke heard the underlying message in his brother's comment. "The difference is I don't plan on buying a wife." Luke couldn't believe a man would force his daughter to marry a man she didn't love just for money. Mary Ann had to be in agreement with this scheme.

"Luke, I think her father knows how to exert his power to bend Mary Ann to his will," Colt said.

"That may be, but she still failed to mention the situation," Luke said.

Colt had no response to that fact. He didn't know why she didn't tell him about Stafford. But he did know his brother, and he knew this situation was gnawing at him, so he said the only thing that came to mind. "You two didn't really spend all that much time with each other before you left for Arizona."

Luke had told himself the same thing. She'd been on his mind from the first day he saw her, so it may have distorted his perception of the situation. It wasn't long after they cooked together that night that Arina came to town and she had occupied most of his time. But after he kissed Mary Ann at the dance, she might have said something then about her fiancé. She had been every bit as passionate as he was, but still she didn't think to mention there was another man with whom she might be sharing such passion. He asked himself what he would have done if she had told him she had a fiancé. If she'd been honest, he wanted to think he might have given Stafford a run for his money. By not telling him, he felt she played him for a fool. It might be unfair to compare her to Arina, but to his way of thinking, both of them deceived men.

"This is just about the same place I camped out with T. J. and Tate before I married Victoria. Young Tate informed me I needed Victoria," Colt said, remembering the last night Tate was alive. Tate was shot and killed that night. Colt had given the young man a job two years before his death and he thought of Tate as a son. He'd even named his youngest son after him.

Luke and Jake smiled. They knew what that young man meant to their brother. "What do you mean he told you that you needed Victoria?" Luke asked.

"He pestered me to death that night asking me if I

intended to marry Victoria. I'll never forget he said I needed more in my life than the ranch. He was a smart kid. Cade and Cody were crazy about him."

Luke and Jake had never heard Colt talk so much about Tate. They took that as a good sign as it'd taken Colt a long time to come to terms with his death. Maybe he could speak about Tate now without the painful memory of the night he was killed.

"The first time Tate saw Victoria I thought he was going to trip over his tongue." Colt recalled the memory that he'd tucked away for a long time. He smiled to himself remembering how Tate couldn't even speak when he first saw Victoria. "He followed her around like a little puppy."

Luke could appreciate how the young man felt. He felt the same way when Mary Ann got off that stagecoach. If she'd spoken to him, he wasn't sure he could have responded. No matter what happened in the future, he knew seeing Mary Ann in that pink hat was one memory that would always remain with him.

Seeing his brother was in such a talkative mood, Jake asked, "Did you know from the start Victoria was the one for you?"

"When I saw her in St. Louis the first time I felt like I'd been kicked by a bull," he recalled. "It took me a while after she came here before I admitted how I felt about her. It took Tate pointing out that I was going to lose her if I didn't do something about my feelings."

Jake laughed. "Yeah, I know what you mean. Not only did I think Promise was the most beautiful woman I ever saw, but she was unconscious and drenched to the bone. There were only men on the trail drive and not a town in sight, so I had to undress her."

"Are we supposed to feel sorry for you?" Colt asked.

"Yeah, you are. All she had was this flimsy stuff, like those things in Mary Ann's shop," Jake said grinning. "It took a lot of self-control for a man that had been looking at grimy men and smelly cattle for over a month."

Luke didn't know Jake had also been in Mary Ann's shop. "You've been shopping for Promise in Mary Ann's shop?"

"I bought her some perfume, but I haven't given it to her yet. It's a surprise, so don't mention it." He looked at Colt. "I gather you bought more than perfume."

"Yeah, women like that stuff from France," Colt said.

"Did you see those corsets? I'll bet the women from L. B.'s will be shopping there," Jake said.

"It wouldn't surprise me," Colt agreed.

Luke had been successful trying to forget it'd be Stafford seeing Mary Ann in those corsets and flimsy camisoles. But his brothers kept bringing up the subject. "I imagine when Mary Ann leaves town George will close the shop. She'll probably take all that stuff to England with her and wear it for Stafford." He didn't intend to say that last part aloud. His blood nearly came to a boil over the thought.

"'*Under love's heavy burden do I sink,*'" Colt quoted.

"What the heck does that mean?" Luke asked.

"Shakespeare?" Jake asked.

"Yep," Colt answered.

"Maybe Luke should read some Shakespeare," Jake said.

"Yep."

"I'm not *sinking* under anything," Luke informed them. "I don't need to read Shakespeare. I don't want a wife."

Colt and Jake exchanged a glance, and Jake said, "I think little brother protests too much."

"Where have you been?" Hardwicke asked Mary Ann when she returned to the hotel later that day.

"Saying good-bye to friends."

"If you've been with that man . . ." Hardwicke started, but Mary Ann interrupted him.

"Father, I've not been with any man!"

"Don't get any ideas about staying with him unless you want to see him in an early grave. Those men who are traveling with me are more than willing to eliminate your friend." Hardwicke wasn't about to let her ruin everything he'd gone through to take her back to England. George had told him that she cared for that barbarian, but there was no way he would allow his daughter to give herself to such a man. With Stafford she would have everything she would want. She would have a life of privilege, not one of lack. And more importantly, the future of the estates would be secure.

She didn't question her father's candor, she knew he would have no problem removing any problem standing in his way and that included Luke. "I am going back with you; there is no need to concern yourself."

"Just remember what I said."

Mary Ann turned her back on him and walked to her shop. While she was disheartened she didn't get to see Luke to say what she held in her heart, she was relieved he was so far away that her father's men wouldn't find him. They would leave in the morning and she wouldn't worry over Luke's safety.

She looked around her shop one last time. Her uncle told her to leave it as it was if she didn't want to pack everything up. George didn't know if he would keep the shop open, but he didn't want her to have additional worries. She thought it would be nice for the ladies in town if he kept it open. Perhaps if Luke saw the shop open, he would think of her occasionally.

Chapter Twenty-Three

The team of horses covered the miles at a pace that didn't seem possible. Mary Ann didn't remember time going by as rapidly when she was traveling to Wyoming. She knew what was waiting for her once she reached England, and all the praying in the world wasn't going to make time stand still. She was wedged between her father and Edmund for hours on end, but fortunately they didn't include her in their conversations. It was the same way her father treated her mother, as if she never said a word that he wanted to hear. Mary Ann didn't care that they didn't converse with her, she had nothing to say to them. Most of the hours were spent with her eyes closed and her mind on one thing: Luke. The stagecoach driver said they would reach the way station in Missouri before dusk. She looked forward to spending the night there since that was where the station keeper's wife, Lillian, taught her to make biscuits. Luke had loved her biscuits. Thinking of the way he'd devoured them made her smile. She wished she was back in Wyoming making lots of biscuits for him.

The stage pulled to a stop and Mary Ann hurried

inside without waiting for the men. Lillian greeted her warmly as if they were old friends.

Lillian hugged Mary Ann, delighted to see the young woman again. "Why honey, I didn't expect to see you again."

"I'm traveling with my father. He came from England to take me home." Mary Ann didn't hesitate to be truthful with Lillian. She was an older woman with a warm and generous way about her and Mary Ann trusted her from the moment she met her.

Lillian could see the sadness on Mary Ann's face. "Don't you want to go back to England?"

Hardwicke and Stafford chose that moment to walk through the door and Mary Ann didn't respond. She introduced them to Lillian, and while they were polite to her they didn't take time for conversation. The stagecoach driver, the two detectives, and Lillian's husband, Henry, came inside after seeing to the horses. Her father asked Henry to show them to their quarters as though he was staying at the grandest hotel in New York. Mary Ann was surprised Henry didn't laugh, but she heard him explain that the men would be sharing a room for the night. It was a small station, but no other travelers were expected, so Mary Ann would have a little space to herself. Mary Ann helped Lillian prepare the meal and told her how successful her biscuits were in Wyoming. It was a relief for her to have a woman to talk with after the long days in the stagecoach in silence.

"It's such a joy to have you to visit with again," Lillian told her. "You remind me so much of my daughter."

"I didn't know you had a daughter. Does she live in Missouri?"

"She died a few years back, but I'd like to think she would be as lovely as you had she lived."

Mary Ann walked over and put her arms around her. "I'm sorry. With you for a mother I'm sure she would have been wonderful." Mary Ann had thought a lot about Lillian on her way to Wyoming. She was the first woman who had spent time with her during her journey. She'd been touched by Lillian's generous spirit and how she treated the travelers like long-lost relatives. Her life wasn't an easy one out here in this desolate place, yet she glowed with an inner joy. The dress Lillian was wearing was threadbare like the one she was wearing before, and she had none of the feminine frills women so enjoyed. Even her home was drab, certainly compared to the McBride parlor. There were no handmade pillows in cheery colors, no paintings adorning the walls, and no lamps with beautifully painted globes on the tabletops. The only colorful thing in the room was a handmade quilt made by Lillian's mother. Lillian told her there was not enough money for such extravagances. "I brought you something." Mary Ann walked to the little room that held her luggage. When she returned to the front room she placed a valise on the table.

"Here you go, open it," Mary Ann said.

Lillian looked at her quizzically. "The valise?"

Mary Ann opened the valise for her. "Yes, everything in there is for you."

Tears filled Lillian's eyes as she looked at the contents inside the piece of luggage. "All of this is for me?"

"Yes, when I knew I would be coming back here, I wanted to bring a few things to you." Mary Ann had purchased items at the mercantile so Lillian would have everything she needed to make a few special things for her home, as well as some cloth to make some new dresses. She'd also packed a bottle of her most expensive perfume.

Lillian's fingers were shaking when she gingerly pulled out each item. By the time she reached the small box that held the perfume, tears were streaming down her cheeks. She pulled out the etched fan-style crystal stopper and sniffed the perfume. "Oh my, this is the loveliest thing I have ever seen. I've never received such a present. It is too much. How can I ever thank you?"

Mary Ann thought about her life in England and how she'd taken such luxuries for granted and she felt ashamed she hadn't appreciated all she had. Just these few items brought Lillian to tears, and to Mary Ann's way of thinking, she was a woman who deserved so much more. "Why, your biscuit recipe alone is worth a small fortune! You should have seen the way Luke . . . the customers at my uncle's hotel gobbled them up. This is the least I could do for you as my uncle will be making a fortune off your biscuits."

Lillian started to put the bottle back in the box when Mary Ann stopped her. "Now put some behind your ears. Henry will like it, I'm sure."

Doing as Mary Ann instructed, Lillian laughed. "He'll be thankful to smell something other than horses." She looked at the beautiful crystal bottle. "I have nothing so magnificent to give you."

"You can write me letters when I get home and tell me how you cook everything." Mary Ann thought that would be the greatest gift even though she would probably never again cook a thing once she was married to Stafford.

Lillian's eyes brightened at the thought of having something of value to offer her. "I can do that! I have recipes from my mother and grandmother. They were excellent cooks."

"That is by far the greatest gift I could ask for." Mary Ann hugged her again.

"Now tell me about the fella that ate all of those biscuits," Lillian urged. "Did you say his name was Luke?" She'd caught how Mary Ann's eyes lit up when she said the name.

It didn't surprise Mary Ann that Lillian was so perceptive. Anyone with that much love in her heart took the time to read people. "He's the most handsome man I have ever seen in my life." Mary Ann told her all about Luke McBride and about everything that happened in Wyoming. She didn't stop until her father and Edmund strolled into the room an hour later.

They all sat around the table enjoying the modest meal of stew and biscuits. Mary Ann was pleased that her father had the good manners to compliment the simple meal. Mary Ann and Lillian chatted about women's fashion while the men discussed horses. The dinner ended and Mary Ann and Lillian were clearing the table when Henry jumped and said, "Riders."

Henry and the stagecoach driver walked to the door to see who was arriving unexpectedly.

Three men reined in at the corral and tied their horses off before walking to the house.

"Hello to the house," one man said.

"Come ahead," Henry replied.

"Thanks. We were wondering if we could pay for a meal and some shelter for the night."

Henry didn't like the looks of the threesome. "We can offer a meal, but we're full up for the night."

"We can bunk in the stable."

Henry didn't think that would present a problem, he'd just have to sleep with one eye open, so he agreed to that arrangement.

When the three men sat at the table, Lillian saw how

they were looking at Mary Ann, and she whispered to her to stay away from the table.

Hardwicke and Stafford paid little attention to the newcomers, they continued discussing the merits of different breeds of horses.

Mary Ann glanced at the men as she washed the dishes. All of them were filthy as if they'd been riding the trail for months without the benefit of a bath. One man was big and tall and there was something about him that made her feel like she was looking into the face of evil. The other two men kept glancing around as though they expected someone to appear from the other rooms. They shoveled their food in their mouths like they hadn't eaten in months.

"Is this all the boarders tonight, old man?" The big man was the one who directed the question to Henry.

"I'm expecting more people in a bit. There's another stage that will be stopping." Henry wasn't about to tell these hombres the truth.

"I didn't know there was another stage through here," the man retorted.

Henry didn't contradict himself. "You been through here before? I don't recall seeing you."

"No, this is new territory to us."

"Where you headed?"

"You ask too many questions, old man." The big man shoved his plate of food aside and stood. The other two men followed his lead. Suddenly, the big man grabbed Lillian as she reached for the plates. He pulled her in front of him and pulled his pistol and held it to her head. His companions immediately pulled their pistols. The stagecoach driver reached for his pistol, but the big man shot it out of his hand.

"What's this?" Henry shouted. His eyes darted to his rifle over the fireplace.

"Don't do it unless you want a dead woman." The big man pointed to Hardwicke with the barrel of his pistol. "Empty your pockets and put it on the table." He looked at Stafford and the two detectives. "You too."

"We don't have money here, mister," Henry told him.

The big man pointed to Hardwicke again. "I bet this old codger has enough to last us a while." He gave Hardwicke a fierce look. "All of you better do it quick or she gets popped."

Stafford took out his pocket watch and put it on the table, but Hardwicke made no move to follow his lead.

The big man glared at Hardwicke. "Put your money on the table too, or do you need some encouragement?"

Speaking to one of his men, he inclined his head toward Mary Ann. "Go get her. I have a feeling that they need to see we mean business."

The man grabbed Mary Ann and pulled her across the room until she was standing in front of the big man.

The big man eyed her up and down. "Let me see that pin you're wearing."

Mary Ann's hand automatically went to the cameo at the top of her dress. It had been a gift from her grandmother.

"Take it off." He gave her a lecherous grin. "Unless you want me to do it for you."

"Leave her alone," Lillian said.

"Don't worry, old woman, we won't ignore you." The big man reached out with one hand to take the cameo from Mary Ann's neck and Lillian slapped his hand away. He shoved Lillian so hard she stumbled and fell to the floor.

"You son of Satan!" Henry started to move to his wife when one of the other men put a gun to his head.

"You people ain't moving fast enough, so this is your fault." The big man directed the barrel of his pistol toward Lillian and Mary Ann thought he was going to pull the trigger. She remembered the man who was going to shoot Luke in the back. This man was going to kill Lillian for no reason. She pulled away from the man holding her and covered Lillian with her body in an effort to shield her just as the gun exploded. The shot stunned everyone, even the man who pulled the trigger. Mary Ann's body went limp. Henry was the only one to maintain his wits and moved quickly to grab the pistol the stagecoach driver had dropped on the floor. Seeing what Henry was doing spurred the detectives into action. They pulled their guns and started shooting. The three robbers ran for the door as bullets started flying in all directions. Hardwicke and Stafford dived for cover behind the table. Henry winged the big man in the shoulder as he disappeared through the front door, but the other shots missed their targets. When Henry ran out of bullets, he ran to get his rifle above the fireplace and headed for the door. The three men were already in their saddles and riding away. Taking careful aim, Henry pulled the trigger. One man fell out of the saddle, but the other two men didn't stop, they hightailed it out of there. The detectives ran to the man on the ground. They wanted to make sure he was dead.

Lillian was already tending to Mary Ann and shouting instructions. She pointed to Stafford and shouted, "Help me carry her to bed!" Hardwicke followed behind them.

Once they got Mary Ann on the bed, Lillian cut her dress down the back to see where the bullet entered.

"Where's the nearest doctor?" Hardwicke asked.

"Clive is not a doctor, but he's as good as any doctor at tending serious injuries. He's about seven miles one way."

Henry came into the room with the boiling water. "How bad is it?"

"I'm not sure, the bullet went in at an angle. Let's pray to the Good Lord that it hit nothing vital, but it needs to come out."

"I'll go get Clive," Henry told his wife.

"I think that is a good idea. Bring whiskey if he has it."

"I have some whiskey in one of my valises," Stafford said.

"Good. I'll clean the wound with it and if she comes around we will give her some for the pain," Lillian told him.

Once Lillian had Mary Ann's wound cleaned and the bleeding stopped, she went to check on the stagecoach driver. Fortunately for him the bullet had just grazed his hand and caused no real damage. She had the whiskey with her and poured him a stiff drink and situated him on a cot to get comfortable.

The detectives sat in the front room with their guns at the ready in the event more trouble arrived that night.

It wasn't long before Henry arrived with Clive, but Hardwicke blocked the bedroom door and questioned the elderly man before allowing him to enter. "Have you removed bullets before?"

"Dozens of times," Clive assured him.

"What has been the survival rate of your patients?" Stafford asked.

"About fifty-fifty." Clive had lived too long not to see his fair share of trouble. He saw no reason to lie to the man. "The way I see it, I'm the only chance she has unless you want to dig that bullet out."

Hardwicke allowed the man to go to his daughter's

side, but not without warning. "Nothing dire better happen to her or you will answer to me."

Clive stared harshly at Hardwicke for a brief moment. He didn't like being threatened, but he wouldn't let the man keep him from doing what he could for his daughter. "Lillian, hold that lantern for me, please." Lillian grabbed the lantern and held it close while Clive inspected the wound in Mary Ann's back. "You did a good job of cleaning this, Lillian."

"What do you think?" Lillian asked.

"I think she is a lucky young woman." Clive turned to address Hardwicke and Stafford. "If you two are squeamish, I suggest you leave the room now." Once they'd left the room, Clive pulled his black bag open and pulled out what he needed. "Lillian, are you ready with that whiskey?"

"I'll be ready. You just be careful with her, she's a special gal," Lillian warned.

"Yes, ma'am. Now hold that lantern close." Clive bent over and went to work. It didn't take him long to dig the bullet out and when he was done he expelled a loud breath. He held it up for Lillian to see. "That did it and nothing vital was hit."

"Thank God." Lillian breathed a sigh of relief. "This little gal probably saved my life."

Clive smiled at her. "Henry told me. Don't you worry, she will be fine."

Lillian set the lantern down and handed him the bandages. "She awoke once, but she quickly passed out again. Do you think she will be out for long?"

"Hard to say, her body has had quite a shock." Clive finished with the bandage and he put his hand on Mary Ann's forehead. "She feels feverish."

"That's not good," Lillian said.

"No. We'll keep a close eye on her. I'll stay for a

while to see how she does." He tucked some quilts around Mary Ann so she couldn't turn over if she awoke.

"Have you eaten?"

"No, I was getting ready to eat when Henry arrived."

Lillian stood and started toward the door. "I'll tell her father how she's doing and warm some stew for you."

"Tell the stagecoach driver to come on back and I'll tend his hand. And if you don't mind, bring back a cup so I can have some of that whiskey."

After Clive ate his meal Lillian told him to get some sleep and she stayed with Mary Ann. She had almost fallen asleep in the chair when she heard a moan coming from Mary Ann. She immediately came alert and grabbed a cup and poured some whiskey in case she needed to give it to her for pain. Mary Ann moaned again and it sounded like she was mumbling something. Lillian leaned over her, trying to hear what she was saying.

"Luke."

Mary Ann mumbled the word, but Lillian understood. "Honey, it's me, Lillian." Just a few hours ago Mary Ann had told her about the handsome man she'd fallen in love with in Wyoming. Lillian figured she was dreaming of him. "Honey, you are with us in Missouri. You're going to be fine. Now just get some rest." Lillian felt her forehead again and thought her fever was even higher, so she ran to get Clive.

"Let's continue to wash her down and hope it breaks soon." Clive heard Mary Ann trying to say something. "Can you make out what she is saying?"

Lillian closed the door and then told Clive the story Mary Ann had told her about her time in Wyoming, and how her father came back to take her home to

England. "She's being forced to marry that man, Stafford."

"That's a shame," Clive said. "I don't understand a man like that."

"I guess it's easy enough to see what man she really loves."

Chapter Twenty-Four

Lillian and Clive worked all night to keep Mary Ann's fever down. The next afternoon her fever finally broke and Mary Ann awoke.

"How are you feeling, honey?" Lillian asked.

Mary Ann glanced around the room, her brow furrowed in confusion. "What happened?"

"Honey, you kept me from getting shot," Lillian explained. "Don't you remember? You shielded me from that bullet and it went in your back instead of mine." Lillian pointed to Clive. "Clive got the bullet out and no organs were hit, but you had a fever all night."

Mary Ann turned her attention on the older man. "Thank you."

"Think nothing of it. Do you think you could eat something?"

"I'm not very hungry, but I would like some water."

Lillian held her head while she drank some water. "Honey, why on earth did you jump in front of that gun?"

"That man . . . I knew he was going to shoot you." She remembered how she felt when that miscreant shot the stagecoach driver and then aimed his gun at

Lillian. It was the same terror she felt that day when Luke was nearly shot in the back. She couldn't explain what she did, she'd just reacted. "Is the stagecoach driver all right?"

"He's fine, the bullet just grazed his hand."

Mary Ann glanced at the door. "Where's my father?"

"He's in the front room. Do you want me to get him?"

"No."

It was just a one-word response, but Lillian heard the immense sorrow it carried. "He has been very worried about you, and that young man as well." She was stretching the truth, but she only wanted the best for Mary Ann. After what she had gone through, the least she could do was tell a little white lie. God would surely forgive her for that.

Mary Ann didn't respond to Lillian's comment. "Can I sit up?"

"Let me have a look at your wound first." Clive was pleased with the condition of the wound so he and Lillian helped her into a sitting position. "Gently now."

"I'm sure Father is displeased that we were unable to leave today."

Lillian didn't confirm her statement even though she knew that Hardwicke was very unhappy that they weren't on their way this morning. "The stagecoach driver wasn't up to leaving either, and it would take a long time for another driver to arrive. So there is no need for you to fret. Everyone will have to be patient."

"You don't need to be traveling right now." Clive left the room to tell her father that very thing. He wouldn't allow Mary Ann's father to jeopardize her health with his impatience to get to England.

Lillian sat on the bed beside Mary Ann. "Do you want me to get your brush from your valise so I can brush your hair?"

Mary Ann's hand automatically went to her hair and she winced in pain from the movement. "That would be lovely."

While they were alone Lillian decided to ask some questions about Mary Ann's father. "Do you think he would change his mind and allow you to stay here?"

Mary Ann explained to Lillian the reason she thought her father was adamant about the marriage. "Edmund wants to marry me and he's very wealthy."

"There's no chance this fellow, Luke, would come for you?" She didn't want to tell Mary Ann that she'd said his name while she was delirious.

"No. I'm afraid he was angry with me for not telling him about Edmund. He thought I was playing him for a fool and he refused to forgive me. I didn't even get to say good-bye to him."

The man had to be a fool if he didn't know how much Mary Ann cared for him. "Then he doesn't deserve you, either. Would you like me to speak to your father? Maybe I could convince him forcing you into a marriage will bring no happiness to anyone. I know I lead a simple life and I'm not a sophisticated person, but there is one thing I do know: Nothing is more important to a parent than the happiness and well-being of their children."

"Thank you for offering, but it is pointless. Father would disagree and tell you that he knows what is best for me." She appreciated Lillian's willingness to intercede on her behalf, though she knew her words would fall on deaf ears. She didn't want to chance her father being rude to Lillian, which he was apt to do. And if he thought she still cared for Luke he might send his watchdogs to hurt him.

Lillian felt sorry for Mary Ann. She couldn't imagine being in a loveless marriage. She'd been married to Henry for forty years and she loved him more today than the day they got married. "Maybe Henry could persuade him."

Mary Ann shook her head. "I will go back with him."

"I'm glad you've come to your senses." Hardwicke stood at the doorway. "That man says you will be able to travel in a few days, so I guess we are forced to stay here until then."

"I'm sorry, Father, but it can't be helped."

Lillian wanted to throw the hairbrush at him for his insensitivity. Instead she stood and walked to the door basically blocking him from entering. "Why don't we allow your daughter time to rest? I'll make some dinner."

Edmund came into Mary Ann's room to see her before dinner. "How are you feeling?"

"I'm fine." Edmund's face held the same impatience as her father's.

"That was a foolhardy thing for you to do." He couldn't believe Mary Ann had put herself in harm's way for a stranger. "How could you risk your own life like that?"

She didn't expect Edmund to understand. "I just reacted."

"You shouldn't be so careless," he admonished.

Mary Ann really didn't want to talk with him. "If you don't mind, Edmund, I would like to rest now."

Edmund left and Mary Ann closed her eyes and thought of Luke. She remembered dreaming of him. He seemed so far away, and it had been so long since she'd seen him, yet she could recall every detail of his face and his unforgettable blue eyes.

Later that night Lillian and Mary Ann were alone in the room and Mary Ann asked Lillian how she met Henry. "I guess the story really begins when I was six years old. My mother made me a doll and I named him Henry. My mother told me it was a girl doll and I should give it a girl's name, but I wouldn't listen. Everyone laughed at me, but I didn't care. Several years later when I was twelve years old, Henry's family moved to a farm near us. I met him at church on a Sunday morning, and when I looked into his eyes I think I fell in love."

"At that young an age?" Mary Ann was surprised by her revelation.

"Yes, but we didn't marry until I was seventeen. My mother told me I would meet many boys before I found the right one. But I knew all along Henry was the one."

It was such a lovely story that Mary Ann started to cry. "I can't believe you named your doll Henry and then married a man with that name. It's almost like you knew he was coming."

"Honey, I didn't mean to make you cry. I do believe the Good Lord told me Henry would be the one."

Mary Ann thought about the first time she looked into Luke's blue eyes the day she arrived in Wyoming. While she thought he was very handsome, she was certain he was a gunfighter wearing that deadly looking pistol on his hip. When he came to her room he seemed friendly enough, but still he was intimidating. "It's such a wonderful story. I don't think I ever believed in love at first sight."

"Henry said he felt the same way. He told his best friend the day he met me that he was going to marry me one day. From the day we wed, we've never been apart."

"Do you ever have disagreements or get angry at one another?"

"Oh, we have our little spats now and again. But the Good Book says never let the sun go down on your anger. We try to live by that. Henry tells me every night that he loves me and I do the same. Life hasn't always been easy, but together we get through the worst of times. We both know we are better together than apart."

What Mary Ann wouldn't give for a love like Lillian and Henry shared. "You have been so blessed to have such a love." She thought of the McBride brothers and their wives. She was certain they shared a love that would last a lifetime.

Three days later the stagecoach pulled away from the station. Lillian was upset that Mary Ann was leaving so soon, but Hardwicke refused to stay another day. She didn't think Mary Ann had recovered enough for the long journey still ahead of her. In just a few short days Mary Ann had lost weight, and Lillian couldn't get her to eat more than a bite or two. She'd mentioned this fact to Hardwicke, but he told her when Mary Ann was hungry she would eat. Lillian had a difficult time understanding a man who was so indifferent to his daughter's welfare. It wasn't only Mary Ann's physical condition that troubled Lillian. She knew the young woman was emotionally spent. The first time she'd seen Mary Ann she was such a vibrant young woman excited about her adventure to the West. She was totally different now, almost as if the light in her eyes had been extinguished.

Mary Ann didn't feel up to leaving, but her father was making their lives miserable with his restlessness and his rude behavior. They were confined in such small quarters that they were getting on one another's

nerves. Both Hardwicke and Stafford could have helped
Henry with some of the work to keep themselves occupied, but they didn't offer. They seemed content to
harp about everything they found inconvenient. And
the list was long.

When it came time for Mary Ann to leave, Lillian
cried and promised to write. Henry thanked Mary Ann
for saving his wife and gently hugged her. They told
her they hoped they would see her again. Mary Ann
was very emotional saying her good-byes to Lillian and
Henry for the last time, but she was so spent she
couldn't even cry. Lillian handed a small bundle to
Mary Ann. "Here's some biscuits and jam. I expect you
to eat them."

Clive instructed Mary Ann to try to keep from
jostling around too much, but that would prove difficult riding in a stagecoach. At this point she couldn't
wait to get on a ship where she could stay in bed during
the entire crossing if she wanted and wouldn't be
forced to look at her father or Stafford.

"That man is an insufferable fool," Clive said when
the stagecoach was out of sight.

Henry laughed. "And that Stafford character isn't
much better."

Lillian wiped her tears on her apron. "I feel like
writing a letter to that cowboy in Wyoming and asking
why he has his head up his tail. Most men wouldn't be
so hardheaded to let such a wonderful gal get away."

Henry and Clive looked at her and laughed. It was
out of character for Lillian to say something so harsh.
"Why do you say that?" Henry asked.

She told them about Luke McBride and how angry

he'd been with Mary Ann over Stafford. "She tried to apologize to him, but he wouldn't listen."

"I agree with you, that cowboy needs his brains examined. But if that English fop bothered him that much, I'd say that cowboy was jealous. I can understand a man being jealous, she's about the prettiest little thing I ever saw," Clive said.

"And she's as lovely on the inside as she is on the outside," Lillian said.

"I don't know why, but I have a feeling we will see her again," Henry said.

Lillian had learned over the years to never underestimate her husband's intuition. She thought he was much more perceptive than most people, and she prayed he would be right this time. It saddened her to think of such a lovely young woman being forced into a loveless marriage. She didn't know how a woman could survive such a union.

It seemed to take forever, and Mary Ann could barely recall the final days of their journey, but at last, she was on the ship. As much as she detested the thought of going back to England, she was thankful for the privacy of her small cabin. She'd been in bed for days and she'd slept and slept, but she remained lethargic. Her wound had healed and it was no longer painful, but her heart hadn't healed. She was eating very little and losing more weight. Occasionally her father or Stafford would come to her cabin to see how she was doing. Their visits were never long and she was relieved when they left. She only wanted to be alone with her dreams.

Chapter Twenty-Five

Colt and Jake missed their wives so they came back to the ranch after two weeks on the range. Luke stayed out on the range with the men.

Victoria saw her husband rein in at the corral so she ran out the back door to greet him. "I'm so happy you are home."

Colt picked her up and kissed her. "You missed me, huh?"

"Yes, I did."

"Where are the boys?"

"Spending some time with Mrs. Wellington."

"Jake and I will have to go back in a day or two," Colt said.

"We'll pick the boys up on the way to church in the morning. Then we can have a nice family dinner in town. Perhaps we should invite George to dine, he's probably missing Mary Ann."

"She's gone?" Colt asked.

"Yes, she left a few days after you left. Did Luke come back with you?"

"He stayed out. I think he needs some more time alone."

"She came here before she left. She said she needed to apologize to him and she wanted to say good-bye."

"I'm not sure it would have made a difference. He's pretty upset with her," Colt replied.

"She was very unhappy when she was here, but I don't think she feels she has a choice in the matter."

"I'm sorry for her if she doesn't want to marry Stafford," Colt said.

"I can't imagine being in a marriage with a man I didn't love." She'd forgotten she had come to Wyoming prepared to marry a stranger so she would have a home for the twins. But God had a different plan.

"Is that your way of saying you love me?" Colt smiled at her. "Do you think you love me enough to let me see that corset one more time?"

"I think we can manage that." Victoria grabbed his hand and led him upstairs.

"It's so nice to see you, but where's your brother?" George asked them.

"He's still out on the range," Jake said.

"Please join us, George," Colt said.

"I know you are missing Mary Ann," Promise said.

George hadn't realized just how much he would miss his niece. "Yes, I am. She was not only a big help, but she's lovely to be around."

"We are going to miss her too," Victoria said.

"She was certainly enjoying her friendship with you two ladies."

"Did she set a date for her marriage?" Promise asked.

"I don't know, I'm sure Hardwicke will set the date soon."

"Why is her father forcing this marriage on her?" Colt asked.

George saw no reason to hide the truth from his friend. "I suspect his estates are in trouble, and Stafford is insistent on marrying Mary Ann. As I told you, she is considered a great beauty in England. Truth be told, I don't even think she likes Stafford. I tried to talk her into staying, but she told me he wouldn't leave until he had his way. I think her father knew she cared about Luke and he used that to pressure her."

"What do you mean?" Colt asked.

"Hardwicke is not above threatening someone to have his way."

"I wish we could do something," Victoria said.

"She was so happy here and proud of her shop," Promise added.

"I told her to leave the shop as it was. I don't think she had the heart to close it."

The next day Colt and Jake left the ranch to go back on the range taking fresh supplies with them. They finally caught up with Luke a week later.

"How's it going?" Colt asked.

"Good. Thank the Good Lord for great weather." Luke was glad his brothers were with him again. He'd had enough alone time, and he was hungry for some conversation.

"Mary Ann left," Jake said.

"Good." Luke had finally come to terms that it wasn't meant to be with Mary Ann. He decided he had to mentally move on. The only thing he needed to do when he got back to the ranch was to go see Sally and set things straight with her.

"George told us she didn't want to go," Colt said.

"Then why did she?" Luke asked.

"George thought Hardwicke threatened you," Colt answered.

"Me? Why would he threaten me?"

"He thought Mary Ann cared about you and he wants her to marry Stafford for his money," Jake said.

"He saw us kissing when he arrived, so he jumped to that conclusion," Luke confided.

His revelation was news to Colt and Jake. "Her old man saw you kissing?" Jake asked.

"Yeah. He grabbed her and slapped her hard enough that she hit the ground. That's when I slammed my fist in his jaw."

"You hit Mary Ann's father?" Colt was beginning to understand why Luke had acted the way he did when he saw Hardwicke at the restaurant.

"Yeah, and the two detectives or whatever those two men were that followed him around."

"I would've paid to see that," Jake said.

"By the way, Victoria said to give you this." Colt reached in his pocket and pulled out the letter. "Mary Ann left it for you."

Luke took the letter and noticed the beautiful script before he stuffed it in his pocket.

"Aren't you going to read it?" Jake asked.

"Not now." For weeks he'd thought of nothing but Mary Ann, but he knew he had to let her go. He wasn't as angry with her as he was at first, so he was making some headway. He'd even managed to chuckle to himself over the night she'd basically dared him to spend so much money on those things for Sally. He knew as soon as he opened that letter all of the anger and regret would surface.

* * *

Over the next week, Luke had pulled the letter from his pocket countless times, but he hadn't opened it. One night when he thought Colt and Jake were asleep, he held the letter in his hands and ran his fingers over his name written in Mary Ann's script. He'd almost thrown it in the fire, but he couldn't bring himself to part with it. It was the only tangible thing he had to remember her by.

"What are you afraid of?" Colt whispered.

The voice surprised Luke, he wasn't aware Colt was watching him. "I told myself I was going to let it go."

"Throw it in the fire then."

Colt always had a way of knowing what he was thinking. "I've thought about it."

Colt saw the hesitation in his brother's face. "If you haven't done it by now, there's a reason. Do you love that gal?"

"Yeah, I did." Luke finally admitted that fact to someone other than himself.

"But you don't anymore?"

Luke thought about his brother's question. He only hesitated since he didn't want to admit it to himself. He'd been so angry with her that he hadn't considered that she might not have a choice when it came to marrying Stafford. But now it was too late. She was gone. He'd been so darn stubborn that he'd let her get away. She could already be married before she sailed to England. He looked at Colt. "I guess I do, but it's too late now. You were right, you know."

Colt moved to a sitting position. "Yeah? I like to hear that. But exactly what was I right about?"

"You told me if I kept playing with fire, I was going to get burned. I guess I never thought I would feel that way about a woman. I've definitely been burned." Right now, he felt like the biggest fool alive.

"Luke, you've lived your life like those horses you broke. Men are sort of like wild horses, we do what we want, fight and buck against getting older and settling down. Then the day comes when the right woman throws that lasso around our neck and we succumb, maybe fighting and kicking all the way, but we still yield. But there's one thing you haven't figured out yet."

Luke looked at his brother. "What's that?"

"When we do give in and stop pulling against that tether, it's the best thing that could ever happen to us. With the right woman you'll be a better man. Look, Luke, I don't want you to ever leave the ranch again, but if you love that gal you need to go get her. You may never feel this way about another woman. I don't have all of the answers, but I know that without a doubt."

"She could be married," Luke said.

Thinking about what he would do if he were in Luke's position, Colt knew he would rather know one way or the other than spend his life wondering if the woman he loved married another man. "Do you want to spend the next year, five years, ten, wondering if she married him?"

"I hurt her and she's probably glad to see the last of me." Luke told him about buying that corset for Sally and kissing her in front of Mary Ann.

Colt couldn't believe Luke had been so callous. For him to do something so out of character, he had to be furious with Mary Ann. "And you were angry at her for not telling you about a man that she ran away from?"

"Yeah. I was crazy jealous. Then when I walked into her shop that night all I could think about was Stafford being the man that was going to see her in those corsets and garters. I guess I went a little crazy."

"A little? I'm surprised she didn't shoot you where you stood."

Luke grinned. "It would have served me right."

Jake whistled and sat up. "Darn straight."

"I thought you were sleeping," Luke said.

"Not with you two jabbering like old women," Jake retorted. "But I have to admit this story is getting interesting, so I'll forgive you interrupting my beauty sleep."

"Well, in that case I guess I should tell you that Mary Ann got even with me in her own way that night." Luke then told them the rest of the story. "I thought she was going to sell Sally everything in her shop. She made sure she sold her the most expensive items. One bottle of perfume cost more than my saddle."

Colt laughed so hard he thought he would break his ribs. "I love that gal! She's a smart one."

"Remind me never to get on her bad side," Jake teased.

Luke laughed with them and when he stopped his voice turned serious when he asked Colt, "What would you do?"

"First of all, I'd read the letter. Depending on what it said, if she gave me an opening and I thought there was a chance, and if I loved her, well . . ." He hesitated, then made it personal. "If it was Victoria, I'd get on that horse and wouldn't stop until I was on a ship." It was an easy question to answer if someone tried to keep him from Victoria.

"It'll take a while," Luke said. He knew he would be away from the ranch for months, not days, if he went to England.

"Most things worthwhile usually do. I waited ten years for you and Jake to come home. Several months is nothing compared to years." Colt envisioned Luke married, living on the ranch, having children, and growing old with his family. He wanted that for his brothers. But most of all he wanted them happy, as happy as he was. He thought Mary Ann and Luke would be very happy together.

"How did you know Victoria was the *one* you wanted to marry?"

That was an easy question for Colt to answer. "I couldn't stop thinking about her. I didn't want to be with another woman. I was furious when she went anywhere with another man. She was on my mind day and night. Not even ranch work took my mind off of her. I didn't even visit the saloon anymore."

For anyone or anything to take Colt's mind off the ranch had to be an eye-opener for him, but Luke knew exactly what he meant. From the first day he saw Mary Ann, he could think of nothing else, and he didn't want to be with another woman. Unless it was to make her jealous. The night he'd been upstairs at the saloon, the whole time he was thinking about her. And he sure as heck didn't want Mary Ann to be with another man.

"I'm going to sleep," Jake said, stretching back out on his bedroll.

"Yeah." Colt leaned back on his saddle and pulled his hat over his eyes. He thought his brother needed time to think through their conversation. It wasn't long before he heard the rustling of paper being unfolded. He hoped Luke liked what she had to say.

Dear Luke,

I came by the ranch to apologize to you before I left. I have little defense for not telling you about Edmund. The few times we were together we didn't spend much time talking. Until the night of the social, I thought you were simply flirting with me as you did with all of the ladies. When you kissed me, I certainly wasn't thinking of Edmund. I thought you spent the night with Arina after the dance, and I felt you were just

*toying with my affections. Then you left for Arizona
and I wasn't at all certain you would not come back
with Arina.*

*On reflection, it is difficult to understand how my
feelings for you developed so quickly. I want you to
know it was not my intention to hurt you. I will never
forget you.*

Mary Ann

Luke read the letter several times. He couldn't
argue that they had not talked much, other than the
night he'd cooked with her in the hotel kitchen. She
admitted she had feelings for him, and she'd even said
she wasn't thinking of Stafford when he kissed her. He
really liked that part. Did she actually think he had
feelings for Arina? He couldn't say he blamed her for
arriving at that conclusion considering Arina was
always hanging all over him, and he'd allowed it to
happen. He'd been one stupid son-of-a-buck. And he
was the one thinking he was owed an apology.

The next morning Luke was up early saddling his
horse when Colt awoke. "Aren't you going to have
some coffee?"

"No time, I have a long ride ahead of me," Luke
replied.

Colt walked over to Luke's horse and checked the
girth as Luke tied down the saddlebags. "Does this trip
include an ocean?"

"Yep."

"You liked what she said in her letter?" Colt questioned.

"Well, she wasn't too clear, but I'm reading between
the lines."

"You want someone to go with you?"

"Not this time, but I appreciate the offer. This is something I need to handle by myself. I'll stop in town to find out from George where I'm going," Luke replied.

"Good, I don't want to go to England." Jake squeezed Luke's shoulder. "Stay safe."

Colt pulled Luke to him. "Come home in one piece and stay out of fights."

"I can't promise to stay out of a fight if I see Stafford, but I will come home in one piece," Luke replied.

"That's all I ask." Colt felt himself getting emotional, so he hugged Luke one more time.

When Colt released Luke, Jake gave him a bear hug. "If you don't come back in one piece, I'll kick your butt, little brother."

"That'll be the day," Luke countered. He knew his brothers would worry about him no matter what. "I'll send you a telegram before I board a ship."

"You do that. When you get to the ranch tell Victoria and Promise we'll be back in two weeks," Colt instructed.

"Sure thing. You want me to tell her to get that corset ready?" Luke teased.

Colt grinned. "You better not, I want to enjoy it when I get home. If you say that I'll be in the bunkhouse."

Luke was laughing for the first time in weeks as he rode away.

Before Luke rode to the ranch he detoured to the Detrick ranch. He needed to apologize and tell Sally the truth about his intentions. He just hoped Old Man Detrick wasn't home so he could have some privacy.

He reined in at the porch, but he didn't have a chance to dismount before the front door opened.

Sally walked to the porch. "Hi, Luke."

"Sally." Luke dismounted, tied his reins, stepped on the porch, and removed his hat. "I need to talk to you."

"Your sister-in-law said you were out on the range," Sally said.

"I was, but I'm leaving Wyoming for a while and I needed to talk to you before I leave." He realized what she'd said about speaking to his sister-in-law. "You were at the ranch?"

"Yes, I wanted to see you."

"Why?"

"To give you back the things you bought from Mary Ann's shop."

"Did your dad see them?" Luke thought that might explain the reason she wanted to return them.

"No, Pa never saw the box. Look, Luke, I know what you were doing."

"You do?" Luke didn't expect she was fully aware of what was happening that night, but what she said next really surprised him.

"Yes, I do. I could tell you were in love with that Englishwoman from the first day you saw her. Don't get me wrong, I don't like it, but there is nothing I can do about it. You never looked at me the way you looked at her. I knew you were purchasing those things to make her jealous, or to hurt her for some reason."

Luke couldn't believe what he was hearing. Sally was a lot smarter than he'd given her credit for. It seemed like everyone knew how he felt about Mary Ann before he did. "That was the reason I wanted to talk to you. I wanted to tell you the truth and apologize."

"You don't have to explain. But I'm curious to know if you were trying to make her jealous or hurt her."

"Both." To his shame it was the truth. He'd been hurt when he found out about Stafford, and he wanted to do the same to her and it was a bonus if he made her jealous. He'd made a mess of everything.

"You know she's in love with you, don't you?"

Luke twirled his hat in his hands. "That's what everyone is telling me."

"I gave the box to Victoria." She reached out and grabbed his hand and gave it a squeeze. "Now I guess you'd best go get her."

"Thanks for being so decent about this, Sally, it's more than I deserve." He got back on his horse feeling better knowing Sally didn't harbor ill will toward him.

Sally smiled at him. "I know I seem desperate to get married, but I don't want someone that doesn't love me. I want a man who looks at me the way you look at her."

"I'm sure you will find him." Knowing how determined she was, Luke felt sure she would find the man for her. "Tell me, did you know what she was doing that night at the shop?"

"Yes, and I thought it was brilliant the way she beat you at your own game. Don't teach her poker."

Luke laughed. "Bye, Sally."

"What do you mean you are going to England?" George asked.

"I'm going to England to see if she wants to marry Stafford," Luke explained. He'd already been to the ranch, packed a valise, and was ready to catch the next stagecoach headed east. "Can you tell me where she lives?"

"You don't have to go to England to find your answers. She doesn't want to marry him," George said.

"I want to hear it from her," Luke said.

"She didn't want to marry him, but that doesn't mean the wedding hasn't already taken place," George said.

Luke had thought of that, but he was still determined. "Did you hear something?"

"No, no, it's just they are probably already in England," he said. "Her father is so determined he may have demanded a quick union. Although, I think it likely that he and Stafford will want a large affair. That's usually the way it is done."

"I'll deal with that if it has happened. Tell me where she lives."

George had been thinking about going to England. He felt sorry for his niece and he wanted to try to talk her parents out of forcing this marriage on her. "I'll do better than that, I'll show you. Let me pack a bag."

"Are you sure?" Luke didn't mind George going with him, but he needed to warn him there would be problems if anyone tried to stop Mary Ann if she wanted to leave with him. "There could be trouble."

"I would love to see you punch Hardwicke again if that is what you mean. I want to go with you. It's past time someone stood up to that tyrant. And I want to see why my sister has allowed this to happen. Coreen used to have some spirit, but I fear Hardwicke has broken her, and he's going to do the same thing to his daughter. Besides, Stafford is not good enough for Mary Ann."

Luke arched his brow at his statement. "You think I am good enough for her?"

"If you love her as much as she loves you I think you are the perfect man for her," George responded.

Luke was surprised to hear such sentimental words from George. "You think she loves me, huh?"

"We English rarely discuss such feelings, but I saw

the way she looked at you. She didn't want to be in the same room with Stafford. He'd behaved dishonorably trying to compromise her before she left England. She didn't want him then or now."

"You mean by *compromise,* he tried to take what she wasn't offering?" He'd wondered if she had been Stafford's lover in England, but he wasn't about to ask George.

"Yes, he ripped her dress and her father assumed the worst. Of course, Stafford most likely encouraged Hardwicke to think something inappropriate happened between them since he wants Mary Ann."

"Her father used that incident to insist she marry Stafford?"

"Yes. Then when he came here and saw her with you he saw his opportunity to have greater leverage. I think he told her things wouldn't go well for you if she gave him any trouble about returning with him. It's all about Stafford's money."

"We'll see who has the trouble."

"Mary Ann was happy here. You and your family were a big part of that. I know she was distraught she didn't see you before she left."

Hearing what George had to say made Luke more determined than ever to get to England as soon as possible. "Go pack your things. I'll be back, I'm going to the bank."

George started to go upstairs, but turned back to Luke. "I don't think Mary Ann planned on returning, but she did leave one thing behind," George said.

"What was that?"

"Come in her shop and I'll show you."

Luke followed George into the shop and everything was exactly as the last time he'd seen it, except for a large box on top of the display case. George opened the box and pulled out Mary Ann's pink hat. "She said you liked this hat and she thought it would bring back sad memories if she wore it again. She told me to sell it."

Luke took the hat from George and ran his hand over the soft pink feathers. It was the first thing he'd noticed about Mary Ann that day, and he wasn't about to let another woman wear it. "How much do you want for it?"

"You want to buy the hat?"

"Yes."

"You can have it, I wasn't going to sell it."

Luke handed the hat back to George. "Put it in her room, she can wear it when we come back."

George chuckled at his confidence. "I'll do that."

Chapter Twenty-Six

"Mary Ann, I know you are dallying, but you can't put this off any longer. The date is getting near, my dear, and it is imperative we start the plans." Coreen swept into her daughter's bedroom determined to put an end to her dithering about. The maid entered behind Coreen and hurried to open the drapes before they delivered breakfast to her room.

Mary Ann quickly shoved Luke's telegram under the pillow. She'd look at that telegram every night and every morning, reading those three words over and over: *I miss you*. Without that telegram she might have thought her time in Wyoming was a dream, but those three words made it real for her. She'd never felt more alive than she was those few times she'd been in Luke's arms. She'd been even more despondent after arriving in England. She had lost so much weight that all of her dresses were hanging off of her. Her complexion was dull and her eyes were lifeless. Her mother compared her to a ghost, and when she looked in the mirror, she thought the description was apt. She didn't care. Nothing about her future garnered her interest. Her existence would be like her mother's, pretending to have the life she dreamed about.

Coreen walked to the wardrobe and pulled out a dress. "Wear this today, we have an appointment with Worth, dear. He's going to design your wedding dress and your gowns for the parties."

Mary Ann turned her head to see her mother was holding up the very dress she wore the first time she saw Luke. Tears welled in her eyes and she turned away so her mother couldn't see.

"Now get out of bed and get dressed. We don't want to keep the designer waiting, he has patrons waiting for months for his lovely creations. We are very fortunate he has agreed to do this for us. Of course, Stafford is the one you should thank. Every tradesperson in London is eager to do his bidding."

"I do not need new dresses, my old ones will suffice, and Father will not have to part with any money," Mary Ann said.

"Nonsense!" Coreen motioned for the maid to leave the room. "I have had enough of this moping about. You need to remember your position. Don't you care if we lose the estates?"

"Mother, I could ask you if you cared about your daughter's happiness."

"You will be happy with Edmund. He has enough money to give you whatever you want," Coreen replied.

Mary Ann shook her head. "Mother, he can't give me love. He doesn't know what that means."

"And I suppose you do with that cowboy in that god-forsaken place." Coreen knew her comment struck home by the stunned look on Mary Ann's face. "Yes, your father told me about that man. I'd say it is a good thing he arrived when he did or you would have been an embarrassment to your family. Did you not think of your position while you were with your uncle in that horrid place?"

"Did Father also tell you that he hit me?"

That was a detail he had omitted, but Coreen would never admit that to her daughter. "Your father has arranged a fine marriage for you and you should be grateful. Would you be happy out in the middle of nowhere, away from civilization to live in some hovel with a destitute cowboy in America?"

She didn't like the way her mother tried to demean Luke. "That cowboy is more of a man than Stafford will ever be! I was happy in the middle of nowhere, as you call it. Uncle George is happy there. Why couldn't you just let us be? Should I be forced to be as miserable as you are for the rest of my life?" Mary Ann almost regretted the words as soon as they left her mouth, but she couldn't take them back now. The Good Book said to honor your mother and father, but it was becoming more and more difficult for her.

"That type of life with *those* people might seem exciting for a while, but I think it would become tiresome fairly quickly."

"You might find you liked that life, you might feel alive for the first time. It's a wonderful feeling to be productive. Uncle George was very brave to go to a new land and carve out a place he could call his own without someone handing it to him. He is to be admired. I found it exhilarating to have a job, to be useful, instead of attending socials and gossiping over silly things."

"I've always felt your uncle was rather silly to leave England. I didn't know my daughter was going to be foolish enough to follow in his footsteps," her mother snapped.

Mary Ann stared at her mother. She was so vastly different from her uncle. "It is sad, Mother. You've become just like Father. I'm glad Uncle George left England, he has a wonderful life in America with a business and friends he can depend on. What do you have?"

Coreen didn't want to listen. She threw the dress on the bed. "I will send the maid back in to assist you. Do be dressed in fifteen minutes."

It was difficult for Mary Ann to keep her focus on the task at hand. Seamstresses were hovering over her, measuring, pulling, and tugging at her until she wanted to scream. The famous designer was sketching designs as he listened to Coreen's banter about the wedding of the century. Mary Ann almost told her mother she should be marrying Edmund since she was as excited as a new bride should be. Her mother whispered in her ear that she was insulting the designer by her lack of enthusiasm. Mary Ann thought her mother's excitement more than made up for her own shortcomings. She didn't know which was going to be worse, suffering through this ordeal, or the dinner that was planned for tonight with Edmund and his parents. Edmund's parents were nearly as insufferable as her own father, and she didn't know how she would manage to sit there trying to pretend she was the most joyful bride in the world.

When everyone left the room to select the fabrics, Mary Ann walked to the table where the designer had been working. She noticed one sketch was a particularly fetching creation with an off-the-shoulder design. It reminded her of the dress she wore to the social. She remembered how Luke complained that the dress displayed too much of her. At first she hadn't understood why he was so upset, but now she knew he was behaving like a jealous husband thinking other men might show an interest. She didn't know why she hadn't realized he wasn't as indifferent as he tried to make her believe. If he didn't care for her why would he have been so upset with her when he found out about Edmund? It made little difference to know that he must have cared for her, he would never forgive her now.

The designer came back into the room and saw her looking at his sketches. He glanced at the paper in her hand. "You prefer this one?"

"It is beautiful," she told him.

"Yes, that is my favorite. It would be lovely on you." He had noticed this beautiful bride-to-be was not thrilled to be planning a wedding. While her mother was over-enthusiastic, the actual bride looked like she would prefer the guillotine. "You are not excited about the wedding?"

"No."

He'd heard the rumors about her father's debts and he was well aware of Stafford's wealth. It wasn't an uncommon practice to marry for money, but he couldn't say he agreed, particularly when it made such a lovely young woman unhappy. This was not a woman in love, at least not in love with the groom. "Wrong groom?"

"Wrong groom," Mary Ann confirmed.

Dinner with Edmund and his parents was an abysmal affair. Mary Ann preferred to be in her room alone with her thoughts. It wasn't necessary for her to be at the table as they didn't include her in the conversation about her big day. She might as well have been invisible. The parents were busy planning everything, and occasionally sought Edmund's input, not hers, but she didn't object. She didn't want to plan this farce of a wedding. Thoughts of the future, tomorrow, or a year from now were depressing. In Wyoming she was excited about her future, but now her entire life looked dismal.

"Your mother said your wedding dress is going to be fabulous," Edmund's mother said to her.

"So Mother says."

"Were you not pleased with the design?"

Mary Ann didn't want to discuss the gown. "It only matters if Mother is pleased."

Edmund's mother thought it was an odd response, but she thought Mary Ann was an odd bird. Any young woman who had taken off for America alone was surely not of sound mind in her opinion. She'd told her son to find another young woman to marry, but his mind was set on Mary Ann.

Listening to their conversation, Mary Ann learned her social calendar would be filled with events leading up to the wedding. How would she ever make it through the days without going insane?

After dinner, Edmund escorted Mary Ann to the gardens so he could speak to her in private. "I want you to have this designer handle your wardrobe for our tour of Italy after our wedding."

"Italy?" This was the first time she'd heard of taking a trip with him.

"Yes, I'm thinking we will take in a few more countries as well. We will be away for several months."

She didn't want to be away, but she didn't want to be in England, so she didn't argue.

"I had planned to take you to America, but you've already been there so the point is moot."

"Did you enjoy America, Edmund?" she asked.

"I enjoyed it less the farther west we traveled," he answered. "What I find interesting is how a lady such as yourself enjoyed it so much."

This was the first time Edmund had a real conversation with her. "I cherished the independent spirit. There were no servants hovering over me every minute. For the first time in my life I felt free."

"Most women take pleasure in having servants, buying new wardrobes every season, and a calendar full of parties."

"Yes, my mother loves that life," Mary Ann agreed. Edmund seemed so rational tonight she thought he might listen to reason. "Edmund, you know we don't suit, why don't you marry someone else?"

"We are going to marry, you might as well adjust to the idea. Your cowboy is not here," he replied.

How she wished Luke were here, that would certainly shake up the evening. She almost smiled at the thought.

Chapter Twenty-Seven

Luke had never traveled by stagecoach and he found the whole experience nerve-racking. He knew he could make better time on horseback. He was thankful that George was an excellent traveling companion, possessing the wisdom to know when to converse and when there was a need for silence. As impatient as Luke was to get to his destination, he did enjoy listening to George's stories about Mary Ann's life in England. Considering her sheltered past, he was even more amazed at her courage to travel to Wyoming by herself. It took a special kind of woman to embark on such an adventure.

After spending time with Luke for weeks, George had developed a deeper respect for the man. He was very much like his brother Colt, a man of integrity, hardworking, and a generous heart. The only difference George saw between the two men was Luke's appeal to the ladies. Colt was intimidating, where Luke was naturally charismatic and attracted women without effort. During one part of their journey a couple was traveling with them, and the woman couldn't keep her eyes off Luke. Luke didn't encourage her attention, he was simply being polite, but the woman flirted shamelessly. George found the woman's actions entertaining, but her husband was not amused. Luke had confided that from the first moment he saw Mary Ann no other woman interested him. George was certain his niece felt the same about Luke, and he prayed her marriage to Stafford hadn't taken place.

The stagecoach pulled into another way station where they would be spending the night and leave at first light. George carried the luggage into the house while Luke assisted the stagecoach driver with the horses. An older man walked from the stables to help them get the horses in a corral. "Thanks, young man. You seem to know your way around horses."

"Yessir, I've spent a lot of time with them."

"Where you coming from?"

"Wyoming," Luke replied.

"Where you headed?"

Luke wasn't offended at the questions. He figured the man enjoyed talking to the travelers when they arrived. The people who ran these stations lived an isolated life, and while most of them had been friendly, some were not as sociable. "Well, I'm headed to England."

"Is that a fact?"

"Yessir."

Luke walked into the house and joined George at the table where a woman was pouring coffee. "That coffee sure smells good."

The woman eyed Luke, noting what a handsome man he was as her eyes moved over his large frame to the six-gun on his hip. When she walked over to pour his coffee she saw his beautiful blue eyes and thought something about him looked familiar. "Have you been through here before?"

"No ma'am."

"I just thought you looked familiar."

"I've never been here."

The older man came through the door and sat opposite Luke at the table. His wife gave him a cup of coffee. "Honey, I want you to meet someone." He pointed to Luke. "This is the man that you wanted to write. The one with his head up his tail."

Luke and George exchanged a look silently telegraphing that these two people had been isolated way too long.

"It isn't possible!" The woman looked at Luke. "I think I knew the moment he walked in! I thought he looked familiar. It must be those eyes!"

"Why would you want to write to me?" Luke found himself asking and not at all impressed that she thought he had his head up his keister.

"You're Luke McBride." It wasn't said as a question, but as a fact.

Luke hadn't mentioned his name to the old man, so he didn't know how she knew unless George told her. "Yes, ma'am, I am."

Lillian sat the coffeepot down and she swiped at her watery eyes. "Oh Henry, is it possible?"

"I think someone needs to explain what is going on here," George said.

"I'm Henry and this is my wife, Lillian. My wife and I have heard all about this young man."

"How so?" Luke asked, truly confused by this woman's emotional outburst.

Lillian sat beside Luke. "We know Mary Ann."

George was the first to speak. "You know my niece?"

"If your brother is that old coot from England, then yes, we know his daughter," Henry answered.

By that description, George correctly figured out they had met Hardwicke. "He's not my brother, but my sister is married to that old coot."

Henry grinned. He liked this Englishman immediately. "The only thing in his favor is he helped to create that beautiful young woman."

"When was she here?" Luke asked impatiently.

"It's been almost two months. You're late to the party, young man," Henry said.

"I'm afraid I have bad news for you," Lillian said.

"Don't tell me she's already married," George said.

"Oh, no. She was shot."

"Shot!" Luke never dreamed he would hear those words. He'd worried about all of the dangers that could befall Mary Ann during the journey on the stagecoach, but he told himself that her father and Stafford would protect her. He should have known better. "Is she okay?"

"Yes, she's fine." Lillian patted Luke's hand. "She was protecting me from robbers. She took the bullet that was meant for me."

"Had she mended by the time they left?" George asked.

"Her wound looked good, but Clive didn't want her jostling around." Lillian told them of their neighbor who had tended Mary Ann.

"I'm sure Hardwicke insisted they leave quickly. He's not a patient man," George said.

"That he did. He was anxious to get home to have a wedding."

"What happened to the man that shot her?" Luke asked, not wanting to think of a wedding that may have already taken place.

"He got away, but I winged him. There were three of them, two rode off. The other one is buried out in the field."

"Who were they?" Luke asked.

"We never saw them before."

Lillian left the table to start dinner and Luke joined her at the stove. She had already prepared the chicken for frying, so she started making dough for biscuits.

Luke picked up the coffeepot and poured himself another cup. "So tell me why you thought I had my head up my rear."

"Mary Ann told me you wouldn't forgive her about Stafford, and that she didn't get to apologize to you, or say good-bye. I told her you didn't deserve her if you didn't accept her apology. You broke that dear gal's heart."

Luke thought about what she said. "I didn't know what I felt at the time."

Lillian thought he must have worked out his feelings since he was going after her. "Well, that girl is crazy about you. I don't think I've ever seen anyone so much in love except for me and Henry."

That made Luke smile. "You been married a long time?"

"Forty years." She gave him a motherly smile. "You can have that too if you get to her in time."

"You said her wound was healed, but you didn't think she should have left. Why is that?" Luke had a feeling Lillian had left some things unspoken.

Lillian started rolling out the dough as she talked. "If I know anything, I know that gal had a broken heart and it was eating her alive. She was skin and bones when she left here. And that father of hers, well, I wouldn't want to walk from here to the stable with him, much less be forced to travel with him across an ocean."

"What about Stafford? Do you think he cares for Mary Ann?" Luke wanted to strangle him for not protecting Mary Ann. He didn't know why he should be surprised, he hadn't even put up a fight when he punched him.

Lillian picked up the tin biscuit cutter and pushed it through the dough. "I think he wants to marry her for her beauty like most men would. I'm not sure what's in his heart. But he's pretty much useless in this country. They weren't armed and they ran for cover when the shooting started with those three men. Of course, none of us expected what happened. Those men ate our food then tried to rob us. But if Mary Ann is going to be stuck with Stafford, it's probably a good thing she will be in England. I reckon men don't carry guns there like they do here."

"She won't be stuck with him if I get to England in time."

"You must love her a great deal." Lillian was thrilled he was going after Mary Ann. Maybe Henry had been right when he predicted they would see Mary Ann again.

"It took me long enough to figure it out." Luke glanced down at the biscuits she was placing in the pan. "You're the one that taught her how to make biscuits."

"Yes, I did. She told me how much you liked them."

"I thought I was going to explode I ate so many. My sisters-in-law are good cooks, but Mary Ann's biscuits are better."

"I promised to write her in England and give her more recipes. Of course, I could just as easily send those letters to Wyoming."

Luke winked at her. "I reckon you could."

* * *

After dinner, George retired for the night, but Luke wanted to hear more about Mary Ann. He spoke with Lillian and Henry for several hours. After they answered all of his questions, Lillian asked about his family. "Mary Ann was very taken with your family. She made life on the McBride ranch sound wonderful."

Luke told them about the ranch and his brothers. "We are not without our own hardships, but we are content. My brothers have married beautiful women and I have three nephews that are real characters."

"Yes, she told us all about them. It sounds as though Mary Ann would be happy there."

Luke prayed she was right. He knew he'd never find another woman like her. He thought of the many times Colt told him he needed to believe that his prayers would be answered. Have faith, Colt had told him. Even his larger-than-life brother said there were times when men couldn't handle difficult situations on their own. He'd never really understood what his brother meant until now. He'd been a stubborn fool to let Mary Ann leave Wyoming, and now he wasn't in a position where he could protect her. Her safety was in God's hands.

Luke was the first one up the next morning and he was outside hitching the team before dawn. He couldn't wait to leave knowing that he was closing in on his destination. He needed to see Mary Ann with his own eyes to make sure she was okay.

"We will see you on your way back," Henry told him.

"You better bring her back with you," Lillian said sternly.

"Unless she doesn't want to come with me, I will bring her back."

"And tell her I was wearing a dress I made with the material she gave me."

"And that's a very pretty dress. Henry best watch his p's and q's before he finds himself with some competition."

Lillian blushed at the compliment. "Go on with yourself now."

After Luke threw the luggage to the top of the stage-coach, he walked to Lillian and put his arm around her shoulders. "I'll be expecting some biscuits on our way back to Wyoming."

Chapter Twenty-Eight

Mary Ann's mother made sure her daughter would make a grand entrance when she arrived at Stafford's ball. She was wearing an ice blue dress designed with a skirt so voluminous that Mary Ann could hardly move. But just as Coreen planned, all eyes were on her and her daughter when they made their appearance in the great ballroom.

Always the perfect gentleman in public, Edmund appeared by Mary Ann's side as soon as she entered. Masquerading as the perfect couple, they roamed the vast room casually speaking with the guests. Mary Ann figured there had to be at least three hundred people in attendance and it seemed Edmund knew them all. Most of the women were openly affectionate with Edmund and barely acknowledged her. But Mary Ann didn't take offense, she actually hoped Edmund would find a woman more to his liking. She hadn't felt that way with Luke. Thinking about the morning when she thought Luke was the man sneaking out of Arina's room, she remembered she had wanted to throw something at him. *Oh Luke! Why are you forever invading my thoughts?* She wished she could stop thinking about him for one night.

Edmund escorted her to the dance floor. "Darling, it's good to see you are not so glum this evening." Edmund reveled in showing off his fiancée to all of the men.

"It is a lovely ball, Edmund, and so many lovely ladies are here who would love to marry you."

"But you are not one of them?" Edmund was tiring of her attitude. He thought she would come to appreciate all of the things he could give her. He didn't dare think she could be in love with that hooligan in Wyoming.

"No, I'm not one of them."

"Tell me, Mary Ann, were you intimate with that cowboy in Wyoming?"

"Of course not! Why would you ask such a thing?"

"I can't imagine a real lady allowing such a man to kiss her in front of everyone. It stood to reason there was much more going on between you."

He had a point. She had allowed Luke to kiss her in the middle of the hotel without a care. And her behavior behind the church the night of the social was purely scandalous.

"Perhaps I'm not a real lady."

"Perhaps not. But I will know soon enough. Why don't we go upstairs now and you can give me what you seemed so eager to give that cowboy. We can put the matter to rest tonight."

Mary Ann was shocked by his statement and tried to pull away from him. "If you remember correctly, I left England after you thought it was your right to take what was not offered."

"Obviously not something you found objectionable with that man."

"Quite objectionable with you!"

Edmund yanked her close to his body. "It won't be long until you have no choice in the matter. And you won't be running away. I will not be as careless as your father. I shall have someone watch over you day and night."

"So I'm to be a prisoner once we are wed?"

"Indeed. I will not be made a fool."

She tried in vain to push him away, but he wouldn't release her. "Edmund, if you think I will ever love you then you are a fool."

Edmund smirked at her. "My pet, I told you before love is not something I believe in. It makes no difference to me what you feel, love or indifference. Marriage is a convenience, nothing more."

That was the only dance she had with Edmund. All of her other dances were with different partners and no one cut in like they did in Wyoming. She'd noticed Edmund had no difficulty finding partners either, and judging by the way they flirted, they found him most charming. She remembered that when Luke had another woman in his arms, she thought her heart would break. When she watched Edmund with another partner, she simply hoped he found her irresistible.

Mary Ann danced so many dances that she was exhausted, and her shoulders ached from the weight of her blasted dress. She went in search of a place where she could sit for a while undisturbed. Working her way around the ballroom she found the hallway that led to the study, and fortunately she was unobserved as she scurried down the corridor. When she opened the door to the study she noticed there was a dimly lit lamp atop a table in the corner. She grabbed her skirt and shoved it inside the doorway, but she came to an abrupt halt when she saw a man with his back to her leaning over the desk. Once her eyes adjusted to the light, she saw the man was leaning over a woman. They were obviously engaged in an amorous assignation. "Oh, excuse me."

Edmund snapped his head around to see his fiancée staring at him. "Mary Ann, what are you doing here?"

The woman jumped up from the desk and hastily straightened her bodice.

Mary Ann could hardly fathom that it was Edmund with the woman, but she quickly composed herself. "I might ask you the same thing, sir." It was rather obvious what he was doing.

"Please say hello to Millicent," Edmund said coolly.

Once Millicent was on her feet, Mary Ann recognized her as one of the women Edmund had been dancing with. "Millie, you might want to pull your skirt down and repair your hair."

Millicent kept a close eye on Mary Ann as she passed her before fleeing from the room.

Edmund pushed his hair from his forehead and picked his jacket up from the desk. "Were you looking for me?"

"No, I thought I would come in here to sit quietly for a minute."

"I see." Edmund walked toward her.

"Why don't you marry Millicent? She must have something you enjoy to risk being seen in your state of dishabille." Mary Ann's future flashed before her eyes. If she had any thought that she would find some measure of happiness in this farce of a marriage with Edmund, it quickly dissipated. And she'd thought Luke was the scoundrel. This man, if she could even call him that, failed miserably compared to Luke.

"Obviously I didn't expect anyone to walk in. And nearly every man in that room has been with Millie so they would think nothing of it." He roughly pulled Mary Ann into his arms. "I want to know how many men you have been with."

"I've answered that question before." Mary Ann averted her head to prevent him from kissing her. "Leave me alone!"

He didn't listen, he forced her against the wall and pinned her arms with one hand and held her by the chin with the other, preventing her from moving.

"Edmund! Stop!" She smelled the alcohol on him. It reminded her of the last time he tried to take advantage of her.

He covered her mouth with his own. He was like a man possessed and she feared he would rip her dress again as she fought him, just like the last time. His lips moved to her neck. "Edmund, do you want your family and your guests to see me disheveled?"

"Stop fighting me!"

Thankfully, one of the servants tapped on the open door and entered.

Edmund released Mary Ann to face him. "Yes?" he snapped.

"Sorry, sir, I saw the light. Is there something I can get you?" The man glanced at Mary Ann.

"No, my fiancée and I were just taking a break from the dancing." He took Mary Ann by the arm and led her from the room.

Once in the hallway, Edmund put on his jacket. "I do apologize, my dear. I'm afraid your charms got the best of me."

"Did Millie's charms get the best of you too?" Mary Ann was furious that he'd manhandled her.

"Are you jealous?"

"Not in the least, but I don't know why you want me when you can have her at your disposal."

"She will always be at my disposal. Our marriage will not change that fact."

They entered the ballroom and Edmund acted as though nothing was amiss as he escorted her around the room.

Mary Ann wanted to scream. She felt like a trapped bird with no place to go. Edmund had made it perfectly clear what she could expect once she was his wife. If she was going to do something to prevent this marriage, she only had a short window of time. If she could escape, where would she go? The first place her father would look for her would be in America. And he would be right. That is the first place she would want to go.

"My, what an absolutely lovely evening. I must say, my dear, you are most fortunate to be marrying Edmund." Coreen began her nonstop soliloquy. If she wasn't expounding on the virtues of being wed to Edmund, she was discussing the silver, the crystal, or the jewels Edmund's mother was wearing. The vacuous comments were endless.

Mary Ann was just thankful the evening had come to an end, and the last thing she wanted was to hear her mother tell her how fortunate she was to have Edmund. "Yes, I must say I thoroughly enjoyed finding my fiancé in the study with some woman in a very compromising position."

"My dear, I am sure you are exaggerating," Coreen

replied. "You must not take premarital indiscretions to heart. Edmund probably has a case of the jitters."

"It amazes me, Mother, that you always make allowances where none are due. If only you showed the same generosity of spirit to your own daughter."

The following weeks seemed to fly by, getting closer and closer to the day she would be lawfully tied to a man she didn't love. The only positive thing about her wedding day would be the end to the mind-numbing socials. She was forced to answer the same inane questions over and over. It was torturous playing the role of the perfect couple with an indiscreet bridegroom. Since the night she'd found Edmund in the study with that woman, she'd considered leaving, but she was never left alone. She had the feeling that Edmund and her father had conspired to make sure she wouldn't have the opportunity to make an escape. She longed to be at the hotel in Wyoming again, and the only man she wanted to be with hadn't even said good-bye.

The ball before the ostentatious wedding was just days away, and she had an appointment for the final fitting of her gown today. She walked downstairs and searched for her mother who was to accompany her. She found her in the dining room amid a flurry of activity. They would be having a dinner before the ball and the servants were scurrying around arranging the lengthy dining table decor under the direction of her conductor mother. The table looked exquisitely elegant, certainly befitting royalty. An enormous sterling silver centerpiece was overflowing with flowers trailing the length of the table in both directions. Countless pieces of twenty-four-carat-gold-encrusted goblets and finger bowls were placed precisely the proper distance from the fine china. Ornate compotiers and candelabras complemented the overall design. Green vines with delicate white flowers were woven through the overhead chandelier. Mary Ann knew under the candlelight the table would be glittering like the huge diamonds in the ring Edmund had given her.

"Mother, I'm ready to leave for the fitting."

"Come here, dear, I want you to see the flowers we have chosen for the ballroom," Coreen said.

"It truly doesn't matter to me." She knew her mother didn't care about her opinion, she just wanted her to say she loved everything she had chosen. Coreen was in her glory overseeing the event and she would never understand her daughter's indifference.

"I'm afraid I can't go with you, I've too many things to attend to."

Mary Ann was delighted. Now would be the time to make her escape. She'd already packed two valises but she needed to figure out a way to get them to the carriage without being seen. She walked outside to see if the carriage was ready to depart and as soon as the butler opened the door one of her father's detectives appeared. "I'll escort you to the shop." There would be no escape.

The ladies at the shop helped Mary Ann into a magnificent silk and satin pale yellow creation. She had to admit that it was the most beautiful gown she'd ever seen. The designer was an unrivaled master. She stared at her reflection in the mirror. Just as it had been sketched, her shoulders were bare and the bodice fit to perfection, with the full skirt accentuating her small waist.

"This color is lovely on you, perfect with the red in your hair," the shop owner said.

"It is a beautiful design." Mary Ann thought of Luke. She wondered if he would like the gown or if he would think it was too revealing. She had to stop thinking about him. Most brides would be worrying if their future husband would like her dress. But it was Luke who'd never failed to tell her she looked beautiful. He always commented on her dresses, her hair, and her scent. Not once in all the years she'd known Edmund had he ever told her she looked beautiful, or commented on her wardrobe. She hadn't realized that before this very moment.

Chapter Twenty-Nine

It seemed all of London was in the ballroom when Mary Ann appeared at the top of the staircase. She had to admit it was a lovely sight with the women in their colorful gowns and the men in their evening wear floating around the room.

"It took you forever," Edmund said as he took her by the hand.

Maybe he was worried that she'd climbed down from her balcony. It wasn't that she didn't think about it, but she was on the second floor. After dinner she'd told him she wanted to freshen up before the ball so she escaped to her room. She spent the entire time clutching Luke's old telegram. Even though he had written the message before he'd learned about Edmund, she clung to the thought that while he was in Arizona he'd missed her.

Edmund looked at her hand. "Where's your ring?"

The magnificent diamond and sapphire ring he'd given her remained in its black velvet box. She had told him that night that she wouldn't wear it, but he refused to listen. She couldn't wear what she felt was tantamount to a shackle. "I don't want to wear it and it's much too large."

"I shall take it to the jeweler tomorrow." He squeezed her hand. "And you will wear it."

She wouldn't waste her breath arguing with him. She was living in a world filled with people and no one heard her.

"Everyone is waiting for us to dance," he said.

She fulfilled her duty and danced her first dance with Edmund. After the dance ended, she lingered near a circle of women she knew and pretended to appear interested in their conversations.

"Tell us, Mary Ann, how did you enjoy America?" Vivian asked.

Vivian was one of Mary Ann's acquaintances since childhood, but she couldn't call her a friend. She was a lovely woman and enjoyed everything Mary Ann detested. "I loved America."

Her comment had all of the women turning to look at her.

"Didn't you go West?" another woman asked.

"Yes, to Wyoming."

"Did you see these cowboys we've read so much about?"

"I saw many cowboys." If they only knew. How she wanted to say she'd even kissed a cowboy! That would give them something to gossip about for at least half a year.

"Oh, my dear, you must tell us if they are as romantic as the novels would have us believe," Vivian said.

"They are more so," Mary Ann answered. "All of you should travel to America if you want to find real men." That should shock them down to their little satin slippers.

"Don't leave us in suspense, tell us about them," Vivian said.

"What would you like to know?"

"How do they look? How do they dress? Do they really wear pistols strapped to their hips?"

Questions started coming from all directions. She'd even had the same questions before she left England, so she understood their curiosity. She answered their questions, describing Luke in vivid detail, down to the color of his turquoise eyes.

Vivian fanned herself with her handkerchief. "Oh my, I feel I may faint."

"You make them sound divine, larger than life," one woman said.

"They are divine, there is no man in this room who can compare," Mary Ann told them.

"Not even Edmund?" Vivian asked.

The question went unanswered when a hush fell over the cavernous room. The music stopped, and Mary Ann turned to see why everyone had stopped dancing. She noticed everyone was staring at the entry-way. "What is it?"

"I don't know; I can't see anything," one woman replied. The women stood on tiptoes, but they were at the back of the ballroom so they still couldn't see what was happening.

Hardwicke's butler recognized George and allowed him and Luke entry into the house. The butler led them to the ballroom and told them he would find Hardwicke for them. George had mentioned to Luke the grandeur of the Hardwicke home, but he was still amazed when he saw the size of the ballroom. From the outside it looked like a large castle and once inside, the opulence of the place left him speechless. He couldn't help but question if he'd made the right decision to come for Mary Ann. George said she'd lived like a princess, but he hadn't fully realized all that she'd left behind. He reminded himself that she'd willingly left England, and George told him she loved Wyoming. Luke took a deep breath, bracing himself for what was to come. He wouldn't back down now, not unless she didn't want him. His gaze passed over the crowd and then he saw her at the back of the room.

Every head was turned to the entry to the ballroom. Mary Ann thought she saw a black hat. Was it wishful thinking? But when the crowd parted Mary Ann saw him. She couldn't believe her eyes. It really was Luke standing in the ballroom, looking even taller than she'd remembered in his black Stetson. And he was staring directly at her. All eyes were on the cowboy from America with his pistol strapped to his hip. The whispers started, no doubt everyone was trying to figure out who he was. The women nearby were commenting on everything from his size, to his hat, his pistol, even his boots. Not one detail missed their notice.

"George, I'll be back. Keep Hardwicke busy for a few minutes." Luke made his way through the throng of people. It was like Moses parting the Red Sea, but instead of a staff, his Stetson and his .45 captivated his audience. His long strides made short work of the distance separating him from Mary Ann, and he didn't take his eyes off her. She was very thin but still so beautiful in that pale yellow dress that his heart started pounding. During his journey, he'd questioned if he was making the right decision to come after her. He'd thought she might not want him considering how he'd treated her. But one look at her and he knew he was exactly where he needed to be.

"Is that the man you were describing?" Vivian whispered.

"Yes." Mary Ann slowly moved toward Luke. He was wearing a blue shirt and even from a distance she could see his turquoise eyes focused on her.

By the time he reached her, the music resumed and Luke removed his hat and held his hand to her. "Would you like to dance, Miss Hardwicke?"

She placed her hand in his and he pulled her into his embrace. She couldn't stop staring at his handsome face. So many times she'd imagined being in his arms once again. Even though he looked tired, he looked wonderful to her. "What are you doing here?"

Luke grinned at her. "I heard you wanted to say good-bye to me."

"That was months ago," she said. "How did you get here?"

"Same way you did. I couldn't ride my horse the whole way. Have you changed your mind?"

"About what?" she whispered.

"Saying good-bye."

"I wanted to apologize for not telling you about Edmund," she said.

"Are you married?" He thought he should find that out before he made any declarations.

"No, we are supposed to marry next week." She expected her father or Edmund to interrupt their dance at any moment. She glanced around to see where they were, and she was surprised that no one else was dancing, everyone was watching them. That meant her father and Edmund were also watching them.

"What are you looking for?"

"I expect Father or Edmund to appear."

"Do you want to marry him?"

Tears started to well in her eyes. "Luke, it's the way it has to be."

When other couples started to dance, Luke thought it was an opportune time to take her out of the room so they could speak in private. "Where's a door out of this place?"

Mary Ann pointed to the doors that led to the garden and Luke escorted her through the crowd. He looked back to see George speaking with Hardwicke and Stafford. He figured he'd have a few minutes alone with her until chaos ensued.

Once they walked deep into the gardens and out of sight from onlookers, Luke put his hands around Mary Ann's waist and pulled her to him. "I've been thinking about this for months." He leaned down and crushed his lips to hers.

Mary Ann wrapped her arms around his neck. The lonely days and nights since she last saw him were instantly erased by his kiss. When they pulled apart she placed her hand on his chest. "We shouldn't be doing this."

"That wasn't the way you'd kiss a man if you wanted to marry another," Luke drawled.

She took his face in her hands and gazed into his eyes. "It has to be this way."

Luke took her hand in his and kissed her palm. "Did your father threaten me?" He remembered what George told him, so he wanted to ease her fears. "Tell me the truth."

The look on her face gave him his answer. "They can't do anything to me. Are you marrying him to save your father from ruin? If you have feelings for Stafford you need to tell me now."

She knew her father wouldn't hesitate to harm him now that he'd come for her. "Luke, I'm so happy to see you, but you shouldn't be here."

"Do you kiss Stafford the way you kiss me?"

"No." She wouldn't lie to him. The thought of kissing Stafford made her stomach turn.

Luke couldn't keep his hands off her. He trailed his finger over her bare shoulder and felt her shiver at his touch. "Do you want him to touch you like this?"

She shook her head as she stared into his eyes. When he touched her, she forgot all of the reasons he shouldn't be here.

He pulled her to him again and whispered in her ear. "Tell me you love him and I will go away and you'll never see me again."

She couldn't say those words. "I don't love him."

"I've carried your letter with me all this time," he told her.

It made her so happy to hear those words. "I've carried your telegram."

"Marry me," he said.

Those were the very words she'd longed to hear for months. "Oh Luke. Don't you see, I can't?"

"You love me," he stated. Even if she hesitated to say the words, he knew she did love him.

"That doesn't mean I can marry you," she countered.

"Yes it does. And I want to hear it from you. Tell me you love me." Before she could answer, he looked into her silver eyes and he kissed her again.

When he pulled his lips from hers, she whispered, "Yes, I do love you, but that doesn't change anything."

Luke took her by the hand and headed back to the ballroom. "It changes everything. I'm going to talk to your father."

"Luke, you can't do this. You don't understand what Father will do to you."

He turned to face her. "Honey, trust me. Your father can't hurt me. The only way I'm leaving here without you is if you say you don't want me."

"What made you change your mind? I thought you didn't want to see me again."

He cupped her chin in his palm. "I figured out I couldn't live without you." It wasn't an exaggeration, he couldn't think of a future without her beside him.

"What about Sally?"

"Sally said she hopes one day a man will look at her like I look at you."

"What about the women at the saloon? I saw you with that woman upstairs that night. I don't want a man who will be with other women."

He could see why she thought he was a philanderer. He had been, but he was a changed man. "I haven't been at the saloon since that night. I don't want anyone but you." He wanted her to know what he felt in his heart. He put his arms around her waist and pulled her to his chest. "I fell in love with you when I saw you under that pink hat. I fought it. I didn't think I was ready for marriage. I wasn't ready before, I was waiting for you. I'll never want anyone but you for the rest of my life."

She threw her arms around his neck. "Oh Luke!"

"When we go inside I want you to go pack a valise for tonight. We will come back to get everything you need later."

"I don't think Father will allow me to leave. They haven't left me alone for five minutes."

"Were they afraid you would take off again?"

"Yes."

"Were you going to leave again?"

"My valises are already packed."

He grinned at her. "Let me handle your father." He turned and entered the ballroom with his arm around her. The sea of people parted again and murmurs filled the room.

Luke saw George was still in an animated conversation with Hardwicke and Stafford. Before he let go of Mary Ann's hand, he winked at her. "Go get your valises."

Mary Ann raced from the room, she didn't even look her father's way. She ran up the staircase to her room and pulled her wardrobe open and grabbed the valises she'd already packed. She didn't know if she would be able to come back for the rest of her things, but she didn't care. The only thing that mattered was Luke was here. He loved her and he'd come after her. She would be going home with him.

The door opened and in walked her mother. "What do you think you are doing?"

"I'm leaving."

Her mother hurried across the room, picked up a valise, and emptied the contents on the bed. "You most certainly are not. In case you haven't noticed, we have a houseful of guests and they are here in honor of your wedding. Now get yourself downstairs and show your appreciation!"

Mary Ann turned to face her. "No! You go downstairs and show your appreciation. This is all for you, not for me. I've told you I don't love Edmund and I'm not going to marry him!"

Coreen drew her arm back and slapped her across the cheek. "You want to ruin everything!"

Mary Ann stared at her for a long time before she

turned and walked to her dressing table. She grabbed the small velvet box that held Edmund's ring and walked back to her mother and placed the box in her hand. "This should be for you." She grabbed her valise and stuffed everything back inside.

"We will see if you get out of this house!" Coreen stomped out of the room and slammed the door behind her.

Luke stopped in front of Hardwicke and Stafford. "Hardwicke, I want to talk to you."

"Don't think you are leaving here with Mary Ann," Stafford said.

Luke turned his icy eyes on him. "Don't think I won't."

Hardwicke saw his guests staring at them and he didn't want to make a scene like they did outside that hotel in Wyoming. "Let's take this conversation to my study."

Luke and George followed Hardwicke and Stafford from the ballroom.

As soon as they reached the study, Hardwicke turned to face them. "What do you think you're doing coming here?"

"I came for Mary Ann," Luke said.

"I came with Luke so I could see my sister. I assume you have no objections," George stated.

"You are not taking Mary Ann," Stafford stated again.

Luke's eyes narrowed and he took a step forward. "I don't think you are going to stop me."

Hardwicke held his hands up as if to separate the two men. He faced Luke and said, "Now see here, Mary

Ann is marrying Stafford in a few days. You can't come in here and think that the marriage is not going to happen."

"It's not going to happen," Luke said pointedly. "I'm taking Mary Ann out of here tonight."

The door opened and Coreen walked in. "George, what in heaven's name are you doing here?"

"I wanted to see what had happened to my sister. You have let this bully turn you into a coward, Coreen. Why on earth would you allow your husband to come after Mary Ann when you knew she didn't want to marry him?" He pointed in Stafford's direction.

Coreen looked stunned that her brother would speak to her in such a way. When she didn't respond, George said, "It's not too late to do the right thing, Coreen. If you don't, you're going to lose a daughter for good."

Coreen slumped to a chair. "George, this marriage will save the estates."

Stafford smiled at Luke. "You see, this wedding will take place."

Luke ignored Stafford and looked at Hardwicke. "How much do you need?"

Hardwicke looked confused. "What?"

"How much money do you need?"

Stafford laughed. "It's much more money than a man like you will ever have."

Losing his temper, Luke grabbed Stafford by the shirt and shoved him to a chair. "Stay there and shut up unless you want a repeat of what happened in Wyoming."

"Sir!" Coreen jumped up and ran to Stafford.

"Do be quiet, Coreen," George told her.

"Stafford is right. It's a great deal more money

than a cowboy from America will ever see," Hardwicke snapped.

"I told you he's as stupid as he appears," George said to Luke.

Pulling out a bank draft from his pocket, Luke picked up a pen and dipped it in the inkwell.

"Give me a figure."

"I'm not quite sure I understand," Hardwicke said.

"Hardwicke, you see a cowboy before you who also happens to own a silver mine in Arizona," George informed his brother-in-law. "I can assure you he is wealthier than Stafford." George didn't know for sure if he spoke the truth that Luke was wealthier, but he suspected as much.

Luke could see Hardwicke's mind working, trying to figure out if what George said was true. "One way or the other Mary Ann is leaving with me tonight. You want money for your estates, I'll give it to you. But this is the only time. If you risk it again, it's your problem."

Mary Ann walked in the room and overheard what Luke said. She was already aware of the reason her father insisted she marry Stafford, but it was still difficult to hear. She felt like a piece of artwork being sold to the highest bidder. "Luke, I don't want you to do this."

Hearing the sadness in her voice, Luke turned to her and said, "Honey, let me handle this."

Hardwicke took the pen from Luke and scribbled a number on a piece of paper.

Taking the paper from him, Luke looked at the figure then tore it up and stuffed it into his shirt pocket. He wrote on the bank draft and handed it to Hardwicke. "Mary Ann will return tomorrow for whatever else she will need." He walked across the room and took the valises from her.

"I won't come back here. I have all I need and I will never have to come back here again." Mary Ann turned her back on her mother and father. She didn't want them to see how much they had hurt her.

Luke recalled all of the luggage she had with her when she arrived in Wyoming. She would be leaving a lot behind, but he understood. He handed George one of the valises so he could pull Mary Ann to his side. "Good, I wanted to buy my wife a new wardrobe."

"I should call you out for this," Stafford said.

Luke's hard stare landed on Stafford. "I wish you would. I'll be happy to meet you at dawn."

Stafford remained silent.

"What on earth are we to say to our guests?" Coreen asked.

"Tell them that your daughter came to her senses," George suggested. He looked at his sister one last time. "If you ever come to your senses you are welcome in Wyoming."

Chapter Thirty

Mary Ann was quiet in the coach on the way to the hotel. Luke knew it had to be difficult for her to hear that her father considered her nothing more than chattel.

"I'm so happy you are going home with us, Mary Ann," George told her. "It wasn't the same after you left."

"Victoria and Promise will be glad to see you. As a matter of fact they told me not to come back if you weren't with me." He didn't know if she would ever want to see her mother and father again, but she had a new family. Family was important to him, but her family had hurt her and he knew it would take a long time for her to forgive them.

"We will have a big party when you get home," George said.

"I'm sorry you had to buy me, Luke." She didn't want the man she loved to feel like he'd purchased her love.

"I didn't buy you. You are going to be my wife and I wanted to help your family. Stafford probably felt the same way. I'm sure with his wealth he had his choice of women." That galled him to say that about Stafford, though it was probably true.

"But Luke, can you afford to do that?" Mary Ann knew about the mine, but she wasn't aware that he was wealthy. And knowing her father, he had probably demanded an exorbitant amount.

"Yes I can, and I don't want you to worry about the money. That's not important to me. You are."

Mary Ann buried her head against his chest and cried.

Luke and George exchanged a look that said they would like to go back and beat the devil out of Hardwicke, but they said nothing. Luke slid his arms around Mary Ann and lifted her to his lap and let her get all of her tears out.

The next morning Luke left the hotel early before they were to leave for the docks. Mary Ann and George were packed and ready to leave when he returned two hours later.

"The ship will depart soon, let's be on our way." He smiled as he held his arm for Mary Ann.

He noticed she was wearing the silver dress she wore when she got off that stagecoach, but it hung loosely on her now. "You look beautiful just like the first day I saw you."

She looked up at him and smiled, but Luke could still see the sadness in her eyes. "Thank you."

"Do you have a cape? It's a chilly morning and the voyage home will be much cooler this time of year."

"No, I forgot to pack one. I'll be fine."

* * *

They boarded the ship and George left them to go to his cabin. Luke escorted Mary Ann to a cabin and when they entered she saw it was much larger than the one she had on the prior journey to England. The bed was also much larger. She noticed two large trunks at the foot of the bed. "Luke, I think someone is already in this cabin."

"Why?"

"There are trunks in here." She turned to leave.

Luke reached out and grabbed her around the waist and pulled her up to him. "Honey, this is our cabin."

Her eyes widened when she looked up at him. She assumed the trunks belonged to him. "But Luke, we can't share a cabin."

"Do you think I'm going to cross an ocean and not be in bed with you?"

She was shocked. Did he think since he paid her father that he had the rights of a husband without benefit of matrimony?

Luke knew what she was thinking. "You said you loved me."

"I do, but . . ." She did love him more than anything, but she never thought he would treat her as he would one of the saloon girls.

Luke reached in his pocket and pulled out a small box. "Then I guess if you do love me you might consider marrying me." He opened the box for her to see the ring he'd picked out that morning.

The diamond ring was almost as beautiful as his sparkling blue eyes. "Oh, yes, I will marry you."

"Good! The captain will be down to marry us as soon as we are on our way. But don't think you will get out of a church wedding when we get home. Colt would shoot me if I don't have a church wedding. And he's a very good shot and you don't want a dead groom, do you?" Luke took her hand and gently pushed the ring on her finger. "Perfect." He congratulated himself on guessing the right size.

"Luke, are you sure you want to marry me?"

He tried to figure out why she asked that question. It didn't make sense to him. He lifted her face to his and looked into her eyes. "If I didn't want to marry you I wouldn't have crossed an ocean for you."

"It's just that you have so many women that you've . . ." She didn't quite know how to say what she was thinking.

"Mary Ann, I've known women, and I know you thought I was a philanderer . . . and maybe I was, but I've never asked another woman to marry me. You are the one I love." Just in case she wasn't convinced, he kissed her.

He pulled away from her because they were alone in a cabin with a large bed. "You better stop kissing me like that or I won't wait for the captain."

"Will it be a legal marriage?"

"Yes, very legal." He really didn't want to offer to wait to get married, but he knew it would be the gentlemanly thing to do. "If you want to wait until we get to Wyoming . . ." He said a quick prayer that she would say *no*. If she said she wanted to wait he didn't know what he would do, maybe jump into the ocean to cool off frequently.

"No, I don't want to wait." She was eager to become his wife.

He expelled a loud breath. "Good." He pointed to the trunks. "Those are yours, so why don't you open them up and see if there is something in there you want to wear to our wedding. The only thing I ask is that you wear the one thing on top when you open that trunk." He pointed to the trunk he was talking about. He'd made sure the lady at the shop placed one particular item on top so Mary Ann would see it as soon as she opened the lid.

She looked at the trunks and back at him. "But . . . how . . ."

He gave her a quick kiss. "Your husband is allowed to surprise his wife. I'll go get George and see when the captain will be here."

Mary Ann walked to the trunks not knowing what to expect. Had Luke gone back to her home and collected her things? After the money he gave her father he'd certainly paid for the right. She opened the trunk and found the most beautiful pink satin corset. She remembered how he'd touched that corset in her shop. Every article of clothing in the trunk was new, he hadn't gone back for her things. All of the undergarments were of the same quality she carried in her shop. Only Luke would notice things like that. Along with the pink corset, he'd also purchased one in heliotrope just like the one Colt purchased for Victoria. She also found a lovely deep sapphire velvet cape.

She lifted the lid on the second trunk and she couldn't believe her eyes. On the very top was a creamy white wedding dress designed very much like the yellow gown she had worn last night. She found a smaller case inside the trunk that held combs and brushes, perfumes and powders. It made her feel guilty that he'd spent so much money. Perhaps she should have taken the time to pack more things from her home. She had been in such a hurry to leave and she thought she would go back, but after she heard the conversation with her father she didn't want to return ever again.

She sat down in front of the mirror and looked at her reflection. She was so pale and thin, but she wanted to look beautiful for Luke. She had so much to be thankful for and she needed to focus on that. The man she loved had come for her and he wanted to marry her. For the first time since she'd left Wyoming she felt genuinely happy. She brushed her hair and secured it on top of her head with the combs that he'd purchased. Nervous excitement filled her. Tonight she would be sharing a bed with her new husband.

She'd just barely finished dressing when there was a knock on her door. "Come in."

Luke and George walked in wearing suits and looking very elegant. She didn't know what she expected Luke to be wearing, but she'd never seen a more handsome man in her life. Just looking at him made her heart beat faster.

Luke couldn't take his eyes off her. It was hard for him to believe that this woman was about to become his wife. His chest swelled with pride. He prayed he would be a worthy husband. "You look so beautiful. Are you ready to take on this cowboy?" Luke asked her.

She looked into his eyes. "Oh, yes. And you look very handsome." She walked over to her uncle and said, "I haven't thanked you for coming with Luke. I don't know what I would do without you. When we get married in the church, I hope you will walk me down the aisle." She kissed him on the cheek.

"It would be my honor." George found himself tearing up by her request.

There was a knock on the door. "That's the captain." Once Luke made the introductions, the captain had everyone take their positions. After he performed the ceremony, he told Luke he could kiss his bride and Luke didn't hesitate. He took Mary Ann in his arms.

"I love you, Mrs. McBride." And then he kissed her to seal their vows.

They received their congratulations and George poured wine to celebrate the occasion. "Welcome to the family," he said to Luke.

Before the captain left he asked them to join his table for dinner that night. George left right after the captain and the newlyweds were left alone.

Mary Ann looked nervously at Luke. "What time is dinner?"

"We have several hours yet." Luke took off his jacket and hung it over the back of a chair. "What do you think we should do?" He moved closer to her.

"Ah . . . well, we could . . ." She didn't finish when she saw the look in his eyes. She recalled the night she'd watched from her bedroom window as he'd removed his shirt when he was with that saloon gal. He wasn't hers then, but he was now. Taking a deep breath she reached up and started unbuttoning his shirt.

Luke couldn't have been more surprised by her bold move. Not that he was disappointed, far from it. While she was unbuttoning his shirt he started kissing her neck, her shoulders, anyplace he could find skin that wasn't covered. By the time he felt her hand on his bare chest he was surprised he didn't self-combust. He pulled his shirt off and Mary Ann stared at his chest. He was magnificently formed, his chest and arms bulging with large muscles. She had been jealous when she saw Luke with that saloon woman touching his chest, but now she was actually angry that other women had seen his beautiful body. She ran her hands over his torso feeling his hard muscles. She was so fascinated by the feel of his body that she didn't even realize he'd unbuttoned her dress, and when he urged her to put her arms down, her dress dropped to a puddle at her feet. She was standing in front of him in the beautiful pink corset and the matching garters holding her stockings. He stepped back and stared at her. No one had ever looked at her the way he was looking at her. He'd told her before that he liked her hair down so she reached up and removed the combs from her hair allowing it to fall loosely around her shoulders.

"I didn't thank you for all of the lovely things."

His eyes traveled the length of her. He didn't know how she could be more beautiful from one moment to the next. "This is all the thanks I want. I want to see you in each piece of clothing, and I want to take them off you." He picked her up and carried her to bed.

Mary Ann was lying on Luke's chest feeling happier than she'd ever thought possible. "Did Sally really tell you she knew you loved me?"

"Yes. She also said she knew I purchased those things in your store to make you jealous."

She raised her head and frowned at him. "You didn't see them on her, did you?"

Luke smiled. He liked to hear that hint of jealousy in her question. He felt the same way about her. When he'd thought Stafford might see her in those corsets it drove him crazy. "No. She returned them to me. Did it make you jealous?"

"Would it make you jealous if you thought some other man might see me in the corset you purchased?"

He pulled her on top of him. "You know it would. I'd be insane." He rolled over with her in his arms so that she was beneath him. He was face-to-face with her when he made her a promise. "You never have to worry,

I will never want another woman. You have my heart and my soul."

His words made her tear up. "Oh Luke, I never knew I could love someone so much."

"I feel the same way."

"Did you care for Arina?"

"No. You don't realize what an evil person she was." It was something that took him a long time to come to terms with.

"I thought you spent the night with her after the dance," she admitted to him.

"That was Creed Thomas."

"I know that now, your brother told me." She told him the circumstances surrounding Colt revealing the truth, and about meeting L. B. Ditty at the ranch.

Luke laughed when she told him about the women drinking whiskey that night with L. B. "I bet you were surprised to meet L. B."

"She was very nice. But you won't be visiting those women at the saloon again, I don't care how nice they are!"

He stared into her eyes. Colt was right, making love to his wife was a completely different feeling for him. He'd never again visit the gals at the saloon. "I have no reason to."

She gathered the courage to ask him the question that had been bothering her. "Luke, did you give Father a great deal of money?"

"Honey, you are worth a million times more than I gave your father. Please don't worry about this."

She ran her hands over his muscled back. "I just don't want you to ever be sorry you married me."

"Nothing in this world would make me sorry that I married you. Nothing." He was enjoying the way she was touching him. "And if you don't stop that I'm going to have to show you just how much I love being married to you."

She laughed, but she didn't stop caressing him. "I love all of the things you purchased for me, but I didn't need so many things."

"Not everything was for you," he replied.

She furrowed her brows at him. "Are you talking about the cloth? I wondered about that."

"That's for Lillian. I thought you might want to take something to her on our way back home. She told me to tell you I saw her in one of her new dresses. It was very pretty."

"Oh Luke, that is so thoughtful of you!" She started to cry again.

"Honey, I don't want you to cry." He rolled off of her and pulled her to his chest.

"They are happy tears," she said, and hugged him.

His mouth tilted in a grin. "Am I wonderful enough that you'll let me see that other corset on you? It sure is a pretty color."

"It's called heliotrope and I love it." She ran her fingers through the hair on his chest. "I think you can see it anytime you want."

Her fingers were driving him crazy. "Well, maybe later." He lowered his lips to hers.

Chapter Thirty-One

Luke was flanked by his brothers and his nephews while he waited for the ceremony to begin. His brothers were as excited as he was to see him repeat his vows in church. His sisters-in-law were busy fussing over the bride's dress outside the church door. Luke didn't mind having another ceremony, he wanted to share this special moment in his life with his brothers.

"You are a very lucky man," Jake told Luke.

"We are all lucky men," Colt added.

"Absolutely," Luke said.

The pastor approached and told them the bride was ready. Victoria and Promise hurried to their husbands and everyone took their seats. Luke stood by the pastor and watched as his beautiful bride walked down the aisle with George. Cade and Cody clapped excitedly when they saw Mary Ann.

The pastor completed the ceremony and told Luke he could kiss his bride.

Luke took Mary Ann in his arms, his eyes filled with love, but before he kissed her he said, "'*My bounty is as boundless as the sea, My love as deep, the more I give to thee,*

The more I have, for both are infinite.'" He then kissed his bride, sealing their union for the second time.

Jake leaned over to Colt. "Shakespeare?"

"Yep."

"Did you tell him that?"

"Nope."

"Did you lend him one of your books?"

"Nope."

Victoria and Promise cried at Luke's romantic words to his bride.

"He's making us look bad," Jake said to Colt.

Colt chuckled. "We'll just have to work harder."

George invited the group back to the hotel for a celebration dinner. The couple didn't have a wedding cake on the ship, so George had asked Mrs. Howe to bake one for this wedding. He had planned a special dinner and when they arrived at the hotel, Eb had the wine and the whiskey on the table.

George filled the wineglasses as Colt poured whiskey for the men. He held the bottle toward the women. "Would you ladies prefer whiskey?"

"No!" they said in unison.

Colt made the first toast. "To the beautiful bride and the groom smart enough to cross an ocean to bring her home."

"I always told you two I was the smart one," Luke replied.

"Uncle Luke, does this mean you narrowed it down to Aunt Mary Ann?" Cody asked.

Mary Ann gave Luke a quizzical look. "What does that mean?"

Luke laughed. "Yes, Cody, that is what I did." He leaned over and whispered in Mary Ann's ear. "I'll explain later."

"Are you gonna have boys now?"

"I'm trying." Luke looked at his wife and chuckled when he saw her cheeks turning a lovely shade of pink.

"When did you start reading Shakespeare, little brother?" Jake asked.

"The captain of the ship seemed to enjoy Shakespeare, so I read some of his volumes on the voyage to England. I figured it couldn't hurt if Colt liked him so much. I wanted to see what makes him so special." He smiled at Mary Ann. "I've found there are times when his words come in handy."

"Today was one of them." Mary Ann had learned there was a very romantic side to her new husband. He'd often quoted Shakespeare to her on the voyage back to America.

"If you're the smart one, tell me why you had to travel halfway around the world when she was right here in front of you for months?" Jake was pleased with himself for coming up with this question.

"Uncle Luke had to narrow it down," Cade reminded him.

Everyone turned their attention on the twins who were nodding at each other in agreement.

Luke laughed. "I'm glad you boys understand."

"I guess we don't have nobody else to get married," Cody said.

"What about you two?" Luke teased.

"No way!" they chorused.

"Pa, I don't understand. Don't girls have to narrow it down too?" Cody asked.

"I suppose they do," Colt responded. "I think that's a question for your ma." He looked at Victoria. "How many men were in the running before you decided on me?"

Victoria smiled at Colt. "That's my secret to keep."

"Come on, Ma, tell us," the boys chorused.

"I think it was too many to count." Colt remembered his wife saying she had received over one hundred replies to her advertisement for a husband.

"Then you must be real special, Pa," Cade said.

"He certainly is," Victoria agreed.

"How many did you have, Aunt Promise?"

Before Promise responded, Jake said, "She had every man on the cattle drive in line for her."

"That many!" Cody remembered the many men who brought the cattle to the ranch.

"That's a lot," Cade said.

"What about your uncle Jake?" Promise asked sweetly. "Aren't you going to ask him how many girls wanted to marry him?"

"Yeah, Uncle Jake, how many brides did you narrow it down to?" Cody asked.

"I only had eyes for your aunt Promise from the start."

"Good answer." Promise leaned over and kissed Jake's cheek.

"Aunt Mary Ann, how many did you have to narrow it down to?" Cade asked.

Mary Ann finally figured out what the boys were asking by everyone's response. "It was your uncle Luke who had his choice of brides."

"Me?" Luke said in feigned innocence.

Mary Ann furrowed her brow at him. "Yes, you. And you very well know what I am talking about."

Luke winked at her. "Don't let her fool you, boys. When I went to England to go get her you should have seen what I had to go through. I walked into this castle where there was this grand ball in this big room and all of the ladies were wearing these huge, colorful dresses." He held his arms wide as he described the dresses causing the boys to giggle. "They looked like dancing flowers. And there was your aunt Mary Ann in her yellow gown surrounded by a thousand beaus in their formal attire. When I saw her she looked so beautiful I was sure she was a princess. I thought I was going to have to fight my way out of the ballroom."

Their eyes widened. "Really, Uncle Luke, what happened?"

"I grabbed her hand and made a run for it through the garden."

Mary Ann smiled at his tale. No one at that ball was looking at her, they only had eyes for the big handsome cowboy from America. "Don't let him fool you, boys, all of the ladies in their lovely gowns were staring at your uncle Luke."

"Did you have to punch that man again, Uncle Luke?" The boys remembered that man who had shoved Cody.

Luke knew they were referring to Stafford. "No, but it was close." That wasn't much of an exaggeration, he was close to giving him a thrashing.

Colt and Jake were as curious as the boys about what had transpired in England. Luke hadn't mentioned his confrontation with Hardwicke and Stafford, but they didn't think everything went as smoothly as he seemed to indicate.

"Aunt Mary Ann, did you punch other brides?" Cade asked.

If only they knew how much she might have enjoyed punching some of those women Luke had been squiring around town. "Well, I must say if I had to listen to your uncle Luke promise one more thing to the other ladies I was going to give it serious consideration."

"What kind of promises are you talking about?" Luke asked, failing to look as innocent as he sounded.

Mary Ann gave him an indignant frown. "Why, Luke McBride! You were the one making all sorts of promises to women from the first moment I got off that stagecoach. Every time I turned around you were making a promise to a different woman. Most of the time you were promising to show them a good time!"

Luke grinned at her. He knew exactly what she was talking about.

"I think she had you figured out from the start," Jake said. "And you're right, Mary Ann, Luke was real popular with the ladies, a renowned flirt who was always making promises."

"Shut up, Jake," Luke said. "You're not helping."

"You don't want me to lie to your wife, do you?"

"What's a flirt?" Cade asked.

"Luke, why don't you explain to the boys what a flirt is, you've had so much more experience than the rest of us," Colt said.

Jake was enjoying this exchange. "Yeah, Uncle Luke, explain that."

If his brothers thought he wasn't up to the challenge, they didn't know him as well as they thought. "Well, boys, before you narrow it down to the one woman you want to marry, you need to pay attention to all the ladies until you find the right one. Some people might call that being a flirt, I call it good sense. You sure don't want to pick the wrong one."

"So when you went swimming with that other lady you wanted to see if you narrowed it down to her?" Cody asked.

That comment shocked Luke to his boots. "How did you know about me going swimming?" *And what did they see?*

The boys glanced at each other and put their hands over their mouths as though they had revealed a secret.

"Whom were you swimming with?" Mary Ann asked Luke. "And when was this?"

"I want to know why you boys were at the river without me," Colt said.

"We went riding with Cole and we saw Uncle Luke at the lake with that lady," Cade responded.

"Yeah, and she wasn't wearing a dress," Cody said.

"She was wearing those things Ma wears under her dresses," Cade said. "'Cept she was all wet."

Colt and Jake both turned to look at Luke and in spite of grinning like fools they did feel some sympathy for him. Unbeknownst to the boys, they'd just given everyone at the table a visual of what happened at that lake.

"It's not easy to swim in a dress," Colt said.

Heaven help me, Luke thought, not daring to look at his wife. This was to be his second wedding night, but he had a bad feeling it wasn't going to go as good as the first one.

Mary Ann remembered on her second day in Wyoming Luke was dining in the hotel with his family and she'd overheard him talking with some women about swimming with Sally Detrick. "That must have been Sally Detrick," she commented. She wasn't angry, she was well aware of her husband's philandering ways before they married.

When Luke didn't deny he was swimming with Sally, Mary Ann said, "I wonder who *swims* with Sally now."

Victoria glared at her husband. "She had set her sights on Colt at one time. Did you *swim* with her too?"

Colt wasn't sure if the women were talking about swimming or something else. Either way, the answer to both questions was a definite no. "Not me." Actually, Sally had invited him to go swimming at the lake several times, but he was always too busy at the ranch. Plus the fact that he was smart enough to know when a woman was trying to rope him into marriage.

"What about you, Jake?" Promise asked. "Did you ever *swim* with Sally?"

"No way." Jake was the only brother Sally hadn't tempted, and right now he was thanking God for that favor.

"Jake wasn't here long enough," Victoria said. "If he had been, Sally would have jumped on him too."

With his brothers glaring at him like the direction of the conversation was all his fault, Luke tried to think of something to say on a different topic. Before he could come up with anything, the boys asked another question.

"Uncle Luke, how come you didn't take your pants off? Ain't it hard to swim in pants?" Cade asked.

Luke looked up and muttered, "Thank you, Lord." He glanced at the boys and answered in a serious tone, "It's not polite for a man to take his pants off in front of a lady."

"You boys remember that," Colt instructed. He was pleased to know his brother hadn't been as reckless as he feared with Sally.

"We don't swim with girls!" Cade answered.

"At least not until you are thirty years old," Victoria told them. "And definitely not with Sally or her offspring."

"Thank goodness Sally will be very old by then," Mary Ann added primly.

"Uncle Luke, you're real lucky Aunt Mary Ann narrowed it down to you 'cause she rides real good and she is the prettiest," Cody said, and Cade nodded his agreement.

"The true test for a bride," Colt teased.

"I am a lucky man for many reasons." Luke stood and held his glass in the air to make a toast to his beautiful wife. Taking her hand in his, he looked into her eyes. "To my wife, my last promise is to love you forever."

Acknowledgments

So many people helped me in this process, and they certainly make me much better than I am. It has been a blessing to work with the Kensington family, and the following people in particular:

A big thank you to John Scognamiglio for your support and your patience with my questions. It is an honor to work with you and benefit from your wisdom.

I am so appreciative to have Jane Nutter in my corner. I'm thankful for your diligence, and I always look forward to your emails!

Thank you, Ross Plotkin. Yes, I nominate you for sainthood! You are always so gracious, and you are much appreciated.

Please turn the page for an exciting sneak peek of
Scarlett Dunn's
next historical romance,

CHRISTMAS AT DOVE CREEK,

coming in November 2016 wherever
print and eBooks are sold!

Prologue

Wyoming Territory, 1868

The small-town one-room church was as hot as Hades. Though the pastor had opened both doors in hopes of lowering the searing temperature a notch or two, not one hint of a breeze filtered through. Thorpe Turlow stood ramrod straight on the makeshift altar, wearing a tailored black suit, a crisp white shirt, and a black string tie, looking more handsome than ever, if that was even possible. The pastor and the town doctor stood beside him, politely conversing as they waited for Thorpe's soon-to-be bride, Evelyn Tremayne, to make her appearance. One glance at the folks in the pews snapping their paper hand fans back and forth said they were as miserable as Thorpe was in the stifling heat. No doubt their patience was also running as thin as his while they waited for the beauty of the territory to bless them with her presence. As it was, patience had never been one of Thorpe's virtues, and after thirty minutes of waiting, his temper was simmering. Tugging at his collar for the umpteenth time, he was tempted to shed his confining jacket, rip off his tie, and unbutton his shirt. "Why does it always take women so da . . ." His eyes met the pastor's and he quickly amended what he was about to say. "Darn long to get ready?"

Considering the circumstances, the pastor overlooked Thorpe's testiness. To his way of thinking, the groom had every reason to be cross. There wasn't another woman in town, other than Evelyn Tremayne, who would have kept Thorpe Turlow waiting. The pastor's own wife had told him every single lady in town would give their eyeteeth to wed the tall, good-looking rancher. "Thorpe, don't try to understand women. One time I heard a pastor say that God offered to give him the desire of his heart. The pastor told God he desired to understand his wife. And do you know what God said?"

Thorpe and the doc both shook their heads.

The pastor leaned in close and whispered, "God asked him what his second desire was."

Eliciting a chuckle from both men, the pastor continued with his nervous chatter. "I'll never understand women. They've planned their big day from birth, so you would think they would arrive on time if for no other reason than to make sure the groom hasn't changed his mind."

"It never fails," the doc agreed. "They harangue you to death trying to get you to the altar and then they make you wait forever once you're there. I think it's their way of making you think you are about to escape that noose." The doc joked, yet silently he hoped the bride didn't show. He'd been at odds with himself all week trying to decide if he would be out of line to tell Thorpe the secret he held about his betrothed. Thorpe was a good man as well as a friend, and he didn't deserve what was about to happen to him.

While Thorpe appreciated their attempt to keep the

mood light, in all truth, he didn't feel like laughing, and it was more than the heat getting to him. He'd almost called off the wedding several times in the last two weeks. He couldn't put his finger on what was troubling him, but he had a deep-seated feeling he was going to regret this union. Only his sense of honor prevented him from doing what that little voice inside his head told him to do.

The pastor turned to look at the congregation wedged elbow to elbow in the pews. "I don't see that Englishman here, the duke or earl, or whatever his title. Did he go back to England?"

"Nicholas Ainsworth. He's still at the ranch. He'll probably ride to church with Evelyn and her father." Ainsworth had been a guest at the Tremayne ranch for several months. Evelyn's father told him Ainsworth was the son of a friend, and he came to Wyoming to learn everything he could about cattle ranching. Evelyn had mentioned several times that Ainsworth was an aristocrat, but Thorpe didn't put a lot of stock in titles. All the same, he figured it was a good thing Ainsworth had inherited wealth because the man wouldn't make a good rancher if that was his aim. After spending some time with the Englishman, it was Thorpe's opinion he could sit a horse well, but he was scared to death of longhorns. And he wasn't inclined to work the long hours necessary to run a ranch.

Hearing the congregation begin to grumble about the heat and the wait, the pastor thought it was extremely rude of Evelyn not to show up on time. He wouldn't dare state his thoughts aloud as Mr. Tremayne was a generous benefactor of the church and he could ill afford to offend him. "Thorpe, do you think I should ask everyone to wait outside under the shade trees?"

Thorpe looked over his shoulder to the entrance of

the church. No buggy in sight. *What in heaven's name was taking the woman so long to get here?* "That might not be a bad idea. I would understand if they all want to go on about their business." It had been his preference to have a small wedding with Evelyn's father and the preacher in attendance, but Evelyn was adamant that they invite everyone in town. Well, everyone Evelyn considered respectable, and that didn't include the soiled doves from the saloon. Now here he stood facing the stewing guests and Evelyn was nowhere in sight. She didn't have a care who she inconvenienced. It was all about Evelyn.

When the pastor stepped away, the doc thought this might be the only time he could speak to Thorpe in private. "Thorpe, I need to talk to you about something."

"Ladies and gentlemen . . ." the pastor began, but was interrupted when Curtis Ryder, Thorpe's ranch foreman, entered the church and hustled down the aisle.

"Thorpe, I need to speak with you," Curtis said.

Hearing the urgent tone in his foreman's voice, Thorpe turned and saw the serious expression on Curtis's face and knew something was wrong. "What is it?"

Reaching the altar, Curtis grabbed Thorpe's arm and urged him near the back door so he wouldn't be overheard. He positioned his back to the now silent assembly and spoke in a low tone.

Thorpe pulled back and stared at him with narrowed eyes. "When?"

"Before dawn."

"Tell the guests to leave, Curtis." Thorpe turned and stalked down the aisle, stripping off his tie before he hit the threshold.

"Thorpe, we need to talk," the doc yelled after him. When Thorpe didn't look back, he added, "It's important."

Curtis put his hand on the doc's shoulder. "Let him be right now."

Thorpe Turlow walked out of that church a changed man.

Chapter One

Missouri, 1876

This is some way to die, Thorpe thought when the arrow slammed through his left shoulder. Slumped over his horse, Smoke, he prayed the arrow tip wasn't laced with poison because it was stinging like the devil. Without any commands from Thorpe, Smoke was still moving fast, but the band of braves were staying with him. Smoke was a strong, stout horse and difficult to outrun, and right now he seemed to have his own plan. Thorpe trusted him to make it to the trees if the two of them were going to stand a fighting chance. He hated endangering Smoke's life, the horse meant more to him than a human friend and that single thought spurred him into action. He wasn't about to let anything happen to Smoke or himself as long as he was still breathing. *It wasn't in my plan to die today, you sons-of-Satan.*

Holding on to Smoke with his thighs, Thorpe steeled himself against the pain, pulled his .45, and turned to fire at the eight warriors closing the distance behind him. His rifle might have been the best option, but the pistol only required one hand. By his third shot, he'd managed to hit one brave, knocking him off his horse. The remaining seven warriors were not deterred, they kept coming. He thought he might have winged another brave, but he'd emptied his gun and he needed to reload or pull his rifle. To keep from making himself a larger target for their arrows zipping by his head, he leaned over in the saddle as he quickly pulled cartridges from his belt.

Holding his .45 against his thigh, he was in the process of opening the chamber when he felt Smoke slow a step. Looking up to see what had alarmed his horse, he saw a black and white Appaloosa in front of the trees about two hundred yards away. The Appaloosa was facing him, standing totally motionless in the drizzling rain, but Thorpe didn't see a rider. The Indians chasing him were also riding Appaloosas and Thorpe thought there was a possibility more braves could be waiting to ambush him in the trees. Instinct told him getting to the cover of the trees was the only option if he wanted to stay alive, so he stayed the course.

"It's okay, son, keep moving." Smoke picked up his pace and Thorpe kept his eyes on the horse in front of him as he loaded his gun. He figured the horse would soon move out of the way with Smoke barreling down on him. Arrows continued whizzing by, but before Thorpe had a chance to fire again, he heard the report of a rifle. With the sounds of the horses thundering behind him, not to mention his blood rushing in his ears from the pain, it was difficult to determine the origin of the shot, but he thought it came from the trees ahead. He prayed whoever was holding that rifle wasn't aiming at him.

When he turned to fire, he saw one brave fall from

his horse. *Someone was lending him a hand.* Aiming as best he could, he fired and another brave hit the ground. He looked ahead to see they were just a few yards from the Appaloosa, and he spotted a rider leaning over the side of the horse holding a rifle trained on the braves. Another shot rang out. *Thud.* Five warriors down. He gave thanks that the rider on that Appaloosa wasn't shooting at him because he was deadly accurate. With a slight squeeze of his thigh he signaled Smoke to pass the horse on the opposite side of the rider. Flying past the Appaloosa, three things struck Thorpe at once: There was no saddle on the horse; whoever was riding that horse was very skilled to be able to make a perfect shot from that position, not once, but twice; and that was one very well-trained animal.

"Don't stop!"

Unless his ears were playing tricks on him, Thorpe thought the voice belonged to a female or a very young man riding that horse like a brave.

The rider turned the Appaloosa and followed Thorpe into the interior of the dense thicket. Several minutes ticked by as they weaved their way through the trees until they happened on a felled tree surrounded by heavy brush. They both slid off their horses and when the rider reached for Smoke's reins to move him out of danger, Thorpe saw his rescuer was a young woman. They took cover behind the cottonwoods, and she handed Thorpe his rifle she'd pulled from the boot. He glanced at the woman holding her rifle to her shoulder. The determined look on her face said she was prepared to give anyone who appeared through the trees a lethal greeting.

Remaining silent, they waited for the warriors. Within seconds, soft rustling sounds told them they were no longer alone in the brush. The woman quickly dropped to one knee and took aim. Thorpe didn't see the braves, but he braced his rifle against the tree to hold it steady as he aimed at the sound. Right after she fired, they heard what sounded like a groan. Two braves remaining. Silence ensued. Minutes later, the woman stood. "They're leaving," she whispered. They listened until the sound of hooves grew faint.

Thorpe figured the warriors might be retreating for the moment, but he wasn't foolish enough to think they wouldn't be back. He slumped against the tree and slid to a sitting position. The woman approached him, propped her rifle next to the tree, and kneeled down beside him. When she removed her hat, long blond hair tumbled down past her shoulders. Large, clear blue eyes met his. Thorpe thought he must be hallucinating, or he was already dead and in heaven because he had to be staring at the face of an angel. Everyone had always told him his ex-fiancée was a beauty, but compared to this woman she was downright homely.

She spoke softly. "Let me see how bad this is."

His gaze met hers and he nodded.

She gently tore a small hole in his shirt to get a better look at his wound where the arrow was protruding from the back of his shoulder. "Why weren't you wearing a slicker?"

Thorpe chuckled. He hadn't expected that question. Now that his adrenaline had abated he was really feeling the pain, and even though he was drenched from the rain, sweat was rolling down his face. He removed his Stetson and swiped his forehead with his shirtsleeve. "The rain came quickly and I had stopped to pull out my slicker when they surprised me." He noticed she wasn't wearing one either and her clothing was so wet it was clinging to her body, but he didn't point that out. She was wearing black trousers and a white blouse, and he figured that was the reason he couldn't see her on the Appaloosa, she blended in with the horse's coat. "Can you break it off and use my knife to push it through?"

"I'm afraid I'm not strong enough to break it off without doing more damage."

Thorpe noticed she was just a little thing, but her size didn't matter when it came to shooting. She was one heck of a deadly shot.

Seeing the perspiration on his face, she put her palm on his forehead to see if he was feverish. She thought most men would have already passed out from such an ordeal.

The contact surprised Thorpe since he hadn't been touched in months. He might have jerked away, but her soft, cool hand felt good against his skin. Their eyes met again and held for several seconds. She definitely had the face of an angel, but her expression was serious. Her eyes flicked over his face and he wondered if she thought he was going to pass out. "I'm not going to pass out."

She smiled at his statement. She was worried about him losing consciousness. She didn't want to leave him alone, but she didn't know what else to do. That arrow needed to be removed and she couldn't do it without some help. But if she left him and those braves came back for a second bite at the apple, he'd be at their mercy, and she knew they'd make sure he died a slow, painful death for killing so many braves. When she came to a decision, she reached for her rifle and stood. "I'd best get Jed. It won't take but a few minutes, he's not far away. Do you think you can stay conscious until I get back?"

Thorpe didn't want her riding out of the trees alone. Granted, he might not be in good shape, but he could still pull a trigger. He grimaced as he pulled himself to his feet using his rifle for support. Whistling softly, Smoke came trotting to him. "I'll go with you. They may be waiting for us."

She knew he was in a lot of pain, but he was obviously a strong-willed man. "We'll ride through the trees. Can you get on your horse?"

He wasn't about to ask her to assist him. She wasn't even half his size, but she sure had grit, he'd give her that. "Yeah." He figured Jed must be her husband, and he wondered why he'd allowed her to ride off alone. Thorpe handed her his .45. "Would you mind loading it for me?"

She placed her rifle against the tree. "Of course." She reached over and without saying a word she started removing cartridges from his belt. When she realized she probably should have asked him before she touched his gun belt, she glanced up and found him watching her with intense dark eyes. She went very still.

Taking the cartridges from his belt was an innocent move, but somehow it felt very intimate to Thorpe. Her head was right at his chest and when she looked up at him, much to his surprise, he had the urge to touch her face. He hadn't even thought about touching a woman in months. How long had it been? Five, six months? Thanks to his ex-fiancée, he'd found out just how deceitful women could be. He'd been angry with all women ever since, and he sure hadn't wanted to put his hands on one.

Lily's mind was racing. The man was so attractive he almost took her breath away. She forced her eyes from his handsomely sculpted face, down his chest, and tried to focus on his gun. Opening the cylinder, she inserted the cartridges with shaking fingers.

Thorpe noticed her delicate fingers as she pushed the cartridges in the chambers. It occurred to him he'd never seen a woman load a gun. Evelyn wouldn't have touched a gun, much less known the business end. This woman handled the revolver like an expert. She was an unusual woman. "Do you live nearby?"

"No, we're on our way to Wyoming." She snapped the cylinder on the .45 in place and handed Thorpe his gun. Pulling a pistol from her waistband, she held it out to him. "If they come back, don't take time to reload, use this."

When she turned away, Thorpe heard her say, "Blaze." Her Appaloosa walked through the trees to her side.

Thorpe tucked her revolver in his belt and reached for Smoke's reins. "You're headed to Wyoming this late in the year?" Thorpe was also headed home and he'd cursed himself for being the biggest kind of fool for traveling so late in the year. Having finished what he'd come to do in Missouri, he wanted to go home and he wasn't inclined to wait until spring. Before he set out for Wyoming, he knew the weather could change in a flash and it wouldn't be in his favor, but he was prepared. The weather wasn't the only challenge travelers had to consider. As he'd just experienced, there were other dangers that could prove far worse and fatal. It was one thing for a man to travel alone under such circumstances, but he only had his own hide to consider, not a beautiful woman's. The way he saw it, her husband was plain irresponsible for risking her life on such a foolhardy journey. Right now, he was thanking the Good Lord that those Indians hadn't seen her long blond hair or he'd certainly have more trouble on his hands.

"It couldn't be helped," she answered. "I'm Lily Starr. Do you live near here?" She'd noticed he was traveling light, just a saddlebag and bedroll was on his horse.

"Thorpe Turlow." He braced himself for the pain he was sure to feel when he mounted. "I'm headed to Wyoming territory. My ranch is there."

Lily didn't want to call him a liar, but he didn't have supplies for such a journey. "Where are your supplies?"

Not only could she ride and shoot, she was also an observant woman. "I imagine those warriors have them by now. I had to let my packhorse go when they gave chase. He's a fine animal and I didn't want him to be shot." He stroked Smoke's neck. "I figured the two of us would stand a better chance of outrunning them, and if we got lucky, all three of us might survive."

His answer satisfied Lily. She understood the way he valued his animals, she felt the same way about Blaze and her mule, Daisy. She jumped on Blaze in one fluid motion, and waited a minute for Thorpe to catch his breath once he was in the saddle.

When Thorpe could speak again, he said, "Thanks for helping me out. But what were you doing out here alone?"

"I heard the shots and thought I'd better check it out."

He wondered why her husband didn't come when they heard the shots, or another man in her party. "How many in your group?"

"Four."

He'd expected her to be traveling with a much larger group. "And you haven't run into trouble?"

"No, we've been fortunate so far." She moved Blaze ahead so Thorpe had to follow. After winding her way through the trees, she pulled her horse to a halt to get her bearings and to see if Thorpe was staying with her. Considering the pain he was in, not to mention the blood loss, she was amazed that he was still in his saddle. "It's just a little farther."

Thorpe didn't want to have lied to her about passing out, but he thought he was close. "We'd best hurry." By the time three wagons came into view, Thorpe was gripping his saddle horn to stay upright.

"Jedidiah!" Lily yelled as she hopped off her horse and ran to Thorpe's side.

A large man came running from one of the wagons with a huge dog beside him just as Thorpe started to slide from his horse.

"Help me with him," Lily instructed. "We need to get this arrow out."

Jedidiah was a muscular man, but he staggered backward from Thorpe's weight. "Mercy, Miss Lily, he's a big one."

"Yes he is. Some braves were running him down, so we need to keep our eyes open. Take him to my wagon."

Together they helped a nearly unconscious Thorpe inside Lily's wagon and situated him on a feather mattress covered with hand-stitched quilts.

"Jed, I can twirl the shaft so I don't think it lodged in bone. We can break off the shaft and push it through, or we can cut around the entry and pull it out carefully."

"Break it off and push the dang thing through." Thorpe could tell the arrow tip missed the bone and he wasn't about to let anyone cut on him.

The sound of his deep baritone voice made Lily and Jedidiah jump. Lily collected herself and pulled

Thorpe's large knife from his scabbard and handed it to Jedidiah. "You can use this to push it through."

"Lily, do you need help?" Isabelle yelled from the back of the wagon.

"What's going on?" Dora asked.

Lily expected the two women would have a thousand questions, but there would be time to explain later. "Bring the whiskey, bandages, and make a yarrow poultice and boil some water. And bring a needle and some thread."

"You'd best be asking for that whiskey to pour down my throat," Thorpe said. He tried to stay alert by reminding himself he'd been hit by an arrow before and been shot a couple of times, so he could handle the pain. If those Indians came back with more braves he didn't want these people facing them alone. *Did Lily say four were in her group?* One man was in the wagon with them, and he heard two other women. That made four people, and that didn't make him feel a whole lot better.

Lily smiled at him. "I'll give you a hefty drink before we start."

Seeing that smile of hers almost made Thorpe forget about his pain. Truthfully, it darn near made him forget his own name.

"Lordy be, I may take a swig 'cause I surely don't look forward to causing you more pain," Jedidiah said.

"Jedidiah, this is Mr. Thorpe Turlow," Lily said. "Can you get his shirt off?"

"Yes, ma'am." Once Thorpe was out of his shirt, Jed inspected his shoulder. "Mr. Thorpe, you sho'nuf got yourself in a real mess."

"That I did, Jedidiah." Thorpe figured Jedidiah wasn't Lily's husband after all.

"Miss Lily knew right away those shots we heard meant business. I thank God we was close by."

"I'm thankful to Miss Lily myself. I thought the Lord sent an angel to help me."

"And he surely did, yessir, he surely did. He sent this angel to help us all," Jedidiah replied.

Thorpe wondered what the big man meant by that statement, but he didn't have the chance to ask because the canvas flap opened. Thorpe whipped his Colt from his holster in one effortless motion and pointed it toward the opening.

In light of Thorpe's weakened condition, Lily was awed by the speed he pulled his gun. She placed her fingers on the barrel of his pistol. "It's okay, it's just Isabelle and Dora. They are traveling with me."

Thorpe holstered his pistol and looked at her. "Sorry, I guess I'm still edgy."

Isabelle shoved the bottle of whiskey and other items through the opening. "We're making the poultice now, Lily."

"Good. Would you see to the horses for me?"

"Sure thing," Isabelle said.

Dora leaned over, trying to get a look at the stranger, but Jedidiah was blocking her view. "Do you need some of my tonic? It'll help relax him."

Lily looked at Thorpe and he shook his head. He figured a tonic meant some sort of opiate and he didn't want to be unconscious for a long time. "Whiskey will do."

After removing the cap, Lily handed the bottle to him. "Here you go, Mr. Turlow."

Thorpe clasped the bottle and looked into her eyes. "Here's to avenging angels." He took a long swig and handed the bottle to Jedidiah.

"No sir, I best keep a steady hand. I ain't much for

spirits. But now you need to take another mouthful before we start."

Thorpe did as Jedidiah suggested, and after he drained a good portion, he handed the bottle back to Lily. "Let's get it over with."

Lily poured some whiskey over his skin and the shaft that was going to pass through his shoulder. After she placed the bottle aside, she positioned herself in front of Thorpe and braced one hand on his right shoulder and one hand on his chest right over his heart to help hold him still. Her face was mere inches from his and she looked into his eyes. "Okay?"

Looking down at the small hand over his heart, Thorpe felt sure it had skipped a beat. His eyes moved back to hers and he gave a nod. Jedidiah didn't hesitate taking the shaft between his strong fingers and quickly snapped off the end. He grabbed the knife and used the flat of the blade to push the arrow through Thorpe's muscled shoulder.

Thorpe didn't make a sound, nor move an inch when the tip of the arrow pushed through his flesh. He was staring into beautiful blue eyes before his head dropped to the curve of Lily's neck seconds later. His last thought was, *Miss Lily smelled better than any flower.*

Under his weight, Lily fell backward with Thorpe on top of her.

"He's bleeding bad, Miss Lily," Jedidiah said.

Lily tried to push Thorpe aside, but couldn't budge him. "Help lift him off of me so I can take care of it." She'd noticed how tall Thorpe was, but when Jedidiah removed his shirt, she didn't think she'd ever seen a more powerfully built man. His chest was broad with well-defined muscles, as were his arms. She estimated he had to weigh over two hundred pounds.

Lily and Jedidiah finally slowed the bleeding just as

Isabelle returned to the wagon with the poultice. Once they had Thorpe's shoulder cleaned and stitched, Lily held the poultice to his wound as Jed wrapped the bandage around his shoulder. Jedidiah tied off the bandage and together they lowered Thorpe to the mattress.

"I ain't seen too many men bigger than me, but Mr. Thorpe shor' is, Miss Lily."

"He's going to need every ounce of that strength considering the amount of blood he's lost." Lily unfastened Thorpe's gun belt and Jedidiah lifted his hips so she could pull it off. She placed the gun right beside Thorpe so it would be within reach if he awoke. The flap opened again, and Dora and Isabelle poked their heads through.

"Who have you brought back this time, Lily?" Isabelle asked.

"She done went and saved Mr. Thorpe here," Jedidiah answered. "Had an arrow through his shoulder."

"Indians are close?" Isabelle questioned.

"We shot all but two and they left," Lily said quickly so they wouldn't be alarmed.

"They'll be back with more," Isabelle warned.

"Oh my, would you get a look at him, Isabelle," Dora said, her eyes roving over the man lying prone on the mattress.

It seemed to Isabelle that he almost filled the entire interior of the wagon. "Merciful heaven! Look how big he is!"

"He'll eat a ton," Dora added.

"I got a feeling Mr. Thorpe can be a big help," Jedidiah commented. He figured any man who pulled a gun as fast as Thorpe was a man who could probably deal with a whole lot of trouble.

"And he told me he was headed to Wyoming. He said he had a ranch there," Lily told them. "It would be helpful to have someone along that is good with a gun."

"You mean if he doesn't die," Isabelle said.

"He is not going to die!" Lily said. "Don't even say such a thing. Quick, say a prayer." She didn't know what it was about Thorpe Turlow, but she could tell he wasn't a man that one arrow could fell.

Dora and Isabelle rolled their eyes at her. "You pray enough for all of us," Isabelle said.

Lily gave them a stern look as if they were two misbehaving children.

"Okay, we'll pray for him," Isabelle said to satisfy Lily.

Jedidiah laughed. "You should know that Miss Lily has a direct line to the Almighty. Why, even Mr. Thorpe said he thought she was an angel came to save him."

Dora couldn't take her eyes off the big man on Lily's bed. He had a striking face and the broadest chest she'd ever seen. "At least this injured critter only has two legs," Dora commented. "And I have to admit he's much more handsome than Blue."

"I guess that's a matter of opinion," Lily said. She wasn't really thinking about Thorpe's handsome face. The comment about Thorpe's appetite forced her to consider their limited supplies. "I have to leave for a little while." She glanced up at Jedidiah. "Look after him, Jed. Make sure he stays put if he comes around."

"I'll get those wet pants off him," Jed told her.

"You just said Indians are roaming around out there," Isabelle said, fear creeping into her voice.

"Keep your guns handy. If you see anything just start firing. I don't expect I will have to go that far," Lily told them. "And I'll leave Blue here to alert you if trouble is coming. Start packing up camp because we need to keep moving for a few more hours." She didn't want to say she expected those braves to come back, just like Isabelle said, but that was what she was thinking.

"Miss Lily, it don't sound safe for you to be out there wandering around by yourself. Where are you going?" Jed asked.

"Mr. Turlow had a packhorse that he had to release and he seems fond of his animals. I'm going to see if the Indians captured him."